Praise for Leslie Gould

"There are some books that seem to just grip you from the first page. Leslie Gould's *A Brighter Dawn* doesn't just grip you from the first sentence—it holds you tight through the entire novel. I couldn't read it researched, thoroughly enjoyab this book is a keeper."

> — Shelley She
> and *U.. Today* bestselling author

"Part mystery, part drama, Gould uses complex events to spotlight the importance of forgiveness. A beautiful story of love, loss, and the bonds that connect a family to its faith."

> —Suzanne Woods Fisher, bestselling author
> of *A Season on the Wind*

"This wholesome time-swap tale will appeal to readers of Beverly Lewis."

> —*Publishers Weekly* on *Piecing It All Together*

"Gould is a fabulous writer . . . this is a charming series debut."

> —*Library Journal* on *Adoring Addie*

"*A Brighter Dawn* is a compelling and poignant time-slip story that exposes corruption during a heart-wrenching era and the abuse of religion to gain political control. Well done, Leslie Gould, for diving with readers into the darkness of both communism and fascism and then resurfacing brilliantly back into the light."

> —Melanie Dobson, award-winning author
> of *Catching the Wind* and *The Curator's Daughter*

"*A Brighter Dawn* is a dual-time story of courage, justice, faith, and forgiveness. By weaving historical and contemporary plot threads, Gould enlightens readers as to how a family's generational struggles may influence relationships and experiences in the present."

—Laurie Stroup Smith, author
of THE POCKET QUILT SERIES

BY
EVENING'S
LIGHT

Books by Leslie Gould

AMISH MEMORIES
• Three •

BY EVENING'S LIGHT

LESLIE GOULD

BETHANYHOUSE

a division of Baker Publishing Group
Minneapolis, Minnesota

Published by Bethany House Publishers
Minneapolis, Minnesota
BethanyHouse.com

Bethany House Publishers is a division of
Baker Publishing Group, Grand Rapids, Michigan

Printed in the United States of America

Library of Congress Cataloging-in-Publication Data
Names: Gould, Leslie, author.
Title: By evening's light / Leslie Gould.
Description: Minneapolis, Minnesota : Bethany House, a division of Baker
    Publishing Group, 2024. | Series: Amish memories ; 3
Identifiers: LCCN 2023059694 | ISBN 9780764240263 (paper) | ISBN 9780764243202
    (casebound) | ISBN 9781493446612 (ebook)
Subjects: LCSH: Amish—Fiction. | LCGFT: Christian fiction. | Romance fiction. |
    Novels.
Classification: LCC PS3607.O89 B9 2024 | DDC 813/.6—dc23/eng/20240103
LC record available at https://lccn.loc.gov/2023059694

Scripture quotations are from the King James Version of the Bible.

Scripture quotations in chapters 30 and 36 are taken from the Holy Bible, New International Version®, NIV®. Copyright © 1973, 1978, 1984, 2011 by Biblica, Inc.® Used
by permission of Zondervan. All rights reserved worldwide. www.zondervan.com.
The "NIV" and "New International Version" are trademarks registered in the United
States Patent and Trademark Office by Biblica, Inc.®

Cover and photography by Dan Thornberg, Design Source Creative Services

Cover images by Shutterstock

Emojis are from the open-source library OpenMoji (https://openmoji.org/) under the
Creative Commons license CC BY-SA 4.0 (https://creativecommons.org/licenses/by-s
a/4.0/legalcode)

Baker Publishing Group publications use paper produced from sustainable forestry
practices and postconsumer waste whenever possible.

24 25 26 27 28 29 30   7 6 5 4 3 2 1

To Natasha Kern,
agent and friend, thank you.

Brighter days are sweetly dawning,
Oh, the glory looms in sight!
For the cloudy day is waning,
And the evening shall be light.

From the hymn "The Evening Light"
by Daniel S. Warner (1885)

· 1 ·

Treva Zimmerman

March 26, 2019
Lancaster County, Pennsylvania

After six months on a mission trip, I was back in Lancaster County.

But not for long.

Tears blurred my vision. Both the white house and red barn seemed to have grown larger since I'd left. So had the green pastures. Even my beloved cows seemed bigger.

"I can't come in." Ivy turned toward me. "I have a client to go see." My eldest sister was a social worker for an eldercare company. "But Conrad and I will come for dinner."

"Thank you for the ride." I opened the passenger door of her twenty-year-old Toyota Corolla, which was my age. Well, almost. I would turn twenty-one on the fourth of June.

As I climbed out and pulled my bag from the back seat, Ivy turned and smiled. "Treva, I'm glad you're home. I really missed you."

Home.

"Thanks." Perhaps she'd just been preoccupied on the drive from Philadelphia—she wasn't her usual chatty self. Then again, neither was I. But I'd need to update her about my life and plans sometime soon. Maybe I could set up a call with the two of us and our sister Brenna, who was living in Ukraine. "See you tonight," I said as I slammed the door.

I inhaled the scent of our family farm. The dairy barn. The alfalfa. The plowed field. It was the smell of hope, even on a cold day. I slung my duffel bag over my shoulder and took another deep breath. And the smell of home.

Exhausted, I trudged toward the back door of the house. A cold rain began to fall. I tried to quicken my step, but my bag weighed me down. Six months on a mission trip in Haiti had aged me by six years. I needed a few nights of solid sleep, and then I'd break it to my family that I was going to take a job in Alaska.

I'd always been the homebody. And the compliant one. The peacemaker. The sister who didn't want to cause any problems. I couldn't be that girl any longer.

The *Dawdi Haus* was to my left and the barn to my right. I kept my eyes on the farmhouse as I started up the steps. The kitchen was Rosene's domain. I hoped she was waiting for me.

After kicking off my shoes on the porch and hanging up my jacket, I dragged my duffel bag into the kitchen.

It was eleven thirty, almost time for lunch. A pot of soup simmered on the burner. Two fresh loaves of bread cooled on the counter.

Tears threatened again.

"Treva! Is that you?" Rosene came around the corner from the hallway. She smiled and opened her arms. "You're home!"

I dropped my bag and ran toward her tiny frame. She hugged me tight and held on for a long minute.

Finally, she released me. "I'm so happy you're here."

She seemed even smaller than she'd been when I left.

"How are you?" she asked.

I swallowed hard, and tears flooded my eyes.

"Treva? What's wrong?"

"I'm tired is all," I answered.

"How about a shower before we eat?" She gestured toward the table. "Arden and Priscilla"—my *Mammi* and Dawdi— "will be ready for lunch in a half hour. Afterward, you can take a nap. Your room is ready."

"*Denki*," I said. "A shower is just what I need. And then a nap. In fact . . ." I hesitated for a moment. "I think I'll skip lunch." I'd flown a budget airline with a nine-hour layover in New York. I was exhausted. "Please tell Mammi and Dawdi I'll be down after I get some sleep."

Rosene's eyes widened. "Are you feeling all right?"

I wasn't. But I didn't say that. "I'm fine. Just tired."

"That's understandable," she said. "I'll tell your grandparents. Get some rest."

As I walked through the living room, Mammi's cuckoo clock chimed the half hour. Our grandmother in Oregon had an identical one that Mammi had given her years ago. Tears sprung to my eyes as my grief threatened to bubble out of me.

I took a long, hot shower. My showers in Haiti had been cold and infrequent, and they'd involved a bucket to catch the runoff to later use to flush the toilet. As tired as I was, I had to force myself to turn off the shower. I put on a pair of sweats that smelled freshly washed, climbed between the clean sheets and under the double wedding ring quilt on my bed, and let my head sink into the feather pillow.

I'd met Pierre in Oregon over a year ago at Christmastime. He was close to our family friends Brooke and Daniel, who served in Haiti as missionaries. He was also friends with Ivy from when she volunteered in Haiti seven years ago, and with our middle sister, Brenna, too, from a Mennonite Global Gathering she and Ivy attended in Germany five years ago. Pierre was four years older than I was and had huge responsibilities when it came to his family and community. His father had been injured in the 2010 earthquake. He had four younger siblings. He worked at the orphanage where I volunteered. His community was overrun by gangs.

While I was in Haiti, I'd suggested he apply for asylum in the US. He'd responded with, *"And never be able to return to Haiti? Maybe my sisters and brother would be able to come to the US someday, but not my parents. How could I live the rest of my life without ever seeing them again?"*

I'd hoped he would do it for me, but I had no idea what I was asking of him.

Pierre spoke softly, his French accent thicker than usual. *"Do you know how many Haitians are denied asylum in the US each year?"*

I shook my head.

"Thousands," he said. *"Thousands and thousands and thousands. More than from any other country. Considering how long and how often the US has interfered in our lives, it seems your government would be more welcoming. But they're not. And this is a particularly difficult time."*

I'd been so naïve when I went to Haiti. About Pierre. About his life. About the work I'd do. It was harder than I'd expected—and more rewarding.

But mostly harder. Sparks had flown between Pierre and me in Oregon, and again when I arrived in Haiti. At first,

I'd imagined us marrying and me staying in Haiti. But after a couple of months, I knew I couldn't make my home there.

Brooke and Daniel decided not to stay either. Too many kidnappings and shootings. Too much instability when it came to supplies and health care. Instead, they decided to raise money to continue the work of the orphanage and hire Pierre to manage it.

I rolled over to my side as my tears started again. Everyone saw me as an old soul and a caretaker of others. I was "beyond my years." Ivy and Brenna saw me as relaxed and easygoing, which I was, compared to them. I'd always tried to be low-key and not take up a lot of space, but I behaved that way even more after our parents were killed in a car accident five years ago, just after I'd turned sixteen. I figured everyone had enough to deal with without me adding to their stress. I wanted to make life easier on Gran, our mom's mother, and Dawdi and Mammi, our dad's parents. And my sisters. I willed myself to accept our parents' death. I wouldn't take up time going through the stages of grief. I'd be strong for everyone else.

One time, Rosene told me that denial and acceptance looked a lot alike on the outside. I was beginning to see her point.

Yes, I was grieving my relationship with Pierre, grieving him. But even more so, I was grieving my parents. It was as if a dam had been breached. I couldn't seem to stop the tears I'd suppressed for the last five years.

I slept until 5:15, awakening to the smell of roasting chicken. My stomach growled as I crawled out of bed. I'd missed the milking. And closing the store. And helping with dinner. I groaned. I hadn't meant to sleep so long.

I contemplated putting on one of my Amish dresses but decided to stay in my sweats. Mammi preferred I wear a dress. I figured she'd care, but I doubted if she'd say anything tonight. And as soon as I told them I was leaving again, it wouldn't matter.

I put my hair in a ponytail and twisted it into a bun on top of my head. Then I headed to the bathroom to splash cold water on my face. As I suspected, my reflection showed red and puffy eyes. I splashed more cold water on my face, patted it dry, and then shuffled down the staircase. As I neared the bottom step, Ivy said, "She seemed really quiet this morning." I stopped as Ivy asked, "Did she open up to you about what's going on?"

"*Nee*," Rosene said.

Ivy added, "I had a text from Pierre that he was really sad to see her leave."

I expected her to say more, but Rosene asked her to fill the water pitcher. The conversation shifted to dinner. I could recognize Rosene's move to change the topic—one she used whenever she feared a conversation had taken a turn toward gossip.

As I entered the kitchen, Rosene said, "There she is. How was your nap?"

"Good," I answered. "Supper smells great."

Rosene smiled. "It's your welcome home dinner. We'll eat in fifteen minutes."

"What can I do?"

"Why don't you see if you can help Priscilla finish up in the store? She must be running late. Conrad went out to help Arden."

I'd much rather help in the barn, but I'd do what Rosene asked. I stepped out onto the porch to put my shoes on.

Ivy said, "See what I mean? She's definitely not her chip-per—"

I closed the door behind me.

A half hour later, we were seated around the kitchen table, passing around roasted chicken, mashed potatoes, green beans, applesauce, and homemade rolls. Mammi had more wrinkles around her mouth, and Dawdi had more gray in his beard. Both seemed a little more stooped over.

"I hope you didn't tire yourself out cooking," Mammi said to Rosene.

"Not at all," she answered. But she looked tired.

"I'll clean up," Ivy said.

"I'll help," I quickly added.

The conversation turned toward my time in Haiti. It wasn't as if I hadn't talked with everyone on the phone once a week, so nothing I had to say was new. I answered questions as succinctly as I could until Ivy asked, "When do you plan to return?"

"I don't plan to."

"Oh. I thought you would."

I turned toward Conrad. "How is Gabe doing?" He was Conrad's little brother and had worked for both Dawdi and Mammi for years. He'd joined the Army Reserve and had been deployed to a US Army base in Kuwait with his unit a few months ago.

Conrad spread butter on his roll. "Okay, I think. He's not very talkative."

I asked, "Is he happy to be there?"

Conrad shook his head. "I don't think so. In fact, I think the whole Army Reserve thing turned out to be a lot harder than he anticipated."

That sounded like my experience in Haiti.

Ivy cleared her throat and asked, "So you and Pierre aren't a couple?"

After swallowing my water, and trying not to choke, I answered, "No. It didn't work out. He doesn't intend to leave Haiti."

"Oh," Ivy said. "I thought he would."

I shook my head.

Ivy stared at me. "So what's next?"

"Staying here, I hope," Dawdi said.

Mammi gave me a pleading look.

It seemed Rosene was trying to appear neutral.

I shrugged. I'd rather tell Ivy and Brenna at the same time than make an announcement now. I pulled my fork through my mashed potatoes. On the other hand, the longer I waited to tell Mammi, Dawdi, and Rosene, the more awkward my announcement would be. "I met a couple from Alaska who volunteered at the orphanage in January and February—I think I mentioned them. Misty and Shawn Wright."

Everyone nodded.

"They own a resort in Alaska." It was called the Resort of the Midnight Sun, which I thought sounded enchanting. "They have a restaurant but also host events throughout the summer—weddings, reunions, and some conferences. That sort of thing." Misty and Shawn's daughter, Lindsay, was getting married in early May. I was excited to help with that event in particular. "They've offered me a job as an event planner."

Ivy's jaw literally dropped, and then she said, "But you're not taking it, right?"

Part of me wanted to hedge, to say, *I'm thinking about it*. But that wasn't an honest answer. It would only delay the inevitable.

"No, I am going to take it." I spoke as confidently as I could. "I start April fifteenth."

Ivy sputtered, "That's three weeks away."

"Eighteen days," I said.

Mammi gasped.

Ivy crumpled her napkin in her fist. "You don't know anything about event planning."

"I do. I planned our events in Haiti. That's why Misty asked me. She said I have a gift for planning and coordinating—for bringing people together."

Ivy shook her head. "That's not the same." Conrad put his hand on her arm. She ignored him. "You can't. You just can't."

"I can." I sat up as straight as I could. "And I will."

The next morning, Dawdi was quiet while we did the milking. So was I as I concentrated on the cows. We didn't have animals, except for dogs and cats, on our Christmas tree farm in Oregon. I found the cows magical in their relationships with one another and with humans too. They adored us. I'd missed them. It seemed like they'd missed me too, and several gave me extra love as they rubbed against me.

I enjoyed working on the farm the most out of the three of us girls. I was tall and had always been strong. Working on the farm had made me even stronger. I was also interested in what it took to run the dairy farm and manage the land. I found the work engaging.

As I looked around, I noticed that everything in the barn was up to code but not up to Dawdi's high standards. Obviously having Gabe and me both gone had taken a toll. "Have you hired someone to help?" I asked.

"*Jah*, several times," he answered. "I just can't manage to find anyone who stays for long." He gave me a woeful smile. "And then I stopped looking when you said you were coming home."

Ouch. I tried to return the smile but failed.

I stepped into the milk room for the bottles Dawdi had already filled and then out to the calf pens on the grassy east side of the barn. With sixty cows in the herd, we averaged five calves a month—unless a cow had twins. We raised the calves in the pens with a hutch for shelter and hand-fed them for a month, until they were ready to join the herd.

The entire process on a dairy farm involved a lot of planning, record keeping, and detailed scheduling, along with an understanding of science and health codes. The results, besides our endless supply of milk, were female calves to carry on the herd, while the males were sold. Some of the female calves were too, depending on how many cows we needed to replace in a year.

Running a dairy farm was a three-hundred-sixty-five-days-a-year, twenty-four-hours-a-day job. The milking had to be done. Calves had to be pulled in the middle of the night. Feed had to be grown. The horses had to be fed and groomed. All the animals needed veterinary care. It was an endless and often thankless job. But I loved it.

At least I had.

I fed two calves at once, standing between the pens with a bottle in each hand held through the wire pen. They butted against the bottle, jarring my arms and making me feel even more connected to them. It was one of my favorite tasks on the farm.

Once we finished the milking, we tackled sterilizing the

milk room. When we were almost done, the barn phone rang in the office.

Dawdi had his hands deep in hot water. "Would you get that? I'm expecting a call from the feed store."

"Sure." I figured it would probably go to voicemail before I could answer, but I hustled around the corner to the office anyway. I snatched the phone off the receiver and said, a little out of breath, "Hello. Zimmerman farm. How may I help you?"

"Hallo. This is Herr Mayer of Frankfurt, Germany. May I please speak with Rosene Simons?" He spoke with a clipped accent and sounded super serious.

"Yes," I said. "May I ask what this is about?" If it was bad news, perhaps it would be better if I told Rosene.

"I must speak with Rosene Simons," he answered.

"All right. Hang on. It will take me a few minutes to get her." I put the phone down on the desk and jogged to the milk room to tell Dawdi the call was from a man in Germany and was for Rosene. "I'll go get her," I said.

He seemed concerned and began peeling off his rubber gloves.

I returned a few minutes later with Rosene. She strode into the office and picked up the phone. "Hallo." Then she began speaking in rapid German. I had no idea what she was saying. Neither did Dawdi, who stood in the doorway beside me.

The conversation continued, and Dawdi wandered back to the milk room. Finally, Rosene said, "*Auf Wiedersehen*," and ended the call. She turned toward me, looking distressed.

"What's the matter?" I asked.

"I've had some bad news." As she took a step toward me, she stumbled.

I hurried toward her but not fast enough. She stumbled

again and then fell, first to her knees and then onto her side, landing on her left arm.

"Rosene!" I exclaimed as I kneeled beside her.

"Oh dear." Rosene sat up. "How clumsy of me." She held her left arm with her right hand.

"Did you hurt yourself?"

"I don't think so." She placed her right hand on the floor and started to push herself up.

"Wait! I need to get Dawdi. Stay right there."

"I'm fine."

I put my hand on her shoulder. "No. You need to stay put. Humor me."

She patted my hand.

"Dawdi!" I called out as I stood and then ran toward the milk room. "Rosene fell! We need you."

He stepped to the doorway. "What?"

"Rosene fell."

He hurried after me to the office.

Rosene still sat on the floor where I left her, her face turned toward the door. "I'm fine," she said. "My knees are sore, and I also landed on my arm." She rubbed it. "It's sore too."

I took my phone out of my sweatshirt. "I'm going to call for an ambulance."

Rosene shook her head. "There's no need for that." She reached out her right hand for Dawdi to pull her to her feet.

Dawdi stepped closer but didn't take her hand. "How about if I stand behind you and lift you up? That's not as abrupt as pulling you."

Rosene nodded.

Dawdi put his hands under Rosene's arms and lifted her slowly. She stood. He let go of her, and she began to sway, clutching her arm.

I said, "I'm calling 9-1-1."

"No," Rosene said. "Take me to the urgent care."

"Dawdi?" I asked.

"I think that's a good plan," he said. "I'll ride along."

Twenty minutes later, we arrived at the urgent care on the edge of Lancaster in the van that I'd inherited from Brenna, that used to be our mother's. Rosene had grown even more pale and hunched over. Thankfully, one of the doctors could see her right away. Dawdi went with her while I stayed in the waiting room.

After ten minutes, he came out and said, "It's her heart. An ambulance is on the way."

· 2 ·

As I drove Dawdi to Lancaster General Hospital, he said, "Lena died." That was Rosene's biological sister, who lived in Frankfurt. "Rosene's doctor said that sometimes the shock of that sort of news can cause a cardiac event."

"Shock? Wasn't Lena over a hundred?"

"One hundred and two," he answered. "Rosene was expecting she'd die sometime soon. It's complicated." Dawdi paused and then added, "They had a strained relationship."

I knew it was difficult, and that Rosene was very grateful for her American sisters—Clare, my great-grandmother, and Martha, my great-great aunt, although they'd both been gone for decades. "What else did the doctor say?"

"That they'll do more tests at the ER. They gave her oxygen and a drug to dissolve clots. The doctor said our quick action may have saved her life."

I winced. "It wasn't that quick. An ambulance would have had oxygen and medication."

"Well, it might have taken a while for the ambulance to get to our house, depending on what was going on. I'm just glad she was in the barn with you. She could have been in

22

the house alone, with no one coming in for hours." He shuddered.

I stayed in the waiting room again while Dawdi went back with Rosene, who had arrived before us.

It was hard to explain to others how a great-great-aunt who was ninety-three years old could hold such an important position in our lives. But Ivy, Brenna, and I didn't have aunts and uncles. And we didn't know Dawdi's sisters, who had both moved away from Lancaster County. We had a few great-aunts and uncles on our maternal grandfather's side of the family, but when Gran and Papa left the Amish when our mother was fourteen, they shunned our family.

Maybe it wasn't just the shock of Lena's death. Why had I declared my plan to go to Alaska last night? I'd tried so hard not to be a problem for my grandparents, Rosene, and my sisters, but now I was anyway. I'd wait to see how Rosene was doing before I actually bought a ticket. Rosene could have a quick recovery, and Ivy, who worked part-time, would be available to drive Rosene to doctors' appointments. I'd leave for Alaska as soon as I could, within reason. I'd text Misty and Shawn once I knew how Rosene was doing. They'd understand.

Dawdi returned and sat down next to me.

"How's she doing?"

"All right," he said. "They just drew blood and will have the results soon. They're going to move her up to the cardiac unit." He nodded toward my phone, which was in my hand. "Would you text Conrad and see if he can help with the milking this afternoon?"

"Yes."

"And let Ivy know what's going on."

I texted her first. She'd hate it if I texted Conrad before

her. I turned my attention back to Dawdi. "I can stay here with Rosene tonight."

"Denki," he said. "That would be a big help." He leaned his head against the chair, making his gray beard jut out over his chest. Tears filled his gray eyes.

I reached out and held his thick, calloused hand. We sat that way for a few minutes.

Finally, he said, "You lost your parents when you were sixteen. I was middle-aged when I lost mine. Here I am, seventy-five, and I still have Rosene, my second mother, aunt, and big sister all in one. I've been blessed by her my entire life. Our relationship has been the least complicated of any I've ever had, except for you girls. I'm not ready to lose her. I can't see ever being ready to lose her unless she's in great pain."

It was the most serious thing Dawdi had ever said to me. I squeezed his hand. "I don't think we're going to lose her yet. I think she's going to get really good care here, and we'll have her with us for more time."

He swiped at his eyes with his free hand. Then he sat up straight, let go of my hand, and took a handkerchief out of the pocket of his jacket. After he blew his nose, he said, "I hope you're right."

Midway through the afternoon, I took Dawdi home, grabbed a few things for Rosene, along with my toothbrush, phone charger, and a change of clothes for myself, and returned to the hospital.

Rosene was in her room, wearing a hospital gown and resting. She looked like a child in the big bed.

"How are you?" I set my bag on the chair.

"All right," she answered. "The blood test confirmed a heart attack. The doctor should be in to talk with me soon."

As she spoke, my phone buzzed. It was Ivy. I'd already spoken with her three times. I answered, and before I could say hello, she asked, "Has the doctor been in yet?"

"No."

"If he comes in before I get there, make sure and take notes."

"I will."

"Conrad is doing the milking. Mammi closed the shop," Ivy said. "I'm going to bring Dawdi and Mammi up to the hospital to see Rosene. We won't stay long, but they are worried. I think it will be good for them—and for Rosene. Hopefully we'll be able to speak with the doctor."

I didn't think that sort of timing usually worked in hospitals, but I didn't say so. "Rosene is resting now," I replied, "but I'll let her know the three of you will be here soon."

"Thank you. Bye."

As I slipped my phone into the pocket of my sweatshirt, Rosene said, "Let me guess. Ivy is bringing Arden and Priscilla to see me."

I smiled. "She is."

I pulled the chair up close to her bed and sat. "I'll let you rest until they get here, but I wanted to say how sorry I am about Lena's passing."

"Denki," she said. "I thought I was prepared. But it shook me." She patted her chest. "I'm the only one left of my generation."

Rosene was in such good physical, mental, and emotional shape that I often forgot she was a generation ahead of Mammi and Dawdi.

"Lena was so tough, it was hard to imagine her ever dying.

25

Her attorney said she died in her sleep. Her heart simply stopped. A perfect death, really. She was still in her home. Sharp as ever yesterday—gone to heaven today. She had a woman coming in every morning to help with the housework and cook her breakfast. She's the one who found Lena."

Rosene's right arm lay against her body, and I reached up and took her hand.

"Herr Mayer said Lena put him in charge of her interment. She didn't want any sort of service." Rosene turned toward the window. "Which makes me sad." After another pause, she said, "I'm Lena's sole heir, which surprised me." Rosene's voice was barely above a whisper. "I expected her to leave her estate to a charity, or perhaps to our cousin Karl's son and his family. Herr Mayer requested I come to Germany to settle everything and decide what to do with the house."

"Will you go?" I asked.

"I don't think I can," Rosene answered.

I'd never known Rosene to say *I don't think I can*. Even at her advanced age, she seemed to be capable of anything.

"Could someone go for you?"

"Would you go?"

That wasn't what I had in mind. "Well, if needed, but I've never been to Germany. What about Brenna? Ukraine isn't that far from Germany."

"That's true." Rosene closed her eyes for a long moment and then she said, "I think that's a good idea. Perhaps I can give her power of attorney. Maybe she can take care of the details, if she's willing."

"Speaking of," I said, "I haven't told Brenna about your heart attack yet. How about if you rest before Ivy, Dawdi, and Mammi arrive, and I'll go give Brenna a call?"

"Jah, please do," Rosene said. "Tell Brenna I miss her.

Don't say anything about her going to Germany yet. Let's see what the doctor says first."

Brenna lived with her boyfriend Johann's mother, Natasha, while he rented a room from a neighbor. Johann worked for the Ukrainian army doing something with cybersecurity. I wasn't sure exactly what. Brenna worked for an American software company.

I really liked Johann—mostly because he was good to Brenna. His love for her played a part in her transformation from being anxious and struggling to being functional, having a good job, and helping others.

I think her relationship with Natasha helped too. My sisters and I longed for parental figures in our lives after losing our mom and dad.

It was nine o'clock in Kyiv, and Brenna answered on the second ring. "What's wrong?" Her voice had a hint of alarm.

"Rosene is in the hospital. She had a heart attack."

Brenna inhaled sharply. "Is she going to be okay?"

"She's out of the ER and in a room on the cardiac floor. We're hoping to talk with the doctor soon. Ivy is on her way here with Dawdi and Mammi."

"What happened? I mean, was she having heart problems?"

"Not that we know of. She'd just found out that Lena died. Rosene fell after speaking with Lena's—"

"Lena died?"

"Yes," I answered. "Her attorney called Rosene this morning. After Rosene hung up the phone, she fell. Dawdi and I took her to the urgent care. . . ." I explained everything that happened.

"Thank you for taking such good care of her," Brenna said.

"I'll text you when we find out what the doctor has to say," I said. "Call me after that if you want to talk more."

"Thank you," Brenna said.

"How are you and Johann doing?"

"Good," Brenna said. "We can talk more soon. Call me during the night if there are any changes."

"I will. I love you."

"I love you too."

By the time I returned to Rosene's room, Ivy, Mammi, and Dawdi had arrived. And so had the doctor. She was speaking to them, saying Rosene had a myocardial infarction. "There's damage to the heart." The doctor spoke directly to Rosene. "Thankfully you received emergency treatment right away or it would be worse."

"What about any upcoming travel?" Rosene asked.

"Where are you planning to travel?"

"Germany, perhaps."

"That's a long trip. You'd be at medium risk," the doctor answered. "If you were in your seventies, I'd say in a month or so you shouldn't have any problems. But you're in your nineties. I wouldn't recommend it for several months, if at all."

Rosene glanced at me.

The doctor said, "We'll run more tests in the morning—another blood test and an echocardiogram. You'll stay tonight for sure, and perhaps tomorrow night too. And then you'll need to do cardiac rehab over the next few weeks."

Rosene thanked the doctor and then turned toward me. "Dr. Lewis, I'd like you to meet another one of my three great-great-nieces. This is Treva."

The doctor stepped toward me, her hand extended. I shook it, and we both said, "Pleased to meet you."

The doctor turned toward Rosene. "I'm happy to see you have so much support."

Rosene smiled. "The Lord has been good to me."

The doctor nodded and then said, "See you tomorrow."

After she left, Ivy and Mammi stepped closer to the bed and began fussing over Rosene. Dawdi stepped to my side. "Did you get through to Brenna?"

"Uh-huh," I said.

"And?"

I think we'd all be a little worried about Brenna for the rest of our lives, even though it seemed like she was thriving. "She's concerned about Rosene, but she sounded good."

A few minutes later, Conrad called Ivy and said one of the cows was in early labor. When Ivy ended the call, Rosene said to Dawdi, "You all go home. Take care of the cow. I'm fine here with Treva. We'll call Ivy if anything changes, and she'll go get you."

Ivy nodded in agreement.

"Are you sure?" Dawdi asked.

"Of course," Rosene said. "Hopefully I'll be home tomorrow. If not, Treva will let you know."

After we said our good-byes, and the three who were headed home traipsed out to the hall, Rosene exhaled slowly. "It doesn't seem I'll be going to Germany anytime soon."

"Do you want me to ask Brenna about going for you?"

"Let's keep that in mind. Perhaps I should speak with Lena's lawyer again."

I nodded. "But in a few days."

"Perhaps so." Rosene slumped down in bed a little bit more. "Having a little more space helps." She turned toward me. "How are you doing? We haven't had a chance to talk since dinner last night. It sounds as if you're hurting over your relationship with Pierre—and now you'll be going to Alaska soon."

"Oh, none of that matters." I was embarrassed she brought it up—from her hospital bed, no less.

"Of course it matters."

"Not now," I said. "I wish I hadn't said anything last night. Now everything feels weird. Dawdi was quiet in the barn this morning. With you ill, it feels even weirder that I said I was going to leave."

"I don't know if your grandparents will bring this up, but they've been talking to Conrad about taking over the farm. And you—if Brenna doesn't come back—would oversee the store."

"What?"

"Jah," Rosene said. "They'd like for the farm to stay in the family. The alternative is to sell it to someone in the community, but it more than likely would go to a stranger."

"Do Ivy and Conrad want the farm?"

"I don't know," Rosene said. "If they do, and you take over the store, you would be a big help to Conrad in running the farm. You have a better idea than anyone, besides Arden, of everything that needs to be done."

"Dawdi doesn't care that Ivy and Conrad are Mennonite and not Amish?"

Rosene paused a moment and then said, "The farm has been run by Mennonites far longer than by Amish, until Jeremiah Zimmerman took it over seventy-three years ago."

I took a step backward, my arms still crossed. "Have Ivy and Conrad indicated they might want the farm?"

"Not that I know of."

I hoped they would take it, but it also stung a little that Dawdi hadn't offered the farm to me. I much preferred the farm to the store. But I was female. Dawdi would never offer me the farm. What was I thinking?

I reminded myself that I would leave for Alaska as soon as possible. I needed a fresh start. It made no sense that I was longing to leave and yet also hurt Dawdi hadn't considered me when it came to passing on the farm.

I hugged myself tighter, trying to contain my conflicted feelings. Ivy had said several times that she'd stay in Lancaster County and take care of Dawdi, Mammi, and Rosene as they aged. It only made sense that she and Conrad would have the farm.

"Sit down." Rosene motioned to the chair that was beside the bed.

I did as I was told.

"I'm sorry about Pierre. I'm guessing that's the cause of you being unsettled."

Again, tears filled my eyes. "It's complicated." I didn't have the energy to go into my new grief over Mom and Dad.

"Are you sure your relationship with Pierre is over?"

"Yes."

"Do you love him?"

I nodded as tears stung my eyes. I couldn't speak. Yes, I wanted to go to Alaska to learn event planning—but I also wanted to get as far away from my grief as possible. It didn't make sense that I was fleeing a failed relationship to coordinate and help plan weddings in Alaska. But that was exactly my plan.

"I loved someone once," Rosene said. "It didn't work out. Lots of things in my life have faded . . . emotions among them. But I remember clearly how much it hurt when

I was in my early twenties to lose the only man I'd ever loved."

I brushed away my tears.

"Would you like me to tell you my story?"

"No. You just had a heart attack." I didn't want to be responsible for digging up memories that might trigger another cardiac event. Or tire her out.

She smiled. "I'll only tell you the beginning right now. I'll save the rest for later."

Judging from the stories I knew she'd told Ivy and Brenna, *later* could span months. I didn't have that much time. But I said, "Just tell me a little. I don't want to make things worse."

· 3 ·

Rosene Simons

Zeke stepped out of the stable, leading two of the workhorses. I stopped at the end of the row of beans and leaned against my hoe. I never tired of watching him.

He squinted toward the garden—toward me—and broke into a grin. Then he waved, a big sweeping gesture with his right hand as he gripped the horses' reins with his left.

My heart skipped a beat as I smiled and returned the wave, although mine wasn't nearly as enthusiastic in appearance. However, it was in spirit. I adored Zeke Zimmerman.

Since the war ended three years before, he had grown into a man. He was taller than Jeremiah, his older brother and my brother-in-law, and a foot taller than I was. He was broadshouldered and strong, and handsome with his bright hazel eyes and golden hair. He was both a hard worker and a kind person. He was everything I wanted in a husband.

Over the last couple of months, as we stole hugs behind

33

the birch trees, I yearned for him to kiss me, to hold me tight. But he hadn't—yet. It didn't matter that I'd never courted anyone else. I wanted Zeke Zimmerman. And I believed with my whole heart that he wanted me too.

I put the hoe away and then slipped through the door into the kitchen. Clare, my eldest sister, who was married to Jeremiah, had confided that she was a few months pregnant and having a difficult time. She was resting in her room with five-year-old Arden. Janice, who was three, slept in the children's room. I tiptoed up the staircase, listening for Janice. When I reached the nursery door, I pushed it open. She sat on her bed, playing with her doll. She glanced up at me. "*Aenti* Rosene," she said. "I was waiting for you."

She was a tiny thing. I scooped her up and held her close, rubbing my face against her braids, first one side and then the other, and taking in the scent of the Ivory soap *Mutter* brought from the shop. "How was your nap, little one?"

"Lonely." She frowned.

"Let's go get a snack," I said.

Halfway down the hall, Arden—who usually looked at books for his rest time—heard us and scampered out of Clare and Jeremiah's room.

I put my finger to my lips. "Your *Mamm* needs to sleep more."

When we reached the kitchen, I put Janice down, and both children scrambled to their places at the table while I dished applesauce into two bowls.

"Where's *Onkel* Zeke?" Arden asked.

"Working." I put a bowl and spoon in front of each child.

"May we go out and watch him?" Arden took a bite of applesauce.

"We can go for a walk." I turned toward the counter, hid-ing my smile, and sliced two pieces of bread from one of the loaves I'd baked that morning. I'd like nothing more than to watch Zeke work too.

Clare came down the stairs as the children put on their boots. "I'll start supper," she said. "Have fun on your walk."

Arden led the way, first heading to the far field and then to the west pasture. He loved everything about the farm. The cows and calves, the fields and pastures, the barns and stable. The horses.

Zeke, who was dragging the pasture, took off his hat and waved it around his head in a greeting. Arden laughed and did the same with his.

"I want to work with Onkel," Arden said.

"Someday," I answered.

Jeremiah allowed Arden to help with lots of chores but not dragging the field. There wasn't a safe place for him to stand.

Zeke had been working on our farm since he was fourteen. He hadn't joined the Amish church yet, but I had no doubt he would. His oldest brother farmed the Zimmerman family farm, with their father's help. I hoped our farm would provide enough work for Zeke to continue working with Jeremiah, and in time, for the two to split the profits.

I was two years older than Zeke. Plenty of Amish married younger than he was now, though. I hoped we'd wed soon, but first we needed to start officially courting.

An hour later, Arden and *Vater* had gone to the dairy barn to help with the milking while Janice played with her doll in the living room. I returned to the garden to cut the early chard for dinner.

Zeke stepped out of the stable, this time without the

horses. He waved again and called out, "Do you have a minute? I want to ask you something."

Of course I had a minute.

He gestured toward the picnic table by the birch trees. I reached it first and sat down.

He straddled the bench beside me. "There's a singing on Sunday evening. Would you like to go?"

I tilted my head toward him. "With you?"

"Jah." His hazel eyes sparkled.

I'd been hoping ever since he turned twenty that he'd ask me. It had only taken him six months.

"What time will you pick me up?"

He chuckled. "Does it matter?"

I raised my eyebrows.

He leaned toward me, bumping my shoulder and sending a jolt down my spine. "Should I pick you up early or on time?"

I hesitated, and then turned my face toward the sunbeam coming through the birch trees and said with confidence, "Early."

He grinned. "I'll pick you up at six. I'll speak with your father today and ask his permission."

"For . . . ?" I was feeling sassy.

He shook his head and laughed. "Taking you to the singing. What did you think?" He stood, bumping against my arm with his leg. I leaned into him. He met my gaze as he stepped away from the bench, his eyes full of warmth. "I'd better get back to work before Jeremiah scolds me."

I stood too. "Will you eat supper with us tonight?" I longed to reach out to him, to take his hand. But we were both already more forward than we should have been—the bumps and the brushes and the hugs.

Zeke motioned toward the birch trees and then stepped behind them. I joined him. He gave me a hug, holding me tighter and longer than he had before. Then he kissed the top of my head through my *Kapp*. I gazed up at him. Would he finally kiss me on the mouth?

He let go of me and stepped backward.

"See you after the milking." Zeke tipped his hat and grinned again.

My heart skipped a beat as I headed to the garden, forcing my feet not to dance along with my heart.

Zeke Zimmerman had finally asked me to a singing.

The night of the singing, I wore a print Mennonite dress, knowing I'd give it up for a solid-color Amish dress if Zeke asked me to marry him.

He showed up in a new buggy—not the old one of his *Dat*'s that he usually drove.

As he came up to the front door and knocked, I stepped away from the window. Vater, who was resting in his chair, stood and said, "Who could that be?"

I answered, "Zeke."

"What is he doing here?"

"I'm going to the singing with him. He spoke with you about it." At least I thought he had.

Vater rubbed both eyes with his fists. "On Friday? Was that what that was about?" He grinned.

I laughed. "Jah."

Mutter came into the living room with a dish towel in her hands. "Are you and Zeke courting?"

"No," I responded. "We're going to the singing."

Mutter threw her hands in the air, launching the dish towel

toward the ceiling. "Am I to lose another daughter to the Amish?" She caught the towel, pivoted, and headed toward the kitchen. But she was teasing me. I knew she adored Zeke too. Mutter had been opposed, at first, to Clare courting Jeremiah. But she wasn't opposed to Zeke.

He knocked again.

I stepped toward the door.

"I'll get it," Vater said. He swung the front door open and motioned for Zeke to come inside. "*Wilkum.*"

"Denki." Zeke clasped his hands together and looked past Vater to me. "Ready?" I'd never seen Zeke seem nervous before—but he did now.

"I just need to get my coat," I said. The day had turned chilly, and it would be cold by the time we returned home.

As I hurried toward the door, Vater asked, "Are you two going as friends?"

Zeke cleared his throat and said, "I've been fond of Rosene—" I couldn't hear any more of his answer.

When I returned with my coat, Vater and Zeke still stood at the front door, but both were silent.

"I won't be late," I said to Vater.

"Zeke said he'd have you home early."

I gave Zeke a coy smile and then turned to Vater. "If you're already in bed, I'll knock on your door and let you know I'm home."

"Get home before I go to bed."

"Vater, I'm twenty-two."

"Are you? I thought you were twenty."

I shook my head. He smiled.

I turned toward Zeke and said, "Let's go."

"*Sehn dich schpeeder*," he said to Vater. *See you later.*

"Tomorrow morning," Vater replied. "Bright and early."

As we walked to the buggy, Zeke said, "Ervin doesn't seem to like the idea of me taking you to the singing."

"He's protective is all—and he was mostly joking." At least I hoped he was.

We reached the buggy, and Zeke helped me up to the bench. "Nice buggy," I said as Zeke climbed up on his side.

He gave me a smile. "I've been saving for a long time. I ordered it a few months ago and picked it up on Monday." Perhaps he'd been waiting until it arrived to ask me to a singing.

As Zeke drove the buggy up the driveway, Jeremiah waved from the pasture where he was checking on a calf. Zeke returned his wave, and so did I. Arden raced alongside another calf. He stopped, took off his straw hat, and waved it in the air. Zeke did the same in response, laughing as he did.

"That kid," he said. "He's ready to take over the farm now."

I agreed.

"He adores you," Zeke said to me.

"Not as much as he adores you," I answered.

"I'm not so sure about that. It's like he has two Mamms." Zeke glanced at me and smiled.

My face grew warm.

Zeke slid toward me. I inched toward him until our thighs touched. I put my hands in my lap, but Zeke reached over and took the one closest to him in his. His hand was warm and comforting. I scooted closer and leaned my head against his shoulder.

"We're a little early," he said.

"Jah," I answered. "We are."

Ahead was the covered bridge that was a mile from our farm. Zeke's horse slowed as it stepped onto the wooden planks. The drumming of the horse's hooves reverberated through the structure. We reached the middle, and Zeke pulled on the reins. "Whoa." The horse came to a stop.

Then Zeke let go of my hand and put his arm around me, pulling me close as he shifted toward me on the bench seat. As he leaned in, I tilted my face toward him. As our mouths met, he pulled me even closer. A jolt of something—energy? passion? desire?—shot through me.

Followed by a sense of panic.

A horn honked. Zeke laughed a little as he pulled away from me. "That's what I get for stopping on the bridge."

I turned my head. A pickup waited behind us.

Zeke clucked his tongue and took up the reins. The horse started across the rest of the bridge. Once we reached the road, Zeke pulled the buggy to the side. As the pickup passed, Zeke waved, and the driver of the pickup nodded. Zeke put his arm around me and kissed the top of my head through my Kapp. Then he said, "I've never been so happy."

I felt the same. Except for that moment of panic I'd felt as he kissed me on the bridge. It had subsided but left me with questions. Should I have told Zeke my secret before? Should I tell him now? Or should I wait until we'd officially started courting?

I shuddered.

"Are you cold?" Zeke asked.

"Not really."

He pulled me nearer anyway.

When we reached the Yoder farm, Zeke dropped me off at the house and said, "See you in a minute." Then he continued on to the barn.

Zeke's sister, Beth, stood by the door. "Rosene!" she called out. Beth was four years older than me and had been working on the other side of the county for several years. I only saw her occasionally. "There you are!" As I met her, she grabbed my hand. "Finally! Zeke's wanted to ask you to a singing for years." Beth and I chatted about how Jeremiah, Clare, and the kids were doing. Then she lowered her voice. "Zeke has adored you for as long as I can remember. He thought he was too young for you, until about a year ago." She grinned and then glanced past me. "I hope you want a lot of children. Zeke has always said he wants twelve." She laughed.

I turned. Zeke was behind us, grinning.

The warmth on my face turned into heat and burned straight through me. Beth didn't notice as she pulled me into the house. Zeke put his hand on my shoulder and followed.

I needed to tell him—but how?

The singing took place in the Yoders' basement. There were twenty-one of us—twelve young women on one side and nine young men on the other. Afterward, we gathered to enjoy oatmeal cookies and popcorn, and to talk and joke and laugh. However, I didn't feel carefree enough to join in. It wasn't that I wasn't comfortable—this was a group of Amish young people I'd known for years.

When Zeke whispered in my ear, asking if I was ready to leave, I answered, "Jah, if you are."

"Let's go," he said. None of the other couples had left yet. I guessed they'd think we were eager to spend time by ourselves.

We stepped out into the waning evening light. By the time Zeke hitched his horse to the buggy and lit the lantern he hung on the side, the first star shone. Then more and more poked out of the dark sky as we rolled down the lane. It was clear but chilly for the first Sunday of June. I began to shiver.

Zeke pulled a wool blanket out from under the seat and handed it to me. "Here," he said. "This will help."

I spread it out over my lap and then flipped the end over his legs too. "Denki," he said and then reached for my hand again. I scooted close as I'd done before, but this time my heart didn't race. Instead, a knot formed in my stomach.

The horse slowed for the covered bridge again. Zeke let go of my hand and put his arm around me, pulling me even closer. "You were awfully quiet at the singing," he said. "Are you all right?"

"I'm fine," I answered. "But I need to tell you something."

He met my eyes. "That sounds serious."

"It is," I answered.

"I'll stop under the tree." There was a pull-out for buggies up ahead that was shaded by a gigantic oak.

By the time he pulled over, my heart pounded, and I felt as if I could barely speak. Turning toward me, Zeke took my hand. "What is it?"

A dog barked in the distance. I was no longer cold. In fact, I was sweating. "As far as children—" I choked on the last word.

"Is that what's wrong?" he asked. "Ignore Beth. She means well." He shifted toward me, leaving his arm around me. "Rosene, I'm crazy about you. But I don't want to rush you. I don't want to assume you feel the same way about me."

"I do feel the same way." I cleared my throat. "But something happened to me while I was still in Germany that you need to know about. It's only fair I tell you now. Unless by some chance you already know. Perhaps someone told you?"

He shook his head. "I don't know anything about your life in Germany—just that Clare brought you here."

"I was part of a study," I said. "My twin and me."

"You have a twin?"

"I had a twin."

His eyebrows shot upward.

"The Nazi doctors—" I paused. "They made it so I can never have children."

Zeke cocked his head. "What do you mean?"

I didn't want to say out loud that they'd sterilized me before I'd even completely gone through puberty. "They did a procedure." Nor could I bring myself to say that Dr. Josef Mengele, who would later be known as the Angel of Death of Auschwitz, performed the surgery. "They didn't want me to ever be able to have children, in case I passed my seizures on to my children."

"But you don't have seizures."

"Not anymore. But I did. That's why I was part of a medical study run by the Nazis." I paused, trying to decide how much to tell him. "When Clare brought me here, she took me to a doctor in Philadelphia who prescribed a new medication, and I stopped having seizures. Perhaps I would have outgrown them anyway."

"Can the procedure—so you can't have children—be reversed?"

"No." I glanced down at my hands, folded on top of the blanket. "I want you to know now . . . before . . ." My voice trailed away.

"Do you want to be a wife someday, even if you can't have children?"

"Jah," I answered. "Of course. Perhaps a child will come another way. Through adoption or . . . something." I knew I would love a child I didn't birth. I thought of all the people who loved me. Jah, Mutter and Vater were also my aunt and uncle, but they loved me and treated me as they did Clare and Martha—perhaps even a little more tenderly because of what I'd gone through. I thought of my deep love for Arden and Janice.

Zeke tilted his head as his brow furrowed.

"Don't say anything now." I continued to stare at my hands. "You should think about it. I just want you to know. I don't want to keep secrets from you."

"I appreciate that." He moved his arm from around me and took the reins with both hands. "If you don't want my answer now, when should I give it to you?"

I scooted a couple of inches to my right. "When you're certain of it." I couldn't bear for him to be dishonest just to make me feel better.

We rode the rest of the way home in silence.

• 4 •

That night, I tossed and turned. Perhaps I'd presented the information to Zeke in entirely the wrong manner. I should have spoken to Clare and Jeremiah before I told him. Perhaps he now felt I'd misled him.

The truth was, I hadn't thought about it as much as I should have. Perhaps I was avoiding having to be honest about being sterilized. I curled up in a ball, pushing away thoughts of Zeke kissing me.

The first I ever saw a diagram of a woman's body was when I took biology class in high school. Uterus. Ovaries. Fallopian tubes. That was when I put together what *tubal ligation* meant. I'd felt violated in the Institute in Frankfurt over and over, but especially after I woke up from my surgery, although I didn't fully comprehend what had happened. I felt violated all over again as I looked at the diagram of a woman's body—and then thought of my body.

An article I read about Dr. Josef Mengele a year ago explained that he originally focused on cleft palates. But when he joined the Nazis and became an SS officer, he focused on genetic research on identical twins and the disabled, which resulted in him taking away my ability to ever conceive a child—and worse, the death of my twin sister, Dorina.

Thanks to Clare, my life had been spared.

The next morning, she greeted me with a wide smile—and then a frown. "You look like you didn't sleep. Did the singing not go well?"

"No, it went fine."

"What's the matter?"

I glanced around the kitchen. Janice sat in the high chair.

As if she could read my mind, Clare said, "Vater and Arden went out to help with the milking." Arden was at the age of repeating what he heard. Janice, on the other hand, showed no interest in the conversations around her. Clare gave her a piece of bread. "Mutter went to the store to check on something."

It was safe to talk. "I told Zeke about what happened in Germany."

Clare had a confused expression on her face. "I think he already knew we had to flee to save your life."

I lowered my voice. "I told him about being sterilized."

"Oh." She sat down at the table. "I'm sorry. I should have . . ." Her voice trailed off. "I guess I haven't thought about that lately." She raised her head. "It wasn't that I forgot. Maybe I didn't want to think about it."

I understood. "I didn't want to think about it either. But if Zeke and I are going to court, I thought he should know."

"What did Zeke say?"

"I asked him to think about it before he responds." I sat down at the table and faced her. "I wish I would have had you tell him. Perhaps he would be honest with you. I'm afraid he won't be with me." My eyes began to burn, and I blinked a couple of times. "When we arrived at the singing, Beth was there. She told me Zeke always said he wanted a dozen children. He confirmed it with a grin."

"Was that after you told him?"

"No, before." I swiped at a tear, and Clare handed me the dish towel that had been draped over her shoulder. I dabbed at my eyes. "That's why I told him on the way home."

"Zeke has been sweet on you for years," Clare said. "I don't think this would make a difference."

"But he wants a lot of children."

"Most Amish *Youngie* want a big family. It's expected." She lowered her voice. "But you don't have to have children to have a happy marriage."

I'd never known of an Amish woman who had my problem. I knew of a few Mennonite and Amish couples that didn't have children—but I guessed no one knew why exactly. None of the women had been sterilized.

"What should I do?" I asked.

"Talk it through with Zeke."

"What if he says he doesn't care? But then resents me later?"

"Well, this isn't your fault. It was done to you without your consent, without even your knowledge. What happened to you was unconscionable." She rested her hands on her belly. "I should have done more. I had no idea what their intentions were that day, but I knew they were no good."

"You did do more—you saved me."

She exhaled. "But not your ability to have a baby."

I closed my eyes, squeezing away the tears.

Zeke, carrying Arden, burst into the kitchen with a grin on his face, as if nothing had happened the night before. "We're ready for breakfast," Zeke called out.

Clare stepped away from the table.

I stood too and gave Zeke a half smile. "I'll start the coffee."

That day, after lunch, Zeke played with Arden and Janice for a few minutes in the living room. I watched from the kitchen as I cleared the table. He stood, and Arden slid off his back. "I need to speak with Rosene about something."

"Don't stop." Arden fell into a heap on the floor.

"You go rest," Zeke said to him, "and then you can help with the milking this afternoon."

Janice stuck out her lower lip.

"Now, now," Zeke said to her. "We'll play longer tomorrow."

Clare came and took their hands. "I'm going to rest too." She turned toward me. "Go talk with Zeke, and then you can do the dishes."

I didn't want to talk with Zeke. I gave her a pleading look. She took the hands of her children and started up the stairs.

"Let's go sit at the picnic table." He motioned for me to go first.

I led the way through the kitchen and down the porch steps. Jeremiah wasn't in sight. No one was. I continued to the picnic table, aware of Zeke behind me.

I sat down, facing the house. He sat down across from me.

He reached across the table and took my hand, which was more of a public display of affection than the Amish allowed. His hand was sweaty. He gazed into my eyes. I couldn't help but look away.

"Rosene."

I forced myself to meet his gaze.

"I've thought a lot about what you said last night."

Here it came.

"Why didn't you tell me you had a twin?"

"What?"

"I thought I knew you. After we talked last night, I realized I don't."

My hand slipped out of his to the tabletop. Out of everything I said last night, that's what bothered him?

"Were you identical?"

I nodded as I put my hands in my lap.

He blinked. "I know nothing about your family in Germany. Your mother?"

"She died."

"Your father?"

I crossed my arms. "I don't want to talk about him."

"You know everything about me." Zeke exhaled slowly. "And about my family."

I doubted I knew *everything*, but I did know a lot.

He continued. "I remember the first time I saw you. I was eleven—" I'd been thirteen. Zeke had come over with Jeremiah a few days after I arrived, to help with the afternoon milking.

He paused a moment and locked eyes with me. "You sat on the porch. You were so small—much smaller than I was—and thin and fragile. I had an urge to take care of you then . . . but soon you brightened and flourished. You were so capable, so spunky, so happy. In no time at all, *you* were taking care of everyone. You didn't need me to take care of you, but I needed you. First as a friend. Now . . ." He smiled. "Now I see that, to me, your existence began that day I first saw you. I wasn't curious about where you came from or what your life was like. In all this time, I never thought to ask. I'm sorry."

"You have nothing to be sorry for."

"I do. I should have asked about your life before I knew you."

49

"That's just it—I didn't want you to ask. I didn't want to talk about it. And I still don't. I only told you what you have a right to know."

"But I want to know. I want you to tell me everything."

I shook my head. "I don't want to remember everything. I don't want to talk about the past."

He leaned across the table. "Are you as happy as you seem?"

I uncrossed my arms and folded my hands in my lap again. If Zeke still wanted to marry me knowing what he did, then yes. I was happy. "Jah," I whispered.

He sat up straight, his biceps bulging against his rolled sleeves. "You don't sound happy."

I brushed away a tear and lowered my head.

"Rosene." Zeke reached across the table again, but I didn't offer him my hand. "Do you trust me?"

"Jah," I answered, but my voice fell flat.

After a long pause, he said, "I'm sorry about your twin. And your German family—whatever happened with them. I'm sorry about what the Nazis did to you. I care, and it matters to me, but it doesn't change how I feel about you."

"Denki." A sob welled up inside of me. I hadn't thought of Dorina, at least not longer than it took to force myself not to, for a long time. "I'm sorry," I gasped, trying to stop the sob. "I need to go back to the house."

I thought of last Christmas, when Mutter had a crate of oranges delivered. She checked the produce and held up a spoiled orange at the bottom of the crate and then another and another. *"Damaged goods,"* she'd said to the delivery-man. *"Give me a different crate."*

That's what I felt like. Damaged goods. Even though Zeke said it didn't change the way he felt about me.

I fled toward the house.

Zeke followed. "Rosene!"

I stumbled but caught myself before I fell. He reached my side and linked his arm through mine. Tears cascaded down my face. Sob followed sob.

"Rosene." His voice was low and tender. He took a bandana from his pocket and handed it to me. I held it to my face.

When we reached the door, he opened it and called out, "Clare!"

The shame, grief, and confusion I'd buried for so long had come out in a torrent of emotions.

Clare appeared, and Zeke left. She helped me upstairs, where I climbed into bed and pulled the covers over my head.

Zeke didn't come in for breakfast the next morning. After I did the dishes, I went to the store to help Mutter. A large grocery store had opened in Lancaster, but people in our area still bought what they couldn't grow at Mutter's store, since it was a long trip into town. She'd added a few new items like work gloves and hats. And women's clothes.

Mutter had decided to rearrange the store that day, something she did at least once a year. She needed my help, which was a good distraction.

As I took cans off a shelf, the mailman stepped into the store. It was a rural route, and we had a box at the end of the driveway for both the store and family. The mailman rarely came into the store, unless it was for something to drink on a hot day.

He held up two envelopes. "I have two airmail letters for you," he said. "They look important. One is for Mrs. Simons."

He handed the first letter to Mutter. "And the other is—" He looked down at the envelope. "For Miss Rosene Simons." He glanced my way.

"That's me."

Mutter said, "Let me get you a soda for delivering these in person. Coca-Cola, right?"

"That's right." He followed Mutter toward the cooler.

My letter was from my sister Martha. The return address was the International Red Cross office in West Berlin, and URGENT was stamped across the front. I craned my neck to see Mutter's envelope, which she'd left on the counter. It was from my biological father, Josef Weber, in Frankfurt.

My pulse began to pound. How unsettling to have a letter from Vater Josef, as I had come to think of him after I was adopted into the Simons family, after my emotional reaction the day before.

I stepped behind the counter and opened the thin envelope, unfolding the letter. Martha was coming home to Lancaster County the next week.

I saw Lena at a meeting in Nuremberg a few weeks ago. She's hoping you'll come visit sometime soon— apparently Onkel Josef is ill. I would be happy to accompany you to Germany and stay with you the entire time. Please think about it—a visit could be good for you—and when I arrive, we can talk about it more.

I quickly refolded the letter and slipped it into my pocket. "What did Martha say?" Mutter asked.

"That she's coming home for a visit." I couldn't seem to move from behind the counter. "Next week."

Mutter smiled. "*Wunderbar!*"

Then she opened her letter. After she'd read it, she said, "Josef isn't doing well." Mutter met my eyes. "He's hoping you'll go to Frankfurt to visit."

I swallowed hard, fighting my escalating panic. I had no desire to return to Germany, not even for a visit. I managed to say, "I'll think about it."

"I hope you'll go," Mutter said. "It would be good for you to have an adventure—especially if you're going to get serious about Zeke." She smiled.

I wasn't surprised she wanted me to return to Germany and have an adventure—she mourned she wasn't able to return to her homeland more. She'd married Vater when he was a student in Frankfurt and then came to Lancaster County with him in 1913. She'd only returned to Germany once since then, in 1927.

Mutter put her letter on the counter. "Did Martha mention George? Do you think he's coming too?"

"I think she would have told us if he was."

Mutter nodded. "I don't understand their work, nor their marriage, but I'm glad she's coming home."

"So am I." I leaned against the counter.

Mutter spoke softly. "Clare said you had a difficult time yesterday."

"I'm fine." I collected myself and returned to the shelf to remove cans. It all felt like too much. Telling Zeke about my infertility. Mourning Dorina again. Thinking about Vater Josef. I couldn't imagine why Martha thought I needed to return to Germany.

I wanted my simple life back.

· 5 ·

I kept my distance from Zeke as I washed Martha's bedding, prepared her room, and cleaned the house from top to bottom. Perhaps I was using these chores as an excuse not to interact with him. Being around Zeke used to make me happy—but now it made me sad. He deserved someone without the baggage I carried. There were plenty of Amish young women for him to court, ones who had grown up in the church and lived in Lancaster County their entire lives. Ones who weren't damaged.

Most days, Zeke would still eat breakfast and lunch with us, but he wouldn't talk or flirt or joke with me. We didn't meet at the picnic table in the afternoon. We didn't go on walks together. We certainly didn't sneak behind the birch trees.

When Martha arrived, Zeke joked with her. They'd always gotten along well. "So, where's George?" he asked.

"In Berlin," she answered. "He couldn't get time off."

"How do we know you and George are actually married?" Zeke teased.

Martha laughed. "I guess you actually can't." She flashed her simple ring at him, just a gold band. "This could be out of a Cracker Jack box, right?"

Zeke smirked. "Nee. It would be fancier if so." It was the most animated I'd seen Zeke in the last week.

After lunch, Martha helped me wash the dishes while Clare took the children upstairs for their rest time.

As Martha took the first glass out of the rinse water, she asked, "Have you thought about going to Germany?" Before I could respond, she said, "You can go with me when I return."

I put another glass in the rinse water. "I don't want to go back."

"Lena wants an opportunity to speak with you. She misses you. And she believes Onkel Josef's health is failing."

I didn't respond.

Martha dried another glass. "What's going on with you and Zeke?"

I shrugged.

She put a hand on my shoulder. "Rosene."

I exhaled. "I told Zeke about being sterilized in Germany."

"Oh." She squeezed my shoulder. "Did he not take it well?"

"No, I think he did. He was mostly upset that I never told him about Dorina. Or my German family. Or what my life was like before I came here."

"Can't you tell him about it now?"

"No." I took a step to the side, causing her hand to fall away. "I don't want to."

"Maybe you *need* to return to Germany. Maybe seeing Lena and Josef will help you work through this and be able to explain it to Zeke."

"I don't want to explain it to Zeke." I washed the last glass and put it in the rinse water.

Martha waited a long moment to respond. "Maybe time

away from Zeke would be a good thing. You'll be with me. We'll spend a night in New York City. And then fly to London and stay a night there. We can see the sights in those two cities, and in Frankfurt. We'd only need to stay at Onkel Josef's for a few days."

When I didn't reply, she continued. "I'll be with you the whole time. I think seeing your German family and your childhood home might put things into perspective. Perhaps it would free you from the past."

Again, I didn't reply.

"Talk to Clare," Martha said. "She knows Onkel Josef and Lena far better than I do. I think she could give you better advice."

I didn't have a chance to speak with Clare that afternoon. Zeke joined us at supper. I guessed it was because Martha was home. The conversation shifted to Germany. I stared at my plate. Vater asked Martha about the European Recovery Program—many called it the Marshall Plan—that had recently been enacted to help Europe, including Germany, recover economically from the war.

"Germany needs to rebuild, or it will be easier for the Soviets to manipulate the entire country, not just the Russian quadrant," Martha said.

Zeke asked, "What's the Russian quadrant?"

Martha explained that after the war ended, Germany had been divided into four zones overseen by the US, England, France, and Russia. Berlin, which was deep in the Russian zone, had also been divided into quadrants. People from the other zones could travel to the city by car, rail, or air.

Martha said, "The people of Germany are more impoverished now than they were during the Depression."

"That's hard to imagine," Mutter said. She grew quiet.

Even during the beginning of the war, Mutter sang the praises of Germany. Toward the end of the war, Martha and I weren't sure where her allegiance fell.

"*Ach*," Vater said. "So many were killed in Germany, and in the rest of Europe." He turned toward Martha. "Do you know how many?"

Martha answered, "Not yet, but hundreds of thousands of civilians were killed by Allied bombing in Germany. But far, far more people—millions—died in the concentration camps from the Nazis' brutality. Jewish people were murdered along with nearly that many Polish and Roma people, Soviet POWs, disabled people, and political and ideological dissidents."

"Goodness," Mutter said. "How many people are displaced?"

"Millions and millions throughout Europe," Martha said. "I've heard over twenty million in Germany alone, including a million lost, missing, and displaced children."

Vater sighed. "I can't begin to comprehend that amount of suffering. What a daunting job you have, Martha."

"And rewarding." She dished up more mashed potatoes. "It's difficult, but I try to focus on one person—one refugee—at a time."

After we finished the dishes, Mutter took the children upstairs for their baths. Martha went out to the barn with Jeremiah to check on a calf, and Clare and I sat down in the living room to catch up on the mending.

I picked up a pair of Arden's trousers that needed the knees patched, and Clare worked on restitching a seam on one of Jeremiah's shirts.

She threaded her needle. "Martha said she asked you to go to Germany with her to see Lena and Onkel Josef."

"Jah." I cut a patch out of a worn-out pair of Vater's trousers. "I don't want to, but Martha said I should speak with you before I decide."

"I could guess why you don't want to go, but would you tell me?"

Why didn't I want to go? Vater Josef and Lena hadn't protected me—in fact, they'd handed me over to the Nazis. "The memories alone sent me to my bed in tears last week. The thought of returning to Frankfurt terrifies me."

"I understand," Clare said. "But the danger is gone. The Nazis can't hurt you."

"I'm not worried about the Nazis. I'm worried about Vater Josef and Lena." And Lena's husband, Garit, but I didn't want to even mention him.

"That they'll hurt you?"

I concentrated on pinning the patch over the right knee of Arden's trousers. "Not physically."

When I didn't say anything more, Clare asked, "Have you forgiven them?"

Forgiveness was important to both the Mennonites and the Amish, but it seemed the preachers in Clare's Amish church talked about it more. I positioned the last pin. "Have they asked for forgiveness?"

"Maybe they will. Maybe that's what Lena wants to speak with you about." Clare stared down at her tiny stitches. "But we're required to forgive whether someone asks for it or not."

When I didn't respond, she said, "If you haven't forgiven them, perhaps seeing them will help. Josef is old and sick. Lena is doing translation work at the Nuremberg Trials—she knows the truth about the Nazis now. Garit is working on his PhD so he can teach at the university. They're trying to move on. They were broken in some way before the war—Josef by what Germany went through after the Great War, Lena by your mother's death, Garit by his own insecurities and determination to prove himself."

Her words surprised me. "What do you mean?"

"About Garit?"

I nodded.

"He always seemed to be scrambling to get ahead. I don't think he felt worthy. Those feelings were common among young men in Germany after the Great War. That's part of the reason why Hitler, who came across as a strong man but was actually a con man, appealed to so many of them. They wanted a great leader, someone to look up to, to make them feel superior, to give them hope. They hoped they, like Hitler, could prevail against a world that had rejected them."

I hadn't thought of that.

"Seeing all of them now that you're an adult will take away any fear that you still have. Seeing them as vulnerable people will hopefully make it easier to forgive."

Perhaps Clare was right about forgiving. Through the years, I'd concentrated on forgetting. Perhaps returning to Germany would allow me to forgive them and then forget them and finally move on.

Later that evening, after everyone had gone to bed, Martha and I sat at the kitchen table. I told her I was interested in going to Germany after all, as long as she would be with me.

"Absolutely," she said. "Until the minute I put you on the plane to fly home."

"I'll have to fly home by myself?"

She nodded. "But you'll know what to do then."

"What about the cost?"

"I'm able to cover it." She sat closer to the kerosene lamp and appeared to glow in the low light. "Please don't give it a second thought."

When I didn't reply, Martha asked, "What do you think?"

"That maybe I should go." I met Martha's gaze.

Time away from Zeke and Lancaster County might be good for me. Perhaps the Lord was leading me to Frankfurt for my own good. Maybe it was time that I did forgive Vater Josef and Lena. And even Garit. I valued Clare and Martha and Mutter's opinions. All of them thought I should go.

Martha smiled at me. "Talk to Zeke tomorrow," she said. "Make sure he understands you're just visiting Germany and you'll be returning. Make sure he knows you want to resume courting."

Resume? We'd only gone to one singing. But I understood what Martha meant. It was as if we'd been courting for years.

"He's hurt," Martha said. "He doesn't understand why you won't share more with him."

"Maybe I will be able to after I return."

"Are you pushing him away on purpose?"

"No," I answered. "I don't think so." But was I? Nothing seemed straightforward.

The next day, I intended to talk with Zeke. But I only managed to say that I'd be gone for a while and when I returned, we should talk. I wasn't sure how to communicate with Zeke anymore.

He agreed and said, "I'll be praying for you."

"Denki." I didn't add that I would be praying for him too, although I would.

As I said, "Good-bye," a dejected expression passed across

his face, but I couldn't think of what to say in response. I'd lost my confidence, my spunk. I felt as if I were thirteen again.

Martha and I took the train from Lancaster to Philadelphia and then on to New York City. We spent the night in a hotel and visited the Empire State Building and Times Square. Then we took a bus to the airport. I wore my Mennonite Kapp and dress and a sweater of Martha's. As the plane took off, I gripped Martha's arm and closed my eyes, certain it would crash. I'd never have to see Lena and Vater Josef. Zeke could marry someone else and have a family. I'd go to heaven.

But the plane ascended without incident, and although we hit turbulence a handful of times and again I was sure my life was over, we landed in London fourteen hours after we left New York. It was so much quicker—and more stressful—than the voyage by ship Clare and I had taken to the US.

In London, we took a bus to Buckingham Palace, Big Ben, and the Tower of London. Signs of the Blitz were everywhere—bombed buildings, gaping cellars, flattened neighborhoods. But other areas were untouched.

I wondered what Frankfurt looked like.

After spending a night in a hotel not far from the airport, we boarded a plane for Frankfurt. From there, Martha hailed a cab to the Weber family home. It didn't take us through Old Town, but many of the neighborhoods we drove through had bombed-out buildings.

It was late afternoon when we arrived at my childhood home. Garit, Lena's husband, answered the door. He stepped backward and then clasped his hands together. "Martha, welcome." Then he looked at me. "Ach, little Dyna Rosene has come home at last."

I blanched at his use of my first name, a name I'd rather never hear again.

"Are they here?" Lena appeared, looking much the same with her blond hair and stylish dress. "Cousin Martha!" she exclaimed, reaching out with a hug and then a kiss. She stepped toward me. "Sister! You have no idea how much we've missed you. Welcome home!"

"I'm only visiting," I answered.

"Oh?" Lena smiled. "I think you'll change your mind."

· 6 ·

Treva

The next morning, a second doctor stopped by and said Rosene would need to spend another night. I decided it was time to send Misty a text explaining what had happened and asking if they could hold my job for a few days past April 15. I needed to buy my ticket to Alaska soon—it would be expensive as it was and would most likely only get more expensive as time passed.

She texted back immediately.

> Of course. We're praying for your aunt and for you. Please keep us updated.

Relieved, I slipped my phone into my pocket. One of my sisters would have to take over Rosene's care, and it wouldn't be Brenna—at least not any time soon. Especially not if she went to Germany to settle Lena's estate.

Mammi couldn't seem to wrap her head around the fact that Brenna now had a career and a boyfriend, one who adored her. Johann was the reason Brenna had moved to

Ukraine almost a year ago. She wanted to get to know him better—and now she had no plans of returning. It seemed Mammi had assumed, since the three of us girls moved to Lancaster County from Oregon five years ago, that Brenna would be the old maid sister who took over the family business. Dawdi told me in a letter he sent while I was in Haiti that Mammi had hired a contractor to convert the storage room above the store into an apartment for Brenna. We couldn't ask her to go to Germany to settle Lena's estate and also take time off work to fly to the States to care for Rosene.

Ivy would have to.

After more tests, Rosene slept most of the morning. The doctor stopped by in the early afternoon. After asking Rosene how she was feeling, she said, "We have your test results. There is definitely damage, but at your age, surgery or a procedure wouldn't be worth the risk."

"Are you sure?" I asked. "Rosene is a very young ninety-three-year-old."

"Yes." The doctor smiled at me kindly. "There are risks with procedures—blood clots and that sort of thing. At this point, because the blockage is minimal, the risk of the procedures is greater than the risk of another heart attack. I'll prescribe a blood pressure medication and rehab."

"Just to clarify," I said, "did stress contribute to the heart attack?"

"Stress can spike blood pressure, which can cause a heart attack." She turned toward Rosene. "Your blood pressure *has* been high. We need to monitor that, so I want to keep you in the hospital for observation for one more day. If all goes well, we'll send you home tomorrow, as long as you can take it easy."

"She can," I said.

The doctor smiled at me and then returned her attention to Rosene. "But will you?"

"I will," Rosene said. "I have plenty of support. But how long should I take it easy?"

"No lifting anything for two weeks—not even a gallon of milk. And then only light activity, such as sweeping, for two weeks after that. No doing laundry or gardening or that sort of thing. It's important that you completely heal. And you'll need to go to a few sessions of cardiac rehab—you'll learn stress-reducing techniques and receive information about nutrition and exercise."

After the doctor left, Rosene said, "That's not so bad. I thought perhaps Priscilla would have to close the store to take care of me. But I can get by."

"No," I said. "You need someone with you."

"The doctor didn't say that."

"She implied it," I said. "Besides, you're in a house without a phone."

"Arden can check in with me every hour or so."

Forcefully, I said, "No."

"Treva, I don't want you to postpone your plans. I don't want you to stay to take care of me."

I took a deep breath, surprised at how agitated I felt. I told her about Misty's text and then said, "I'll give it some time and then decide."

<hr>

While Rosene ate her dinner in her room, I headed down to the cafeteria, thinking it was time I ate a real meal. As I bit into a cheeseburger, Ivy appeared in the doorway of the cafeteria, searching the tables.

I waved.

She smiled and headed toward me. "There you are. Rosene told me to come down and keep you company."

I swallowed and asked, "Have you eaten?"

She shook her head as she sat down across from me. "I'm not hungry," she said as she reached for a fry and then dragged it through the ketchup on my plate. "That's good news that Rosene is doing so well."

"Did she tell you she needs to take it easy for the next month?"

"No. She said she didn't need surgery, and she's going to be fine."

I relayed exactly what the doctor's instructions were. "We can't leave her alone. Someone needs to be with her."

"Oh." Ivy picked up another fry. "Maybe Brenna will come home."

"Rosene might need Brenna to go to Germany and settle Lena's estate," I answered. "I was hoping you could take some time off."

Ivy wrinkled her nose. "Conrad and I are leaving for Oregon on Saturday for two weeks."

"What?"

"We've had this planned for a couple of months. It's spring break."

"It's spring break for a week."

"Yeah, Conrad managed to get another week off. A couple of personal days and unpaid days."

"What's going on?"

"I've been missing Oregon and Gran."

"And you couldn't wait until summer?"

Ivy picked up another fry. "No, I couldn't. Can you postpone your trip to Alaska?"

"I already have by a few days."

"Have you bought a ticket yet?"

I shook my head.

"By the time I'm home from Oregon, Rosene will be doing better," Ivy said. "Between Dawdi, Mammi, and me we can check in on her multiple times a day. In another three weeks or so, you can most likely go to Alaska."

"Most likely? Why wouldn't I be able to if you plan to take over the farm anyway?"

"Which farm?"

Was she playing dumb? Exasperated, I replied, "Dawdi's."

She wrinkled her nose. "We're not sure what we plan to do. We have an idea, but we need to figure out some things first. I think we can all make that work. You should plan to go to Alaska in a few weeks."

Baffled, I said, "I will."

When we returned to the room, Rosene had her eyes closed, and Ivy said she needed to go home. "Conrad just got done with the milking."

"Does he help on the farm often?"

"Quite a bit when Dawdi's between farmhands," Ivy answered. "If Dawdi does the milking on his own, it takes hours." Ivy gave me a hug. "I'll tell Rosene good-bye tomorrow before we leave for Oregon. Let me know if she's here or on the farm."

After Ivy left, Rosene opened her eyes and said, "You should go home for the night. Help Arden with the milking in the morning. Hopefully I'll be able to go home tomorrow."

"All right." I grabbed my bag and then asked, "Did you know Ivy and Conrad were going to Oregon?"

Rosene gave me a slight smile. "Not until just now. That puts more pressure on you, doesn't it?"

"No," I answered.

She tilted her head and met my gaze with her watery eyes.

"Well, maybe a little, but that's okay," I clarified. "I already texted Misty. She said it would work for me to arrive later."

"I really will be fine in the house alone."

"Maybe so," I said. "Maybe not."

The thing was, I wouldn't be fine if Rosene was alone. I needed someone to be with her, even if she didn't. What if she'd made it to the house yesterday morning and then had her heart attack? It could have been an hour before I'd gone inside.

The next morning, as Dawdi and I did the milking, he yawned several times. Then he stumbled as he dumped feed into one of the troughs.

"The coffee is done." I'd started it before we came out and let it percolate on low. "Why don't you go in and get some? I'll be fine until you get back."

"Good idea." He handed me the feed shovel. "I'll bring you a cup too."

"Denki." I resumed shoveling feed into the troughs of the cows that I'd just hooked up to the milkers.

As I worked, I couldn't help but note that the milking stalls needed to be cleaned from the night before and that the concrete floor needed to be scrubbed too. Gabe had been Dawdi's farmhand for years before he was deployed. I hadn't realized what a difference Gabe made on the farm, but now it was obvious. I'd taken his work for granted.

When Dawdi returned, we stood side by side and drank our coffee. "How did you sleep last night?" I asked.

"Great." He smiled a little. "During the couple of hours I managed to sleep."

"What kept you awake?"

"I keep thinking about what's going to happen to the farm."

"What do you mean?"

"I know you're going to Alaska to work, but do you plan to return here afterward? Running the store is wearing Priscilla out."

"Rosene said you've offered the farm to Ivy and Conrad."

He nodded. "Whether they decide to take it over or not, we could use your help."

"If Conrad and Ivy take over the farm, will he quit teaching?"

"I think he'd have to," Dawdi answered. "I'm hoping a family effort can help make the place more profitable—and sustainable."

"The farm isn't profitable?"

"We're on a downward trend." He grimaced. "If this keeps up, we won't be profitable in a few years. It's going to take a concerted effort, but I don't have the energy to take the lead. We really could use your help in the store. Priscilla needs to retire too."

"Do I have to decide now?"

Dawdi took a sip of coffee and then said, "No. Let me know when you know."

"It won't be until I've spent a while in Alaska." I wanted to see what I thought of it there before I made any other commitments. I rubbed the side of my neck. "Will Gabe work for you again when he returns?"

"There's no guarantee he will return."

A little alarmed, I asked, "What do you mean?"

"Perhaps he'll move on to greener pastures." Dawdi smiled wryly at his joke.

I didn't respond. A cow mooed.

"I'm afraid I'm going to have to sell the farm if Conrad and Ivy don't want it."

"Dawdi, don't say that."

"It's true," he said. "I'd like it to stay in the family." He shrugged. "But maybe that's not God's will."

I felt a little sick to my stomach but remembered Brenna telling me not to take responsibility for everything. "Any other reason you didn't sleep well?"

"Well, I hate to admit it, but I was worrying about Rosene. I know I'm not supposed to worry. . . ." He took another drink of coffee.

"I understand." I held my mug with both hands, drawing warmth from it. "She's seemed invincible for as long as I've known her." Another cow mooed.

Dawdi sighed. "Jah, Rosene has seemed as if she'd live forever. Even though we know no one does."

I thought about what Dawdi said as I drove to the hospital. No one was invincible. I knew that better than anyone.

After the accident that killed our parents, I'd been worried about Gran, who had cancer at the time, and about Brenna, who had already been depressed and having panic attacks. I worried about Ivy too, who mostly seemed out of sorts.

I first started trying not to be a problem in our family when Mom lost a baby—our little brother—when I was seven. He was stillborn at six months. I'd been naughty that morning, making a scene because the dress with the pink flowers I wanted to wear wasn't clean. Gran ended up having to dress me as if I were three and then carried me out to the van. Mom taught at the school my sisters and I attended, and when she climbed into the driver's seat, she said, "Treva, I'm extra tired today. I need you to do a better job cooperating."

I pouted the entire way to school and then didn't tell Mom good-bye before marching down the hall to my second-grade classroom. Mom taught kindergarten for a half day, and Dad had been picking us up from school. But Gran and Papa picked us up that day, saying that Mom and Dad were at the doctor.

"Mom didn't have an appointment scheduled. Is everything all right?" Ivy asked, already a know-it-all.

"As far as I know," Gran answered.

We didn't hear from Mom or Dad until several hours later, when Dad arrived alone. My sisters and I were doing our homework at the kitchen table after we'd finished the supper dishes. Dad's face was red and his eyes puffy. Papa and Gran sat down at the table with us as Dad said, "I have some bad news."

He told us the baby had died in utero, that it was a little boy, whom they'd named David. He said Mom would stay in the hospital overnight and then come home the next day. Ivy and Brenna both rushed into Dad's arms, while I froze. It was my fault. I'd been naughty. Mom was tired. The baby had died.

I vowed never to be naughty again.

As I parked the van in the hospital garage, my anxiety began to rise. What if Rosene had another heart attack soon? What if she was sicker than the doctors thought? My baby brother hadn't been invincible. Neither was Rosene.

A month ago, a baby in the orphanage in Haiti grew sick, a little boy who was four months old. His mother had died in childbirth, and the family didn't have the resources, without the mother, to care for him. He'd always been a little sickly.

Underweight. Prone to catching viruses. But, nevertheless, he'd been smiling and interacting. Coincidentally, his name was David.

I tried not to have favorites and never would admit it, but David was my favorite. Maybe because of his name. Or maybe because he was sweet and cuddly. Or maybe because I'd finally admitted I couldn't stay in Haiti and was beginning to accept Pierre wouldn't leave, and I was finding comfort in caring for David.

At first, he slept more. Then he became lethargic. Brooke called the doctor, who prescribed antibiotics. But then David developed thrush. And then diarrhea. And a horrible diaper rash. And he didn't get better. His fever spiked. The doctor changed the prescription to another antibiotic. David broke out in hives and began vomiting.

The next day, when I arrived at the orphanage, he wasn't in his crib. I turned around, alarmed. Brooke stepped to my side. "He didn't make it." Her voice was low and kind.

"Didn't make it?" I stuttered.

"He passed away early this morning."

For a moment, the old numbness returned, but then I broke through and began to cry. To wail. Brooke quickly escorted me to the office. "It happens," she said. "We've been fortunate this year. This is our first death. Sometimes by now we've had three or four."

I continued to wail. She hugged me and then held me. After a while, someone came to the door and said, "Brooke, we need you. . . ."

She gave me another hug. "Go to your room," she said. "Take whatever time you need."

Misty and Shawn had already returned to Alaska. The next group of volunteers wasn't arriving for a few days.

The rest of the babies in the orphanage needed me. "No." I took a shaky breath. "I'll be out in a minute."

Now, as I reached the entrance to the hospital, I took another shaky breath as I stepped through the sliding doors. Death was inevitable—and it happened at all ages. "She survived the heart attack," I said out loud. "She's not going to have another one soon." A woman heading toward the exit gave me a sympathetic glance. I quickened my pace.

When I reached Rosene's room, she was dressed and sitting in a wheelchair instead of on the bed. "I'm ready." She smiled.

"Does that mean you've been released?"

She nodded, holding up several pieces of paper. "I have my instructions. Let's go."

• 7 •

When Conrad showed up to help with the milking that afternoon, I thanked him but said I could do it.

"I want to," he said. "Besides, Ivy is bringing dinner here after work."

"She is?"

He nodded. "She put a roast in the Crock-Pot this morning." That sounded like Ivy.

"Thank you," I said. "I'll go tidy up in the house." My plan had been to help with the milking but run into the house every fifteen minutes to check on Rosene. With Conrad here, I wouldn't have to do that.

Rosene was at the table when I hurried through the kitchen door.

I asked, "Shouldn't you be resting?"

"Shouldn't you be doing the milking?"

"Conrad's here," I answered.

"Then go help Priscilla. She's doing inventory today."

I shook my head. "I'm going to clean the kitchen." The stove needed to be scrubbed down from breakfast. "Ivy's on her way. I'll go help Mammi once she arrives."

I barely had the stove scrubbed when Ivy came through the back door, carrying a huge Crock-Pot. "Hi!" she called out. "How's everyone doing?"

"Good." Rosene stood. "Do you need help?"

"Please sit down," I said to her, miffed.

Surprisingly, she obeyed me. "Not doing anything is going to be harder than I thought."

"Treva." Ivy put the Crock-Pot on the counter. "Can you go get the basket from my trunk? I have rolls and a salad in it."

"Sure."

She'd have to transfer the roast into a pan to heat it in the oven since there was no electricity for the Crock-Pot. Living with Amish grandparents had made me much more adaptable in Haiti to rolling blackouts and lack of resources than other workers—but not adaptable enough to stay.

After I brought the basket in, I told Ivy I was going to help Mammi and headed to the store. I'd only seen it late in the afternoon at closing time the first day I came home. Rested and in the sunshine, I now saw that the exterior needed to be stained. As I came around the front, I could see the steps and porch needed to be stained too. It had been a hard winter. Maybe Mammi would have to hire someone instead of having Dawdi do it. It seemed he had enough to do with the farm.

Or maybe it could wait until Gabe came home. Then again, maybe Dawdi was right. Maybe after working on a US military base for a year Gabe *would* move on to something more exciting than working on the farm.

The thought made me sad. I had taken Gabe for granted—not just his work, but who he was. I hadn't taken him very seriously, but now I could see how much he added to the farm. Stability for Mammi and Dawdi and Rosene. Dependability. Loyalty.

We assumed he wouldn't work on the farm forever, and joining the Army Reserve definitely seemed a step in that direction. But he'd never said exactly what he wanted to do.

I opened the door and called out, "Hello, Mammi!"

When I didn't hear a reply, I said, "Hello!" again.

"I'm back here."

I continued through the store, past the oak counter with the cubby shelf and Rosene's clock on top of it. Past the grandfather clocks and the wall clocks. Past the tables and chairs and hutches and racks of old quilts to where the woodstove and chairs were. Mammi sat in one of the chairs.

"Are you feeling okay?" I asked.

Her Kapp was a little askew. "Just tired."

"Did you finish the inventory already?"

"I decided to do it next week."

It was an hour until closing. "Go to the house. Ivy's getting dinner ready. I'll close up the shop."

She sat up straight. "Oh, I'm fine."

"I'm happy to close."

She stood and let out a sigh. "Denki."

As I followed her toward the front, the clocks began to chime four o'clock, which reminded me of something I wanted to ask. "Mammi, wait."

She turned toward me, speaking over the cacophony of chimes. "What is it?"

"Why do you carry so many clocks?"

"Well, because I like them."

"But why do you like them so much?"

"Because they're dependable, functional, and practical. But also decorative and a little whimsical. The Amish like them because they were one of the few decorative items approved by the church. And tourists like what I carry because the Amish like them." She grinned, which she didn't often do. "It's a win for me, a win for our Amish customers, and a win for tourists. What is there not to like?"

I laughed.

She grew serious. "Denki for coming over so I can go home early."

I was tempted to give her a hug, but she wasn't affectionate. Instead I said, "You're welcome."

After Mammi left, I pulled the duster out from under the counter. Just like the barn, things weren't in the usual tip-top shape here either. I began by dusting the clocks. I took extra care dusting the one Rosene had brought from Germany. It was a mantel clock made out of cherrywood with a curved top, and it sat on the top shelf behind the counter. It wasn't for sale.

The door dinging startled me.

"Hello?" It was a man's voice.

I stepped toward the front of the store.

He appeared to be in his late thirties. He was tall with broad shoulders, wore his light brown hair short, and had a square chin and dark eyes. He wore jeans and a down jacket.

"How may I help you?" I asked.

He extended his hand and then shook mine as he said, "My name is Drew Richards. I'm looking for a place to rent—hopefully furnished—for a few months while I do research in the area."

I let go of his hand. "Are you looking for a place on an Amish farm?"

"Yeah, I guess this looks a little weird." His eyes shone as he smiled. "I'm a PhD student at Duke University. I'm doing my dissertation on Anabaptists in the US during times of military conflict. I'm hoping to find lodging in an Amish area."

"I see," I said.

"Do you know of anyone in the area who might have a Dawdi Haus to rent out?" he asked. "That sort of thing?"

I thought of the apartment above the store. "I can ask around," I said. "Do you want to leave your phone number? I'll call if I hear of anything."

He took out his wallet, removed a card, and handed it to me. It read *Drew J. Richards* and had a phone number under the name and an email address. That was all. I met his eyes.

He smiled. "The sign outside says *Amish Antiques*. But I'm guessing you're not Amish."

I glanced down at my sweatshirt and jeans and then up at him. "My grandparents are Amish. I'm Mennonite and although I sometimes"—or used to—"wear a Mennonite dress and Kapp, or an Amish dress and Kapp, today is a jeans-and-sweatshirt day."

He smiled. "Well, thank you for your help. Please call if you hear of anything."

I slipped his card into my pocket. It seemed weird he had a card, but he probably had them made for Amish people. Since he was studying nonresistance, he was most likely doing research at the Anabaptist museum in Lancaster.

After Drew left, I turned the sign to *Closed* and opened the cash register drawer. It had been a slow day. I put the cash and checks in the drawer into a bank bag and then locked the front door and headed toward the back. Mammi left the key hanging to the left of the door in an alcove. Next to it was another key, and the label above it read *Apartment*.

I took both keys and then stepped out onto the porch,

where my curiosity got the best of me. It would only take a minute to check out the apartment. I dashed up the steps, unlocked the door, and stepped into the apartment.

A large window lit the living area furnished with a couch, a coffee table, and an empty bookcase. The floor was hardwood, and there was a large rag rug in the middle. I stepped to the middle of the room. To my left was a kitchenette with a mini fridge and a stovetop, both fueled by propane. The cupboards were made of wood, and the countertop was granite. There were a small table and two chairs against the far wall, under a window. Across the living room was a hallway, which led to a small bedroom and a bathroom. The entire apartment was adorable.

I just needed to find out if Drew Richards was legit.

After hugging Ivy and Conrad good-bye and telling them to say hello to Gran for me and to send pictures from Oregon, I offered to help Rosene get ready for bed.

"Don't be ridiculous." With a wave, she headed down the hall toward her bedroom.

I headed out to the barn to look up Drew Richards on my phone. Before I left for Haiti, I decided not to use my phone in the house, even after Mammi and Dawdi went to bed. I sometimes had, but it seemed disrespectful. Of course, I'd use it in an emergency to call 9-1-1 but not for other things. I figured they used the phone in the barn, so it seemed reasonable for me to do the same.

I found an article Drew had written that was published in the Goshen College newsletter entitled "Conscientious Objectors from Elkton County, Indiana, During the Great War." I found him listed as an adjunct professor of history at

Hesston College in Kansas, along with a photograph. It was definitely him. I knew both Goshen, which was where Conrad went, and Hesston were Mennonite colleges. He hadn't specified that he was Mennonite when I shared that I was.

Perhaps he was getting his PhD so he could get a position that was more than an adjunct. Duke University was a long way from both Kansas and Indiana.

Mammi was scrubbing the counters when I returned to the kitchen. I began prepping the coffeepot for the morning. Dawdi sat at the table.

I told them about Drew Richards looking for a place to rent.

"Who is he?" Mammi asked.

I explained that he said he was working on a PhD. "He goes to Duke University."

"Is that around here?" Mammi asked.

"No," Dawdi said. "It's in North Carolina. That's probably why he needs a place to stay."

"Sounds suspicious," Mammi said.

"I just did some research on him." I relayed what I'd found.

Mammi stepped to the sink. "What if Brenna comes home?" She started to rinse the dishcloth.

"She won't," I said. "And if she does, she can stay here in the house for a couple of months."

"The money would help," Dawdi said.

Mammi turned off the water.

"How much could we get a month?" Dawdi asked me.

"I'm not sure. I'll look into it and let you know tomorrow."

"Regardless," Dawdi said, "I think it's a good idea. It would help us and help Drew Richards. Plus, scholarly research into our history and nonresistance is a good thing, right?"

I agreed.

Mammi shrugged. "I'm going to bed."

"So am I." Dawdi followed her toward the hallway. "Good night, Treva," he called out. "I'm glad you're still here."

For the moment, so was I. But I hadn't changed my mind about leaving. My delay was only temporary.

I slipped out to the barn to use my phone again, this time to catch up on my texting.

First, I texted Brenna to let her know Rosene was home.

I didn't expect an answer from Brenna since it was four o'clock in the morning in Ukraine. But she responded immediately.

That's so good to hear. How are you?

Why are you up?

We had a security breach. I took the night shift.

I didn't know dealing with security breaches was part of her work. It sounded serious.

I'll let you know how Rosene is tomorrow. Call me sometime soon.

Okay. So how are you doing?

I didn't respond. I'd tell her when she called.

Next, I researched how much small, one-bedroom apartments were going for in the area. It seemed $700 would be reasonable.

If Dawdi wanted to rent out the apartment—and Mammi agreed—I'd recommend they do it. Drew was who he said he was. He wouldn't be a threat to anyone here, and if Dawdi thought they needed the money, then they definitely should do it.

After the milking, over breakfast, I reported what I'd found out about apartments to Dawdi, Mammi, and Rosene. "I think you should rent it to him."

"How about for five hundred a month?" Dawdi wiped his beard with his napkin. "He's a student. He's probably not making any money right now."

"Okay," I said. "I'll call him in a little while. What about the Dawdi Haus? Do you want to rent that out too?"

"Absolutely not," Mammi said as Rosene said, "That's a great idea."

Dawdi grinned. "We'll see. I'd like to have more people around. It's so good to have you home, Treva."

A bolt of guilt stabbed at me. "We could rent the Dawdi Haus out to tourists," I added. "That way we could decide when and for how long. I bet Brenna would make a website for us."

Mammi shook her head.

Dawdi's eyes twinkled. "Let's take this a step at a time."

Midmorning, Dawdi came in for another cup of coffee, and as he sat with Rosene, I slipped out to the barn and called Drew Richards.

"Hello," he answered. "This is Drew. How may I help you?"

"This is Treva Zimmerman. I met you yesterday in Amish Antiques. I'm calling about a room to rent."

"Oh. Great!"

"My grandparents have an apartment above the store. One bedroom, with a bath and a kitchenette. Five hundred a month. It's furnished. Are you interested?"

"Yes, absolutely."

"There's one caveat. It doesn't have electricity."

He laughed. "I suspected that would be the case."

"Are you still interested?"

"Yes."

"When do you want to see it?"

"Tuesday would be great."

"I'll show you the apartment then."

"Sounds good," he said.

I panicked a moment, wondering what I should say next. Then it came to me. "I'll draw up a contract and have it at the store on Tuesday morning. The store opens at ten. If I'm not there, my grandmother will show you the apartment and offer you the contract, if you want to take it."

"Thank you. May I ask you a question about something else?"

"Sure."

"I'm looking for Anabaptist people—Amish or Mennonite—to interview about their experiences during wartime in Lancaster County. Do you know of anyone?"

Rosene had stories from World War II. "Let me ask around," I answered. "Are you interested in secondhand stories or only firsthand accounts?"

"Both."

"Great," I answered. "I'll let you know."

On my way to the house, my phone dinged with a message from Ivy.

We're in Chicago. Conrad had a message from his mom when we landed. Gabe was in an accident in Kuwait three weeks ago. He just called her today. He's on his way home.

What was up with Gabe that he took three weeks to let Sharon know he'd been injured? My phone dinged again.

By Evening's Light

Did I tell you Sharon downsized to a one-bedroom apartment last month? Gabe hurt his back and shouldn't sleep on her couch—and Sharon's having back problems too, so she shouldn't either. Would you ask Dawdi if Gabe can stay in the Dawdi Haus for a while?

I stared at my phone for a long minute. So many complications.

Sure. I'll let you know what Dawdi says. When will Gabe arrive?

Wednesday. Sorry for the short notice.

Let me know when you land in Portland. Give Gran a hug!

When I reached the barn, I found Dawdi in the office at his desk.

"Ready for lunch?" I asked.

He glanced up at the clock on the wall and then stood. "I lost track of time."

As we walked to the house, I told him about Ivy's texts.

"So Gabe is coming home early?"

"Yes," I answered. "Do you think he could stay in the Dawdi Haus?"

"Of course."

"Do you want to ask Mammi first? She seemed resistant to renting it out."

"No, she'll agree. It's Gabe. Of course we'll help him." Dawdi seemed energized at the thought of Gabe staying on the farm. I was pretty sure Dawdi saw both Gabe and Conrad as grandsons. They'd both enhanced Dawdi, Mammi, and Rosene's lives, probably as much as my sisters and I had.

He'd been lonely with all of us gone. "Do you think he'll want to work for us again?"

"It sounds as if he has some healing that needs to happen first."

"Right," Dawdi said. "We'll get him well. And see what he needs."

After lunch, I gathered cleaning supplies to spruce up the Dawdi Haus.

"I'd like to go out with you," Rosene said from her chair at the table.

"Absolutely not," I said, "I'll come in and check on you."

"I wasn't offering to help. I just want to keep you company."

"Oh."

"I could tell you more of my story."

I grinned. The Dawdi Haus was small enough that she could sit on the couch and speak in a normal voice and I could hear her while I cleaned the kitchen.

· 8 ·

Rosene

After Martha and I had a chance to bathe and rest, Lena came up to my room, which I used to share with Dorina, with a box of clothing—dresses, shoes, stockings, and sweaters. "Your Plain dress and Kapp will draw too much attention. This can be the start of your new wardrobe. Go ahead and change, then come down for dinner."

I looked toward Martha for advice. "What should I do?"

She shrugged. "Whatever you want. If you want to wear your cape dress and Kapp you should. People will stare, but it doesn't matter. If you want to wear the dresses Lena purchased, that's fine too."

"I'll wear one of the dresses today and see how I feel." I put on a blue shirtdress and a red cardigan sweater along with stockings and pumps. I had admired the clothes Lena wore when I was little. I didn't mind dressing Plain back home, but I might as well dress in the same manner that Lena and Martha did while I was in Germany. Otherwise I would draw unwanted attention to myself.

As I descended the stairs, my mouth watered at the smell of *sauerbraten*. Lena stopped dishing it up from the pan on the stove as I walked into the kitchen. "Sister," she said, "you look beautiful in that dress. I'll help you with your hair after dinner."

Once we were seated, Vater Josef led us in a simple prayer, saying, "Lord Jesus, we thank you for safe travels for Rosene and Martha and thank you for this food. Amen."

He sounded humble and sincere, and I cautioned myself against judging him. He was thin and didn't look well. And he was referring to me as Rosene, my middle name and the one I chose to use when I left Germany, instead of Dyna, the name he'd always called me.

As Lena dished up the sauerbraten, she said, "I'm afraid it's not as good as Clare's. I don't have time to learn to cook the way she did, with working and all."

I took a bite and said, "It's delicious." But she was right—it was dry and overcooked. And the red cabbage undercooked. I said another prayer, asking the Lord to help me be gracious. It didn't matter if the food was tasty or not.

"Tell us more about your work in Nuremberg," Martha said.

"It's been incredible." Lena dabbed at the corners of her mouth with her napkin. "What a privilege to work with the Americans and bring justice for so many."

My stomach roiled.

"I'm finishing that work now and transitioning to re-settling refugees." She nodded toward Martha. "I'll be working with the International Red Cross. I'm a little sur-prised our paths haven't crossed more than the meeting in Nuremberg."

"Yes," Martha said. "I've mostly been in Berlin."

"How awful for you." Garit scowled. "Aren't you frightened to be in such close proximity to the Russians?"

"No," Martha answered. "We're focused on helping refugees."

"Of course." Lena spoke quickly. "We don't want them to be trapped by communism."

"The Soviet Union wants all of Germany." Garit's voice grew louder. "And our vast resources. They're afraid we'll invade them again—and succeed."

Vater Josef said, "That may be true, Garit, but let's not dwell on that now." He turned toward me and said, "Rosene, how do you spend your time in Lancaster County?"

"I work in the store," I answered. "And tend to the house and the garden. Sometimes I help with the farming, and I help care for the children."

"The children?"

"Clare's—Arden is five and Janice is three."

"That's right. Monika has written about her grandchildren. . . ." Vater Josef took a drink of water. "Were you able to attend college?"

"I finished high school but didn't go to college." I enjoyed school but hadn't considered continuing, even though Martha had.

"It seems you've followed more in Clare's footsteps than Martha's," Vater Josef said.

I quickly took a bite of cabbage to prevent myself from answering. I'd never take after Clare. I'd never be a mother.

Perhaps Martha understood my discomfort because she said, "Rosene is very much her own person with her own gifts. She's been Mutter's right hand in the store. She's the best auntie anyone could ever dream of having. And the best daughter and sister."

Lena made an odd sound.

"Garit." Martha seemed eager to change the subject. "Tell me about your studies."

He happily did, going on about his classes and the fact he'd already been offered a professorship after he received his doctorate in history, which would take another two years. "I've been studying the Great War and the Russian Revolution," he said. "Watch the Soviet Union. Worse things are coming. We must unite against them. If only the US hadn't allied with Russia during the war."

Martha let out a laugh. "Goodness, where would we be now if we hadn't?"

"Not in the sights of Russia," Garit replied. "They'll try to take all of Germany soon and then the rest of Europe. Just watch."

"Well, I think we can have benefited from the alliance during the war and be weary of them now postwar," Martha said. "Both can be true. Plus, the US has come up with the Marshall Plan, and it will soon benefit Europe."

"Do you think it will stop Russia?" Garit had an expression of disgust on his face. "They wouldn't have the strength and the territory now if they'd been ostracized by the Allies instead of embraced."

I kept silent. If Russia and the Allies hadn't fought together, Germany would have won. Perhaps that was what Garit wished for.

Martha and I went for a walk early the next day, having awoken before dawn. We found rubble just four blocks away in the direction opposite of the airport. I'd read that over five thousand people had been killed in Frankfurt during the war.

Later, when I asked Lena about the state of Old Town, she frowned. "It was heavily bombed, and there's no money for restoration now. It could be years before it's repaired."

"How about *Alte Nikolaikirche*?" I kept mixing my English and German.

"Old St. Nicholas?" She preferred speaking in English. "Miraculously, it was barely damaged." She opened the door. "Step outside and you can hear the bells."

I did. The sound of my childhood serenaded me. I continued into the street, by the fountain. The sound of the water tumbling over the sides of the bowl accompanied the bells. My childhood hadn't been entirely bad. Could I appreciate the good amid the heartache?

"I've arranged for a driver to take us to the farm tomorrow."

I turned toward Lena. "How is everyone?"

"We've only exchanged a few letters," she said. "Onkel Klaus and *Tante* Olga seem to be doing well. *Kusine* Karl has married, although last I heard they don't have any children."

That night, I had a nightmare and woke up crying—but I couldn't remember what the dream had been about. The next morning, I felt weepy and anxious. I tried to hide how I felt from Martha, but she asked me several times how I was doing.

Vater Josef didn't go to the farm with us, nor did Garit. On the way through town the next morning, we saw more of the ruins. Homes. Businesses. Churches. As we left town, on the hill to our right was the University Institute for Hereditary Biology and Racial Hygiene, where I'd been part of the study on twins and had been sterilized. Lena sat up front and stared straight ahead. Martha sat on the left-hand side of the car and didn't see the Institute. Perhaps she had no idea what the building was. I choked on my tears, but this time out of anger. Returning to Germany hadn't been a good idea.

Lena planned for us to spend the afternoon at the farm and return in the evening. She didn't want to hire the driver for two days.

When we arrived, Onkel Klaus came out to greet us, followed by Tante Olga. "Lena, *Willkommen*," Onkel said. "You must be Martha." He took Martha's hand. I came around the other side of the car. "Dyna Rosene, is that you?"

"Jah," I answered.

He stepped forward and wrapped his arms around me. His body shook a little as he said, "Thank God you got out of here. Bless Clare for taking you."

Embarrassed, I didn't say anything to him.

Tante Olga said, "My turn."

Onkel let go, and Tante put her arm around me. Speaking in German, she said, "Our prayers have been answered. You've grown into a lovely young woman."

Cousin Karl stepped out of the kitchen. I grinned. He'd grown into a man—a big one—since I last saw him when he was seventeen. "This is Hilda." He motioned to the young woman behind him. "My wife."

"I'm pleased to meet you," I said.

"I've heard so much about you." She wore her dark hair in a bun. "I'm pleased to finally meet you too."

The day was blustery and cool, so we ate inside the house at the kitchen table. Neither Onkel Klaus nor Tante Olga asked about Vater Josef, nor about Garit. However, they did ask about Mutter, Vater, and Clare. Martha and I took turns updating them and telling them about Arden and Janice.

"How are things in the United States?" Karl, who was more talkative than he was nine years ago, asked. "Can you get new cars? Enough food? Store-bought clothing?"

Martha glanced at me.

I shrugged. Vater had parked our car in the shed after Jeremiah took over the farm. We didn't buy store-bought clothes. But we had plenty of food.

Martha answered, saying, "I haven't been living in the US for the last three years, but I know the rationing ended, including sugar, last year. The factories converted from war-time goods to making cars and washing machines and that sort of thing. People had to put their names on lists for big items, but those are now being delivered."

"How fortunate for you not to have been bombed," Onkel Klaus said.

Martha agreed. "Yes. Our infrastructure wasn't affected at all, and the only refugees we have are the few being allowed to immigrate."

"Why just a few?" Onkel Klaus asked.

"There's opposition in Congress," Martha answered. "I hope that will change."

Martha, who had never been to the Kaufman farm, was interested in a tour. Lena stayed inside with Tante Olga while the rest of us ventured out into the windy day.

Onkel Klaus showed us the barn, the five cows, the goats, the chickens, and then the orchard that was beyond the barn. As we stood admiring the apple trees, Karl asked, "Is Josef doing well?"

"He's been ill," Martha said. "And he's aged since I saw him three years ago."

Karl kicked at the soil with his boot and kept his head down. "How about Garit?"

"He's studying history at the University of Frankfurt," Martha said. "He plans to teach at the college level when he receives his PhD."

Karl turned to me. "Did you know he came after you and Clare? Came here to the farm looking for you after you left?"

"Did he?" I sputtered. A memory came to me of Garit at the depot in Kaiserslautern in the spring of 1939, where Clare and I waited to take the train to France and flee Germany for good. Clare and I both wore disguises—she was dressed as a peasant woman and I was dressed as a boy in clothes we'd gotten here on the farm. Garit had yelled, *"Has anyone seen a young American woman with a thirteen-year-old German girl? They're wanted by the Gestapo."*

Not once had Clare and I discussed Garit being at the train depot. By the time we arrived in the US, I was so relieved we'd escaped that perhaps I buried the memory. But it had come back now. What if he had caught us? What would he have done?

Karl asked, "How can you stay in the same house as him?"

"Son," Onkel Klaus said, "that's not our business."

I shuddered, not sure how to answer Karl. So I didn't.

When we arrived in Frankfurt late that evening, I asked Lena what time we'd need to be ready for church the next day.

"We don't plan to go," she answered.

Surprised, I asked, "Why not?"

"Garit and I have been going to the Lutheran church near the college. We ride with friends who have a car. It would be difficult for so many of us to go."

"We could take the bus," I said.

"It would take too long."

"What about Vater Josef?" I crossed my arms. "We could walk with him to the Mennonite church."

"He no longer goes," Lena said. "That congregation has dwindled to nearly nothing. Several of the families have left Frankfurt. Some have been able to immigrate to Canada. Others have gone to the country."

"I see." I never missed church back home. Sometimes I went to the Amish service with Clare and her family, but usually I went to Vater and Mutter's Mennonite church. The only time I missed was if I was ill.

"We'll have a late breakfast and rest," Lena said. "We'll be tired after our long trip today."

That night, as I slept in my childhood bedroom, I dreamed I was in the Kaiserslautern train depot again, alone and not dressed as a boy. Terrified, I awoke. This time, instead of crying, I was shaking. I glanced across the room, looking for Dorina. Then I began to cry. Martha didn't stir. I curled into a ball and muffled my sobs as best I could.

The next day was clear and bright, and Lena declared we'd have our breakfast out on the patio. She'd already gone to the bakery and had a box of pastries on the counter, along with boiled eggs, slices of ham, and coffee. With ongoing food shortages and rationing, I guessed Lena had saved coupons or bought on the black market to feed us.

Martha had a phone call from George while I helped Lena arrange the food on platters. The call didn't take long, and

Martha came to the kitchen doorway and said, "Rosene, may I speak to you for a moment?"

I washed my hands and joined her in the living room.

"I'm needed in Berlin," Martha said. "I need to go tomorrow."

"You're leaving me?"

"I'll return by Friday and get you to the airport on Saturday."

I couldn't bear to stay in Frankfurt alone. "I can't stay here without you."

Martha pressed her hand against the side of her face. "Let me think about it."

Vater Josef wasn't feeling well, so he didn't join us out on the patio. Garit was even more talkative than usual. Once we served ourselves, Garit said, "Have you heard that Hitler is still alive?"

Martha carefully put down her coffee cup. "I've heard the rumor but haven't seen any evidence."

"He's in Argentina. So are many of his officers."

"What are they doing there?" Martha seemed to be humoring Garit.

"Collaborating," he answered. "Coming up with a plan to keep Russia from taking over all of Germany."

"Really." Martha picked up her cup.

"It's also been proven that the Jews started the war. Hitler was simply defending us. He'll do it again."

Martha's eyes narrowed. "None of that is true." She shook her head. "Hitler's dead, by his own hands."

Garit smirked. "You'll see." He glanced at me. "All of you will see."

I felt ill.

"Let's speak of cheerier things," Lena said. "Rosene, do you have a beau? Are there wedding bells in your future?"

I shook my head. Zeke was the last subject I wanted to talk about with Lena, especially when I wasn't sure what the status of our relationship was. If only she and Vater Josef hadn't turned me over to the Nazis.

· 9 ·

Martha placed a call to George later that afternoon while Lena rested and Garit worked on his studies in the office. Vater Josef hadn't come out of his room at all. I sat out on the patio, watching an orange butterfly flit about the garden, and thought of the child's wagon that Clare used to pull to Klein and Son with Dorina and me trailing behind. Dorina had a seizure at the grocery store that landed her as a patient in the Institute again. She never came home after that.

Once I left Germany with Clare, I did my best not to think about my life in Germany. When we'd receive a letter from Lena or Vater Josef, I would feel ill for a few hours, but even then I wouldn't dwell on what happened to me as a child.

Now I was fighting the memories. How close Dorina and I were. How much we mourned our mother after she passed away. How gutted I felt when Dorina died. I didn't know how I would have managed to go on without Clare.

I missed Clare horribly. Mutter and Vater too. And Arden and Janice. And Jeremiah.

And Zeke. Especially Zeke.

Martha joined me on the patio. "George said it would be fine if you come to Berlin."

Relief swept through me.

"We have Red Cross work to do. You'll need to stay in the apartment while we're working. You'll be safe. But I need you not to tell Mutter and Vater that I took you there."

I must have given her a questioning look because she said, "Believe me, it's for the best. Can you reassure me that you won't?"

"What if Lena or Vater Josef writes to Clare or Mutter that you took me to Berlin?"

"If they do—or it comes up some other way—tell them I'll explain what happened next time I'm home." She gave me a tender smile. "I just can't say more now."

That evening, Vater Josef joined us for dinner. He was pale and quiet. As we ate, Martha said, "Our plans have changed, unfortunately."

I marveled at her tact.

"I've been called to Berlin."

Garit crossed his arms and turned toward me. "You'll stay here with us."

I froze.

Martha cleared her throat. "Rosene will be going with me."

"Whatever for?" Lena asked. "I've taken time off work. You can't deprive me of my sister." She turned toward Vater Josef. "Vater, please don't allow this."

He shrugged and then stared at his plate.

I couldn't seem to speak.

"Lena." Garit spoke firmly. "Perhaps it's for the best. . . ."

Martha gave me a questioning look. Perhaps my eyes gave me away because Martha said, "It's settled. Rosene will accompany me."

"She'll have to return here to fly home," Lena said.

"I'll look into getting her ticket changed to fly from Berlin or perhaps Hamburg. We'll say our good-byes in the morning."

I had a nightmare again and cried most of the rest of the night. I couldn't wait to leave the Weber home and Frankfurt. And yet I was homesick for Lancaster County and dreaded going even farther east, farther from home.

The next morning, Garit left for the university before breakfast and Vater Josef didn't come out of his room again. We ate with Lena in silence. When we finished the dishes, we carried our luggage down the stairs and Martha called for a taxi.

Then she said, "Thank you for your hospitality" to Lena.

Lena ignored Martha and turned to me, putting both hands on my shoulders. She was only a few inches taller than I was, but it was enough she could look down at me. "Someday you'll have an understanding of what happened beyond your childish perspective."

I didn't reply. Lena hadn't changed; she'd always been cold. Martha thought Lena might want to apologize to me, but nothing could be further from the truth. Lena felt no remorse for not protecting me when I was a child.

I picked up my suitcase and took a couple of steps toward the front door.

"Thank you again," Martha said in a frosty voice. "We'll go ahead and wait outside."

I led the way, and Martha closed the door firmly behind us. When we reached the sidewalk, it began to rain. And I began to cry.

I imagined Lena standing at the window, watching my shoulders shake.

Mortified, I took several deep breaths and tried to stop.

"It's all right," Martha said. "Just cry. Especially if it helps. I'm so sorry. I thought Lena had grown more sympathetic."

I cried all the way to the train station and then went into the restroom while Martha bought our tickets. When I came out, I managed to keep myself composed but not enough to talk with Martha. I fell asleep on the train. I woke when it stopped but soon fell asleep again. By the time we reached Berlin, my anxiety had decreased.

As the train slowed, Martha said, "The main depot is in the Russian quadrant. We'll have to get on another one to go into the US area."

I followed her, carrying my suitcase, watching the other passengers. Most of their clothes were worn, and some were downright ratty. We boarded a subway and then, a few minutes after the train took off, it stopped. Again, I followed Martha, and this time we exited the station, into the rain.

Someone shouted, "Martha!" A man wearing a trench coat and a hat waved at us. "Rosene!" It was George. He ushered us into the back seat of a taxi and loaded our suitcases into the trunk. Then he climbed into the front and gave the driver an address.

I leaned my head against Martha's shoulder and closed my eyes.

"How is she?" George asked.

Martha answered, "Tired."

I'd only met George once, in June of 1945, before he left Lancaster County for Europe, but I knew Martha wouldn't have married him if he wasn't a good man. I wasn't surprised that he was concerned about me.

When the taxi stopped, George paid the driver and then jumped out of the cab and opened my door, offering me his hand. I took it. Then he grabbed both of our suitcases from the trunk. Martha pulled a set of keys from the pocket of his coat and motioned for me to follow her. We hurried up the steps into the building and then up three flights of stairs. Martha unlocked a door, switched on a light, and then motioned me inside the apartment. There was a sofa, a table with two chairs, and a kitchen all in one room.

"It's only a one-bedroom apartment," Martha said. "Will you be comfortable sleeping out here?"

"Of course," I said.

George came in with the suitcases and left mine beside the table and headed down the hall with the other.

"We're fortunate to have a private bathroom," Martha explained, "instead of having to go down the hall."

For the first time since we left the US, anxiety turned to excitement. Here I was, in Berlin on the edge of the Iron Curtain. Leaving Frankfurt with Martha had been the right thing to do.

The next day I awoke to Martha making tea in the little kitchen. I asked, "Is George still sleeping?"

"No," Martha said. "He was called away during the night."

I vaguely remembered hearing the telephone ring, followed by George's voice. "On Red Cross business?"

"Yes." Martha poured boiling water into the pot. "There's a rumor that the Soviets might block travel in and out of West Berlin. Stalin isn't happy with the Marshall Plan. It seems he hoped the US would withdraw from Europe entirely, leaving the Soviet Union as the biggest influence in the area."

"What would happen to you and George if Stalin prevents travel here?"

"It depends on when he does it," Martha answered. "George is trying to secure a car for us to leave in case the trains are stopped sometime in the near future."

"What would happen if Stalin gained control of Europe?"

"Well, we have an idea of what he did in Ukraine in the early 1930s. He starved millions. And there have been reports of millions more killed in Russia at his command." She paused a moment and then said, "So many have suffered for so long, and still are. We need to do all we can to ensure Stalin doesn't cause even more to suffer by gaining any more territory than he already has."

"But how?"

She exhaled. "There are US agencies dedicating themselves to making sure he's not successful. But you and I have no control over any of that. We must focus on getting out of Berlin."

My eyes must have grown large because she smiled and said, "Nothing will happen to prevent your leaving. I'll put you on the train. I'll change your flight to leave from Hamburg instead of Frankfurt. I'll call now."

Martha made the phone calls while I dressed. When I came out of the bathroom, she said the airline arrangements had been made. I didn't ask about costs, and she didn't mention them. As we had our tea and pastries, she said, "I have a Jewish refugee leaving soon—Esther. In fact, I've gotten her on the same train as you and the same flights out of Hamburg and London. She's being resettled in Lancaster County."

"Really? How did you manage that?"

"A woman who used to volunteer with the Red Cross and

her family are sponsoring her. Esther will live in Lancaster; there's an apartment waiting for her."

I was intrigued. I had, in many ways, been a refugee myself, fleeing for my life. A doctor at the Institute had procured a fake passport for me. Clare had risked her life to get me out of Germany. "Can you tell me Esther's story?" I asked.

Martha smiled a little. "Hopefully, Esther will be able to tell you her story. I can tell you she lost her immediate family in the war. She has an uncle, but she needs a fresh start. A place with more opportunities than she has here."

"The Red Cross does so much good," I said. "Mutter often talks about what a good organization it is."

Martha poured more tea into my cup. "The Red Cross, like most organizations, hasn't always lived up to its ideals."

"What do you mean?"

"All Red Cross workers are to remain neutral, but there are rumors that Red Cross workers in North Africa were spying for the Nazis at the beginning of the war. And although the International Red Cross requested Germany to allow them to inspect concentration camps, they didn't keep pressing the Germans when denied." She set the teapot on the table. "The International Red Cross did send food parcels to some captives and deportees, saving lives, but many in need received no parcels, medical care, or protection. As you know, millions died." She looked up at me across her teacup. "I'm determined to do all I can for survivors and refugees now."

I could see that.

That afternoon, Martha and I took the subway back into the Russian quadrant of Berlin. The day was clear and bright and growing warm. Once we reached the station, we walked for a half hour, passing old men dressed in threadbare clothes sitting up against buildings. Older children carried younger children. Women stood in a long line at a bakery.

"There's little food here," Martha said. "A paycheck only buys a loaf of bread. The Americans introduced a new currency, Deutschmarks, which have started to show up here, infuriating Stalin. He flooded East Berlin with billions of printed notes, but of course they're worthless. People have been living off the black market, fueled by American cigarettes, aid packages, and—" A woman walked around the corner wearing a dressing gown. Martha didn't finish her sentence.

Instead, she said, "The people are barely getting enough calories to survive. Certainly not enough to actually fuel their bodies."

I thought of the food in Martha's kitchen. "How have you and George managed to buy things?"

"The Red Cross provides our supplies."

The next block had been decimated. A woman and a boy came up the steps of a basement. "Are they living there?" I whispered.

"Yes," Martha said. "Many people live in the basements of bombed buildings."

That sounded damp and dreary. And unsafe.

Martha said, "Over ten percent of Berlin was completely destroyed by the bombing. It will take years to rebuild. The Marshall Plan is absolutely necessary, otherwise much of Europe will never recover and that could lead to another war soon."

"How horrible for the children."

"Jah, it is." Martha spoke quietly. "Although . . . it's difficult to explain, but war is all the children remember. All they know is suffering. At least now there are no bombs. I hope their lives will soon grow easier."

Finally, we reached an apartment building. Windows were covered with plywood or blankets, but the building was intact. I followed Martha up the steps and into a dimly lit hall. Then we climbed two sets of stairs. Martha turned down another hall that had only one bulb at the end that flickered on and off.

Martha stopped at a door labeled *314*. "Here we are." She knocked. Then knocked again.

A young woman opened the door—a young woman my height with dark hair and brown eyes. She was terribly thin. "Martha, I thought I'd been forgotten." She spoke in German.

"*Nein.*" Martha motioned to me and introduced me as her sister from the United States.

Esther motioned for us to come into the apartment. There were a wooden table, two chairs, and a mattress under the window.

"Do you have my papers?" Esther asked in German.

"Jah." Martha took an envelope from her purse. "I was able to get an Austrian passport for you, based on your father's citizenship. The US was more likely to accept that than a German one, which they did. I have your train ticket to Hamburg. I've also arranged for airline tickets from Hamburg to London, and London to New York. From there, you and Rosene will take the train to Lancaster, Pennsylvania."

"Wunderbar." Esther smiled at me.

I couldn't help but smile in return. I'd be able to help someone—another refugee. I had a purpose. My worries and sorrows over Vater Josef and Lena began to subside. In fact, I put that visit entirely out of my mind, determined to focus only on being in Berlin.

"Meet us at the train station tomorrow at noon," Martha said. "George and I will make sure you and Rosene are both on the train and on your way to Hamburg."

A voice came from down the hallway of the apartment.

Esther pointed toward the door. "Quickly." She led the way and once Martha and I stepped into the building hall, Esther closed the door. "My Onkel says that the Russians are serious about closing off Berlin to the Americans, English, and French. I hope tomorrow will be soon enough."

"It's only one day away," Martha said. "Surely nothing will happen before then."

Esther pursed her lips together. "Things seem to be moving quickly."

"Plan to meet us by the café at the station unless you hear otherwise," Martha said.

Esther nodded as she slipped her documents into the pocket of her apron. "I need to go." As she stepped into the apartment, someone inside asked, "Where have you been?"

"Taking out the trash," Esther answered.

I followed Martha down the hall. Perhaps Garit was right. It appeared Berlin wasn't safe. What if Esther and I made it out—but Martha and George didn't?

· 10 ·

Treva

I sat on the far end of the sofa in the Dawdi Haus, facing Rosene, who leaned against a couple of pillows.

"Mammi always said you brought the clock in the
shop from Germany in 1949, not 1948. Is she mistaken?"

Rosene smiled. "Priscilla isn't mistaken, but that's getting
ahead of the story."

"It's June 1948, in the story, right?"

"Correct."

"What date was that Wednesday that Esther was supposed
to meet you at the train station in the Russian quadrant of
Berlin?"

"June 23, 1948."

"What day did the Berlin Blockade begin? Wasn't it right
around that time?"

"You know your history," Rosene said. "But you're also
getting ahead of the story."

"You went to Germany twice in the late 1940s?"

Rosene sighed. "Yes, I went to Germany twice, but the

trip in 1948 was so difficult as far as my time in Frankfurt that I blocked it out for years—grief compounds grief, and my dilemma with Zeke combined with the memories that had surfaced from my childhood threatened to overwhelm me. So I shut down as many memories as I could. In fact, it wasn't until after I went to Germany with Ivy and Brenna five years ago that I allowed myself to think about that very first visit. I was better prepared for Vater Josef, Lena, and Garit the second time."

"In 1949?"

Rosene laughed. "Well, obviously you know I brought the clock back in 1949. So you already know the answer to that."

I nodded. "Was it common for people to fly to Europe in the late 1940s like that? It's as if you and Martha were jet-setters or something."

Rosene sighed. "It wasn't common. If it hadn't been for Martha and her work—"

"For the Red Cross? It seems odd they'd fly her back and forth, or that she made enough money to pay for that sort of travel."

Rosene stood. She was small but mighty, even at ninety-three years old. Even recovering from a heart attack. "Now you really are getting ahead of the story. I'm going to go back to the house."

Chagrined, I said, "I'll go with you." I'd clean the bath-room and change the sheets on the bed later.

The next day was an off Sunday for Mammi and Dawdi's church, but they attended church at a neighboring district, as they often did, since I already planned to stay home with Rosene. We read scripture together—the Sermon on the Mount—and then spent some time in silent prayer. I prayed for her, for Gran, for Ivy and Conrad, for Brenna and Johann, for Mammi and Dawdi. And for Pierre. Then I felt melancholy. But I remembered to pray for Gabe too and felt better.

Rosene rested while I started lunch for the two of us—heart-healthy chicken curry salad that used yogurt as the base.

As we ate, Rosene said, "I need to go out to the barn and make a phone call."

"Could I do it for you?"

"Oh, it would do me good to walk out there. I need to call the refugee center and leave a message. I'm scheduled to volunteer tomorrow."

I put down my fork. "What?"

"I've been volunteering at the refugee center on Mondays, working with a group of women."

"What inspired you to volunteer?"

"Well, I volunteered in the late 1940s to help European refugees. Then again in the seventies to help settle Vietnamese refugees in the area. I volunteered for a few years with Iraqi refugees before you girls came."

"Did you quit because of us?"

She wiped her mouth with her napkin and then smiled. "I took a break is all. Now I'm working with mostly Syrian refugees and some from Afghanistan and Somalia too. Did you know that Lancaster County started welcoming refugees three hundred years ago? Some call it America's refugee capital because it settles twenty times more refugees per capita than the rest of the nation."

"Really?"

She nodded. "The world is currently experiencing the biggest refugee crisis since World War II. Seventy million people have been displaced."

That was a hard number to fathom. "What exactly do you do at the refugee center?"

"First, I help serve the noon meal, which the refugee women take turns cooking. Then I help them with their English, filling out forms and reading their mail. That sort of thing. I hate to miss it. The center is always short-staffed."

"Could I volunteer for you?"

"Oh, you have plenty going on right now without taking over my duties."

"No, I'd like to." I thought of Rosene at twenty-two, looking forward to helping Esther and how it took her mind off herself. Maybe that was what I needed.

She said, "You need a background check."

"I had one before I went to Haiti. I have a copy of it."

"Hopefully that will work. Take it with you. I think the young women I work with would love to meet you," she said. "I'll leave a message and tell the director to expect you instead of me."

On Monday morning, after breakfast, I put on one of my Mennonite dresses and a Kapp. At ten thirty, when Dawdi came into the house to stay with Rosene, I left.

The refugee center was in the heart of downtown Lancaster and not far from the hospital. When I arrived, I checked in at the office and introduced myself as Rosene Simons's niece.

"I've been expecting you," the receptionist said. "I'm so sorry to hear about Rosene's heart attack but thankful she's recovering. I'm Cheryl, and the director is Pamela." She motioned to the woman behind her, who was speaking on her cell phone.

I gave Cheryl my background check, and she made a copy. By then Pamela was off the phone.

"Come on," she said to me. "I'll show you around and introduce you to a few of the women." She led me into a dining hall and then into the kitchen, where two women worked.

"Treva," Pamela said, "I'd like you to meet Zaida and Cala."

After we exchanged greetings, Pamela said, "They're in charge of the meal today. The other women are in English class, and the children are in their class."

"How can I help?" I asked.

"You can put out the napkins," Zaida said in perfect English. "And the forks." She pointed to a set of drawers. "Put them on the counter by the plates. We have twenty-five women eating today. The children will be served in their classroom." She stepped to the stove. "We're just finishing up the rice and bread."

Cala placed a large round circle of dough on a stone and slid it into the oven. She took out another stone and slid a piece of baked flatbread off of it and onto a stack of cooked bread.

After the women—most of whom wore hijabs, although Cala and Zaida didn't—had been served, Zaida motioned toward the food. "Dish up a plate," she said.

I sat with the two of them at the table closest to the kitchen and took a bite of the bread and hummus—both melted in my mouth.

Cala asked me how old I was. "Twenty," I answered.

She grinned. "So am I." She patted Zaida's arm. "My sister is twenty-eight."

Zaida smiled. "So you are in Rosene's family?"

"Yes," I answered. "I'm her great-great-niece."

"Amish?" Zaida pronounced it with a long *A*.

"I'm Mennonite, but the two groups are similar."

"But two different religions?" Cala asked.

"No," I answered. "Both are Christian and much the same, but different groups."

"Oh."

I guessed it was kind of confusing, but I thought it would be pointless to explain how the Amish and Mennonites both broke off from the Swiss Brethren in the 1690s. I didn't always understand it all myself.

"Are you Muslim?" I asked.

Zaida nodded and glanced around the room. "Most of the women here are. We're from Syria. Others are from Iraq and Afghanistan. A few from Somalia and some from Sudan."

"Are you married?" Cala asked.

I nearly choked on a piece of bread. "No," I said. "Are you?"

She shook her head. "Zaida is. She has two children, a girl and a boy."

"Aww, that's wonderful," I said.

Zaida smiled again.

I held up the bread. "And so is the food." The rice and beef were seasoned with cinnamon and other spices. They also served a salad—tabbouleh—made from parsley and tomatoes. "What's the grain in the salad?"

"Bulgur," Zaida answered.

"All of it is delicious."

"Thank you," Cala said. "We hope to open a restaurant someday. Zaida's husband has a cousin in New York who wants to open a restaurant with our help." She shrugged. "Perhaps we'll end up there."

I asked Zaida, "What is your husband doing now?"

She shrugged and answered, "Looking for a job."

"What kind of job?"

"Anything. Driving. Construction. Loading trucks."

"What did he do in Syria?"

Zaida hesitated a moment and then blinked a couple of times. "He was a student. At Damascus University. So was I."

"I'm sorry," I said.

Zaida exhaled and then said, "We are here and safe. That's what matters."

"We're thankful for the help we've had," Cala said. "And for people like you. And Rosene. We adore her. She's like the grandmothers we all"—she swept her hand wide—"left behind."

After we washed the plates and cleaned up the kitchen, I helped the women with their English homework, as did Zaida, while Cala packed up their things in the kitchen. I guessed Zaida had learned English as a young child.

Some of the women had mail for me to read. One woman had a preschool application to fill out for her four-year-old for the following September.

At two o'clock, the women went to collect their children. On my way out, Pamela stopped me for a moment and handed me a card that the women had signed that morning in their English class for Rosene.

I pressed it to my chest. "What a lovely gesture. This will mean a lot to her."

"Will we see you next week?" Pamela asked.

"Yes. I'll be here." I was already looking forward to it.

When I reached the parking lot, someone called my name. It was Cala, standing beside a sedan and waving to me. I started toward her. A man stood beside Zaida on the other side of the car. He held a little girl in his arms.

"Treva," Cala said. "This is Kamil Hamad, Zaida's husband."

"I'm pleased to meet you," I said.

"Likewise," he answered.

"And their daughter, Gamila." The little girl in Kamil's arms smiled. Cala pointed inside the open door of the back seat. "And Ahmad."

I waved at the little girl and then the boy. "I'm pleased to meet all of you."

Zaida told Kamil that I was Rosene's niece.

His eyes grew serious. "Zaida told me Rosene is ill." He spoke with more of an accent than his wife and sister-in-law.

"Yes," I said. "But she's getting better."

"Please give her our regards," he said. "Tell her we hope to see her soon."

After I left the center, I stopped by the library and researched rental contracts. I found a simple, generic one, and after editing it, I printed out two copies. Then I looked up power of attorney forms and printed off a few of those too, in case Rosene needed one. As I drove to the farm, I realized I hadn't thought about Pierre once in the last three hours. A record for me over the past year and a half.

The next day, I worked in the store in the morning again while Mammi stayed with Rosene. Just after eleven, Drew Richards came through the door.

After I greeted him, I said, "Let's go look at the apartment." I grabbed the file with the contract and a pen. Then I locked the front door, put up the *Be Back Soon* sign, and led the way through the store and to the back door.

As we climbed the steps, I said, "My grandfather redid

this staircase a couple of years ago, and the apartment was finished last year. No one has lived in it yet."

I unlocked the door and then held it open, motioning for Drew to go through first.

"Nice," he said.

I stepped in too.

He walked toward the window. "The light in here is perfect."

I smiled. "It will be pretty dim once the sun sets." I motioned to the lamp. "It's battery operated so you won't have to bother with kerosene or propane. But it's not very bright."

"I'll make do," he said.

I showed him the bedroom and bathroom, then opened the hall closet and the cabinets in the kitchen.

He sat down at the desk.

"You'll need a better chair," I said.

"I'll buy one." He stood and turned toward me. "I'll take the apartment. How soon may I move in?"

"Today." I held up the contract. "We can sign it here." I put it out on the kitchen counter.

He read through it, and then we both signed it, and I handed him the apartment key. "I'd like you to meet my grandparents and Aenti Rosene. Do you have time now?"

"Yes," he answered.

Once we reached the bottom of the outside staircase, I said, "Mammi and Rosene will be at the house for sure. Dawdi may be in the barn."

As we walked along the path, I asked Drew where he grew up.

"In Wisconsin. We had Amish neighbors who hired me as a farmhand throughout high school. I became fascinated with Anabaptists and attended Goshen College in Indiana."

"My brother-in-law went there." I didn't tell Drew I already knew he went to Goshen from my online search. "He graduated five years ago."

"I graduated fifteen years ago."

"So I guess you two don't know each other," I joked.

"No," he answered. "But no doubt we know some of the same people."

"Are you Mennonite?"

"I've belonged to Mennonite churches. I'm currently going to a nondenominational church, though." He pointed at my dress. "It looks as if you're Amish today."

"Yes," I answered. "I probably shouldn't switch back and forth like I do. Some might find it disrespectful."

"Are you on some sort of *Rumspringche*?"

"No. For a few years I strictly went to my Mammi and Dawdi's Amish church, but I still consider myself Mennonite." I shrugged. "I don't know what I'll do for sure." Except go to Alaska once Rosene was better.

I led the way up the steps into the kitchen. As I opened the door, I said, "Hi, Mammi. Hi, Rosene. I'd like to introduce you to our tenant. This is Drew Richards."

Drew stepped forward and shook their hands.

"Drew is going to be doing research on Anabaptists in times of military conflict," I said. "He'll also be conducting interviews."

"I have several lined up," he said. "But do you know of anyone who served in the military or as a conscientious objector?"

"My husband's father served as a CO at the mental hospital in Philadelphia," Mammi said. "Rosene has his story."

"Would you be willing to tell it to me?" Drew asked.

Rosene hesitated.

"Rosene is recovering from a heart attack," I said.

"Oh, well then, I don't want to tax you. Give the interview more thought."

"Thank you," Rosene replied. "I will. Or Arden could tell you the story."

I gestured toward the door. "I'm going to go introduce Drew to Dawdi right now. I'll be back in for lunch in a few minutes."

When we reached the barn, Dawdi was in the far corner, moving sacks of grain.

As we approached, I asked, "Need some help?"

Dawdi spun around. "Treva, you're just in time," he joked.

"This is Drew Richards," I said. "Our new tenant."

Dawdi extended his hand. "Arden Zimmerman. It's a pleasure to meet you."

Drew pumped Dawdi's hand as he grinned. "I'm *so* pleased to meet you." Drew seemed as if he'd met a long-lost friend.

Perhaps it was because Dawdi's dad had been a conscientious objector. I couldn't think of any other connection.

• 11 •

Wednesday morning, Mammi worked in the store, and I finished readying the Dawdi Haus for Gabe, putting sheets on the bed and cleaning the bathroom. A half hour after I finished, when I was back in the kitchen with Rosene, I heard a car door slam.

"That must be Sharon and Gabe." Rosene sat at the table, peeling potatoes. She stood and headed to the sink to wash her hands.

I turned the burner off. I'd been browning stew meat.

"You don't need to come outside," I said to Rosene.

"Oh yes, I do." She started toward the door. I followed her. When we reached the last step, Gabe started to climb out gingerly from the van.

"Welcome home!" Rosene called out.

Gabe turned toward us and smiled, just a little. "Thank you." He wore sports pants, running shoes, and a sweat-shirt. His face was tanned, and his short brown hair seemed lighter. He also seemed taller, but perhaps that was because of the way he carried himself. I guessed he had a brace on his back.

LESLIE GOULD

I gave him a wave and then said hello to Sharon. "The Dawdi Haus is ready. What needs to be carried inside?"

"Gabe has a bag of clothes. And some groceries. That's all."

I opened the back of the van and grabbed the Army green duffel bag, putting the strap over my shoulder, and then grabbed a box with milk, cereal, bread, fruit, veggies, and sandwich stuff.

Rosene led the way to the Dawdi Haus.

"How are you feeling?" Sharon asked her.

"Just fine," Rosene answered.

Gabe followed along behind them, walking slowly.

As we walked into the Dawdi Haus, Sharon placed her hand on her chest. "This is perfect. Thank you so much."

"Of course," Rosene said. "We'll always have room for Gabe."

"Yes, thank you," he said.

I put the groceries on the counter and then said, "I'll put the bag in the bedroom." I headed down the hall. When I returned, Gabe was putting the groceries away in the fridge.

"How's your mobility?" I asked.

"Decent." Gabe stood up straight. "It's limited right now by my brace. I have exercises to do that help with movement and pain and all of that. But they're hopeful about my recovery—not to the point of serving again, though."

"Oh?"

"I'm in the process of being honorably discharged."

I couldn't tell how he felt about that. Gabe, who was usually loud and sometimes a little obnoxious, seemed quiet and withdrawn.

"We're having stew for lunch." Rosene glanced from Sharon to Gabe. "We'd love to have both of you join us."

Sharon said, "Thank you, but I need to get back to work." She worked as an aide at a nearby school.

Gabe leaned against the counter. "I don't want to be a bother."

"Gabe," Rosene said, "you could never be a bother. We're so glad you're here."

He smiled a little. "Thank you, but I'll just make myself a sandwich. Please tell Arden and Priscilla hello."

Rosene wrinkled her nose. "Tell Arden and Priscilla hello? They'll want to hear it in person, from you. Either come to lunch or they'll be marching over here as soon as they know you've arrived."

Gabe exhaled. "I'll come over at noon. Thank you." This new Gabe seemed humble. Or maybe resigned.

Sharon gave Gabe a hug and said, "Call me if you need anything. I'll come get you tomorrow evening for dinner."

He returned the hug, a little stiffly, and said, "See you then. Thank you for everything."

"See you soon." I followed Sharon and Rosene out the door.

When we reached the van, Rosene asked, "Does Gabe seem different to you?"

"He's definitely not himself," Sharon said. "And I can't get him to talk about what's bothering him."

"Besides having a broken vertebra and being discharged from the army?" Rosene asked.

"True, that would be enough to make most people quiet and withdrawn, but I think there's something else going on. Maybe Conrad will be able to get him to talk."

I hurried into the kitchen to get the stew assembled and started on the stove. Then I made biscuits and a salad while Rosene rested.

Gabe seemed to lighten up a little around Dawdi and

Mammi while we ate. Dawdi, in true Dawdi fashion, gave direct orders, such as "Tell us about the accident."

"It was just one of those things." Gabe buttered his biscuit. "I was riding in the back of a truck, and a sandstorm blew up. Sand is worse than ice. The driver lost control, and the truck rolled."

"Goodness," Mammi said. "You're fortunate your injury wasn't worse."

Gabe nodded. "Definitely."

"Was anyone else badly injured?" Dawdi asked.

Gabe shook his head. "There were three others in the truck. They were bruised a little, but nothing bad. We weren't going very fast."

"Anyone from your unit?" I asked. We knew two of them—Marko and Viktor, who had become friends of Brenna's before she left for Ukraine.

"No." Gabe shifted in his chair. "I was working on a garbage detail with another unit."

"Interesting," Rosene said. "We don't think much about what needs to be done on a military base."

"Yeah," Gabe said. "It's basically a little city. Some services are contracted out to civilian businesses, but others are taken care of by soldiers." He grinned. "I basically went all that way to be a garbage hauler."

"Well." Rosene smiled kindly. "That's important work. Imagine what would happen if no one did it."

"Exactly." Gabe smiled wryly, showing a glimmer of his old self. "At least that's what I kept telling myself."

I worked in the store that afternoon while Mammi stayed at the house with Rosene. I sold a new clock to a tourist and then an antique quilt to a collector. Halfway through the afternoon, I heard footsteps on the outside steps and then above in the apartment.

A few minutes later, Drew came in through the front door of the store. After saying hello, he said, "I'm off to interview your grandfather about his dad's service."

"Nice," I said. It made me a little sad Rosene wasn't going to tell him about Jeremiah. She had always been the keeper of the family stories.

"I want to thank you again for renting the apartment to me." Drew placed a hand on the counter. "It's an answer to my prayers."

"I'm so glad." I smiled. "It's nice to have you on the Zimmerman farm. How are you doing without electricity?"

He laughed. "It takes some getting used to. I keep trying to flip a switch when I walk through the door. But overall I appreciate the experience."

After Drew left, I thought of Gabe and hit my forehead with the heel of my hand. Gabe had grown up Mennonite and then joined the Army Reserve. He'd be perfect for Drew to interview—if Gabe was willing to do it. He might not be.

Mammi came to relieve me at the shop at four. "Rosene's resting," she said. "Go help Arden with the milking."

I'd have to speak with Gabe later. The day had turned warm, so I hung up my coat in the barn office and put a vinyl apron over my dress. As I walked toward the milking area, I heard voices—Dawdi's and then Drew's. I stopped.

Drew asked, "Did your father talk much about his work at the mental hospital?"

"No," Dawdi said. "Rosene was my main source as far as the story, but before he died, I asked him to tell me what his experience was in his own words. It followed Rosene's exactly."

"How did he feel about serving?"

"Good, I think. It was a difficult time—nonresistant or not, he wanted to help our country."

"Did he consider serving in the military?"

"No," Arden said. "I'm certain he didn't. No one's ever mentioned that, but you could double-check with Rosene to be sure. He would have had to leave the Amish church to do so."

I stepped into the milking parlor. "Hi."

Dawdi gave me a wave, and Drew, who held a shovel in his hand, said, "Hello."

Dawdi motioned toward Drew. "He has experience with milking."

"The Amish farmer you worked for in Wisconsin had a dairy?" I asked.

Drew smiled as he dumped a shovel of grain into the trough. "Yep. It seems to be a skill one doesn't forget."

"You can go get dinner started," Dawdi said. "We're fine in here." I guessed Dawdi was happy to have another man around.

I untied my apron. "See you soon."

On my way to the house, I detoured to the Dawdi Haus and knocked on the door. No one answered. Perhaps Gabe was resting—I didn't want to wake him. But as I turned to go, the door opened. Gabe stood in front of me, bleary-eyed.

"Sorry," I said. "I didn't mean to wake you."

"No worries. I needed to do my exercises anyway. What's up?"

I told him about Drew. "He interviewed Dawdi this afternoon and has other interviews lined up. But a current story, like yours, would probably be helpful."

Gabe made a face and shook his head. "I don't think I should talk to Drew."

"Why not?"

"My story's pretty boring. He wouldn't be interested."

"Yes, he would."

Gabe shook his head.

"Would you think about it?"

He frowned. "Probably not."

"Are you okay?"

"Yeah. I'm fine."

I took a step forward. "How were Viktor and Marko when you left?"

"Good. Well, concerned about me. The accident kind of freaked them out, with what happened to Rylan and all. But once they got word that I'd be fine, they felt better." He ran his hand through his hair. Rylan was a friend of theirs who had lost a leg while serving overseas.

"Well, if you change your mind about talking to Drew, let me know. He's staying in the apartment above the shop."

Gabe cocked his head. "Brenna's apartment?"

I grimaced. "I doubt she's coming back."

"Does Priscilla know that?"

"If she doesn't, she's deluding herself."

Gabe looked so sad. Had he been sweet on Brenna? "I'm going to the house to fix dinner. Come eat with us."

"I just had lunch with you."

"Yes," I said. "And we'd love to have you join us for dinner too."

He glanced over his shoulder, perhaps toward his little kitchen.

"Dawdi, Mammi, and Rosene have been pretty lonely with all of us gone." I smiled. "You'd be doing them a favor."

He exhaled. "They're doing *me* a favor by letting me live here. They've been doing me a favor for years. I never really realized everything they'd been doing for me until I landed in Kuwait."

I kind of wanted to give him a hug. "I think the favors have been mutual. Dawdi's had a hard time keeping a farmhand since you left. He's missed your work—and you as a person."

"Maybe I should go hang out with him in the barn."

"You should." I gave him a sassy smile. "You could meet Drew—he's helping with the milking."

Gabe groaned. "That feels like a setup."

"It's not. Really. We'll eat at five thirty. Just show up if you change your mind."

Gabe didn't join us for dinner, but Drew did, at Dawdi's invitation. Thankfully, I'd roasted a chicken and made mashed potatoes. With home-canned green beans, applesauce, yeast rolls Mammi had started that morning, and an Amish apple goodie—otherwise known as an apple crisp—that Rosene had insisted on making, it was a pretty typical Amish meal.

Drew was the perfect dinner guest. He asked questions and encouraged Rosene and Dawdi to tell more stories, while also graciously answering Dawdi's questions. Drew was an only child, and his parents had divorced when he was young. His father passed away three years ago. He had a sweetheart named Stephanie who taught at nearby Elizabethtown College.

That gave us something to root for when it came to Drew.

"Don't wait too long," Dawdi said.

"Jah," Mammi said. "You're not getting any younger."

I guessed Drew was around thirty-five.

He grinned. "Thank you," he said. "I hope to get hired at a college in the area after I get my PhD." He glanced from Mammi to Dawdi. "How long have the two of you been married?"

Mammi turned toward Dawdi, who said, "Let's see."

"Fifty-one years," Rosene said. "In June."

"What?" I gasped. "Your fiftieth anniversary was last June?"

Mammi nodded.

"Why didn't you say something?"

Dawdi smiled. "We celebrated it. I picked Priscilla a bouquet of sweet peas."

"And I made Arden a strawberry pie."

I remembered the bouquet of sweet peas on the table and the strawberry pie we ate. I shook my head. "You should have told us."

Mammi reached over and put her hand on my arm. "We have our ways."

Drew hesitated a moment, most likely not wanting to butt into the middle of a family conversation, and then said, "I thought the Amish mainly got married in the fall, after the harvest is done, especially years ago."

"Jah, that was true," Mammi replied. "Now couples get married throughout the year; there are too many weddings to keep them to certain months. Back then, most people were married after harvest, but it wasn't unheard of to marry at other times. June worked for us."

I asked, "Why?"

Mammi said, "It worked better for my parents."

It hit me that I'd never heard Mammi talk about her parents. All of the family stories had been from Dawdi's side.

"How's that?" I asked.

"My Dat was ill," she said. "He passed away two months after we married."

"Oh. What about your Mamm?"

"She was at the wedding." Mammi glanced at Dawdi. "She remarried about six months later and moved to Ohio. She passed away twenty years ago."

I was dumbfounded that Mammi had never mentioned her parents before. And dumbfounded that I'd never asked.

She stood. "Let's get these plates cleared. Treva, would you go get the ice cream?"

"Sure."

Dawdi stood to help clear the plates too, before Rosene could. Then Drew did too. I headed to the basement to the propane-powered freezer.

The next morning, after breakfast, I drove Rosene into Lancaster for her follow-up appointment. The office was close to the hospital and not too far from the refugee center. She asked me to come into the appointment with her, saying, "It's always good to have another set of ears."

The doctor was the same one who saw her in the hospital and seemed genuinely happy to see Rosene doing so well. After checking Rosene's vitals and asking her a few questions, she said, "I recommend starting your regular walking again and, if you choose, adjusting your diet some. Fewer saturated fats. Olive and avocado oils are good. Lots of fresh fruits and vegetables. Lean meats. Legumes. Unrefined flour. Whole grains."

Rosene nodded.

"How is your stress?"

"Better."

The doctor smiled at her. "Gradually increase your activity," the doctor said. "Don't lift anything heavy for another week. Keep taking your blood pressure and blood thinner medications, and come see me again in a month. Also, make an appointment at the front desk for your cardiac rehab."

After we made the appointments and then headed toward the van, Rosene took a slip of paper from her purse. "May I use your phone to call Herr Mayer? It's late there, but I thought I'd leave a message asking if Brenna could represent me, if she's willing. May I give him your email address in case that's an easier way to communicate?"

"Of course." I handed her my phone.

I listened as she rattled off a message in German. I understood *Herzinfarkt*—heart attack—and *Nichte*—niece—and a few other words, but I couldn't keep up with Rosene's rapid speech. Finally, she rattled off my email address and said, "Danke." Then she ended the call and handed me my phone. "It's a relief to leave a message. It's been weighing on me."

"How's your grief?" I asked.

"Oh, you know how grief is. It comes and goes. The shock—which shouldn't have been a shock—is gone. Now I just have that ache. And regrets."

"Regrets?"

Rosene sighed. "I doubt I would have made any different decisions. And I guess I'd have regrets no matter what decisions I made. . . ." She squared her shoulders. "I'm not just grieving Lena. I'm grieving Martha and Clare again too. My three sisters were so different. All were strong women. Clare and Martha nurtured me. Lena antagonized me. But the older I get, the more I realize how wounded Lena was, not just by our mother's death but also by the war and the aftermath. I wish I'd seen that more clearly, sooner. When I last saw her five years ago, I knew she was wounded. But

I still couldn't get through to her. It was as if she had some sort of force field around her."

I smiled and tilted my head at her choice of words.

She laughed a little. "Gabe explained force fields to me a few years ago."

"Nice." I started the van.

Rosene leaned against her seat. "Would you like me to tell you more of my story while you drive?"

"Yes," I answered. "Absolutely."

· 12 ·

Rosene

On Wednesday, Martha took the subway with me to the train station in the Russian quadrant. Esther held a single small suitcase and waited for us in the crowded lobby. She seemed nervous. She spoke in German when we reached her, saying, "The platform is packed with people trying to leave by train. So is the subway."

"What's going on?"

"There are rumors that today is the last day the train will run."

"I heard it's tomorrow."

Esther said, "Either way, you and George need to get out."

"He's secured a car." Martha turned toward the platform. A crowd blocked the door to the train.

Esther whispered, "They'll cut the road off too."

Martha took both of our free hands. "We need to get the two of you on the train." She started toward the platform, but the door was blocked. "We have tickets," Martha called out in German. The crowd didn't budge. She began pushing her way through, but she couldn't pull us with her. Our hands slipped from hers, and a man knocked Esther down. I pulled her to her feet as I called out, "Martha!"

She turned and elbowed her way back through the crowd. We had no problem going in the opposite direction.

"We should take the subway," Esther said.

I added, "To your apartment. You and George need to leave."

"Our work . . ." Martha pursed her lips together.

"What good can you do if Berlin is cut off?" I asked. "You won't be able to get anyone out—and nothing will get in. You'll starve."

After a moment, she nodded decisively. She grabbed our hands again, and we started to run toward the subway. As we reached the platform, we were again stopped by a crowd. We had to wait for four trains, and when we finally got on, we were smashed together, barely able to breathe.

By the time we reached Martha's stop in the midafternoon, I felt panicked. But once we neared her apartment, I breathed a little easier. We turned the corner, and there was George, loading a box into the front of a two-door car. It looked like the engine was in the rear of the car, and the trunk was in the front.

"George!" Martha called out. "We need to leave."

He waved. "Put your suitcases in the car. Martha, we have a few more things we need to take. I've packed a suitcase for us."

"Did you pack food?"

He shook his head.

"Rosene, go get the bread and cheese," Martha said. "And anything else you can find. Esther, help her."

Ten minutes later, George pulled the car away from the

curb. Martha sat up front with a box on her lap. Esther and I sat in the back seat with two boxes stacked between us. We held our suitcases on our laps and had baskets of food at our feet.

The streets were clogged with vehicles. "Do you have a full tank of gas?" Martha asked George as we inched along.

"Yes, but it's a small tank," George answered. "I have two cans of gas in the trunk."

"It's a hundred miles, right?"

"Yes. We'll be fine."

"But then we'll need to continue on to Hamburg. It will be night with nowhere to gas up."

"We'll be fine," George repeated.

We inched along for two hours. Finally, on the outskirts of town, we picked up speed to twenty miles an hour. Thirty minutes later, the traffic slowed drastically again until it barely moved. Ahead was a checkpoint.

Martha turned toward us. "Get your papers out."

My hands shook as I retrieved mine from my purse. What if we weren't allowed to continue? Being stuck in Germany was my worst nightmare. Even worse was being trapped in the Russian quadrant.

Forty-five minutes later, we reached the checkpoint. George greeted the guard in German and handed him our papers. He spoke rapidly, telling the guard that he and Martha worked for the International Red Cross and were being transferred to Hamburg. Then he told them I was Martha's sister, in Germany for a visit, and that Esther was a refugee on her way to the US.

The guard asked what goods we were carrying.

George answered, "Household goods and some work papers."

The guard ordered George to exit the car. Then he pushed the driver seat forward, reached over me, and flipped open the top box between Esther and me. I could see files with *Red Cross* stamped across the top.

The man grabbed a handful of files, stepped back with them, and then after a moment, shoved them back into the car over my suitcase that I still held on my lap, and sent them cascading over the basket of food at my feet and onto the floor. Then he said something to George.

George pushed his seat into place and climbed back into the car.

"Can you put the papers into the box?" Martha asked me as George started driving. "No doubt we'll be stopped again soon."

I began picking up the papers. Some had the names of people. Others had only numbers. "What will happen to the refugees remaining in Berlin?"

Martha glanced at George. "Whatever the Russians are up to will only be temporary. We'll be able to return. Hopefully soon."

I picked up a paper that had some sort of code on it. I glanced at Esther. She shook her head. I put the paper in a file.

"Don't try to sort all of that," Martha said. "It doesn't matter what file you put papers in. Just get it in the box. Then hand it to me."

George glanced in the rearview mirror, and then he patted Martha's leg.

"Everything will work out," he said. "You'll see."

I'd never seen Martha anxious before.

I must have dozed because when I opened my eyes, the sun was going down.

Esther leaned toward the middle of the seat, around the box between us. "Are those Russian tanks?"

I leaned toward the middle so I could see around George too. The tanks traveled toward us.

"Yes," Martha said.

George pulled the car to the side of the road as a black car passed the tanks in our lane and zoomed past us.

"They're most likely headed to Berlin to close the road." George waited until the tanks passed and then pulled back onto the road. He soon picked up speed.

An hour later, George said, "The gas is getting low."

"We should stop." Martha shifted in her seat. "We can have something to eat too."

A few miles later, George pulled over under a tree. He walked around the front to the hood and pulled out a gas can as Esther and I wriggled out of the back seat and then pulled out the baskets of food.

Martha crawled out of the front seat and stretched her arms. "Put the baskets on the hood."

We ate cheese and bread and then passed around the bottle of milk. The sun was setting in the west.

"By evening's light," Martha said.

"What does that mean?" Esther asked.

Martha translated it into German. "We used to sing a song in church by that title," she added. "Do you remember, Rosene?"

I nodded.

Martha sang the first verse. "'Brighter days are sweetly dawning, Oh, the glory looms in sight! For the cloudy day is waning, And the evening shall be light.'"

I joined in as Martha sang the chorus. "'Oh, what golden glory streaming! Purer light is coming fast; Now in Christ we've found a freedom, Which eternally shall last.'"

"Christ?" Esther asked. "Your Messiah, correct? I remember Him from when I went to Mass with my father."

I assumed it was her mother who had been Jewish. I hoped we hadn't offended Esther.

"Yes," Martha said. "Jesus Christ."

Esther said, "I have nothing against your Christ, nor His teachings—even though the Nazis claimed Him."

"They didn't follow His teachings," Martha said. "It was as if they made up their own religion."

Esther pursed her lips together.

When we'd finished our food, Esther and I piled into the back seat and Martha handed us the baskets, which we put at our feet again.

George turned on the headlights, and we continued on. Night fell, and it seemed we were the only car on the road.

A *thump, thump, thump* jarred me. The telltale sound of a flat tire.

"Do we have a flashlight?" Martha asked.

"I have a candle," Esther said.

"How about a match?"

"Jah," Esther said.

"The burning question is—" George opened his door— "do we have a spare?"

Thankfully, we did. George changed the tire by candlelight.

When we settled in the car again, George said, "We're almost at the hundred-mile mark. We'll be at the border soon." It was the inner border of Germany, the one that separated the Russian quadrant from the American quadrant. From there, we would drive north to the English quadrant.

As we approached the border, George slowed. Two guards stood at a checkpoint. Again, we showed our papers. This time, the Russian soldier went to the trunk and opened it.

"What's he doing?" Martha whispered.

"Going through papers."

The soldier returned to the window with a file. "What is this?"

George opened his door. "Did you find what I brought for you?"

"What are you talking about?"

George climbed out of the car. "American cigarettes. I have three cartons. You can share them with your comrades or keep them for yourself."

The soldier hesitated but then handed over the file and followed George to the front of the car. A minute later, the soldier stepped to the booth with the cartons, and George slammed the hood and climbed back into the car. He waved at the soldier, and then he slowly accelerated, leaving the Russian quadrant behind.

We stopped one more time for George to empty the second gas can into the tank. I couldn't stay awake any longer. When I awoke again, we were in a city. My legs were asleep from the weight of my suitcase.

"Hamburg," Esther told me. "We made it." Then she began to cry.

———

I expected that George and Martha would find a hotel but instead they drove to a house—a rather big one. George climbed out of the car and went and knocked. First gently and then harder. A man wearing a robe over his pajamas finally opened the door.

"Red Cross colleagues live here," Martha said. "George and I will be able to stay for as long as we need, and you can sleep some before you catch your flight to London."

It was the middle of the night and no one was on the street, but we carried everything into the house. The man in the robe helped with the boxes. Once we finished, Martha introduced him as Robert Jones. "His wife is Candace," she said. "You'll meet her in the morning."

Robert showed Esther and me to a bedroom down the hall, pointing to the bathroom on the way. In just a few minutes, Esther and I climbed into a bed with a down mattress and comforter, still with our clothes on. It was light when Martha woke us in the morning. "We need to hurry to get to the airport," she said. "Change your clothes. There's food ready for you."

Once we were dressed, we ate bread, sausage, and stewed plums. Candace and Robert were nowhere to be seen. Once we were in the car, Martha said, "If you can't find your gate in London, make sure and ask. Stay together at all times. And don't converse with strangers." Martha glanced at me. "If anyone asks about us, play dumb."

I opened my mouth to ask what she was talking about.

She shook her head.

George parked the car, and he and Martha walked us into the airport. After we stopped at the counter for our tickets, George stepped to Esther's side and asked how she was doing.

"I'm sad. . . ." She spoke softly and I couldn't hear what she was saying.

Martha stepped closer to me. "I'll write soon and give you our new address. You may have questions about some of what you've seen. . . ."

I nodded.

"Please don't say anything to Mutter or Vater. Or Clare and Jeremiah. I don't want them to worry. Our Red Cross work has grown . . . complicated. I'll explain later. But we are safe and doing what we need to do. Getting refugees out of Germany and all of Europe is important work."

"It is," I agreed. "I trust you. And George. Please take care of each other."

"We will." She put her arm around me and pulled me close. "I'm sorry things didn't go well with Lena and Onkel Josef. I'll be praying for you."

"And I for you." I hugged her in return.

They walked us to our gate. As I turned to wave one last time, Martha blew me a kiss. I had a sinking feeling as I blew a kiss back and then walked toward the plane, staying close to Esther. I doubted Martha would ever move home. She seemed to be thriving in Europe. And she was doing important work, no doubt, even if I didn't know the details.

Together, Esther and I navigated our flight to London, the six-hour layover, and then our flight to New York. We were both exhausted by the time we reached Grand Central Station, and even more so when we finally reached the Lancaster train station.

Martha hadn't said anything about whether she was going to contact Mutter and Vater about our arrival, but she must have because Jeremiah was waiting on the platform for us. I looked past him for Zeke. Surely he would be waiting for me. But he wasn't.

Someone called out, "Esther?" It was a woman wearing a skirt, sweater, and pumps. And a string of pearls around her neck.

The woman met my eyes. "Is that Esther Lang? From Germany?"

"Yes." I introduced myself.

"Are you George's sister-in-law?"

"That's right." I introduced Esther to her and then Jeremiah.

The woman introduced herself as Peggy Meyer.

I asked, "Do you speak German?"

She held up her finger and thumb. "Just a little." She turned toward Esther. "Do you speak English?"

Esther smiled and held up her finger and thumb. Then she said, in English, "I actually speak quite a lot." They both laughed.

Mrs. Meyer handed me a card. "This has my address and phone number. Would you come visit sometime soon? Esther will stay with me until her apartment is furnished."

I took the card and nodded. Then I turned to Esther and said, "I'll come see you in two days. You can let me know what questions you have." I gave her a hug. She hugged me back and then left with Mrs. Meyer.

Jeremiah took my suitcase from me. "You must be exhausted."

"Jah," I answered. "I'm ready to go home."

"I hired a driver."

As we walked out of the depot, I said, "I hoped Zeke would be with you."

Jeremiah exhaled and then looked down at me, his eyes full of kindness.

"What's wrong?" I asked.

"Zeke left a week ago, for Illinois. He's taken a job there."

"When will he come home?"

"He didn't say."

It seemed I had my answer. *No*.

"He left you a letter," Jeremiah said. "Clare put it in your room."

"Has she read it?"

"No," Jeremiah answered. "Of course not."

I wished she had.

Jeremiah patted my shoulder as I fought back tears, trying to keep my grief from my past and my grief over Zeke from colliding.

· 13 ·

Treva

Early Monday morning, I headed out to the barn before Dawdi and checked my email on my phone. Herr Mayer had sent an email in response to the voicemail Rosene had left on Thursday. It was in German. I'd show it to Rosene later, when Dawdi and Mammi weren't around.

After helping with the milking and eating breakfast, I headed to Amish Antiques to work while Mammi stayed with Rosene.

As I emptied the bank bag into the old-fashioned drawer of the register, I heard footsteps on the porch. It was 10:01. I hurried to flip the sign and unlock the front door. Then I opened it. Gabe stood in front of me.

"Need some help?" he asked.

"Umm." I looked behind myself into the store. Could he help with the sweeping? The dusting?

"Today is the first day I don't have to wear my brace," he said. "And I'm bored. I'd like to help. I don't expect to be

141

paid. I offered Arden rent money, but he refused. I can help in the store, but I can't help with the milking. Not yet."

I swept my arm wide. "I'd be delighted for you to help in the store. Please come in."

"But I won't be wearing the pants and shirt Priscilla used to make me wear—well, wanted me to wear. Which I did."

I glanced down at my Mennonite dress. Mammi hadn't said anything about what I wore to the shop since I returned, whether it was jeans or a dress. Mennonite or Amish. Perhaps she was getting over that.

Gabe dusted while I wound the clocks, including Rosene's. A few customers came in, and we took turns waiting on them. When we finished with the winding and dusting, we stood at the counter. "How do you feel about being out of the army?" I asked.

He didn't answer immediately.

"Conflicted?" I asked.

"No." Gabe started pacing.

"What's wrong?"

He didn't answer but kept pacing. Finally, he said, "I don't know what's wrong. That's the problem. And I don't know what I should do with my life."

"You should rest," I said. "And get well. Then you should start helping Dawdi with the milking so I can go to Alaska."

"You want to go to Alaska?"

"I'm *going* to Alaska."

His face fell. "See, even Treva—the youngest of all of us—knows what she wants to do."

"It's just for the summer," I said. "I think."

"Are you running away from something?"

I froze. Was it that obvious? "No."

He cocked his head. What had Ivy and Conrad told him?

Perhaps Pierre had texted Ivy. Or Conrad. Perhaps everyone knew.

"I need something new," I said. "Does that make sense?"

"Yes," he said. "Because I need something old. I need to be here. I do understand. Just in reverse."

A lump grew in my throat. Gabe seemed to be humbled, without an ego. I wanted that—my ego was deeply bruised.

Footsteps on the porch ended the conversation before I could respond.

Drew opened the door. "Treva," he said. "Hello."

"Hello," I said. "Is everything all right?" Maybe a clogged drain or a problem with the lamp.

He smiled. "I just stopped by to say hello."

I motioned toward Gabe. "This is Gabe Johnson. He's—" I hesitated a moment. "He's worked for Mammi and Dawdi for years. He's living in our Dawdi Haus and is helping in the shop this morning."

Drew stepped forward and shook Gabe's hand. "I'm pleased to meet you," he said. "Arden mentioned that you were staying in the Dawdi Haus. He said you grew up Mennonite but just returned from Kuwait, where you were serving in the army."

Gabe gave me a wry look.

I shrugged. I hadn't said anything.

"That's right." Gabe crossed his arms.

"I'm doing research for my PhD dissertation on Anabaptists in times of military conflicts. Could I speak with you sometime?" Drew tilted his head a little as he spoke. "Ask you some questions about your service?"

Gabe was silent for a minute. "I guess so. When would you like to chat?"

"How about this afternoon?"

Gabe nodded. "Come to the Dawdi Haus at two. If that works for you."

"Perfect." Drew nodded toward me. "See you soon, Treva. And Gabe, I'll see you this afternoon."

━━━━━━

I left the store at 10:30, leaving Gabe in charge, and stopped by the house to let Mammi know she didn't need to go to the store until after lunch. Then I left for the refugee center for Rosene's Monday shift. Cala greeted me at the door when I arrived. "How is Rosene?" she asked.

I gave her an update.

"When can we visit her?" Cala asked. "We'd like to bring dinner."

"Aww," I said. "That's so nice of you."

"How about tomorrow?"

"I think that would work." I took out my phone, and we exchanged numbers. "I'll text you this afternoon and let you know for sure."

Three women from Somalia prepared lunch—spongy, pancake-like flatbread; deep-fried, cone-shaped pastries stuffed with vegetables; and a spicy pasta dish with peppers and a little beef. I set out the plates and forks. And poured glasses of water. After we cleaned up, I helped the women with their homework and paperwork again.

After I answered a few questions Zaida had about filling out medical forms for her family, I asked if Kamil had found a job.

"Not yet," she said. "He's been doing rides to get us by."

"Doing rides?"

"From the app."

"Oh." A rideshare app.

"Do you know of any jobs?" Zaida asked.

"Has Kamil ever worked on a farm?"

"He grew up on a farm." She smiled. "He had goats."

"Did he enjoy the work?"

She laughed. "The goats, not so much. But the farm, yes."

"I'll ask around," I said, "and see if anyone needs a farmhand."

"Your farm?"

"I don't know," I answered. "I'll ask. I'm going to text Cala about you bringing a meal to Rosene tomorrow. I'll let her know if anyone in our area is looking for a farmhand."

"Thank you," Zaida said.

I hated to think of Zaida, Kamil, and Cala buying groceries for a dinner for us, but I wasn't sure about offering them money for the ingredients. I'd ask Rosene what I should do.

On the way home, I stopped by the store. I needed shampoo. Mammi asked me to pick up dish soap. Rosene needed avocado oil.

Supermarkets in Haiti were expensive. The food we couldn't grow at the orphanage we bought at an open-air market, along with other necessities too. I wore Mennonite dresses in Haiti—they were cool, easy to wash, and quick to dry. Wearing a Kapp helped keep my hair cleaner than it would have been otherwise, with the dust on the roadways and in the yard.

I stared at the shampoos, wondering which version of myself I'd be in Alaska. Shawn had grown up Mennonite, but he and Misty went to a nondenominational church now. Misty's parents had owned the resort, and she grew up working on it. And then inherited it a decade ago. She and Shawn worked hard in the spring, summer, and fall and then usually volunteered somewhere for a couple of months in the winter, which brought them to Haiti and the orphanage. Misty wore dresses in Haiti because they were cooler, but I knew she wore jeans and sweatshirts in Alaska. Under her parka.

Summers in Alaska could be pretty cool. I'd probably wear jeans and a sweatshirt too.

I finally made a decision as far as which shampoo, and then found the other things on my list and headed home.

When I pulled into the driveway, Drew and Gabe sat at the picnic table. I thought of Zeke and Rosene sitting at it all those years ago. Now, in Rosene's story, Zeke was gone. Poor Rosene.

Gabe waved. I waved back and continued toward the shed to park the van. As I turned off the engine, my phone dinged. Pierre. My heart lurched.

Thinking about you. I hope you're doing well.

I slipped my phone into my pocket. I'd return his text later.

I stopped by the barn first, but Dawdi wasn't there. I continued on to the house and into the kitchen. Dawdi and Rosene sat at the kitchen table.

Rosene stood as I came in. "How did it go?"

"Great." I explained that Zaida and Cala wanted to bring a meal by the next day.

"Oh, I don't want them to use their groceries on us."

"Me neither, but I really think they want to. Could I give them money?"

"I don't think so." Rosene pursed her lips together. "Maybe we could give them some meat from the deep freezer. They don't have dietary restrictions, so I think they might accept that."

"Should I text Cala and let her know?"

"Jah." Rosene walked toward the stove, where something simmered on the front burner. "Actually, wait. I hope this doesn't sound contradictory—first I'm worried about using up their groceries and now I'm going to propose something."

What was she going to propose?

She took the lid off the pot. "What if we invite Gabe and Drew to dinner tomorrow?"

"I think that would be really nice," I said.

"Great. We'll try to give them several packages of meat."

I sat down across from Dawdi. "Are you looking to hire a new farmhand?"

"Are you still planning on going to Alaska?"

"Jah," I answered.

"Then I guess so. If Gabe wants to work in the store again, I think that would help, but I don't want him farming until a doctor clears him for more strenuous work. Do you have someone in mind?"

"Zaida's husband, Kamil, is looking for a job."

"Does he have any experience working on a farm?"

"Zaida said he grew up on one. They had goats."

"Ach," Dawdi said. "Cows are easy compared to goats. I'd only need him to help with the milking, twenty hours a week at the most."

"I guess it would depend on if that would be enough hours for him," I said. "Perhaps he'd still do the rideshare work he's doing too. I'm assuming he'll give Zaida and Cala and the kids a ride here tomorrow. Maybe you could ask him."

"I'll take him around the farm," Dawdi said. "And see if he seems interested. Are you ready to help me with the milking?"

"I just need to change my dress," I said. "I'll be right back."

As soon as he left, pulling the door shut behind him, I

pulled my phone from my pocket and showed Rosene the email from Herr Mayer.

I waited as she read it.

"What does it say?" I asked.

"Oh, you could have read it yourself."

I laughed. "I tried. My German isn't good enough." I knew quite a bit of Pennsylvania Dutch, and I'd picked up some German from the Bible readings at church and following along in a German Bible, but I wasn't fluent.

She smiled. "Herr Mayer wrote that communicating by email would be fine. He said that he was sorry to hear about my heart condition and that it made it difficult for me to travel—he was looking forward to meeting me. As far as Lena's estate, he said I need to submit a certificate of inheritance issued by a German probate court and that he could mail me the needed documents to settle the estate. But that if Brenna could come to Germany and represent me, the process would be much quicker and less cumbersome. Plus, she could see to leasing out the house once everything is settled."

"I'll ask her if she'd be willing to do that."

"I don't want to bother her."

"I don't think it will be a bother. Perhaps Johann can go with her. That would make it easier—and enjoyable for them."

"Maybe they can stay in the house."

I wrinkled my nose. "I don't think Mammi would be okay with that."

"Maybe Natasha could go with them."

I said, "I'll message Brenna about going to Germany after we're done with the milking."

An hour later, my phone dinged. I tried not to use my phone around Dawdi, so I didn't check who it was from.

After we finished, I told Dawdi I'd be in the house in a few minutes. Once he left the barn, I checked my phone. The text was from Ivy.

How is Gabe doing?

> Better, I think. He helped in the shop today.

Next, I texted Cala.

> Tomorrow works great to bring dinner. Would you mind if I invited two others to join us? That would make six of us altogether, plus your family. That's a lot. We have some meat in our freezer we'd like to give to you to help make up for the groceries you use. Is Kamil coming too? My grandfather would like to speak to him about a possible farmhand job.

Cala texted back.

Six of you is no problem. We will arrive around five and have dinner ready to serve at 5:30. I will tell Kamil about the possible farmhand position, and, yes, we will accept the meat. Thank you. ☺

Next, I messaged Brenna.

> Would you be willing to go to Frankfurt and meet with Lena's attorney, Herr Mayer? Rosene would give you power of attorney to make decisions for her. She'd also need you to look into leasing the house, through a property agency most likely. I think it would be pretty straightforward.

I waited a few minutes until Brenna answered my text.

Would I be attending to the financial side of
the estate only, or would I need to go through
Lena's things too?

I had no idea.

> I'll ask Rosene and get back to you. She was
> thinking maybe Johann and Natasha could go
> with you.

Let me know what Rosene says about exactly
what my duties would be. After I have the
needed information, I'll consider it.

That was Brenna. To the point.

⁓

The next day, as Dawdi and I finished up the afternoon milking, Rosene appeared in the open door with Kamil at her side. "Arden," Rosene called out in a strong voice. "I'd like you to meet Kamil."

Dawdi stepped forward with a smile on his face, then slipped off his glove and shook Kamil's hand.

"Kamil, this is my nephew, Arden," Rosene said.

In unison, both said, "Pleased to meet you."

Rosene nodded toward me. "Have you met Treva yet?"

"Yes." Kamil smiled. "Hello."

"Good to see you," I answered.

"I was just going to finish in the milk room," Dawdi said to Kamil. "Would you like to join me?"

"Of course," he answered.

Dawdi turned to me. "I'll finish up."

I walked with Rosene toward the house. She stumbled a little but caught herself. I gave her my arm for support.

Perhaps she hadn't gained back as much strength as she claimed.

After I greeted Cala and Zaida and complimented them on how good everything smelled, I ran up the back staircase to shower and put on clean clothes—another Mennonite dress and Kapp.

When I came down to the kitchen, Mammi was setting the table, and Gabe was pouring water into each glass.

Zaida and Kamil's children were playing with a set of old-fashioned blocks in the living room. "Hello, Ahmad and Gamila," I said.

They each waved but didn't speak.

I asked Gabe where the blocks came from.

"Rosene pulled them out of there." He motioned to the staircase, where there were storage cupboards. Had Mammi, Dawdi, and Rosene kept those around for when children came by? Had Dad played with the blocks as a child?

Mammi's cuckoo clock chimed the half hour—five thirty. Both children glanced up at it but then returned to their play. When my sisters and I first arrived in Lancaster County, there were two recliners and a rocking chair in the living room, but they soon added a sofa for us. I sat down on it for a moment, thinking about Dawdi, five-year-old Arden, and his little sister Janice in Rosene's story.

Dawdi and Kamil arrived, and Dawdi headed down the hall to clean up. When he returned, after being introduced to Zaida, Cala, Ahmad, and Gamila, he directed us to sit around the table. Cala lifted Gamila into the old high chair that Dawdi had carried to the table from the corner of the kitchen. Had Dad used it too? I'd never thought to ask.

Dawdi explained our tradition of a silent prayer and led us in one.

After Dawdi lifted his head and Rosene said, "Amen," Dawdi asked Zaida to tell us about the food.

She smiled as she pointed to the chicken shawarma, falafel, roasted vegetable salad, and *yabrak*. "Stuffed grape leaves," she explained. "We have *swar* for dessert, which is like baklava."

My mouth watered as we passed the dishes around.

Gamila sat between Mammi and Cala, while Ahmad sat between Gabe and me. I dished up for him and then passed the serving bowls to Gabe. I cut Ahmad's chicken into smaller pieces for him. Drew sat on the other side of me, next to Mammi.

Dawdi exclaimed how good the food was. "You should open a restaurant," he said to Zaida.

"Thank you." She beamed. "That's exactly what we would like to do."

Rosene clapped her hands together. "You know what we should do first?"

We? Rosene shouldn't be doing anything.

Rosene said, "We should host a community meal."

"What is that?" Zaida asked.

"I read about someone across the county doing one recently. We would invite neighbors—Amish and Mennonite and *Englisch*—to meet you, a refugee family. You would make the food and eat with our guests, providing a cultural experience for them. You would learn about our guests, and they would learn about you. We could charge twenty-five dollars per person. The money would pay you and Cala for your time and cover the groceries, and then the rest could go to the refugee center."

Zaida beamed. "Cala, what do you think?"

"The idea sounds good," she answered.

Zaida looked across the table. "Kamil, what do you think?"

He gave her a nod. "If you'd like to do it, you should."

Zaida turned her head toward Rosene. "What day works for you?"

Rosene glanced from Mammi to Dawdi. "The sooner the better. How about Saturday?" That was only four days away.

Mammi started to open her mouth, but Dawdi spoke first, saying, "I'll go around and invite our neighbors personally. The ancestors of every farmer in this area came here as immigrants, and many as refugees. I think they'll be thrilled to meet a recent refugee family."

I admired Dawdi's optimism.

Mammi opened her mouth again but then shut it.

After we had our dessert, Gamila grew fussy, and Ahmad wanted to go outside.

I'd already put together a box of meat from the freezer and brought it upstairs after dessert. "I'll do the dishes," I said to Zaida. "You should go home and see to the kids."

Zaida asked Kamil if he'd bring her out the next day to plan the community meal with Rosene.

He smiled. "I'm working here tomorrow. I'll bring you when I come for the afternoon milking."

After a round of thank-yous and good-byes, our friends left and Mammi excused herself, saying she had a headache. Dawdi went out to check on a cow who was in labor, and I began running the dishwater. Gabe poured himself another cup of coffee. Rosene stepped up to dry.

"Absolutely not," I said.

"This is ridiculous," she answered. "I promise to sit if I become tired."

"No need." Gabe stood. "You sit. I'll dry."

I glanced at Rosene. "I have a few questions from Brenna

for you, about working with Herr Mayer. Do you mind if Gabe hears the conversation?"

"Of course not," Rosene said.

I relayed what Brenna needed more information about.

"Jah," Rosene said. "She would need to attend to both the finances and the material goods in the house."

I moved the water faucet to the rinse pan. "What about a power of attorney for Brenna? I printed a few copies at the library."

"I'll sign it and have it notarized. Carol Smith is a notary, so that will be easy, and I can send it by express mail to him." Carol was our neighbor.

"Okay." I started washing a stack of plates.

"Brenna will need to meet with Herr Mayer," Rosene said. "She should plan to be there for a week or so."

"I'll let her know and see what she says." I rinsed the plates and then Gabe began drying them.

"I can tell you more of the story as you two work," Rosene said. "Gabe, would you like to listen?"

He answered, "I'd never pass on one of your stories."

Neither would I.

· 14 ·

Rosene

Once we reached the farm, I told Mutter and Vater hello, hugged Clare, and picked up Janice and swung her around and then Arden too, although he was getting too heavy for me to lift. Then I headed up to my room with my suitcase in search of Zeke's letter. It was on my bureau, where no doubt Clare had put it.

I put down my suitcase, picked up the folded piece of paper, and sat down on my bed.

Dear Rosene,

I had a difficult time waiting for you to return, wondering if you will return at all. I decided to go on my own adventure to make the time pass faster. I'll be gone a couple of months or so.

Zeke

That was all. Difficult time? I'd never seen Zeke get antsy about anything, let alone have a difficult time. Had he been jealous that I was on an adventure? Or what seemed to him as one, even though half of it was a nightmare to me.

I refolded the letter and stuffed it in my top drawer. Then I put away my things. Mutter came up the stairs, telling me it was time to eat. I couldn't bear to face them. They all knew Zeke hadn't waited for me.

The way Lena and Vater Josef had treated me made me angry. But Zeke leaving filled me with pain. How could he ask if I trusted him and then not wait for me to come home?

I crawled into bed and pulled the covers over my head. At some point, Arden knocked on my door and said, "Aenti Rosene, it's time to eat."

I didn't answer.

Clare came up and sat on my bed. I turned toward her. She brushed my hair from my eyes. "Are you all right?"

I nodded. "Just tired."

"How did things go with Lena and Onkel Josef?"

"I'll tell you in the morning."

But I didn't get out of bed in the morning. I stayed under my covers, even after Clare came to check on me again. "What's wrong?"

"I'm exhausted," I said.

Finally, driven by hunger, I got up midmorning and trudged down the stairs. Janice played with her doll while Clare sat at the table, peeling carrots.

I concentrated on sounding cheery. "What can I do to help?"

Clare smiled at me, and Janice ran to hug my legs.

"Get something to eat," Clare said. "I saved you a couple of eggs and a sticky bun from breakfast. They're on the sideboard. And then you could brown the meat for the stew for dinner."

I slipped back into our normal routine, but life on the farm seemed drab without Zeke, even with Arden and Janice clamoring for my attention and Clare needing my help.

I answered Clare and Mutter's questions about Germany as best I could. Vater Josef didn't seem to be in good health, but no one talked about what was wrong with him. Garit hadn't changed—he was still opinionated and bossy. Lena hadn't changed either.

Mutter asked, "Did George go to Frankfurt while you were there?"

I shook my head.

"Where are they living?" Clare asked.

"Hamburg." Somehow I hadn't had to lie.

"Did anyone see the blockade of Berlin coming?" Mutter asked.

"Garit seemed to believe the Russians would make trouble," I said. "What exactly is going on in Berlin? I saw a headline at the train station."

Mutter explained that Russia had closed off the roads and trains to Berlin. The US was flying in supplies to feed people. "They're going to have to increase the amount of goods they're flying in or people will be starving again."

I didn't say it appeared many were already starving, or close to it. Relieved that Martha, George, and Esther were out of Berlin, I smiled a little. But not for long when I thought of the people in Berlin who were barely surviving as it was.

"A refugee girl that Martha helped flew home with me," I said.

Clare nodded. "That's what Jeremiah said."

"I'd like to go see her." I felt too tired, too spent to go to town, but I needed to. It would be good for Esther, and it would take my mind off Zeke. "She's staying with a family in Lancaster. I'm hoping I can help explain things to her. She'll be in an apartment on her own soon."

"How old is she?" Mutter asked.

"My age."

"What became of her family?"

"They were killed during the war, except for an uncle. She came from Berlin, from the Russian quadrant."

"Goodness," Mutter exclaimed. "Is she a Communist?"

"Mutter!" Clare said.

"No," I answered. "She's not. She's Jewish."

Sometimes it seemed to me as if the world was going mad. As I tidied up the living room, I went through a stack of newspapers. President Truman had signed the Displaced Persons Act of 1948. But he wasn't happy about it. The act would assist in the resettlement of thousands of European refugees, but it placed strict limits on the number of people and excluded anyone who entered a refugee camp after December 22, 1945. The stipulation would actually prohibit Jewish refugees who survived the Holocaust and then fled the pogroms in postwar Poland, arriving in Germany after 1945. The so-called generous congressional act was actually anti-Semitic.

I sat down as I continued reading, feeling ill.

Truman's speech about the Act was quoted in the article. *It is with very great reluctance that I have signed . . . the Displaced Persons Act of 1948. . . . The bad points of the bill are numerous. Together they form a pattern of discrimina-*

*tion and intolerance wholly inconsistent with the American
sense of justice. . . . The bill discriminates in callous fashion
against displaced persons of Jewish faith. . . .*

I thanked the Lord that Esther had gotten out of Germany,
out of East Berlin specifically, but mourned for those who
were stuck.

I kept going through the newspapers. On the positive side
of another negative story, US pilots were dropping bags of
candy for the children of Berlin. There was still good in the
world. I said a silent prayer for God to bless those pilots and
all the pilots flying in and out of West Berlin. The English
had joined in the efforts too.

I put the newspapers in the bin by the woodstove in the
kitchen and then went down the back steps and turned
toward the store. I didn't dare glance at the picnic table—
every time I did, I expected Zeke to be there, waiting for
me. When I reached the store, I told Mutter I needed to call
Esther and then call for a driver.

"You should learn to drive," she said. "Then you could
be the driver in the family." She sighed. "It's ridiculous to
be without a car."

I didn't want to learn to drive. I wanted to marry Zeke
and join the Amish. Or if Zeke wasn't coming home, I
wanted to go far, far away. But where? Certainly not to
Germany.

"Call Esther," Mutter said. "Then I'll give you the number
for the driver we used last week to take us to Vater's doctor
appointment."

Mrs. Meyer answered the phone. I told her hello and
who I was. "We met at the train station when Esther and I
arrived."

"Of course," she said. "I remember. How are you?"

"I'm fine. I'm calling for Esther."

"She's not here," Mrs. Meyer said. "She moved into her apartment yesterday."

"Do you have a phone number for her?"

"No. But I have an address." She rattled it off. "I'm going over tomorrow, and I'll tell her you called. But I think you could just stop by. She speaks so fondly of you. I know she'd want to see you."

"Thank you," I said. "I'll plan to see her the day after tomorrow at nine thirty. Please tell her for me."

After we hung up, Mutter gave me the name of the driver, a Mr. Moore. I called and left a message with the man's wife, asking if he could pick me up the next morning at nine.

When I arrived at the apartment building, Esther was waiting for me on the stoop. As I climbed out of the car, she rushed toward me.

"Rosene." She kissed me on one cheek and then the other. "I've been waiting for you." She grabbed my hand and pulled me toward the building. "Come see my new home."

She led me up to the top floor of the three-story building and into a studio apartment, furnished with a daybed that doubled as a couch, a small table with two chairs, and a dresser.

"Isn't it lovely?" She pointed toward the daybed. "Mrs. Meyer gave me the quilt." It was obviously handmade, but I didn't recognize the pattern.

Tears filled Esther's eyes. "It's been so long since I've had a real home." Esther made tea, and we sat at the little table and talked for an hour, mostly in English. She insisted. Then she said, "There's a refugee center that I visited yesterday.

They're serving lunch today. Would you like to go there with me?"

"Jah," I answered. "I'd like that very much."

Located in the basement of a downtown church, the refugee center consisted of tables and chairs, a station with literature about local services, and an American Red Cross staff member and a couple of volunteers, along with three kitchen staff. Around thirty refugees gathered for a meal of soup, bread, cookies, and coffee.

A few of the refugees were quite elderly, but most were in their twenties and thirties. And while there were a couple of families, most seemed to be single. There were refugees from Austria, Poland, and Romania.

We sat next to an older woman from Austria who was also Jewish. As she and Esther struck up a conversation, the Red Cross staff person sat down next to me.

"I'm Lorraine Purcell. I understand you're the younger sister of Martha Simons."

"Yes," I answered. "Martha Hall now."

The woman smiled. "That's right. I knew she and George had married." She spoke softly. "We're looking for volunteers at the refugee center. Perhaps every other week?" She explained the duties would be to take turns with the cooking and cleanup, and to help the refugees with paperwork and accessing what they needed. "Would you be interested?"

"I'll speak with my parents." I was interested, but perhaps they would need me to help on the farm or in the store. Plus, I might need to hire a driver, which would be costly over time. Mutter had begun paying me some for my work in the store, but it wasn't much. And I didn't want to take money from the household budget.

Lorraine took a card from the pocket of her dress and handed it to me. "I work out of the office not far from here. Give me a call and let me know. The meal is always on Wednesdays. If that works, you could help here. If another day works better, I have other things you can volunteer for at the office."

I took the card. "I'll let you know." But I was already planning what I'd like to do: Make better meals. The soup was thin and tasteless. The bread was store-bought. And the cookies were dry. Perhaps Vater and Mutter would donate some meat and produce from the farm to feed the refugees.

That night, when I explained what I wanted to do, both Vater and Mutter gave me their blessing. It dawned on me that they were worried about me, both because of how emotional the trip to Germany had been and because Zeke had left.

"Volunteering would be good for you," Mutter said.

"But you need my help in the store."

"I can spare you one day a week."

"What about the money for the bus or a driver?"

"You can use what you make in the store, if you wish. But hire a driver. It will take too long on the bus."

I asked Vater about using extra produce from the garden and other food. "Could I make bread here to take? Do we have cuts of meat I could use to make soups and stews? I'll ask others to contribute too—perhaps a baker and butcher in Lancaster."

"Yes, as far as the bread. Check with Clare about what we can spare when it comes to produce. Also, yes, as far as the cuts of meat. I believe we could contribute. Share what we have."

Clare and I came up with a plan for the food.

For the first time since returning home, I felt I had purpose. The next day, I called Lorraine at the Red Cross office and told her I could volunteer. "I'd like to do a meal every other Wednesday and start as soon as possible. My family will donate some of the food."

Lorraine's breath caught. "Are you sure?"

"Yes," I said. "It's what the Lord would want us to do."

· 15 ·

I made bread, prepared soup with vegetables from our garden, tossed a cucumber salad, and baked three German chocolate cakes for that first meal. Then I boxed it up and hauled it in the driver's car to the refugee center. Not only would the bus have taken too long, but I also wouldn't have been able to haul the food.

Esther, Lorraine, and another volunteer helped me reheat the soup and serve the meal. The menu was a hit with the refugees, especially the cake.

Afterward, Esther and I planned the next meal. She said she would stop by the Jewish deli in her neighborhood and ask if they would donate bread for one meal each month. I found another baker who said he would do the same. A butcher who'd emigrated from Poland thirty years ago offered to donate ground beef or stew meat once a month. A produce man offered me his vegetables that were close to going bad.

Esther would pick up the food and store it in her apartment, and I would collect it from her. I decided cooking the meal at the church the morning of the meal would work best.

Zeke's Mamm started to come over on the days I was gone so she could help Clare, which I felt badly about, but not enough to stop my volunteer work. It kept my mind off Zeke. And off Lena and Vater Josef.

I tried to think of the good that had come from going to Germany—helping get Esther to safety. I had a relationship with her now. If I hadn't gone to Germany, I wouldn't be as invested in caring for her and other refugees.

That was the way God worked. *The Lord giveth and the Lord taketh away. Blessed be the name of the Lord.* That seemed to be the story of my life.

One Wednesday morning as we cooked, Esther said, "I've been thinking about going to New York City. Would you want to come with me?"

"To visit?"

"No, to live."

"Why?"

"I'd have more of a community there," Esther said. "A bigger synagogue. More refugees from Germany."

"How is the synagogue here?" I'd only seen it from the outside—a small building on Duke Street.

"The service is in English with some Hebrew. But quite a few of the members speak German. I was surprised that the first Jewish congregation in Lancaster didn't form until 1856."

I was surprised it had formed that early. I wasn't aware of Jewish people around, except when we drove by the building.

"I want to go to a bigger synagogue," Esther said. "That's why I'd like to go to New York."

Part of me wanted to leave Lancaster County. Perhaps in a new place I could forget Lena and Vater Josef, Dorina and my first Mutter. But from what I'd seen when I'd spent a night there with Martha, I couldn't imagine living in New York.

"You're more German than Amish," Esther pointed out. "You lived in a city before. Frankfurt isn't Berlin, but it's big. Don't you miss it?"

I shuddered. I didn't miss anything about Frankfurt. "Do you plan to go to New York soon?"

She sighed. "I doubt I'll go at all. It's just that I feel restless here. And I need to find a job, but so far I haven't been able to."

Gradually, I'd begun to learn Esther's story. She'd grown up in Berlin not far from where her uncle's apartment was. Her father had been Gentile and from Austria, but Esther's mother was Jewish. "She and I didn't go to synagogue, though," Esther said. "I sometimes went to the Catholic church with my father, but we had no religion in our home. However, there was a large Jewish population in Berlin. Soon, many began emigrating, and the population of Jews in the city visibly fell. Vater said Mutter was safe—no one even knew she was Jewish. When Jewish people had to start wearing yellow stars, Vater insisted that Mutter not leave the apartment. But then Vater was drafted into the army, and soon the Gestapo came to our apartment, perhaps based on a tip from a neighbor, for both my Mutter and me."

Esther explained that they were taken to Sachsenhausen, a concentration camp in Oranienburg, about an hour north of Berlin. In the camp, her Mutter told her everything she could remember about Judaism, and then other women in their barracks taught her more. Her Mutter died—probably from cholera. Esther was near death when she was forced to march away from the camp with tens of thousands of other prisoners. The SS shot anyone who collapsed. Finally, the Red Army and US Army arrived and liberated the group.

After she recovered enough to make her way to Berlin, Esther found her uncle, who said her father had been killed in France during the Battle of the Ardennes. She wasn't close to her uncle and found solace with a group of Jewish people who had also returned to Berlin and had begun to worship at the nearby bombed-out synagogue. Through information she acquired there, she applied to emigrate through the Red Cross, which was how she met Martha.

"Now the Communists have taken over." She hesitated a moment and then said, "I'm pretty sure my uncle is working for the Russians. He knows too much not to be."

"Have you heard from him?" I asked.

"Yes," she said. "I had a letter in response to my letter, letting him know where I am. He thinks I should return."

Shocked, I managed to ask, "To East Berlin?"

"Jah," she answered. "He said German people should stay in Germany and help rebuild. He thinks I made a cowardly decision to leave."

"What do you think?"

She shrugged. "When I was in Germany, it certainly didn't feel as if I was cowardly to leave. I felt as if I were brave. And I don't want to go back and live in the Russian-occupied territory. The Nazis were horrible, but that doesn't make the Russians trustworthy."

When she asked me my story, I hesitated. I hadn't told anyone the entire thing. "I had a twin," I said to Esther. "Her name was Dorina. We both had seizures." I told her about our mother having a seizure and dying. About the testing done on Dorina and me at the Institute. About how invested Vater was in the research, so much so that after Dorina died . . .

Tears filled my eyes and I blinked several times. I wouldn't tell Esther that Dorina had most likely been killed. "And then Clare, who was my cousin but is now my sister, saved me. She worked with a kind doctor at the Institute who got me a passport with my new name, Rosene Simons. Clare and I fled on a train to France in 1939 while we still could."

"How fortunate for you," Esther said. "I can see why you don't miss Frankfurt." She wrapped her arms around herself. "I never felt at home with my uncle, but perhaps I should have tried harder. He's the only family I have left." She sighed. "I don't want to return to Berlin, but I feel as if I'm without a country now. Without a home. Americans have been good to me to take me in, but I don't feel as if I'm home."

I understood why she felt that way. I also realized I didn't. I had a home with Mutter and Vater and Clare and Jeremiah.

I found purpose in my relationship with Esther and working at the refugee center. The meals I planned and prepared were healthy and appetizing. One of the older women told me that my food nourished both her body and her soul. "It tastes like home," she said. "Especially your bread and desserts."

In the middle of October, Esther finally agreed to visit our farm and stay overnight. She said she'd come on a Saturday afternoon. When I told her we would have church the next day, she said she'd like to go with us. Which surprised me. But then I remembered she sometimes went to a Catholic church with her father as a child. Perhaps she expected something like that.

Mutter chattered away in German with Esther, asking her about Berlin and the state of the city and how long she thought the barricade would last. Clare spoke with her too, and it seemed Esther felt comfortable and thankful to be with two women older than she was who spoke German.

At dinner, as we ate sauerbraten and red cabbage, Esther said, "I haven't had such a fine meal since before the war."

"Wait until dessert," Mutter answered. "Clare made a Black Forest cake."

Esther smiled. "Sounds delicious." She had a good appetite, and she was definitely gaining weight.

"What do you miss the most about Germany?" Mutter asked.

"My mother." Esther choked up a little.

"Of course." Mutter reached over and put her hand on Esther's. "You were so young to lose your mother."

Esther nodded toward me. "Rosene lost her mother even younger—but now she has you."

"And you will find another family here—or make one. But you will always feel the loss." Mutter squeezed Esther's hand and then let go. "My own mother was killed during the war, in a bombing raid. I didn't find out until two years after she died. She was on in years but spry and healthy. The war was horrible," Mutter said. "It's unbelievable what humans can do to one another. I'm so sorry for how it changed your life."

"Jah," Esther said. "The war changed life for everyone in one way or another, but some of us don't have the choice to return to the life we had before. It's not that I'm not grateful to be here, and with your family in particular. But I can't seem to shake the horrors that I saw and endured." She glanced at me. "Working with Rosene at the refugee center helps. My mother used to cook for the poor in Berlin before the war. Now I can see why she did. Serving others helps us forget ourselves."

We rode with Jeremiah, Clare, and the children in their buggy to Jeremiah's parents' farm for the church service. Arden sat on my lap, and Janice sat on Esther's. When we reached the farm, Jeremiah helped Clare down and then Esther and me. We led the children toward the shop while Jeremiah took care of the horses.

Clare went into the kitchen to help Jeremiah's Mamm, Elizabeth.

When Jeremiah reached Esther and me as we played under the fluttering leaves of the willow tree with the children, he took Arden to sit with him during the service. Clare and Elizabeth joined us, and then the members of the congregation filed into the shed.

We sat for three hours on the wooden benches. Halfway through, Clare took Janice out of the shed. Probably more for Clare's comfort than Janice's. Clare had another month until the baby would be born, and sitting on the bench had to be uncomfortable.

We sang songs in High German, and the preacher read scripture in German. Esther seemed to follow along, at least some. She stared ahead and sat with her back straight.

The elder spoke about the first and greatest commandment, according to Jesus: "Thou shalt love the Lord thy God with all thy heart, and with all thy soul, and with all thy mind. . . . And the second is like unto it, Thou shalt love thy neighbour as thyself. On these two commandments hang all the law and the prophets." He thumbed backward in his Bible. "Jesus was quoting from Deuteronomy when He said to 'love God' and from Leviticus when He commanded us to 'love our neighbor as ourself.' All of scripture can be found in those two commandments."

Esther glanced at me and smiled. Then she continued to listen, but the preacher was now speaking in Pennsylvania Dutch exclusively, which I doubted Esther could comprehend much of, but I understood.

Still my mind wandered. The Amish taught loving your neighbor. I doubted they would have ever supported anyone like Hitler, not like the Mennonites in Germany had and most of the other German churches too.

After the service, Esther and I helped with Arden and Janice and the other children while Jeremiah and the men set up tables and benches in the shop, and Clare, Elizabeth, and the other women finished preparing the meal in the kitchen.

None of the Zimmermans mentioned Zeke, and I didn't ask. We ate bean soup, homemade bread, and sugar cookies for our lunch, and then it was time to go home so the children could nap. We waited under the willow tree for Jeremiah to come around with the buggy. Arden chased the falling golden leaves while Janice cuddled against me, sucking her thumb.

Esther said, "I didn't understand most of your service, but I recognized the scripture references I learned while in the concentration camp." She folded her hands. "Your people seem gentle and kind. Like Martha."

"Would you want to come to church with me again?"

"It was a long service." She laughed. "My bottom hurts. Ours is much shorter."

The Mennonite service was shorter too. Not any longer than an hour and a half.

A man started walking up the driveway. He wore dungarees and a cowboy hat and boots.

I stood. Jeremiah came up behind him with the buggy and slowed. Then he stopped and spoke to the man. The man jumped up into the buggy.

Zeke.

He'd come home.

· 16 ·

Treva

That night, after I said my prayers, I kept thinking about Rosene's story. She'd lost her mother and sister. Then her remaining biological sister and her father betrayed her.

All of that left scars. Although thankful for her new family, she'd felt abandoned by her original one. And then abandoned by Zeke too.

I curled up under my quilt, fighting off my own emotions. My parents hadn't betrayed me—and never would—but I'd lost them, and in some way, I felt abandoned too. When things hadn't worked out with Pierre, I'd felt abandoned again. But because I didn't want to make life harder for those around me, I'd stuffed my grief down.

I couldn't stop the tears. My grief over losing Mom and Dad and my relationship with Pierre all seemed woven together. Rosene had said that grief can compound grief. She'd buried her grief over losing her twin. But her grief over her uncertain relationship with Zeke, along with seeing her German family, had brought it back.

Was compounded grief what was happening with me? The loss of baby David in Haiti had stirred up my grief over my baby brother David—and my guilt. The loss of Pierre had brought up my grief over my parents' deaths, grief I'd tried to deny at the time. Finally, I ran out of tears, turned my pillow over, and fell asleep.

The next morning, Kamil arrived to do the milking. I helped for a half hour and then left, going to the shed first to text Brenna and then back to the house to fix breakfast.

Gabe helped me in the store during the morning while Mammi stayed with Rosene and saw to the housework and fixed lunch. As we swept and dusted, he said, "That's some story that Rosene told us last night."

"Isn't it? Want me to tell you what happened before the part you heard?"

"Please," he answered. As we worked, I caught him up on Rosene's story. Although I couldn't do it justice, I did my best.

In the early afternoon, I helped Dawdi pull a calf. Zaida, Cala, and the children arrived with Kamil in the midafternoon. I already had an enchilada casserole prepared in advance for dinner, so I made tea and put out a plate of snickerdoodles for Rosene, Zaida, and Cala. Then I put cookies in a plastic bag for the children and asked if I could take them outside.

The children smiled up at me but didn't speak.

Zaida spoke in Arabic, and both children nodded. Gamila reached up and took my hand as I grabbed the bag of cookies with my free hand. Ahmad opened the door for us, and we ventured outside. The afternoon was warm, and baby birds tweeted from a nest up in the branches of the birch trees above the picnic table.

"Papa?" Gamila asked.

"He's in the barn," I answered, "milking the cows. He'll be done in a couple of hours."

After we ate the cookies, I asked, "Would you like to go see the ducks on the pond? There might be some geese nearby too." Ducks stayed on the farm year-round, while the geese were on their way north.

"Yes, please," Ahmad said.

Gamila held my hand again as we headed to the pond. I opened the gate to the pasture and passed through first, telling both children to stay close to me. After I closed the gate, Gamila put her hands up to be held, and I lifted her into my arms. A goose started toward us, and Ahmad squealed. Then he turned toward me and wrapped his arms around my legs. I somehow managed to lift him into my arms too.

We retreated from the pond and walked through the pasture to the store. As we stepped inside, clocks marked the half hour. Three thirty. Mammi smiled at the children and greeted them with a hearty "Hallo!" Gamila gave her a little wave, and Ahmad said, "Hello, Mrs. Zimmerman."

"Oh, call me Mammi," she replied. "That means 'grandmother.'"

After the children walked around the store, I took Gamila's hand. "Let's go back to the house."

"Pull the blocks out again," Mammi said. "And there are some books in the cupboard." As she walked us to the door, she added, "It's so nice to have children on the farm again."

Once we were in the house, I pulled out the blocks and then a basket of books. Gamila grabbed the top one and handed it to me. Ahmad headed for the sofa.

The book was *Mother Goose Treasury*. Inscribed on the title page was *To Isaac, on your first birthday Love, Uri, Laurel, and Malinda*. Wow. The book was to Dad, from Papa, Gran, and Mom, who was just a baby too.

I turned the page and began reading "Twinkle, Twinkle, Little Star."

I read book after book to the children and then set up the blocks for them to play with. Just before five, Dawdi and Kamil stepped into the kitchen.

"Ready?" Kamil asked Zaida.

"Yes." She stood and put her notebook in her purse. Cala stepped into the living room and summoned the children.

Ahmad groaned and said, "But we're having fun."

"We'll be back," Cala said. "Let's put the blocks away and then tell Rosene, Treva, and Mr. Zimmerman thank you."

Rosene said, "We'll see you on Saturday."

After they left and Dawdi went to get cleaned up, I asked Rosene about the blocks, the books, and the high chair. "Were those Dad's?"

"Well, yes, he was the last to use those things, although Clare bought them when her children were little. Jeremiah made the high chair for Arden and then Janice and Lydia both used it."

"Lydia?"

"She's Arden's youngest sister."

"That's right." I'd heard of Lydia but had never met her. I'd finally met Janice right before I went to Haiti.

Rosene nodded. "Lydia lives in Canada."

I said, "Obviously she's not Amish."

"No, she's not. She and her husband are Mennonite."

"Is she the baby Clare's pregnant with in the story?"

Rosene smiled. "You'll find out."

I changed the subject so Rosene wouldn't chide me for jumping ahead in the story. "What do you need me to do to help with the dinner on Saturday?"

"Drive Arden around tomorrow afternoon to invite the neighbors. If we don't have guests, we won't have a dinner."

Rosene walked with Mammi to Amish Antiques the next afternoon, saying she would sit the entire time she was there, and I drove Dawdi around to invite the neighbors. At the first place, I waited in the van, but it took twenty minutes for him to appear. He held a plate of cookies in his hand.

"What took you so long?" I asked.

"I can't just get to the point right away," he said. "We need to visit first."

"Oh."

"Come into the next house with me."

"Only if I can tap my wrist when fifteen minutes is up. Otherwise we'll never get to the other neighbors."

"It's a deal."

At the next house, Carol Smith answered the front door, and we could hear the sound of the TV in the background. "Arden, so nice to see you! And Treva, what a surprise."

The Smiths were Englisch, although Rosene told me that Carol's ancestors were Amish. Her great-grandparents left the church in the early 1900s.

"Bill, Arden's here," Carol called out. "Turn off the TV."

"Oh, I don't mind if you leave it on." Dawdi winked at me. He wasn't joking. I think Dawdi kind of liked seeing what the neighbors were watching. I couldn't see the TV, but by the sound, it seemed to be a news show.

But the sound stopped, and Bill Smith came around the corner of the kitchen. "Arden! Treva!" He extended his hand. "How are you? How's Priscilla? And Rosene? Is she recovering?"

After Dawdi answered Bill's questions, Bill invited us into the kitchen. "How about a cup of coffee?"

"Thank you," Dawdi said. "I'd appreciate that."

"How about you, Treva?"

"Yes, please."

The four of us sat around the table, chatting about the weather and the alfalfa crop and Bill's sick calf. Dawdi offered some advice and then said, "We're having an event at our house on Saturday evening. It's a fundraiser."

Bill cocked his head.

"We're trying something to help our new neighbors. The Good Book says to love them as ourselves."

"That's true," Carol said.

"Rosene has long been volunteering at the refugee center in town." Dawdi nodded at me. "And Treva's taken over for Rosene while she's recovering. They've befriended a family from Syria."

Carol leaned forward a little as Bill leaned backward.

"The family brought over a meal the other night on account of Rosene and all. Delicious food." Dawdi licked his lips. "I can't compare it to what Priscilla, Rosene, and Treva make because it's very different, but it was tasty."

Carol said, "I can imagine. We ate at a Syrian restaurant in Philly a few years ago. Wasn't it good, Bill?"

He agreed.

"So, Rosene came up with the idea of having the women—Zaida and Cala—fix a Syrian meal and serve it at our house to us and a few of our friends. We'll be taking donations—

twenty-five dollars per person is suggested—and all of the money will go to the refugee center, plus our family will donate the food. I'll pay Zaida and Cala for their time."

That surprised me. We hadn't talked about Dawdi paying them—that was very generous, especially when the farm wasn't bringing in as much income. "Would you be interested in joining us?" he asked. Before they could answer, Dawdi said, "You don't have to let me know now. Just leave a message by tomorrow at noon so we can let Zaida and Cala know how much food to buy."

Carol glanced at Bill, who said, "We'll be there. What time?"

"Five thirty," Dawdi answered. "Come hungry!"

We repeated the process eight more times. Altogether, seven couples said yes. Two couples already had plans for the evening.

"Let's see how it goes," Dawdi said on the way home. "Maybe we could do it again and invite more people from church, plus more Englisch neighbors. In the meantime, let's ask Gabe and Drew too. And Sharon. I'll make sure they know it doesn't have to be a donation. I know their budgets are tight."

Sharon volunteered to help us get ready for the dinner, Gabe said he'd think about attending, and Drew said he was honored to be asked and would join us.

Sharon came over Friday afternoon to help clean the house. I hadn't realized how much Rosene did that I never knew about, such as washing the woodwork and cleaning the door handles and the tops of doors. She had a special duster for that on a telescope handle. We also scoured the kitchen to make sure everything was clean for cooking. I polished the oak table when we finished.

Bill Smith came over, and he and Dawdi moved the living room furniture into the downstairs spare bedroom. Then we set up four folding tables in the living room. We'd have twenty-five people altogether.

Zaida and Cala arrived Saturday afternoon. Kamil took the kids out to the barn with him, and he and Dawdi started the milking a half hour early. Zaida and Cala had already made the dips—*muhammara*, which was a roasted pepper and walnut spread, and baba ghanoush, which was mashed grilled eggplants with garlic, tahini, and yogurt. They'd also made the desserts—date brownies and the Syrian baklava again—and prepped the chicken, lamb stew, grape leaves, and green beans. The dough was already prepared for the bread too.

First, they dressed up the tables with colorful cloths and candles, which was really fancy for our Plain household and also really beautiful. They used Mammi's set of china, Clare's china, and our plain white everyday dishes, which together was enough for all. Then they began cooking, filling the house with the scent of unfamiliar spices. Sumac in the chicken. Cardamom in the stew. Allspice in the grape leaves. And the smell of the bread baking on the stones in the oven brought the mouthwatering scents together.

By five thirty, Dawdi and Kamil had cleaned up from doing the milking and the guests had arrived. After introductions, we gathered in a group in the kitchen. Dawdi explained our silent prayer before our meal to our guests and then led us in one, leaving each person to pray what they felt most comfortable with. When he raised his head, Rosene said, "Amen."

Then Zaida directed the guests to their tables. She, Cala, and I served the food family style at each table, which used every one of our serving dishes. Zaida, Cala, and I ate between serving the courses. By the looks of how much everyone ate, they enjoyed the food. We refilled the bread baskets several times.

After the meal ended and we cleared the plates, Kamil and Zaida told their story, some of which I could hear from the kitchen as Cala and I made tea and readied the desserts.

Kamil had grown up on a farm outside Aleppo, while Zaida had grown up in the city. Her father was a lawyer, and her mother was a university professor. Her mother wore skirts and jackets to work and no headscarf. Zaida and Cala attended the best schools.

Kamil excelled in his village school, so much so that he was able to go to Aleppo for his university studies, where he met Zaida. That was in 2011, the year prior to when the Battle of Aleppo began. They married in 2012 before the violence started and then fled the country to Jordan later that year with Zaida and Cala's parents. Their father died in the refugee camp the week after Ahmad was born in 2014. A week later, they began applying for asylum in the US. In 2016, Gamila was born, and they had to redo their applications. In 2018, they were granted asylum in the US, and they came to Lancaster County just six months ago. Zaida and Cala's mother passed away a month before they traveled.

"From a broken heart." Zaida placed her hands over her own heart. "We are grateful to be here and to be together and to have a chance to raise and educate our children. Kamil and I couldn't continue our education, but we hope to be able to finish college in the years to come." She paused and glanced around the room. "Do any of you have any questions?"

Carol Smith raised her hand and asked, "When did the two of you learn English?"

"I began studying it when I was a little girl, by the time I was six," Zaida answered. "Our mother taught English at the university, and she enrolled Cala and me in classes. She read us books in English from the time we were tiny."

Kamil added, "I was older, twelve or so, by the time I started to study English."

A few other people asked questions and then the children, along with their parents, sang a Syrian lullaby in Arabic. After they finished, Dawdi stood and said, "My family first came from the Palatinate area in what is now Germany to Lancaster County, where they received a land grant. Ongoing persecution caused them and thousands of other Amish and Mennonite families to flee to a place that offered religious freedom." He glanced around the group. "I imagine most of our ancestors arrived in the US as refugees or immigrants, in search of a better life. Sometimes out of fear for their lives."

A few heads nodded. Dawdi glanced from Kamil to Zaida to the children to Cala. "Our ancestors were welcomed with open arms, which changed the trajectories of our families. In return, we want to welcome all of you." He looked at the Hamad family, speaking each of their names. "Kamil, Zaida, Cala, Ahmad, and Gamila, we're glad you're here. We're your neighbors—and your friends."

Kamil placed his hand over his heart. "Thank you, Mr. Arden Zimmerman." He stood straight and said, "Thank you, everyone."

After that, Cala and I served tea and dessert while Zaida sat down next to Kamil and their children. As I cleared the tables a final time, I insisted Cala stay in the living room, where she could interact with the guests.

I overheard Dawdi tell Bill Smith that Kamil was working for him. Bill turned to Kamil and asked, "Do you know other refugees who would be willing to do farm work?"

"Yes." Kamil smiled. "Well, if they knew it was a possibility, I think they would be."

"I'm interviewing a possible farmhand tomorrow," Bill said. "If that doesn't work out, I'll be in touch."

After our neighbors left, Drew said he occasionally wrote freelance articles. "I've written some for national publications and local ones too, including a few here in Lancaster County. Could I contact a couple of editors I've worked with about writing an article about tonight?" he asked Dawdi and Kamil.

"Yes," Kamil said. "If you write about Zaida and Cala. Not me."

"How about you, Arden?" Drew asked.

"Only if you focus on Rosene's role in this and not mine," Dawdi said. "She's the one who is committed to working with refugees. Ask her what she thinks."

Drew headed across the room to Rosene and began talking. A minute later, she nodded and then responded, though I couldn't hear what she said. Next, he spoke with Zaida. She smiled and nodded too.

After we cleaned up and everyone left and Dawdi, Mammi, and Rosene went to bed, I sat down at the table and marveled at the success of the dinner. I'd felt like such a failure leaving Haiti, feeling as if God would never ask me to serve again. But here, without planning to, I was working with refugees.

Just as working with World War II refugees had given Rosene purpose in a difficult time, I was finding purpose too, even if it was temporary. But the thing was, Cala and Zaida were giving me far more than I was giving them, I was sure.

· 17 ·

The next morning was the off-church Sunday for Rosene, Dawdi, and Mammi, which was good timing. My grandparents seemed tired from the evening before and decided not to visit another church in the area. Before helping Dawdi with the milking, I started yeast dough. After the milking, I made a breakfast of eggs, bacon, and sticky buns.

After I cleaned up the kitchen, I decided to go to the Mennonite church that Ivy and Conrad attended. I knocked on Gabe's door to ask if he wanted to go with me. I knocked and then knocked again. Finally, he came to the door wearing sweatpants and a sweatshirt, his hair sticking straight up.

I asked, "Want to go with me to your church?"

He glanced down at his sweatpants. "I haven't showered."

"You have time. I'm not leaving for a half hour."

He shook his head. "I'm going back to bed."

"Okay. See you later."

I dressed in a jeans skirt, blouse, and sweater and put a scarf over my head. Some women wore *Kappa* at the church, and some left their heads uncovered. It was a pretty progressive place.

As I walked out to the van, I heard someone yell, "Wait!" I turned.

Gabe walked toward me. "I decided to go." He'd showered and wore jeans and a jacket. "Thank you for asking."

On the way there, I asked how he was doing. "Just fine," Gabe said.

"Is it hard to be here and not in Kuwait?"

"Do you want a canned answer? Or the truth?"

"The truth," I answered. "For sure."

"The entire time I was in Kuwait, I wished I was here."

I stole a glance. He was staring out the side window. I shifted my gaze to the road. "Really?"

"Yep. I'm relieved to be home. I'm not happy that the truck rolled or that I was injured. Just that I'm out, even though I'm embarrassed to admit it." He looked over at me. "Don't tell anyone."

"I won't," I assured him.

"Not even Ivy. Especially not Conrad."

"I promise."

"Being in the army was a lot more than I expected. I wasn't cut out for it. I never felt comfortable. . . ." His voice trailed off.

"Because?"

"Because I never should have joined. I'm impressed with people who do—who make a life out of it. I thought I could shake those teachings we grew up with—the 'turn the other cheek' and 'love your enemies.' All of it. But I couldn't. Not even on a military base when I was far from any battlefield and not around any 'enemies.'" He put air quotes around the word. "I can't imagine what combat would have been like. I probably would have gone AWOL." He stared straight ahead. "I'm shameful."

185

"I don't think you're shameful."

"I made an impulsive decision. And even though I have education benefits, I've realized I don't want to go back to school."

"Dawdi was afraid you wouldn't want to come back to the farm. That you'd be off to greener pastures." I slowed for a buggy ahead of me.

He shook his head. "I keep thinking Arden is going to push me off the farm at some point, like a bird out of the nest."

"Why would he do that?" I asked.

"Because I'm twenty-five," he answered. "I need to get a grown-up job—not the one I've had since I was fifteen."

"When you were in Kuwait, did you want to be back on the farm working or just back in Lancaster County?"

"On the farm." He glanced toward me. "When you were in Haiti, did you want to be back on the farm?"

"At first I did," I answered slowly. Was I like Gabe? Feeling as if I should have a grown-up job? One that wasn't because my grandparents owned a farm and store? "But then it seemed like somewhere far, far away was a better idea."

"Maybe it will be for you," Gabe said. "But not for me." He sighed. "I'm no further along in figuring out my future than I was when I was fifteen."

We were a few minutes early for church and managed to sit in the last row instead of up front, where Sharon always sat. The final song before the sermon was "Great Is Thy Faithfulness."

"'Sun, moon and stars in their courses above, Join with all nature in manifold witness, To Thy great faithfulness, mercy and love. . . .'" The scripture reading that followed was from Job 17. *My days are past, my purposes are broken off, even the thoughts of my heart.*

The song and scripture seemed to contradict each other.

I leaned forward in the pew, wondering where Pastor Mike was going to go with the sermon. "It's never too late to start anew," he said, launching into a sermon about the disciples leaving their previous lives to follow Christ.

"Everyone feels like a failure at some time or another too," he said. "And yes, we do fail at things, but it doesn't make us a failure. It's part of the process of living and growing and becoming the person God wants us to be. We fail for all sorts of reasons. Perhaps because we didn't have a plan. Perhaps because of circumstances beyond our control. Or perhaps, even, because we weren't willing to take a risk. Perhaps your failure has made you feel as if your days are past, as Job says. Or as if you have no purpose." He paused a minute and then said, "What I want you to remember is that God is always faithful. You can count on God's mercy and love, not on what you've done or not done, or how you feel."

After the service, Gabe and I slipped into the lobby—and ran straight into Ivy. She gave Gabe a hug first and asked, "How are you?"

"Good."

"You're back," I said to her.

"We came home yesterday."

"A day early?"

She nodded. "I wasn't feeling very well, so we got an earlier flight. I'm better now, though."

"You could have texted."

Ivy shrugged. "I didn't think I'd see you here today."

Conrad came out of the sanctuary and joined us, hugging me and then Gabe.

"Can you stop by the farm tomorrow?" I asked Ivy.

187

"I've been really tired and need to catch up on work," she answered. "What do you need?"

"To talk about when I can go to Alaska. Rosene is doing much better, but I wanted your opinion."

"How about Tuesday?" Ivy asked. "Is that soon enough?"

"Sure," I said. "You and Conrad should come for dinner. I know everyone would like to hear about your trip."

"Sounds good." Ivy gave me another hug. "We'll see you then. Tell everyone hello."

Conrad stepped to Ivy's side and put his arm around her. She leaned her head against his chest because she was too short to reach his shoulder. They were sweet together.

Gabe gave me a nod, gestured toward the door, and then walked out of the church foyer. He most likely wanted to sneak out before being accosted by the old ladies who adored him. I gave Ivy a wave and said, "See you Tuesday."

She nodded and waved. It wasn't like her not to come straight out to the farm after a trip to tell Mammi, Dawdi, and Rosene all about it, nor to cut her trip short. I wasn't sure what this new behavior was about, but something was up.

Gabe was quiet as we drove home. When I asked him to come to dinner on Tuesday evening, he simply nodded.

"Want to come for lunch today?" I asked. "I think we're having leftovers from last night."

He shook his head. "That dinner was delicious, but I have some thinking to do."

"About what?"

"Oh, you know." He stared straight ahead. "Who am I? What am I going to do with my life? Why am I such a loser? That sort of thing."

"You're not a loser."

"I am."

"It's never too late to start anew, right?" I hurt for Gabe. "Like Pastor Mike said. We're all in process. It's about moving forward."

"That's why I need to do some thinking."

I wasn't used to having Gabe be so serious. He used to be a jokester. "Anything I can do to help?"

"No. Maybe." He turned to look out the window. "You could pray for me."

"Absolutely," I said. "Out loud? Right now?"

"No," he said. "Silently. Later." He turned toward me and smiled. "You know. The unpretentious Amish way."

I grinned. I didn't think praying out loud was pretentious— Mom and Dad prayed out loud with us, even though they'd grown up Amish. But I liked the quiet way the Amish prayed too.

I dropped Gabe off in front of the Dawdi Haus, but Rosene called to him from the porch and he headed toward her. As I parked the van by the shed, my phone dinged with a text from Brenna.

I can go to Germany next week. Johann and Natasha will go with me. Text me Herr Mayer's information. I'm going to contact him about us staying at the house. I also presume you'll send the power of attorney before we get there.

Yes on the power of attorney. I'll email you a copy of it too. I'll forward you the email Herr Mayer sent Rosene. It has his email and phone number. Thank you! Please tell Johann and Natasha hello.

I will.

189

We'd need to take care of the power of attorney in the morning. Then I'd scan it at the library and email it to Brenna and Herr Mayer, and then overnight it to him too, which was bound to be expensive. But worth it.

I found the email from him and forwarded it to Brenna. Then, as I climbed out of the van, my phone dinged again.

I expected it to be Brenna, but it was Pierre.

> I hope you're doing well. I'm just checking in. I've been thinking about you and missing you.

I swooned a little. He missed me. Before I could respond, my phone dinged again. Another text from Pierre.

> I wanted to let you know I've been seeing someone here. She's a midwife working at the birthing clinic about five miles away. She's from Washington State. She's been here for a year and has decided to stay permanently. I met her several months ago, when I went to get a baby at the clinic, but we've just started seeing each other recently.

Recently? I'd only been gone three weeks, although Pierre and I had been at odds the last three months I was there. And I certainly hadn't expected him not to pursue a relationship with someone else. But still . . . it stung.

I slipped my phone into the pocket of my skirt.

In my head, I chanted, *Alaska, Alaska, Alaska.* That was my best course of action. I needed a new location.

My stomach fell. Gabe had said that going far away hadn't worked for him. He'd wanted to return to the farm the entire time. He hadn't found purpose by joining the Army Reserve and going somewhere else. Would I find purpose in Alaska?

The only way to find out was to give it a try. At the mo-

ment, being that much farther from Pierre seemed like a
great idea.

I texted back.

> Thank you for letting me know. I wish you the
> best. Please keep in touch.

Definitely. Above all else, you are my friend.

That stung a little too.

When I reached the house, Rosene sat on the front porch
in one of the rocking chairs. Gabe sat in the other one, eating
a sandwich from one of Mammi's plates.

"Treva," Rosene said, "I made a plate for you. It's on the
counter. Grab it and come out on the porch. I'll tell you and
Gabe more of the story."

· 18 ·

Rosene

I froze as Jeremiah drove the buggy toward us. Zeke sat beside him, grinning.

"Whoa," Jeremiah called out to the horse.

The buggy stopped, and Zeke jumped down. His golden-brown hair was nearly blond. "Rosene," he said to me. "You're home."

"Of course I'm home." My voice sounded harsh, even to me.

"I didn't think you'd come back."

"Why would I stay in Germany?"

He shrugged.

Frustrated, I said, "I gave you no indication I would. I was surprised to return and find you'd gone to Illinois."

His eyes lit up. "I went all the way to California."

"California?"

He nodded. "To the Pacific Ocean. It's amazing."

Esther cleared her throat.

I crossed my arms. "Zeke, this is my friend Esther. She came to the US from Germany with me."

Zeke looked at Esther, then at me. "You were friends when you were little?"

"No. Martha knows Esther and made it possible for her to immigrate here. Esther traveled with me."

Zeke grinned. "Pleased to meet you."

"Hallo," Esther replied. "I am pleased to meet you too."

Jeremiah climbed down from the buggy, and Clare and Arden and Janice stepped forward. Were they waiting to give Zeke and me a chance to speak? Elizabeth came out of the house and called out, "Zeke? Is that you?"

He turned toward her and called out, "Jah, Mamm. It is." He grinned at me and said, "I need to go explain myself to Mamm. Would it be all right if I visit you tomorrow?"

"Jah. . . ."

During the buggy ride home, no one mentioned Zeke, not even Arden. Was everyone that concerned about me that they wouldn't bring him up? Zeke seemed carefree. And happy. Was he happy to be home? Or had traveling made him happy?

I rode with our driver, Mr. Moore, to take Esther back to Lancaster later that afternoon. On the way, she asked about Zeke. "Are you interested in him?"

I shrugged, not wanting Mr. Moore to hear my answer.

"You should be," Esther said. "He's cute. And he likes you. I can tell."

I smiled, but my stomach sank. He *had* liked me. Did he still?

Esther poked my arm. "I can tell you like him too."

I changed the subject to our upcoming lunch at the refugee center on Wednesday. "Can you pick up the bread from the baker on Twelfth Street on Tuesday? We'll pick you up on Wednesday morning at nine to give us time to cook the chicken and dumplings."

Esther said she could, and we talked more about the lunch. I'd bring bouquets of asters for the tables. And I'd make three pies the night before from a few of our garden pumpkins.

Monday morning, Zeke showed up to do the milking with Jeremiah. The farmhand Jeremiah had hired in the spring had quit a few days before, so it was good timing. Then Zeke ate breakfast with us as if he hadn't been away at all.

"What was your favorite place that you visited?" Vater asked Zeke.

"Chicago was amazing with the river running through the middle of the city. When I got to the farm I was supposed to work at, they'd given the job to someone else—so I kept hitchhiking. California was my favorite place. Orange and lemon trees. Endless beaches. The Pacific Ocean. And there's a boom going on. I built houses in Los Angeles—these small houses for veterans who are going to college and getting married and starting families. Some aren't so small, and some even have swimming pools. It just depends on the neighborhood. But most have an orange tree in the backyard."

I couldn't imagine picking an orange off a tree to eat.

"Was it hot?" Vater asked.

"Some, but a breeze blows in off the ocean. I'd go to the beach on my days off." He grinned. "I even learned how to surf."

"Surf?" Clare asked.

"You ride a board over the waves," Zeke explained.

Jeremiah put down his coffee. "But you don't know how to swim."

Zeke laughed. "I do now. It was sink or swim. And riding those waves was too much fun to sink."

Arden laughed with him and then Janice did too. I'd get out the atlas and show them where California was after I cleaned up from breakfast.

Zeke went out with Jeremiah to harvest the corn, and at noon he came in to eat. When the afternoon milking was done, I stepped outside to collect the pumpkins for the pies I planned to make the next day. Zeke was nowhere in sight. He'd said he wanted to talk with me, but I was beginning to doubt it. Even though Zeke was home, it felt as if he were still in California, riding the waves.

The next afternoon, after the milking, Zeke came to the door and asked if I had time to talk.

"Not right now. I'm in the middle of cooking dinner. Plus I have pumpkin boiling for pies."

He asked, "How about tomorrow?"

"I won't be home until late in the afternoon, but it should work."

Zeke nodded. He wasn't as chipper as he'd been the day before. "We'll talk then."

I stayed up late to get the pies done. Zeke didn't appear for breakfast, and Arden asked where he was.

"He's helping on your Dawdi and Mammi's farm this morning," Jeremiah answered. "He'll be back this after-noon."

I boxed up the pies, flowers, cans of peaches, and ingredients for the chicken and dumplings and waited for my ride. And waited.

Finally, I hurried to the store to call Mr. Moore's house.

His wife answered and said, "Oh dear. I forgot to call you. There was an emergency, and he ended up taking a neighbor to the hospital. I'm sorry."

Here I was with most of the food for the lunch—and running late. Desperate, I asked Mutter if Vater could drive me in the old Studebaker that we kept in the shed.

"No," she said. "It's not good for his blood pressure."

As I turned to leave, Zeke came into the store to buy a soda.

Before I even said hello, Mutter asked him, "Did you learn to drive along with how to swim during your travels?"

He grinned. "I did."

"Would you take the Studebaker and drive Rosene into town?"

"Jah, of course." He smiled at me. "I'd be happy to."

"Will it start?" I asked. No one had driven it in a year.

"Your father starts it once a week. It should be fine."

Ten minutes later, Zeke pulled up as close to the kitchen door as he could and helped me load the boxes. Then we were on our way to pick up Esther. He wasn't a good driver. The car lurched forward when he accelerated, and when he braked, it came to an abrupt stop and then jerked forward a little. I held on. He laughed. "It'll take me a little while to get used to this car."

I didn't speak, not wanting to distract him. By the time we were on the highway, his driving was better. Once we reached Lancaster, he lurched the car again as he shifted down, but he didn't brake as hard—until we reached Esther's apartment. He slammed on the brakes, sending me against the dash, and then killed the engine.

He reached toward me. "Are you all right?"

"Yes." I reached for the door handle.

As I opened the door, Esther came running, the loaves of bread in a box. "You're late. Whose car is this? What's going on?"

I opened the back door for her. "Get in." I took the box from her, and once she was sitting down, placed it on her lap.

"Oh, hello, Zeke," she said.

Once I climbed in, I gave Zeke directions to the church. Then I told Esther what happened. "We can still get everything done in time."

"I'll help," Zeke said. "Just tell me what to do."

Esther said, "First, we need to pick up a box of apples at Mrs. Fogel's. She can't come today." Mrs. Fogel was a woman from the synagogue who sometimes invited Esther to her house for Shabbat dinner.

Esther directed us to a row house a few blocks away. She hurried up the path. Mrs. Fogel met her at the door, carrying a box of apples. After Esther took the box, Mrs. Fogel waved to me, and I rolled down the window and called out, "Thank you!"

Lorraine, the Red Cross worker, helped us carry everything into the church. I worked on assembling the chicken and dumplings, and Esther helped Lorraine set the tables. I sent Zeke to put the flowers on the tables and when he returned, I instructed him to cut the bread. Then I started slicing the pumpkin pies.

The refugees began arriving before the dumplings were done, but it only took ten more minutes until we were ready to serve lunch. I introduced Zeke to an older man from Poland named Szymon, who began talking about the Soviet blockade.

Zeke sat across from him. "Rosene was in Germany in June."

"I know," Szymon said. "She was in Berlin when the block-ade started. That's what Esther told me."

Zeke turned toward me with a questioning look. "You were?"

I nodded.

"Why?"

"I was with Martha and George."

"Oh." He frowned. "That doesn't sound safe."

"It was safe enough." I took a step away. "I survived."

We had to hustle to get the fellowship hall cleaned up and Esther to her apartment and then return to the farm for Zeke to help with the milking.

On the way, I asked him not to tell the others I was in Berlin.

"Why?" he asked.

"I'm just following Martha's instructions. I don't think she wants Mutter and Vater to worry about her."

"I can't believe she took you to Berlin when the blockade was happening."

"She didn't know it was going to start so soon."

"Still." Zeke was a half hour late, so I changed into a milking dress and helped. Before I went into the house to clean up and help Clare, I asked Zeke if he wanted to stay for dinner.

"I'd like that," he said.

Clare was growing heavy and slow, but she'd already started the mashed potatoes to go with the round steak that was browning in the largest cast-iron skillet. I pulled jars of applesauce and green beans from the pantry and a loaf of bread I'd made the day before. I'd also made a pumpkin pie for us.

Zeke didn't talk much during dinner. After Jeremiah led

us in a closing prayer, I began clearing the table and said, "Clare, I'll clean up and do the dishes."

Zeke stood. "I'll help."

"Can Onkel Zeke read us a bedtime story?" Arden asked.

"Not tonight," Clare answered.

"I will," Jeremiah said.

Zeke and I didn't talk much as we did the dishes. Mutter and Vater sat in the living room, and I didn't want them to overhear our conversation.

After Zeke dried the last dish and I put it away, he asked, "Do you want to go on a walk?"

"Yes," I said. "I'll tell Mutter and grab my coat."

A couple of minutes later, we stepped out the door. Stars glimmered in the black sky.

Zeke asked, "How did you get out of Berlin?"

"George secured a car, and we were able to drive to Hamburg. That's where George and Martha are now."

"Wow," Zeke said. "You wouldn't think being on staff with the Red Cross would be so dangerous."

"Jah." I buttoned my coat against the cold as we walked. I wouldn't share my suspicions about Martha and George's work.

"How was your visit in Frankfurt?"

"Scarier than Berlin." I shivered. "I don't want to talk about it." I cringed. Me not wanting to talk about my past had hurt Zeke before. Now I didn't even want to talk about what happened four months ago.

Zeke didn't respond to what I'd said. But he did ask, "Was it good to come home?"

"It was." Although it hadn't been good to come home and have him gone. I didn't tell him that. I didn't tell him how unsettled I felt. And restless too, until I started volunteering at the refugee center.

"How about you?" I asked. "Is it good to be home?"

He laughed. "It's good to see everyone, but to be honest, it's boring."

I stopped. "Boring?"

"Uh-huh." He turned toward me. "It's the same thing every day."

"You've only been home three days. Was today at the refugee lunch boring?"

He smiled. "No. That was the most exciting thing yet." He started walking again. "I never felt bored before I left."

I skipped a couple of steps and caught up with him. "Why did you leave?"

"Because I convinced myself you weren't coming back."

"Why?"

He shrugged. "I panicked." Zeke had never seemed the type to panic. He smiled at me and changed the topic. "Did you know before I hitchhiked west, I'd never left Lancaster County?"

"No." He'd never been to another state. A neighboring county. To Philadelphia. I wondered if that was part of his drive to travel. Here I was, going to Europe, while he'd never even been anywhere in the US.

"I feel as if I'm ruined," he said.

"What do you mean?" I was the one who was ruined.

"I've seen so much."

I nearly laughed. We had very different definitions of ruined.

"No one told me what was out there," he said. "Great Lakes. Mountains. Deserts. The ocean."

"Didn't you pay attention during geography class?"

He smiled. "Not enough, obviously. It's just so much more impressive than I ever imagined." He kicked at a rock as we reached the lane. "My father, in his sixty-one years, has never been out of Lancaster County. Can you believe that?"

I guessed his father probably didn't care, but I could see Zeke's point. His Dat didn't know what he was missing.

Zeke stopped walking again. "Come with me."

"Come with you where?"

"To California."

"Just the two of us?"

"Yes."

I had so many questions. "Is there an Amish church in California?"

He grinned. "I'm pretty sure there's not."

"Mennonite?"

Zeke paused a moment and then said, "That's more likely."

What would he do for work? More construction? What would I do? I shivered again.

He lifted my chin and met my eyes. "What do you think?"

"What church did you go to while you were in California?"

"I didn't."

"Why not?"

He shrugged. "I didn't want to. And you know what, nothing bad happened to me. God didn't strike me with lightning. I didn't get hit by a truck. I didn't drown in the ocean." He grinned again. "I'm thinking maybe God loves me more than I thought—or more than I was told."

That surprised me. Not that God loved Zeke more than he thought. I believed that was true of all of us. But that he didn't go to church. We were raised to go to church. "Would we go to church together in California?"

"Sure," he said. "I'll do whatever you want."

What did *Zeke* want? "I need to think about this more."

"I understand," he said.

"One more question." I crossed my arms against the cold. "When do you plan to leave?"

"Not for a few months."

A few? Three or four? January or February? Why couldn't I seem to be able to speak? I'd never had a difficult time asking Zeke questions and telling him how I felt. But all of a sudden, he felt both familiar and foreign at the same time.

I was desperate to change the subject. "Did you go to Hollywood when you were in Los Angeles?" The sun was setting, streaking the sky with pink and orange. I turned around to head to the house. Zeke matched my steps.

He laughed. "See, you do know about California. Have you been reading the movie magazines?"

"Not regularly," I joked. I'd seen a couple at Esther's apartment. She was fascinated by American movie stars.

"I saw the Hollywoodland sign, but that's all."

"Did you go to any churches on your trip?"

"A couple," he said. "A Mennonite one in Indiana. A Presbyterian church in Colorado with a family that let me sleep in their barn."

Someone yelled my name. "Rosene!" Mutter shouted it a second time.

I increased my pace.

"Hurry!"

I began to run. So did Zeke. As we reached the driveway, Mutter met us. Behind her, the Studebaker was parked by the back door with the lights on.

I grabbed Mutter's hand. "What's wrong?"

"It's Clare. She's hemorrhaging." She let go of my hand.

"Zeke, would you drive her to the hospital? I don't want Ervin to."

"Yes." Zeke started jogging toward the car.

"Rosene, you go with them. Vater and I will stay with the children."

· 19 ·

Clare had a healthy little girl that night, but Clare didn't fare as well. Her blood pressure plummeted, and she lost consciousness. A nurse came into the waiting room and then led Jeremiah to the delivery room just after midnight. After the doctor and nurses revived Clare, the doctor told Jeremiah he thought they were going to lose her. That's why he sent the nurse to get him.

By the time Jeremiah came out to the waiting room three hours later to tell Zeke and me about the baby and Clare, he looked as if he might collapse.

He told us to go home, and he'd call the store the next day and give Mutter an update. First, we stopped by the nursery. Baby Girl Zimmerman was in the front row. She had a head of dark hair, a perfectly round face, and a button nose. I fell madly in love with her immediately, but I also felt my loss intensely. More than I ever had before.

Zeke drove us home. "I'll do the milking in the morning," he said when we reached the farm. He parked the car in front of the house instead of driving around to the shed. It already *was* morning.

"Sleep on the sofa," I said. "I'll wake you up in an hour."

As we shuffled into the kitchen, I heard Mutter and Vater's door open. By the time I had grabbed the quilt off the sofa and handed it to Zeke, Mutter was in the living room.

"Well?" she asked.

"A little girl. Clare had a hard time, though." I explained what had happened.

"Oh, dear Lord," Mutter said.

"I think she's going to be all right." I hoped so.

"We're going to sleep for an hour," I said. "And then do the milking."

"I'll have coffee ready for you," Mutter said. "And then breakfast when you're done."

"Jeremiah's going to call in the morning."

Mutter said, "I'll see if Nancy can watch the store. I should be here with the children." Nancy was a neighbor who'd helped Mutter in the store while I was in Germany.

Zeke and I slogged through the milking. After breakfast, Mutter went to the store to call Nancy. Zeke went home to give his parents the news about the new baby and take a nap. "I'll be back by early afternoon," he said.

Just after eleven, Nancy came to the house. I held my breath, expecting the worst. But she said, "Jeremiah said Clare is doing better than last night. They'll keep her at least a week."

After our noon meal, Zeke returned and then drove Mutter to the hospital. After they left, I sat down on the sofa, pulling the quilt Zeke had used the night before around me. His scent—the castile soap his family used and a hint of smoke from the woodstove—enveloped me. Zeke was home. And yet he wasn't, not entirely. He'd seen a part of the world he hadn't known existed. And now he wanted to go back and see more of it, with me.

But did he really want to go with me? Had he met other girls—women—on his travels? Someone who could give him more than I could?

"Rosene?"

I awoke to Zeke standing over me, and the children playing on the living room floor. Arden must have gotten Janice up from her nap but not awakened me.

Zeke said, "It's time to do the milking. We can take the kids out with us."

"Where's Vater?"

"He must be resting," Zeke answered. "Jeremiah didn't come home from the hospital."

"Did Mutter stay?"

He nodded.

I didn't want to wake Vater, so I gave Arden and Janice a snack and then we went out to do the milking. Arden helped, and Janice sat on a hay bale with a couple of books and her doll.

As we worked, I asked how Clare was doing.

He glanced toward Arden. "I'm going to go pick up Jeremiah this evening. Perhaps your mother too."

"What's going on?" I asked.

"Jeremiah thought Clare was doing better earlier, but it seems she's about the same as she was yesterday."

"Was Mutter allowed to see her?"

"Yes."

"How is the baby?"

Zeke smiled. "Good. Even cuter than last night."

"Have they named her?"

"Not yet," he said. "Jeremiah is waiting for Clare to feel better."

We finished the milking, and Zeke stayed for sandwiches

for supper. Vater prayed out loud for Clare before we ate. Zeke helped me do the dishes again, and then we put the children to bed.

After we finished, he said, "I better go get Jeremiah."

"Do you need money for gas?" I asked.

"No, I have enough."

I sat with Vater in the living room after Zeke left, mending Arden's pants. When Vater went to bed, I moved from the rocking chair to the sofa and soon fell asleep.

I awoke to Jeremiah saying my name. I sat up straight, asking, "How is Clare?"

He sat down beside me. "She had surgery this afternoon. She had some complications during the birth. They had to do a hysterectomy."

I'd heard a woman in the store tell Mutter about having a hysterectomy, so I knew what it was. But the woman was Mutter's age—Clare was so young. "I'm sorry," I said.

"Denki." Jeremiah sighed. "I'm just thankful Clare survived. She lost a lot of blood."

I said, "I'm thankful for the three children you have."

Jeremiah sighed. "So are we." Then he hesitated, as if he might say more. But instead he stood. "I'm going to get to bed. Zeke will be here in the morning, so you don't have to help with the milking."

"I'll care for the children," I said. "See you at breakfast."

For the next week, Mutter and Jeremiah took turns going to the hospital, with Zeke driving them back and forth. We juggled the kids and the milking and cooking and cleaning. Thankfully, Nancy saw to the store.

Finally, Clare and the baby were able to come home. Clare

looked horrible—pale and thin for having just had a baby. She walked gingerly. Mutter had made up the spare bedroom on the main floor for her.

Mutter handed me the baby as soon as they came into the house. The little one looked up at me, right into my eyes, and held my gaze.

"What is her name?" I asked, not looking away.

"Lydia Rosene," Mutter replied.

My heart melted as I sat down on the sofa.

A few minutes later, Zeke came in with Elizabeth, laughing. Then he said, "Look who accepted a ride from me when it meant seeing the baby a little sooner."

Elizabeth marched straight toward us and scooped the baby out of my arms. Then she sat down beside me and called Zeke over. "She's a beauty," Elizabeth cooed, cradling the baby. "She looks like you did, Zeke, when you were a newborn." Zeke was her youngest.

I didn't think the baby looked like Zeke, although of course I hadn't known him as a baby. She didn't even look like Arden or Janice. I thought she looked entirely like herself.

After a while, Zeke said, "I'd better get you home, Mamm. I need to help Jeremiah."

Elizabeth handed Lydia back to me and whispered, "You'll be next."

I was too alarmed to respond. No one had told Elizabeth I couldn't have children. She expected Zeke to stay in Lancaster County. And she expected us to get married. If she knew I couldn't have children, would she want us to wed? Perhaps. She had plenty of grandchildren as it was and would no doubt have many more.

But Zeke wasn't going to stay. Elizabeth would be hurt and disappointed.

Clare's milk never came in, so we gave Lydia evaporated milk in a bottle. I got up at night to feed her so Clare could regain her strength. I gave the baby her baths, kept her in the kitchen in a basket with me during the day while I cooked, and rocked her as I read books to Arden and Janice.

Vater was taking three-hour naps every afternoon and was in bed by eight, and his blood pressure kept inching higher and higher despite the bromide he took. Mutter's health seemed to be deteriorating too. When I went to the store to call Lorraine and Esther to tell them I wouldn't be able to help with the refugee lunch for a few months, Mutter sat in a chair by the woodstove, dozing.

I called Nancy first and asked if she could come watch the store so Mutter could rest. Then I called Lorraine. Finally I called Esther, who had recently gotten a phone.

"Oh, I'm so sad," she said. "What will I do without you?"

"Would you like to come out to the farm for a few days? We could use the help."

She paused. "I'm not *that* sad—besides, I just got a part-time job at the Red Cross office. Call me next week and let me know how your sister is."

I awoke Mutter and told her Nancy was on the way and for her to come home and rest as soon as she arrived. As I walked to the house, a car pulled into the driveway. A blue coupe I didn't recognize.

I quickened my pace.

A woman wearing a long coat and a felt hat climbed from the passenger side of the car. She turned toward me.

"Martha!"

She hurried toward me as I ran toward her.

"Why didn't you write that you were coming?" I asked.

"It was a last-minute trip." Martha hugged me. "If I'd sent a letter, it wouldn't be here yet."

"Is everything all right?"

"Yes," she said. "I have some Red Cross work to see to."

"Where's George?"

"Still in Hamburg. It's a quick trip for me. I need to check in with Esther and some other refugees. I'll be here a night or two."

She opened the trunk and pulled out a small suitcase. "I received your letter about Lydia Rosene. How is Clare doing?"

"Better, but still weak. She'll be so happy to see you. Everyone will." I grabbed her hand and pulled her toward the house.

As we came through the door, Martha called out, "I'm home!"

Arden, followed by Janice, came running out of the living room and straight into Martha's arms. I continued on to the living room.

Vater, his eyes wide, sat in the rocking chair with Lydia in his arms. "Is Martha really here?"

I took the baby from him. "Jah," I said. "She really is."

After detouring into the bedroom where Clare rested, I returned to the kitchen and handed Martha the baby.

She held her for a moment, cooing, "Hello, Lydia Rosene," and then handed her back to me. "Where's Clare?"

"In the spare bedroom."

Clare, wearing her nightgown and robe, stepped into the kitchen. Then Mutter came through the door, followed by Jeremiah and Zeke.

"Who's here?" Mutter asked. Martha turned toward her, and Mutter gasped. As I stood in the middle of the kitchen—my kitchen—with those I loved most, I'd never felt so safe and secure and loved and needed. It was a comforting moment for me. This was where I belonged. The memory of seeing Vater Josef, Lena, and Garit had almost entirely faded.

Later that afternoon, Martha donned her old overalls and went out to help with the milking. She didn't come in with Jeremiah, and when I went out to cut the last of the marigolds for a bouquet for the table, she and Zeke sat at the picnic table, deep in conversation. Ten minutes later, she came in for dinner, but Zeke didn't.

That evening, after everyone else was in bed, I sat in the rocking chair, giving Lydia her bottle. Martha stepped into the living room and sat down on the sofa.

"Do you have time to talk?" she asked.

"Jah." I took my eyes off the baby.

"I had a long conversation with Zeke while we were milking and then afterward."

"I saw you sitting at the picnic table." I put Lydia on my shoulder to burp her.

"I'm going to be blunt," Martha said.

I wrinkled my nose. "That's exactly what I would expect from you."

She chuckled a little. "I've only gotten worse." She leaned forward. "You can't help who you fall in love with, but you can help who you marry."

I kept patting the baby. "You don't think I should marry Zeke?"

"I didn't say that. What I think is that you should think this through carefully. He wants to go to California. Will you be happy to have Zeke be your *whole* life? Not that you won't find community wherever you go, but it might not be a lasting community."

"Isn't that what you're doing?"

Martha exhaled. "I guess I am."

Before she could say more, I blurted out, "He doesn't seem to mind that I can't have children." The irony of the baby in my arms weighed heavily on me.

Martha's brows came together. "Do you think you won't find someone else who doesn't mind?"

I shrugged, but the truth was, I didn't.

"Don't let that be what you base your decision on. Children aren't a guarantee in any relationship," Martha said. "It seems George and I might not be able to have children."

"Do you want children?"

Martha paused. "Well, yes. We'd welcome children. We'd be overjoyed. But if we don't have a child, we'll still have fulfilling lives." She lowered her voice more. "Zeke isn't exactly aiming to follow Christ's teachings."

"What do you mean?"

"I'm not saying he's aiming *not* to—but he's very much wanting to run around instead of making a commitment to the Lord and a community."

"I'm hoping Zeke comes around."

Martha's eyebrows shot up.

I pursed my lips together. "Are you and George committed to the Lord and a community?"

"We're trying to be," she answered. "We read scripture together and pray. We seek out a church wherever we're living. Of course, we don't have the choice of a Mennonite church nor a Methodist one. Right now, we're attending a Lutheran church in Hamburg."

That was good to hear. Perhaps Zeke would be willing to attend another type of church besides an Anabaptist one.

"His parents are worried about him," Martha said. "They're afraid he'll never join the Amish, that they'll lose him forever. They're hoping you'll keep him here."

"Elizabeth doesn't know I can't have children." I met Martha's gaze. "Perhaps if I could, Zeke would want to stay."

Martha hesitated a moment and then said, "I don't think that's true. Maybe the thought of not having children someday has made him want to travel more. He won't be weighed down by as many responsibilities. But I think his motivation is that he simply wants to see more of the country. With you."

"Do you really think he wants me to go with him?" I continued to pat Lydia.

"I think he loves you," Martha said. "I think he has for years. And if he'd never left Lancaster County, he'd be ready to settle here. But now that he's seen other places and ways of life, he's not ready to settle down, neither in his faith nor in one place," Martha said. "I'm not going to give you advice except for you to give this a lot of thought. You value church and faith and family and community. You're willing to join the Amish. At the least, you'd like to stay Mennonite."

She leaned toward me. "I hope this doesn't sound odd, but you value being with family far more than I do. Besides following the Lord, who you marry and where you live are two of the most important decisions you'll ever make. Don't ever marry someone hoping they'll come around or, even worse, that you can change them."

I nodded. I knew she was right. "If you had a child, would you come home?"

Martha folded her hands together. "Perhaps. But I don't know for sure. I think the difference for us is that George, even though we're from different religious backgrounds, very much wants to pursue faith together. It doesn't matter where we are. I didn't gather that from Zeke when I spoke with him."

I hadn't gathered that either. The baby burped. I cradled her and continued rocking. I had a lot to think about.

· 20 ·

Treva

The next morning, Rosene and I walked over to Carol's to get the power of attorney form notarized. I'd been thinking about Zeke since the day before. Where had he ended up? Obviously Rosene hadn't gone with him. And obviously she wouldn't get ahead of the story and tell me what happened to him.

Did she even know? Maybe so. Perhaps he lived nearby. Or not. No doubt he would have kept in touch with his parents and Jeremiah. But they had been dead for decades.

As we walked, I said, "I know you won't tell me how the story ends, but do you know what happened to Zeke? Do you know if he's still alive?"

"I don't want to give the story away, but I will say I have no idea where Zeke is," she said. "I tried to reach him when Jeremiah passed away. I sent a letter to the last address we had for him, but it was returned."

We'd reached the Smiths' house. Rosene knocked and then opened their kitchen door. "Hello!" she called out.

"Come on in!" Carol called back.

After a few minutes of chatting about the weather and then Carol telling us how much she enjoyed the refugee dinner, Rosene signed the document and Carol notarized it.

As we walked home, I asked Rosene, "Have you searched for Zeke in the last ten years or so?"

"No. I did an online search at the library when I first learned about the Internet but didn't find anything." She took my arm as a car zoomed by. "I don't think there are many Zeke Zimmermans out there—I think he would have shown up. Last I checked with any of his other older nieces and nephews, none of them had heard from him either. I'm guessing he's deceased." Her voice grew softer. "I hope he had a good life. I hope he found his way back to the Lord and serving God and others."

"I hope so too," I said. "Would you like me to do a search?"

Rosene tightened her grip on my arm. "Jah. I would like to know this side of heaven what happened to him."

I decided to stop by the library on the way to the refugee center. After I made copies of the power of attorney form, I scanned it and emailed an attachment of the document to Brenna. Then I took a moment to search for Zeke Zimmerman. A person by that name popped up on a social media app. An Ezekiel Zimmerman popped up on a business app. An article about Zeke Zimmerman, a soccer player in Australia, was listed, along with information about a psychologist in Colorado named Zeke Zimmerman. None of them were the Zeke Zimmerman I was looking for.

The name was more common than I'd expected. I'd have to spend more time looking for him later.

I had enough time on the way to the refugee center to stop at a shipping company store and send the hard copy of the power of attorney to Herr Mayer. Then I sat in the parking lot and texted Misty and Shawn.

> Just checking in. I'm still interested in the job if you can hold it for me awhile longer. I should know by next week when I can come.

My phone dinged before I could put it in my purse. It was Misty.

> If you can't come in two weeks, one of our employees who was holding off until May will be able to come now. However, we need you here by the first week of May so you can help with the details for Lindsay's wedding. We don't have anyone who can take your place for that. Let us know your plans as soon as possible. I hope your aunt is improving!

> Thank you. I'll update you next week.

Misty didn't sound as flexible as before, which was understandable. They had a business to run. And a wedding to host. They were taking me on, someone without any experience, out of kindness.

I pulled out of the parking lot, feeling down. Perhaps, like Zeke, I'd seen more of the world and was determined now to keep going.

I arrived at the refugee center a few minutes later. Zaida and Cala both gave me hugs when they saw me, and we talked about what a success the dinner had been. "We should do it again," Zaida said. "It felt so good to give the money to the center this morning. We're helping others."

"And ourselves," Cala said. "It was good of your grandfather to pay us."

"He's a good guy," I said. "And we should do it again."

"How about in two weeks?" Zaida said.

I cringed inside. Why was I planning ahead when I might not even be here? But they could do it without me. "I'll talk with my grandparents," I said, "and let you know."

After lunch was served, I helped clean up and then assisted with homework questions. When I returned home, Dawdi and Rosene sat at the table.

"We were remembering," Rosene said.

"About?" I asked.

"Onkel Zeke," Dawdi said. "He was always my favorite."

Rosene smiled. "Mine too."

Dawdi stood and patted Rosene's shoulder.

The next day, I did a couple of loads of wash in the basement before breakfast and hung them on the line, then worked in the store. After lunch, Rosene took a nap. She wanted to be rested when Ivy and Conrad arrived. Several times, I stepped to her open doorway and checked to make sure she was still breathing. She was.

In the midafternoon, as I stood at the counter and chopped onions, the kitchen door swung open and Ivy appeared.

"You're early," I said.

"I'm just stopping by," she said. "We'll be back."

"What's going on?"

She held up her phone. "I need to tell you and Brenna something before we tell everyone else this evening." Brenna waved at me from the screen.

I put my knife down. "Shouldn't we go out to the barn to talk?"

Ivy stepped to my side. "Nah. This will be quick."

"Hi, Brenn." I waved and turned toward Ivy. "What's up?"

She grinned and stepped to my side, holding the camera so Brenna could see both of us. "I'm pregnant."

"What?" I broke out into a smile. "Really?"

She nodded and grinned.

Brenna clapped her hands together. "That's wonderful!"

I wrapped my arms around Ivy, careful not to actually touch her with my oniony hands. "Congratulations."

She hugged me in return. Then, as I pulled away, Ivy said, "I have other news too that I wanted to tell both of you at the same time."

Ivy repositioned the phone so Brenna could see both of us. "Conrad and I are moving to Oregon to take over the tree farm."

I lurched forward. "What? Dawdi asked you and Conrad to take over this farm and help save it. You said you'd take care of Rosene, Dawdi, and Mammi when the time came."

Ivy shook her head. "We never said we'd take over the farm. And I said I'd care for our elders before I was married. Now I need to take care of my own family."

I glared at her. I'd appeal to her sense of family since she didn't seem to care about duty anymore. "You can't take my niece or nephew to Oregon."

Ivy locked eyes with me. "You're moving to Alaska."

I leaned against the counter and crossed my arms. "Am I? If you're moving to Oregon, don't you think someone needs to be here?" The Amish took care of their elderly. We couldn't abandon our grandparents and aunt.

Ivy clapped her hands together. "Yes! You can run the farm *and* take care of Rosene, Dawdi, and Mammi."

"Who said I'm going to run the farm?"

"You love the farm. Why wouldn't you?"

"I'm only twenty—"

"Almost twenty-one."

I dropped my voice to a hiss. "Dawdi's not going to give me the farm. And how could I take care of the farm *and* our elderly relatives?" It would be impossible if any of them needed serious care.

"Hey!" Brenna said. "Stop fighting."

I snapped, "We're not fighting." But I was still glaring at Ivy.

She didn't flinch. She didn't even acknowledge Brenna had said anything. "Treva, you've always loved this farm, this land."

"Always? I've only known this land existed for the last five years."

"Look." Ivy glanced from me to Brenna. "I know this is a surprise."

Brenna leaned forward, her face filling the phone screen. "When are you moving?"

"July."

I groaned. That was three months away.

"I gotta go," Ivy said. "I have another client to see before I'm done with work."

"Wait." I turned to Ivy. She hadn't asked Brenna about herself or her trip to Germany. I hadn't given them an update about going to Alaska. "You can give us five more minutes. Brenna, what's up with you? Are you looking forward to going to Germany?"

"Are you going for sure?" Ivy asked.

"Yes," Brenna said. "Johann and Natasha are going with me." Brenna gave us an update about her plans, then she said, "I have news of my own. Johann and I are getting pretty serious."

Ivy squealed. "How serious?"

"Really serious," Brenna said. "We're talking about marriage. Hopefully soon." She grinned. "The two of you will be first to know." Brenna's phone began to ring. "Oops. Gotta go. It's a work call."

We said a quick good-bye. I guessed Brenna and Johann were already engaged—at least informally. She didn't usually share much personal information unless it was definite.

"See you in a couple of hours." Ivy headed out the door. "Oh, and I asked Gabe to join us for dinner."

I returned to chopping the onions, trying not to cry. I was going to have a niece or nephew. And probably a new brother-in-law too. I was thrilled about both, but I was also feeling the loss of Pierre—again.

Perhaps Ivy learned from telling Brenna and me her news because at dinner, before Dawdi said the closing prayer, she told everyone they were moving to Oregon first.

Shocked, Dawdi, Mammi, Rosene, and Gabe sat dumbfounded, and before anyone spoke, before Dawdi could bring up the farm, Ivy beamed and said, "There's more. We're having a baby! It's due in October."

All anyone dwelled on after that was that there would be a great-grandbaby in the family. Dawdi and Mammi were both beside themselves. Rosene wiped away tears.

Gabe didn't look so happy, though. "When are you moving to Oregon?"

"Not until July," Ivy answered.

"Have you told Mom?" Gabe asked.

"Not yet," Conrad answered. "We'll do that tomorrow."

"Have you told Brenna?" Rosene asked.

"Yes. This afternoon." Ivy pursed her lips together. "I was surprised she's going to Germany so soon."

"Herr Mayer is ready to settle Lena's estate," Rosene explained.

Ivy asked, "Do you think Brenna's up to that?"

"Absolutely," Rosene said.

I reached for Gabe's plate to stack on top of mine. "Johann speaks German. Herr Mayer speaks English. She'll have plenty of help to sort through everything."

Ivy leaned back in her chair. "I'm glad Johann's going with her."

Dawdi led us in a closing prayer, and then I began clearing the table. Mammi stood and started helping me.

Everyone was silent for a long moment, but then Gabe said, "Is anyone going to bring up that Ivy and Conrad are moving to Oregon, leaving behind four grandparents in Pennsylvania?"

"Three," Rosene said.

"No, four." Gabe stood. "You, Rosene, count as a grandparent."

"Gabe, don't," Conrad said. "We'll talk later."

"And an aunt and an uncle." Gabe pointed to me, then himself. "Does anyone else care?"

Dawdi stepped to Gabe's side and put his arm around him. "Of course we care. But this is Conrad and Ivy's decision. It's our job to make the best of it."

Gabe exhaled.

"I'm thinking maybe a road trip to Oregon is in our near future," Dawdi said. "Or a talk with our bishop about flying. Or both."

Rosene stood. "I like the way you're thinking, Arden."

Ivy clapped her hands together. "That would be so much fun. You could come for Thanksgiving. Fly out in the winter and then do a road trip in the summer."

Not everyone would be able to go. Someone would have to stay to do the milking. Where would I be?

"We'll visit one or two times a year," Ivy said. "You'll see the baby. I promise."

The next morning, while I was working in the store, Gabe came in to help. He waited to talk with me until the customer at the counter paid for the tea set and tablecloth she was buying. As soon as the door shut behind her, Gabe said, "We need to talk to Ivy and Conrad."

"Why?"

He ran his hand through his hair, which was growing out. "They can't move to Oregon."

"Why not?"

He glared at me.

I sighed. "You're in a mood." But part of me was happy to see Gabe angry. At least he was showing some kind of emotion. I could see a glimpse of the old Gabe.

"Conrad told me before I left for Kuwait that Arden asked him and Ivy to take over the farm." Gabe leaned against the counter. "That's all I thought about while I was there—getting back here. To this farm. I was sure Conrad and Ivy would tell Arden yes. After I'd been in Kuwait a week, I told Conrad I'd work with him when I came home."

"You told him you wanted to work with him when you got home?"

Gabe stood up straight. "Not exactly."

"What do you mean?"

"I think I made it sound more like I'd be *willing* to help him."

I crossed my arms. "As if you'd be doing them a favor?"

"It might have come across that way."

"So Conrad didn't know that you *wanted* to work with

him on the farm?" I asked. "That it would be your prefer-
ence?"

Gabe shoved his hands into the pockets of his jeans. "I
would have been clearer about it if I had any idea they were
thinking about moving to Oregon, but never—not once—did
Conrad mention that was a possibility." He shook his head.
"Maybe there's something wrong with me."

"Why do you say that?"

"There's a whole big world out there, and all I want is to
work on this farm. I keep making my world smaller instead
of bigger."

"I think it takes just as much courage to contract as it does
to expand," I said. "Adults always have expectations that the
youth will go out and change the world, but someone needs
to stay close to home and maintain what's already been es-
tablished. The important thing is to be honest with yourself
and do what you feel God wants you to do. Remember that
verse? 'Delight in the Lord and He will give you the desires
of your heart'? We desire things for a reason."

Gabe rolled his eyes. "This isn't my farm."

I gave him a sympathetic smile, not sure what to say.
Dawdi needed someone to run the farm. If he knew Gabe
wanted to stay here, would he hire Gabe to do it? He could
keep living in the Dawdi Haus. He wouldn't be able to run
both the farm and the store, but at least it would keep the
land in the family for a little longer. I could see it wasn't a
long-term solution.

Gabe grunted and then said, "Come with me tonight to
talk with Conrad and Ivy. They need to stay here."

"No," I said. "I don't want to get involved in their business."

Gabe grimaced. "I suppose I shouldn't either, but why

would they do this? Conrad told me they planned to stay here."

I nodded. "I know. Ivy said she'd take care of Mammi, Dawdi, and Rosene."

"Is your Oregon grandmother sick again?"

"No." At least I didn't think she was. I stepped to the counter.

"Would you at least give me a ride over to Ivy and Conrad's place tonight?"

"Aren't they going to talk with your mom this evening?"

"Probably not. She has her book group. Please give me a ride."

I shook my head but then said, "I'll think about it." Nothing would change Ivy's mind once she decided on something, but I understood how Gabe felt.

Blindsided.

I was the one who was supposed to be leaving—not Ivy.

Now that it was on my mind, I texted Ivy to find out how Gran was doing. She texted back.

Okay.

That didn't sound promising.

> Can we talk sometime soon about you moving to Oregon and all of that?

Of course.

> How about tonight?

That works. Sharon has book group. We'll tell her our news tomorrow.

I smiled. Gabe kept track of more than I expected. Actually, I found the fact that he was so unsettled about Conrad and Ivy moving endearing too.

Okay. Gabe is going to come too.

When Gabe and I arrived at Ivy and Conrad's apartment, they both met us at the door. "I picked up ice cream on the way home from work," Ivy said. "Come on in."

As we sat in their living room with our bowls of peanut butter and chocolate ice cream, Ivy asked, "So, what's up?"

I glanced at Gabe.

He put his bowl on the coffee table. "What made you decide to move to Oregon just like that? Is your other grandmother not doing well?"

"She's healthy," Ivy said. "But she's getting older, and she doesn't have anyone there with her." Ivy nodded at me. "Treva's here. It seemed one of us should be in Oregon."

"I'm only here because Rosene had her heart attack. Otherwise I'd be in Alaska—and I will be soon."

"But that's only temporary."

"You don't know that," I argued. "And you knew before you went to Oregon that I planned to go to Alaska."

Conrad cleared his throat and then said, "We decided to move to Oregon right after we found out about the baby, before we knew you were going to Alaska. Or that Gabe was coming home. I applied for teaching jobs while we were there, and Ivy looked into some part-time work. I like Oregon and the tree farm. Ivy wants to raise our family there. And, yes, Gran could really benefit by having a granddaughter around."

"I feel ridiculous saying this." Gabe rubbed his arm. "But I just never thought you'd move. I thought the two of you would take over the Zimmerman farm. I hoped I'd be able to help you work it."

Conrad shook his head. "You never told me that."

"I said I'd help you. . . ." Gabe's voice trailed away.

"*If* we decided to take over the farm. You never *said* you wanted to actually farm."

"Well, I do. I did."

Conrad leaned back against the sofa. "I'm sorry about that, but we've decided on Oregon."

Ivy turned toward Gabe. "Treva can take over the farm. Maybe you can work with her."

I exhaled loudly. "Ivy, have you ever seen a woman in charge of any of the farms around here?"

She shrugged. "You could be the first."

"Well, Dawdi hasn't said anything about me taking over the farm, so it's a moot point." My voice rose in volume. "He only mentioned the store. Besides, I'm not even twenty-one yet."

Gabe glanced at me. "I need to go."

I stood and grabbed my empty bowl and Gabe's nearly full bowl. "Thank you for the ice cream." After I'd taken the bowls to the kitchen sink and returned to the living room, Gabe was already gone. I gave Ivy a hug, then Conrad.

"Is Gabe okay?" Conrad asked.

"I'm not sure. . . ."

Conrad exhaled. "I need to spend some time with him."

"That's a good idea."

· 21 ·

The next day dawned bright and chilly. But by noon, it had grown warm. As I walked toward the shop, Gabe sat across from Drew at the picnic table. The two were deep in conversation. I hoped maybe Drew could help Gabe work through some of his angst and figure out what he needed in life.

I gave both a wave and then continued on to the store. A half hour later, Gabe stepped through the front door.

"How are you doing?" I asked.

"Hanging in there," he answered.

"I was just getting ready to dust, sweep, and then polish. Want to help?"

"Sure."

"I saw you talking with Drew."

Gabe nodded. "He's a good guy."

"Did he have any advice for you?"

Gabe cocked his head. "Why do you think I'd ask him for advice?"

I suppressed a smile. The old Gabe—or a version closer to the old Gabe—was definitely inching his way back. "Oh,

I don't know. Maybe because you disclosed you feel a little unsettled. And Drew seems like a good listener."

Gabe frowned. "He said to give myself some time. To figure out where I need to feel comfortable and where I can stretch myself."

That sounded like good advice. "How are you feeling about Conrad and Ivy moving to Oregon today?"

"The same." He sighed. "I didn't explain all of that to Drew, though." Gabe paused a minute and then said, "Rosene's story is helping some. It's easy to think that everyone had life figured out in the old days. But they didn't. Some knew they wanted to stay on their childhood farms. Others left and went far away. There wasn't a right or a wrong."

"Did you tell Drew about Rosene's story?"

Gabe shook his head.

"You two talked for quite a while."

"Yeah," Gabe said. "And it wasn't me doing all the talking. He asked several questions too."

"What about?"

"The Zimmermans. Arden's father, in particular. It was almost like he was fishing for information but in a really nice way." Gabe met my eyes and shrugged.

That seemed odd. Not the nice part—Drew was the epitome of nice. But that he was fishing. "He hasn't asked me anything," I said.

"I told him he should. Or Rosene. I know her last name is Simons, but she seems to know a lot about the Zimmermans too."

Gabe left after a couple of hours. As I was closing, Drew parked his car at the far end of the parking lot, where he always parked, and came toward the store.

I stepped onto the porch. "Hello," I called out.

"Oh, Treva. How are you?"

"Good," I answered. "Isn't it a nice day?"

"Gorgeous. I went for a drive east of here, toward New Holland. The pastures are so green and full of new lambs and calves. I don't think I've ever seen anything like it."

"Wisconsin doesn't look like this?"

"Oh, it's still cold in Wisconsin. It goes from snow to mosquitoes. There's no in between."

I smiled. "Do you mind if I ask you a question?"

"Not at all."

"Gabe said you were asking about the Zimmerman family. How come?"

Drew put his hands in the pockets of his jacket. "I thought about that on my drive. I should have asked you or Rosene or Arden instead of Gabe. Sorry about that."

"What do you want to know? And why?"

"Do you have a few minutes?"

"Yes." I nodded toward the steps leading up to the store. "Want to sit?"

"Sure."

I sat down on the top step and he sat a few feet away and turned toward me.

"Whenever I'm in an area with Amish people, I look up the name Zimmerman," Drew said. "When I found out that a family with the last name of Zimmerman operated the antique store, I stopped by."

"What's the attraction to the name Zimmerman?"

"My father passed away three years ago. He was adopted and never knew who his birth parents were." Drew wrapped his hands around one knee. "All he knew was that his father—my grandfather—had grown up Amish and that his

230

last name was purported to be Zimmerman. I joined a couple of different ancestry apps and had a DNA test done before my father passed. I have a significant percentage of Germanic ancestry, leading to the Canton of Bern in Switzerland, where the Amish church originated. I believe the information that my biological grandfather was Amish is correct."

"Was your father born in Wisconsin?"

"No. He was adopted by a couple who lived in Wisconsin. He was born in Tennessee."

"Have you looked for Zimmermans in Tennessee?"

"Yes. I found some but not the right age. The first group of Amish settled in Tennessee in 1944, and the first Zimmermans didn't arrive until twenty years or so after that, long past when my father was born. I've found Amish Zimmermans in Kentucky, New York, Ohio, Illinois, Wisconsin, and Colorado too." He rocked backward a little. "And in Pennsylvania. Pretty much all over."

"I'm sorry you haven't found what you're looking for."

"Any chance that any of your relatives were born between 1915 and 1930 or so?"

"My great-grandfather—Jeremiah—had multiple brothers. You'd have to ask Dawdi or Rosene how many for sure. I'm guessing that Jeremiah was born before 1920."

"From what your grandfather told me about Jeremiah, I'm guessing I can rule him out."

I agreed. "I've heard enough of Rosene's stories to second that."

"Did any of his brothers leave this area?"

"One did for sure. I don't know about the others. The one I know about traveled west and spent some time in California." I thought for a moment. "I don't know if he ever went to Tennessee or not." Perhaps Rosene hadn't gotten that far in the story. "You should ask Rosene. I think she would know more than Dawdi."

"Thank you," Drew said. "I will."

"What are you hoping to accomplish if you do find your grandfather?"

He sighed. "Answers. It's one of the reasons I'm interested in the Amish—in the Anabaptists in general. My dad didn't tell me about my biological grandfather with the last name of Zimmerman. His adoptive mother did when I was twelve or so. I was close to my grandmother. She always hoped Dad would look for his biological father, but Dad didn't seem to care. I do, though. That's why I worked for the Amish man in Wisconsin. Went to Goshen. Taught in Kansas. That's why I'm at Duke now and doing the research I'm doing." He shrugged. "I probably sound obsessed."

"No," I said. "I think everyone deserves to know where they come from." I'd spent my entire childhood not knowing Mammi, Dawdi, and Rosene and having no idea about the Zimmerman farm in Lancaster County. All of those things were missing pieces. I ended up losing my parents but gaining my grandparents and great-great-aunt. I just wish I could have had all of them at once.

"I really hope you find what you're looking for." I stood.

"Thank you." He stood too. "I need to grab a few things from the apartment, and then I have another interview this evening. I'll talk with Rosene tomorrow."

I walked to the house, thinking about Zeke. Had he gone to Tennessee? What if he was Drew's biological grandfather? How would that make Rosene feel?

Perhaps it wouldn't matter after all these years.

On my way to the house, I stopped by the barn and found Dawdi working by himself.

"Where's Kamil?" I asked.

"He had some business he needed to attend to."

"Oh." I hoped he hadn't found another job. "I can help now."

"I started early so I'm nearly done," Dawdi said. "But you can help me scoop manure."

I smiled. "My favorite thing."

He laughed. "Mine too."

We each grabbed a scoop shovel and got to work. Dawdi stopped a few times to rest while I kept working. He really needed to not have to work so hard.

Once we finished, we headed into the milk room. As we washed our hands, I said, "Gabe's upset that Ivy and Conrad decided not to take over the farm."

"It seemed he was." Dawdi pulled his hands out of the water and shook them over the sink. "I understand. Now I'm without a plan." He grabbed paper towels to dry his hands.

I turned off the faucet and grabbed paper towels too. "Gabe had hoped to work on the farm with Conrad."

"Really?"

I nodded. "Could you make the farm profitable if Gabe could work for you full-time again?"

Dawdi's brow furrowed. "I wish I could, but we need someone for the store, plus another farmhand—at least a part-time one."

"Would you be willing to have Gabe work for you again?"

"Of course," Dawdi said. "Until I figure out what to do. I'm guessing we'll have to sell sometime soon. Hopefully an Amish or Mennonite family will want to buy the farm."

My heart lurched.

Once I was in the house, I didn't say anything to Rosene

about my conversation with Drew. She went to bed right after dinner. The next morning, she didn't get up until it was time for breakfast.

Because she seemed extra tired, I asked Gabe to sit with Rosene while I went to the pharmacy to pick up her prescription. When I returned, Rosene—who had a quilt tucked around her—and Gabe sat on the front porch in the two rocking chairs.

I headed toward them as Drew came around from the direction of the store. Rosene waved at Drew, and then at me. Drew and I reached the front steps at the same time.

"Come sit," Rosene said. "We're enjoying the sunshine."

"Thank you." Drew pulled chairs around to the rail for him and me. As we sat down, he said, "Did Treva tell you I haven't been completely honest?"

"No." Rosene glanced at me and then back at Drew.

Gabe shifted in his chair and stared at the steps.

Drew told Rosene about his father being adopted. "All he knew was that his father's last name was Zimmerman and that he'd grown up Amish."

Rosene smiled a little. "When was your father born?"

"December 1949."

Rosene rocked in her chair. "Do you have any reason to believe that the man who grew up Amish and had the last name of Zimmerman was from Lancaster County?"

"No," Drew said. "But I don't have any reason to believe that he wasn't."

Rosene thought for a moment. She didn't seem upset, although it could all feel shocking to her. The last date in the story was November 1948, and Zeke was still in Lancaster County.

"My father was born in Tennessee," Drew said. "Although

that could have more to do with his biological mother than his biological father."

"Is your father still alive?" Rosene asked.

Drew shook his head. "He died three years ago."

"How about your grandparents?"

"No. They passed away when I was in college."

"And your mother?"

"She and my father divorced when I was young. I don't have much of a relationship with her."

"Siblings?"

"I'm an only child," Drew answered. No wonder Drew wanted to find his father's biological family. He didn't have any family left.

Rosene's brow creased.

"Did your father want to find his biological father?"

"No," Drew said. "But I do. I've had my DNA tested, and there weren't any matches."

"Give me some time." Rosene smiled at him. "I'll put more thought into it."

He stood. "Thank you. I don't expect you to have an answer for me. But if you have ideas, I'd appreciate any information you can give me."

Rosene nodded and then said, "I'm sorry your dad never found his biological father before he died, whether he wanted to or not. Knowing the past is helpful."

"As someone who studies history, I agree." Drew reached out and took her hand. "Thank you."

I went into the house to start lunch, and after a few minutes Rosene came in too.

"How are you doing?" I asked.

"Drew's question caught me off guard." I expected her to say more, but she didn't.

I took the ground beef I'd defrosted out of the refrigerator. "How are you feeling?"

"Good," she said. "Rested. What can I do to help?"

"I was going to make a carrot salad. Would you like to peel and grate the carrots?"

"Jah," she said. "I would. I'll tell you more of the story while we work."

· 22 ·

Rosene

Martha was right about Zeke. He didn't seem to be in pursuit of anything that had to do with faith or God or church. He wasn't attending Amish services with his family, nor Mennonite services. I continued to go back and forth between the two, but now I questioned whether I should eventually join the Amish. Would I be welcome without Zeke? Would anyone believe I wanted to join on my own?

Autumn would soon turn to winter, but there were a few glorious days in November that made it seem the golden and scarlet leaves would hang on to the maple trees forever. Overhead the Canada geese flew south, keeping in formation.

Martha had gone into Lancaster on business, but when I mentioned that to Lorraine when she called to see if I could help the next Wednesday at the Red Cross office, she didn't know what I was talking about, saying, "I haven't seen Martha in years, and she's certainly not here today. But I did hear that she'd come home because of illness. How's her health?"

"Fine," I said. "But it's our sister who is ill."

"I must have misunderstood," Lorraine said. "Can you help on Wednesday?"

"No," I answered. "I'll let you know when I'm able to volunteer again."

The next day, Martha went into Lancaster again. After Lydia's nap time, Zeke and I sat at the picnic table as I held the baby. Arden and Martha played in the roots of the birch trees.

"Have you decided to go with me?" he asked.

I glanced down at the baby.

Zeke came around the side of the table and sat beside me, taking Lydia in his arms. "These aren't the only children in the world. I worked with a man in California. He and his wife couldn't have children, so they adopted. Two. A girl and a boy. It's not like they're rich people. There are babies who need homes."

"But would we take the children to church?"

"Jah," he said. "I'm just taking a break from all of that for a while. Trying to figure out who I am."

"Do you want me along for that?"

"Jah, I want you with me." Zeke met my eyes and held my gaze. He seemed sincere.

Lydia began to stir, and Zeke stood up with her. He began humming, and she stopped fussing.

"I like it here," I said. "I've seen other places. This is home."

"Well," he said, "maybe we'll return someday."

Maybe. I'd already lost one family. I didn't want to lose another. Zeke was two years younger than me. Obviously, he still needed a running-around time. He needed to know who he was and what he wanted.

But I didn't.

Zeke slid the baby back into my arms. "It's time to get started on the milking."

"Will you eat dinner here?" I asked.

He shook his head. "I told Mamm I'd eat at her house tonight."

I summoned Arden and Janice. "You can play by the steps until it's time to set the table."

As we started toward the door, a car stopped in the driveway in front of the house. I expected it was Martha, although she usually parked by the shed. Arden and Janice ran ahead, but then they came back.

"It's a man," Arden said.

I quickened my pace. As I came around the side of the house, the man started up the front steps. He was tall and wore a long coat and a hat.

"Hello," I called out. "May I help you?"

He turned toward me. "I'm looking for Martha Hall."

"She's in town," I said. "But she should return before dinner. Whom should I say is looking for her?"

"No need," he said. "I'll return."

When Martha arrived, I told her about the man and described him.

"Oh, that's probably Stephen Wilson. He's a colleague who works in Philadelphia. He told me he was coming down this way," she said. "I gave him our address in case he needed to find me."

As we sat down to eat, someone knocked on the front door. Rather forcefully. "I'll get it," Martha said.

Muffled voices reached us in the kitchen and then came the

sound of footsteps. Martha appeared at the doorway. "Rosene, do you have Esther's phone number? Stephen needs it."

"Jah." I rattled it off.

"Mutter, it's Red Cross work. Could we use the phone in the store?"

"Jah." Mutter nodded toward the key by the kitchen door.

Martha retrieved the key and then walked to the front of the house. The door clicked shut, and they were gone.

Around twenty minutes later, as we finished eating, she returned. She motioned me into the kitchen. "Esther didn't answer. Where do you think she is?"

"It's Friday evening. Maybe she's at dinner with one of the families from her synagogue."

"Would you go into town with us to find her?"

I had no idea what was going on, but I couldn't imagine a Red Cross worker coming down from Philadelphia to speak with a refugee in person. It didn't make sense. Nor did Martha coming all the way from Germany to check on a few refugees either. I couldn't even guess at what was really going on.

Ten minutes later, I sat in the back of Stephen Wilson's car, and Martha sat up front. No one spoke. I'd been up a couple of times during the night before with Lydia and soon dozed. I awoke as Mr. Wilson slowed at the city limits. It was completely dark now.

"Let's start at Esther's apartment in case she's home now," I said.

Mr. Wilson drove straight to it, which I thought was odd.

"You go up by yourself," Martha said. "If she's there, tell her I'm out in the car and need to speak with her."

I did as Martha instructed. When I reached Esther's door, I knocked. And then knocked again. She didn't answer.

I went back down to the car. "One of the families that Esther sometimes has Shabbat dinner with lives a few blocks from here. Let's go there."

As we rounded the corner, Martha said, "Stop." Ahead was a woman with long brown hair who was Esther's height. Mr. Wilson pulled up beside her. The woman turned toward us. It wasn't Esther.

I continued to direct Mr. Wilson to the Fogel residence. When we arrived, Martha turned toward me and said, "Would you go up and see if she's there?"

"Jah." What had I involved myself in? I knocked, hoping I wouldn't offend the family by interrupting their Shabbat. An older man answered the door, and I asked about Esther.

"She's here," he said. "Just a minute."

A few minutes later, Esther stood in front of me. "Rosene? What's going on?"

"Martha's in town," I answered. "She and a Stephen Wilson need to speak with you."

"I'll get my coat," she said, "and meet you in the car."

· 23 ·

A half hour later, Martha and Mr. Wilson dropped me off at the farm, saying they would take Esther to her apartment. If I didn't trust Martha implicitly, I'd suspect she was up to something nefarious. I watched as the taillights of the car disappeared.

Esther hadn't seemed alarmed. Obviously they wanted—needed?—to speak to her in private. Martha and Mr. Wilson hadn't wanted anyone in Esther's apartment building to see them. Nor had they wanted anyone in the Fogel family to see them either.

I hung my coat and then went into the kitchen. The kerosene lamp sat on the table, casting soft light around the room. The dishes were done. The house was quiet. Then Lydia began to cry from the living room.

I walked toward the sound. Clare sat in the rocking chair, tears streaming down her face as she held the baby.

"What's the matter?" I asked.

She nodded. "Just a little sad tonight." She moved the baby to her shoulder. "I've missed out on so much of taking care of Lydia. And I still feel so tired. I wish I was better by now."

"Do you want me to take her?"

"Jah," Clare said. "If you don't mind."

"Not at all."

"She just had a bottle." Clare handed me the baby and then stood. "I'm going to go to bed. Jeremiah's upstairs with Janice. She's having a hard time settling down."

I took the baby and walked her back and forth across the living room until she fell asleep. I put her to bed and then went to bed myself, knowing I'd be up in a few hours to give her a bottle.

The next morning after breakfast and while Lydia napped, Martha asked if I would go for a walk with her. Arden and Janice had gone with Jeremiah to fix a fence post, Clare was resting, Vater read the newspaper at the table, and Mutter was at the store.

The day was bright but cold. It had frosted that morning, and the world still had a silvery hint to it. We walked down the lane toward the road.

"I'm guessing you're wondering what's going on," Martha said.

I nodded. "Whatever you're doing doesn't seem like Red Cross work."

"It actually is." Martha spoke softly. "But there's also some crossover work with a government agency. Some of the refugees have information the government needs."

"Oh." I had no idea what she was talking about, though I did recall that Esther still corresponded with her uncle in East Berlin. Perhaps Martha needed to speak with her about that. "Is what you're doing safe?"

"Yes," Martha said.

"Does George know what you're doing?"

"Yes," she said again. "He's involved with it sometimes too."

"Is Esther working for someone?"

"No. She truly is a refugee."

I hesitated for a moment and then said, "Lorraine, who works at the Lancaster Red Cross office, heard you came home because of illness. I thought you came home for work."

Martha responded without hesitation. "I came because of Clare—but decided to combine work with my trip too. It made sense to get as much done as possible while I was home." Then she paused. "Please don't say anything to anyone else. Not even to Vater. Especially not to Mutter. I don't want Mutter writing to Josef about anything and having someone in Germany intercept the letter."

Martha hadn't completely trusted our mother during the war when it came to where Mutter's allegiance was—her home country of Germany or her adopted country of the United States. There was no way Mutter would hold any allegiance to the Russian quadrant of Germany, but she might write something to Josef that could fall into the wrong hands and endanger Martha.

"Don't even tell Clare," Martha pleaded. "I don't want her to worry. I'm telling you because I know it was obvious Mr. Wilson and I needed to speak with Esther about something."

"Thank you for letting me know," I said.

"I'm leaving this afternoon for a week or so for more Red Cross business." Martha put her hand on my shoulder. "But then I'll come back here before I return to Germany."

After Martha left, Mutter talked about her good work with the Red Cross. "Those refugees need her. How wonderful to have someone who helped you in Germany come to America to make sure you have what you need."

Clearly Mutter thought Martha's work was all for the Red Cross. When I didn't answer her, Mutter crossed her arms. "Don't you think so, Rosene?"

"Jah," I answered. "She's doing good work." At least I hoped she was.

Our Englisch neighbors, the Smiths, had purchased a brand-new set of encyclopedias from a door-to-door sales-man a few months ago. They had a boy around Arden's age and were always friendly with us. Mrs. Smith had told me I was welcome to use the books anytime. The next week, I visited our neighbors while the children were resting.

Mrs. Smith showed me the encyclopedia set in the book-case in the living room. I sat on the floor and took out the *U* volume, flipped to *United States Government*, and scanned through the different departments—agriculture, education, treasury, war. I kept reading. I came to the Federal Bureau of Investigation, the Office of Strategic Services, and then the National Security Council.

I startled as I realized Mrs. Smith was looking over my shoulder.

She asked, "Are you interested in US intelligence?"

My face grew warm. "I'm interested in what's going on in Germany with the blockade and all. I was wondering what agencies might be working there."

She sat down in the nearest chair. "There's a new agency— one that was formed last year. Mr. Smith was telling me about it. A friend of his cousin works for it. It's called the Central Intelligence Agency. This friend has been sent to Europe. I don't know where, though."

"Interesting." But I doubted a woman—especially a Red Cross worker—would be gathering intelligence for the new agency. Although Martha had been in Berlin.

I thanked Mrs. Smith, told her good-bye, and started home. We'd hoped the end of World War II would bring peace, but now a new kind of war waged. I hoped Martha truly was safe. And I hoped she wasn't going against our tenets of nonresistance, whatever she was doing.

A week later, Jeremiah's mother came over to help Clare, and I managed to go into town to help with the refugee lunch. Esther planned it, and Mrs. Fogel helped her. Zeke drove me and helped out. After we finished, we gave Esther a ride to her apartment.

"Come up for a minute," she said to me. "I have something I need to give you."

I followed Esther into the building and up the staircase to her apartment. She closed the door behind us and then motioned me toward her little table with the two chairs. After we both sat down, she said, "I'm going back to Germany."

I gasped. "Why?"

She spoke softly, even though no one else could possibly hear her. "I'm going to help Martha."

"But why? She barely got you out before."

"I can help," she said. "At least I think I can."

"But how?"

She pursed her lips together. "I can't say."

"Where are you going?"

"Berlin. My uncle . . . I know you won't say anything. He works as a guard and travels with scientists who are working on a special project." Her eyes grew large as she spoke. "If I can find out where he goes with the scientists, that will help your country."

"Oh, Esther," I said. "That doesn't sound safe." Why

would Martha allow Esther to do such a thing? I shivered. "How will you get there?"

"On one of the American counter-blockade planes." She took a piece of paper from the top of her bookshelf. "You can write to me at an address in West Berlin, where I hope to live. Although I'll be going into East Berlin, maybe even staying there some." She slid the paper across the table. "Will you write to me?"

"Jah, of course." I took the paper. "Do I need to be careful about what I say?"

"Don't ask any questions except how I'm doing. Write about your daily life—that's what I want to read about." She handed me another piece of paper and a pencil. "I need your mailing address."

I wrote it down.

"I'll write to you as soon as I get there," she said. "I'm leaving next week. I can't tell anyone else where I'm going. Once I'm gone, when Mrs. Fogel and Lorraine ask about me, tell them a family member in Germany contacted me in need of help, and I returned."

She stood. "Thank you."

I stood too.

She stepped forward and kissed me on one cheek and then the other. "I'm indebted to you for all you've done for me. I hope we'll meet again someday."

"I hope so too," I said. "When will you come back?"

"I'm not sure," Esther said.

"*Will* you come back?"

"Jah, I believe so."

I hugged her. "May God keep you."

"And you," Esther answered.

On the way home, Zeke kept quiet. Thankfully he didn't

ask me what Esther had given me. When we reached the farm, the blue coupe Martha had been driving was parked alongside the shed.

"Martha returned," Zeke said.

"Jah."

Zeke spoke slowly. "She's not working for the Red Cross, is she?"

"She says she is." I thought of Martha telling me that Red Cross workers were required to remain neutral. It didn't appear she was meeting the requirement. I opened the car door. "I need to start dinner. Would you eat with us?"

Zeke smiled. "Sure. Maybe Martha will tell us what's really going on."

Zeke did come to dinner, but Martha didn't. She came down the back staircase from her room and told me she had another refugee she needed to see in Lancaster. "Tell everyone I'm sorry to miss out," she said. "And sadly, I'll need to leave tomorrow. I'll see everyone at breakfast."

Zeke raised his eyebrows when I relayed the message but didn't say anything.

Clare sat at the table with us, beside Janice, while Lydia slept on top of a folded quilt in a wooden box near the stove. When Arden knocked his glass of milk over, Clare jumped and then burst into tears. Arden started to cry too. "There, there," Jeremiah said. "It's just milk. We have plenty of it."

Clare tried to smile at his joke but instead cried more. I cleaned up the milk and then comforted Arden. When Clare couldn't stop crying, Jeremiah helped her to the bedroom.

"I think she has the baby blues," Mutter said.

"What's that?" I asked.

"Sometimes mothers of newborns get it," Mutter said. "Especially when they had a hard delivery and recovery. I read about it in a magazine."

That made sense. And I guessed the fact Clare couldn't have any more children probably weighed heavily on her too. No one talked about it, and I was afraid perhaps it was because of me. Clare had three children—I'd never have any. Did everyone think I'd be offended if they felt sympathetic toward Clare? It was a loss for her and Jeremiah and for the entire family, including me, that she couldn't have more children.

The next morning, as I cooked breakfast with Lydia sleeping in her box by the stove, Martha came down the back staircase again, this time with her suitcase. She put it down by the door and then stepped to my side.

"Is anyone around?"

I shook my head. "Vater isn't up yet. Neither is Clare." Mutter was upstairs with Arden and Janice, but Martha would already know that. "And Jeremiah and Zeke are still doing the milking."

"Good. I have a proposition I need to speak with you about."

I set the pot of porridge on the stovetop to keep warm. "What is it?"

"I need a translator in Germany, someone I can trust. In Hamburg—where it's safe. Would you be willing to come for six months and see if you want to stay on permanently?"

My head spun for a moment. *Germany*. "No." I was surprised at how easy it was to say that word when normally I'd do anything in the world to help Martha. "I can't. I don't want to go back."

For a moment, she seemed disappointed but then appeared to shift to being concerned. "Do you plan to go with Zeke?"

"I—" The baby began to cry. As I picked her up, I had a moment of clarity. I couldn't go with Zeke either.

"Will you think about coming to Germany later?" she asked.

"I'll write to you," I said, "and let you know."

She stepped toward me and rubbed the top of Lydia's head. "Speaking of writing, if you get letters from Esther, would you send the last two pages of hers with the letters you write to me? It will make sense when you see her letters."

"Jah," I answered. "I can do that."

"Thank you," Martha said. "Please tell Vater and Clare good-bye. Tell them I didn't want to wake them. I'll stop by the barn and tell Jeremiah and Zeke I'm leaving."

She hugged Lydia and me at the same time.

"Be careful," I said to her.

"I will—what I'm doing isn't dangerous." She laughed a little. "They don't let women do any of the dangerous work, believe me."

I hoped what she said was true.

Life went on. Zeke continued working with Jeremiah on the farm. Lydia kept growing. So did Arden and Janice. And Clare slowly regained her strength. I continued to care for the children, cook, and clean. I didn't help with the refugee lunches, and no one contacted me about Esther, thankfully.

The first of December, I received a letter from her. She wrote that she was doing well and settling into life in Berlin. She wrote about the weather—cold—and meeting an Englishwoman who was an aid worker. The letter was short, just a few paragraphs. She wrote that she hoped I would enjoy her poetry and then signed the letter *Esther*. The next two pages were some sort of German poem that didn't make sense to me, about goblins and dark forests. I wrote a letter to Martha and put the two pages of poetry in the envelope.

Was Martha promoting peace?

Was I promoting peace by forwarding Esther's poetry?

As the weather grew colder, Zeke grew more restless. A few times, he asked Vater if he could borrow the Studebaker, and because Zeke had been so kind about driving us places, Vater allowed him to.

He didn't ask me to go with him, and I didn't ask him where he went. The rift between us grew wider.

Three days after Christmas, after the milking and break-fast, Zeke played with Arden and Janice in the living room. Then he came into the kitchen and lifted Lydia from the big-ger box she now slept in and cradled her for a few minutes. She smiled up at him. Then he put her back down.

"I'm leaving," he said.

"Where are you going?"

"South for now—somewhere warmer. Probably Texas. Then west, back to California." He brushed his fingers against my cheek. "I know I asked you to come with me, but I don't expect you to. I'm sorry for how things worked out, but I can't stay."

I nodded. I could see that.

"And I don't think you can leave."

I nodded again. I couldn't speak.

His eyes grew misty. "Maybe I'll come home at some point. I'll write and let you know. I don't want to leave you hanging. I need more time is all."

I'd thought I'd known Zeke as well as I'd ever known

251

anyone, but standing in the kitchen I realized I didn't know him at all. His inner life seemed as big and vast as the entire US. And I realized mine must seem as big and foreign as the world to him.

I thought when we were contained to Lancaster County our two inner worlds overlapped. And maybe they did. But it wasn't enough. He was leaving. I was staying.

Only God knew if he'd ever come back.

· 24 ·

Treva

When Rosene stopped the story, she said, "I'm going to go rest for a bit."

I turned down the heat on the green beans. "Would you like me to wake you when it's time to eat?"

"No." Rosene stood. "I'm not hungry. I may just sleep through."

"Are you feeling all right?"

"Jah," she answered.

I watched as she shuffled toward the hall, her heart-shaped Kapp nearly as big as her shoulders. Was she shrinking? She seemed smaller than ever. Did telling the story make her tired? Or had Drew's questions, along with the story, brought up too many sad memories?

I understood what Rosene meant when she described her and Zeke's inner worlds. There was so much that Pierre and I shared—our faith and wanting to help others, mainly. But there were things we couldn't comprehend about what the other needed and wanted. Committing to someone took more than common interests. It took more than love. It took a shared vision. Rosene and Zeke didn't have that—at least not at that moment in time. And Pierre and I didn't have it either.

I found it interesting that Zeke said he was heading south first in December of 1948. Tennessee was south, although I doubted it was that warm in the winter. He'd have to keep going to South Carolina or Georgia or Florida to find that. But he'd said he was going to Texas. Had he changed his mind and gone to Tennessee instead?

As I pulled the meatloaf out of the oven, Dawdi opened the kitchen door. "Treva," he called out, "you have a phone call from Bennie's Buggy Rides." He grinned. "If you need to borrow a buggy, you can use mine."

"Ha ha. I'll be right out." I turned off the burners on the stove as I puzzled over why someone from Bennie's Buggy Rides would call me. I saw their buggies around, giving tourists rides. And sometimes they stopped at the antique store.

Dawdi and Kamil were finishing up the milking as I stepped into the office.

"Hello," I said. "This is Treva Zimmerman."

The woman on the other end of the line introduced herself as Eliza Yoder. "I'm Bennie's wife," she said. "We're in need of someone to do an Amish dinner for a group of ten tourists tomorrow. Our usual family had an emergency and canceled. I heard from the Smiths—my cousin is married to Carol's nephew—that you put on a fundraising dinner recently. Would you be interested?"

A tourist dinner wouldn't be much different from a refugee dinner—except I wouldn't have Zaida and Cala to do the cooking. But I thought Sharon might help me. And hopefully Mammi would too.

"Let me have your phone number," I said. "I'll check with my grandparents."

First I called Sharon. After I explained the situation, she said, "Sounds like fun. I'd like that, as long as I can dress normal."

"Of course," I said.

Normal for her was a simple dress. She wore her hair short, and I'd never seen her wear a Kapp or even a scarf.

"If you need more help, ask Gabe," Sharon said. "He got cleared to drive and can do some shopping as long as the bags aren't heavy. He can't set up tables, but he can set up chairs."

"I'll ask him." Maybe I'd ask Drew too. Perhaps he could talk about Anabaptists and nonresistance and what he'd learned in his research about Lancaster County.

During supper, I told Mammi and Dawdi about the request. Rosene stayed in her room.

Mammi frowned. "I think that would be too much for Rosene. The dinner last Saturday evening made her tired, and Zaida and Cala did most of the work."

"I wouldn't want Rosene to help," I explained. "In fact, she could stay completely out of sight—but I'll talk with her first, of course. Sharon said she would help me. And I'll ask Gabe too. I thought I'd ask Drew if he'd like to talk with the guests about what he's researching and learning. We can do our usual roasted chicken, mashed potatoes, green beans, creamed corn, applesauce, and bread. Two pies will be plenty. I'll do cherry pies since the filling is already made."

Dawdi said, "Priscilla, I understand your concerns, but if Treva wants to do it, I think it would be a good experience. Several families increase their incomes with these dinners. If Treva—"

If.

"—does want to stay on the farm—"

How could I stay on the farm if he planned to sell it?

"—it might be a way to make it more stable." Dawdi gave me a nod.

That sounded like a lot of dinners, but I guessed every bit helped. But above that, was Dawdi coming up with a new plan? Perhaps one involving Gabe taking over more responsibilities, along with me staying on the farm, if I chose to do so?

After I finished the dishes, Rosene came out of her room. "I'm a little hungry after all," she said. "I'll help myself to some leftovers."

As she took the meatloaf out of the refrigerator, I told her about the phone call from Bennie's Buggy Rides.

"That's a wonderful opportunity," she said. "I think you should do it."

"We're worried it will wear you out."

"If I'm tired, I promise to stay in my room."

"How would you feel if we included Drew? And asked him to share about his research?"

"That's a great idea."

"Will you speak more with him about Zeke?"

She shook her head. "I can't think of anything that might help."

"You said Zeke was headed to Texas."

"That's what he said, but I have no idea. He also said he'd write within six months, but I never heard from him. His mother received a few letters over the years." Her shoulders drooped. "Probably more than that. After a while, Clare stopped telling me when someone heard from him. I don't want to speculate about where he went."

My heart hurt for Rosene. How could Zeke be so cold? She didn't deserve that.

"I don't know why Zeke didn't write, but I forgave him a long time ago. He was young and full of life. I don't hold it against him. And if Drew is Zeke's grandson, I want to know the truth. That's what's best for Drew—and for Arden and all of you. You would be cousins." She smiled. "And no one can have enough cousins. There's actually a bit of a shortage in this branch of the Zimmerman family."

That was true. "I'll go speak with Gabe and see if he'd like to help."

A few minutes later, I knocked on the Dawdi Haus door. Gabe answered, and I got right to the point. "We might have a tourist dinner at our house tomorrow evening. Your mom is going to help. Do you want to?"

"Sure."

"She said you could help with the shopping, as long as the bags aren't too heavy."

"I can do that," he said. "I can go in the morning."

"We won't need much. I'll make a list and give you the money. You can drive my van."

He seemed pleased. "I'll help with the setup tomorrow afternoon too."

"Thank you." I started to leave, but then turned toward him. "How are you doing with Conrad and Ivy leaving?"

He shrugged. "About the same." He smiled a little. "But honestly, it helps to be staying here. And it helps to be needed, both in the store and with your events, even if I can't do what I used to do."

"You'll be able to soon," I said.

"Yes. In a couple of months, I should almost be as good as new." He laughed. "Although I wasn't that great before."

"No, you were," I said. "And you will be. You and Conrad both have been so good to Dawdi and Mammi. And Rosene. You've been the grandsons they never had."

Gabe looked as if he might cry. "Don't say that. We're not family. Well, Conrad is, but I'm not."

"You are." Mammi and Dawdi adored Gabe as much as they did Conrad.

He shook his head a little. "Regardless, I'll stick around as long as your grandparents will have me. Although I know I need to start coming up with a plan soon and looking for a real job. That sort of thing."

"I need to figure that out too."

"But if you wanted the farm, don't you think you could have it?"

I shrugged. "Dawdi hasn't offered it to me. And like I said, I don't know any women running a farm around here. Especially not a Mennonite woman."

"You'd be good at it."

I met Gabe's gaze. "Thank you. That's one of the nicest things you've ever said to me."

He flashed me an impish grin. "Don't let it go to your head."

As I walked to the barn to call Eliza, I wondered if my grandparents would have considered leaving the farm to Conrad and Gabe if Ivy, Brenna, and I had never come into Mammi and Dawdi's lives. Or would they have left it to us girls even if they'd never met us? Most likely it would have gone to Dad, and then he would have had to decide whether to sell it or keep it and leave it to us.

That night, as I made a menu, a shopping list, a prep timeline, and a production timeline for the tourist dinner, I thought of Misty and Shawn's Resort of the Midnight Sun.

Planning a tourist dinner was sort of like planning a wedding dinner, I imagined, but not as stressful.

I enjoyed farming, but event planning had piqued my interest. Now that I'd helped put on the refugee dinner and was getting the experience of planning a tourist dinner, event planning appealed to me even more.

I texted Drew to see if he'd be interested in coming to the dinner tomorrow at five with a group of tourists and then giving a fifteen-minute talk. I added,

> Dinner is on us!

I'd love that. Thank you. Do you mind if I bring my girlfriend? I'll pay for her.

> We'd love to have her join us. We'll cover her cost too.

I remembered that her name was Stephanie and that she was a professor at Elizabethtown College. I looked forward to meeting her.

Gabe bought the few groceries I needed the next morning. Rosene rested that afternoon and then peeled potatoes while I made the pies. Sharon prepared the chickens and put them in the oven, then made the cucumber and onion salad and put on the green beans and creamed corn to heat.

Dawdi and I extended the kitchen table for sixteen—Sharon and I would serve while Dawdi, Mammi, Gabe, Drew, and Stephanie sat with the guests—and Rosene too, if she felt up to it.

Dawdi and Gabe greeted the guests as they arrived and offered them lemonade on the porch. Rosene stayed in the kitchen, and Mammi hadn't arrived from the store yet. She was our wild card—would she be warm to the guests? Or annoyed they'd invaded her home? Sometimes it was hard to tell with Mammi.

Sharon and I had the food ready to go by five fifteen. Gabe came in to tell us that the guests had arrived, including Drew and Stephanie, and Dawdi led them into the house through the front door.

Drew introduced Stephanie to me. She wore jeans and a sweater and wore her long hair in a ponytail. She smiled as she shook my hand. "I'm so pleased to meet you," she said. "Drew has told me so much about all of you."

I smiled back. "Welcome. I'm so glad you're here."

As she and Drew joined everyone else around the table, I wondered what it was like for Drew to be in a state of limbo, wondering if perhaps Zeke could be his grandfather. I hoped we could find out for sure. If nothing else, I could always take a DNA test.

Dawdi welcomed everyone and then explained that we gave thanks with a silent prayer and led us in that. Then, as Sharon and I brought out the food, Mammi slipped into the house and took her place at the table.

As the guests began to eat, Dawdi introduced Sharon and me, and then Gabe, Drew, and Stephanie. He talked about the farm and the history of it a little, and then he introduced Mammi. "Priscilla operates Amish Antiques. You may have noticed it as you reached the farm."

"We did," a woman from New York said. "Are you open tomorrow?"

"No," Mammi answered. "But we'll be open on Monday morning at ten." She paused a moment and then said, "But if you would like to see the store, we could go over after dinner. The building is over one hundred years old, and the women in the family have been operating a store on the premises since the 1920s." It was quite the monologue for Mammi. She added, "I met Arden's mother at the store when I was five—she gave me a peppermint stick. I met Arden and his sister Janice that day too."

I'd never heard that story.

"I'd love to see it," one of the women said. Immediately, the other guests, except for the two tweens, added their agreement.

One of the men asked Dawdi about his dairy herd. Dawdi gave him some information and then said, "We can go out to the barn after dinner too."

Another woman asked me what my tasks around the farm were. I explained that I helped where I was needed—in the house, at the store, and on the farm.

"What are your plans for the future?" she asked.

"I'm working on that." I smiled, hoping that would dissuade her from asking more.

"Are you still in school?"

"I've taken classes at the community college," I said.

Dawdi cleared his throat. "We have an unconventional Amish household. Treva has two older sisters, and all of the girls are Mennonite. Ivy, the oldest, has her master's degree in social work. Brenna has a degree in computer security and now lives and works in Ukraine."

The woman's eyebrows shot up. "No grandsons?"

Dawdi shook his head.

She asked, "Who will take over the farm?"

Dawdi shrugged. "We'll see."

"Would one of the girls be allowed to take it over someday, as a Mennonite?" a man asked.

"Jah," Dawdi said. "The farm was passed from my Mennonite grandparents to my Amish parents in the 1940s. It can be passed back to a Mennonite family."

"But would a woman be allowed to farm it?"

"I'm not sure," Dawdi answered, his voice low.

Gabe caught my gaze, but I didn't respond.

⌇

A half hour later, Drew spoke about his research into nonresistance and Anabaptists in Lancaster County and their varied responses—from a conscientious objector during World War II to a man who had grown up Mennonite and recently served in the Army Reserve. Sharon and I worked quietly to dish up the pie, and I thought about the farm.

A few times lately, Dawdi had come inside during the day to take a short nap. Farming was hard work—from feeding and milking the cows to calving to caring for the horses, mucking out the stables and dragging the fields, to growing silage and alfalfa to feed the cows. Then there was tilling and planting the garden and taking care of it and the flower beds. Because Mammi ran her own business, Dawdi was responsible for things that a farm wife would usually take care of. Not to mention the paperwork involved with the dairy farm and managing the herd.

Now with Rosene ill, we were taking on her household responsibilities too. It was incredible all the work Rosene had still been doing, really. The current workload of the barn and farm wasn't sustainable for three elderly people, even with help. A final decision about the farm was probably going to have to happen sooner rather than later.

When Drew finished his talk, he asked if anyone had any questions.

One of the men asked, "How did Anabaptist people in Europe respond to World War Two?"

"I've been researching that this week." Drew glanced at Rosene. "Would you want to answer the question?"

"Sure." Rosene folded her hands in her lap. "I was born into a Mennonite family in Frankfurt, Germany. My mother's family was part of a Mennonite community, and my father joined as an adult. He was a college professor, and he also worked to settle Mennonite refugees from Europe in other countries, such as the US and Canada. By the mid-1930s, he worked with the Nazis on policies affecting Mennonites. Young men in our Mennonite church were conscripted into the German army or joined on their own, including my future brother-in-law. My sister ended up working as an assistant to a Nazi officer. It was a complex situation, but one factor was the Mennonites in Ukraine had been persecuted and starved by the Russians, so Mennonites in Germany believed that the Nazis were the better option, compared to communism."

"When did you come to the US?" a woman asked.

"Nineteen thirty-nine," Rosene answered. "Arden's mother, Clare, brought me to the US."

"Do you mind if I ask how old you are now?" the woman asked.

"Ninety-three." Rosene smiled. "And yet sometimes it feels as if it were yesterday."

I decided to step in with the plates of pie on a tray, afraid the conversation would be too taxing on Rosene, but it shifted to people sharing about their family's World War II stories as the guests ate. A woman's grandmother served in the Women's Army Corps. Another woman's father survived Pearl Harbor and went on to fight in the Pacific. A man's father fought in North Africa.

After they'd finished their dessert, Sharon and I cleared

and scraped the plates and added them to the pile of dishes ready to be washed while everyone else followed Mammi to Amish Antiques. I told Sharon and Gabe to go too. I figured the more people to interact with the guests the better. Drew and Stephanie went along also.

Once everyone left the kitchen, I turned to Rosene, who still sat at the table. "You should go rest. You must be tired."

"I'm not," she said. "How about if I tell you a little more of the story before Arden and Priscilla return."

I grabbed the dishcloth to clean the table as I said, "I'd love that. I've been thinking about Zeke. About all of you."

Sometimes it felt as if Rosene's Mutter and Vater and Clare and Jeremiah were still on the farm with us. I couldn't see them—but I could feel them.

· 25 ·

Rosene

Zeke left Lancaster County right before a snowstorm hit. I longed to go after him, to tell him I'd made a mistake. To beg him not to leave me behind. But I had no idea where to go. I hoped he was traveling by train or bus and not looking for rides along the way in the winter storm.

On New Year's Day, Clare fell ill. Then the children. Then Vater. It was soon obvious it was the flu. We closed the store, and Mutter and Jeremiah and I cared for the sick, but then Mutter caught the flu too. The farmhand Jeremiah had scrambled to hire to replace Zeke also became sick. I helped Jeremiah with the milking and then cooked and cleaned, delivered aspirin and meals, and took care of Lydia.

A week later, I rocked Lydia in the living room. With each back and forth, I felt worse. First my head. Then my throat. I needed to start dinner. I needed to help Jeremiah with the milking. I needed to give the baby a bottle.

Jeremiah came in to see why I hadn't gone out to help, finding me in the chair.

"I can't move," I said.

He felt my forehead and then took Lydia to Clare. He helped me to the sofa, covered me with a quilt, and brought me an aspirin. He went out and did the milking by himself.

Mutter managed to fix milk toast for dinner. Clare saw to Arden and Janice while Vater held Lydia.

The others continued to get better while I grew worse. Jeremiah sent for the doctor, who declared that, besides having the flu, I was exhausted. Caring for Clare and the children, along with cooking and cleaning, had caught up with me, not to mention Zeke leaving. I was spent.

Jeremiah helped me up to my room, where I collapsed in bed and slept twelve hours straight. Mutter brought me aspirin and soup. Clare came in and mopped my forehead with a cool cloth. Still, I continued to run a fever. Jeremiah sent for the doctor again.

I heard Mutter say to Clare, "We've expected too much from Rosene."

"I'm better now," Clare said. "I'll care for her."

"I'll keep the store closed as long as needed," Mutter said.

"And Jeremiah's farmhand said he'd be able to return tomorrow. We'll get through this. But Rosene must rest."

I did. Slowly, I began to regain my strength. But it took months.

In May, when the Berlin Blockade ended and land access to West Berlin reopened, I wondered if Martha and George would return. I thought of Esther. Perhaps she'd return to Lancaster now that the crisis was over.

Or was it?

On a warm mid-July day, I was sitting on the porch, holding a sleeping Lydia in my arms, when a car turned into the driveway. It was Martha.

She climbed out of the car and waved, then she bounded up the steps. She seemed even taller and more confident than ever. "How are you feeling?"

I hadn't written to her since I fell ill. I hadn't had a letter from Esther to forward and hadn't felt up to writing Martha without that incentive. "How did you know I've been unwell?"

"Clare wrote and told me."

"Oh."

I *was* better and doing more. I'd done the wash. I'd gone on walks with Arden and Janice. I'd cooked dinner a few times and had been doing the dishes for a few weeks.

Martha sat down beside me. "I have a surprise for you."

I blinked a couple of times but didn't answer.

"I'm taking you to the Maryland shore for a vacation."

"Why?" We didn't take vacations. It wasn't a word we even used. When you lived on a dairy farm, you stayed on the farm.

"Because it would be good for you. I need a vacation too. I already wrote Clare about my plan. Jeremiah's mother will help her with the children and the cooking and cleaning."

I hadn't seen Elizabeth since before Zeke left. I wondered if she blamed me.

"We're going to leave tomorrow," Martha said.

"How long will we be gone?"

"It depends," she answered. "We'll need to see how you're feeling and talk more."

I sighed. "Are you up to something?"

She stood. "We'll talk. Right now, I need to go in and say hello to the others."

I stood too, holding on tightly to Lydia, who had begun

267

to stir. Martha took the baby out of my arms. Lydia opened her eyes and smiled up at her.

As Martha stepped through the front door, she called out, "Look what I found on the front porch."

Martha and I did go to Maryland, to Chesapeake Beach. We stayed in a cottage a block from the ocean and walked on the boardwalk over the water and picnicked in the park. We rode the carousel and had dinner at a restaurant one night.

With a camera Martha brought, we took photos of the ocean landscapes and the town. We even took a few photos of each other.

I'd always been close to Clare, but in many ways I felt safest with Martha. She'd always been capable and confident, but her travels and work had empowered her even more. And, frankly, the mystery of what her work entailed fascinated me.

One evening, as we walked on the boardwalk, I said, "I haven't had a letter from Esther in over six months. Have you heard from her?"

"That's why I'm here," Martha answered. "I need your help."

A sea gull swooped down in front of us. "Is Esther in danger?" I asked.

"I don't know." Martha slowed her pace. "I wouldn't ask you what I'm going to if I could think of another solution. And I can only tell you my plan a step at a time." She stopped walking and looked behind us and then ahead. We were completely alone now, and dusk was falling. "Would you be willing to go back to Germany with me?"

"Does this have to do with Esther?"

"Yes. I can't say more than that, though. Not here."

I started walking. Martha fell in beside me. Surely she could do whatever needed to be done to help Esther. How would I, a Mennonite woman from the US, be able to do what Martha couldn't? But Martha wouldn't ask me if she didn't think I could help. And Esther had no one except Martha. And me.

Martha asked, "If you decided to go, do you feel well enough to make the trip?"

I nodded.

"I thought I found someone who could help, but her German isn't good enough. I had to come to the US on other business and decided I had to at least ask you."

"What are you planning?"

Martha glanced around and then said, "I need someone to make contact with Esther in East Berlin."

"This isn't Red Cross work, is it?"

Martha shook her head. "I can't say more. But to be honest, this plan isn't without risks."

I hesitated but then said, "I'm willing to take a risk for Esther."

"Denki." Martha leaned toward me, her arm bumping my shoulder. "We'll need to go to Frankfurt first, to have a cover for you being in Germany."

I pursed my lips together. I'd planned to never return. "How long do we need to stay in Frankfurt?"

"A couple of days, both going and coming."

I shivered, even though the evening was warm and muggy. "How will we get to Berlin? On the highway?"

She shook her head. "I'm going to try to get seats on a flight going in, although now that the blockade has ended, there aren't as many flights in and out."

"Have you been to Berlin since a year ago?"

She nodded. "A few times."

"What will I tell everyone back home?"

"That we're going to Frankfurt to see Onkel Josef, whose health is deteriorating. I'll call Mutter in the morning."

"Will I be home in two weeks?"

"I believe so, yes. That will give us two days of travel on each end, three days in Frankfurt, coming and going, and a couple of days in Berlin."

"What about Vater Josef and Lena? Have you contacted them?"

"I have." She put her hand on my shoulder. "Josef is eager for you to come. It's true his health is worse. He's been diagnosed with congestive heart failure. Lena doesn't think he has much longer."

"What about Lena? Is she eager for me to come?"

Martha shrugged. "She's not opposed to it."

Perhaps Lena wouldn't interact with me this time. "I'll go—for Esther."

Two days later, we arrived at Vater Josef's at three in the afternoon. I noticed the house was shabbier than the year before. More peeling paint. A crack in the stoop. No flowers planted in the window boxes.

Martha knocked several times before the door finally swung open. Vater Josef stood before us, wearing trousers that hung loosely, a baggy sweater, and slippers.

Tears sprang into his eyes. "Rosene," he said. "Have you come to tell me good-bye for good?"

~~~~~~~

The time with Vater Josef, Lena, and Garit was tense, even worse than before. Lena didn't take any time off and wasn't around during the day, but in the evenings, she was terse and snippy. Garit worked on his thesis and mostly locked himself in the study. The pounding of typewriter keys seemed constant. Vater Josef shuffled when he walked and spent most of his time in his room.

Lena hadn't shopped in preparation for our arrival. There wasn't much food in the house, so Martha and I purchased groceries at the neighborhood store, a stein of beer at the closest *Kneipe*, and a metal can of cream from the milkman. We made a dinner of bratwurst, red cabbage, potato gratin, and Bavarian cream for dessert. No one spoke of anything of consequence, not even of Vater Josef's health. Martha took photos of Vater Josef and Lena, the house and garden, and me.

The next afternoon, Martha and I walked back to the neighborhood store, where she bought the Frankfurt newspaper. As we retraced our steps, she showed me the front-page article. The United States Senate had approved NATO—the North Atlantic Treaty Organization.

"It's a military alliance," Martha explained. "Between the US and European countries—but not West Germany. Not yet. Perhaps in time. All the members will agree to defend each other against third parties."

"Even the Soviet Union?" I asked.

"Yes. Especially the Soviet Union."

Martha had managed to secure a plane ride for us from Hamburg to Berlin, but that meant a train ride to Hamburg. The day we left, she packed one suitcase for us to share. We took a taxi to a house near the Hamburg train station, and Martha gave me clothes to change into. A plaid skirt, a white blouse, and a worn sweater. The shoes were scuffed.

She instructed me to brush my hair out. Then she took out a pair of scissors. "May I cut your hair to your shoulders?"

"Why?"

"I need you to match a specific description."

I nodded.

After she finished, she brushed my hair again. Then she stared at me in the mirror and said, "Perfect." She grabbed her camera and took a photo.

She put the scissors and my clothes in the suitcase and took out a passport. But it wasn't green. It wasn't mine.

It was a new West German passport—for Esther Lang, born February 12, 1925. In the photograph, she wore her hair shoulder-length. And she wore a sweater and a white blouse.

I glanced in the mirror. Martha stood behind me. "I'm to be Esther?"

She nodded. "If you're up to doing this."

"I have no idea what I'm doing."

"I need you to go to Esther's uncle's apartment and see if she's there."

"Can you go with me?"

"No," Martha said. "I'd be recognized. I don't want anyone to connect Esther to me, especially someone who may have seen us together previously. Initially, I didn't think it would be dangerous for you to go in, but I spoke with one of our colleagues while we were in Frankfurt and a few things have grown more concerning."

"Such as?"

"It seems Esther's uncle is working with high-ranking Soviet Communists, more deeply than we realized. We're afraid he became suspicious that Esther was looking for information."

"What do you think could go wrong?"

"Someone might know right away that you're not Esther, especially if she's left the area."

"'Left the area'? That sounds as if she may have been kidnapped." Or worse, killed.

"She's been silent. We don't know if it's by her own volition or imposed by someone else." Martha rubbed the side of her neck. "We need information, that's all. If you can determine if she's at her uncle's apartment, that would be helpful. If you can get her out, that would be best."

"Don't you have people watching the apartment? Can't they tell?"

"Yes, but no one has seen her in over two months. She was living in West Berlin and went to visit her uncle in East Berlin. She was spotted going into the apartment building but not coming out."

"I'm to go knock on the apartment door?" I asked. "If the uncle has done something to her, then he'll know I'm not Esther."

"We're going to draw him away. Try the door, and if it's not unlocked, you'll have to break the lock. We'll give you a file—the lock won't hold. All you have to do is go in the apartment and look for Esther. If she's not there, come out immediately."

Doubts swamped me. "Are you sure someone else can't go?"

"I can't find anyone else who can walk into East Berlin in broad daylight without being suspicious, who also looks similar to Esther and is fluent in German."

"But I don't have a Berlin accent."

"It's close enough—speak as little as possible," Martha answered. "Everyone in East Berlin is suspicious of everyone else. They won't be any more suspicious of you." Martha took a purse from the suitcase and handed it to me. "Are you willing to do this?"

I thought it through for a minute and then said, "Yes. For Esther."

"Thank you." She gave me a hug. Then she put Esther's passport in a false bottom in the purse and mine in the main section. "My colleague who picks you up will give you instructions. Listen to them carefully." Martha closed the suitcase. "We need to get going."

We went straight to the airport, to an area with a fleet of US military airplanes. We were soon on board, along with crates of supplies and ten or so military personnel, strapped to seats positioned parallel to the wall of the plane. The engines of the plane were so loud we couldn't talk.

When we landed, Martha told me she would get off first and then a middle-aged woman wearing a blue velvet hat would take me to her apartment for the night. "Her name is Betty. You can trust her. There are pajamas and toiletries in the suitcase for you."

"Where are you going?"

"To our apartment."

"Is George here?"

She nodded. "Betty will take care of you. She'll make sure we're reunited. Don't worry."

• 26 •

Treva

Dawdi and Mammi came through the kitchen door, laughing, and interrupted Rosene's story.

"What's so funny?" I'd finished the dishes and sat at the table, and I was a little annoyed to have the story stop.

"We made more in an hour in the store with the dinner group than we did in the last week," Mammi said. "That alone made the dinner worth it."

"Would you want to do it again?" I asked.

Mammi glanced at Dawdi, who shrugged.

"Jah," Mammi said. "I'd do it again. I enjoyed it. How about you?" she asked me. "Would you do it again?"

"I would. I thought it went well." I stood. "Did Drew and Stephanie go to the store?"

"Jah," Mammi said. "Drew is taking her home."

"I like her. I hope we see more of her," Dawdi said.

Both Mammi and Rosene agreed.

Mammi said, "Well, we have church in the morning. It's off to bed for us."

Rosene yawned and stood. "For me too."

"Bed or church?" I asked.

"Hopefully both," she answered.

After breakfast the next morning, I checked with Gabe to see if he wanted to go to the Mennonite church. He didn't, so I put on one of my Amish dresses and went to church with Mammi, Dawdi, and Rosene. I'd gone to their church exclusively the first few years I lived in Lancaster. Last summer, before I went to Haiti, I'd started going to the Mennonite church some too.

Everyone was overjoyed to see Rosene. She was one of the oldest members of the district and deeply loved. After the service, as the benches were being switched, Rosene chatted with a woman I hadn't seen before. As I approached them, Rosene said in English, "This is Treva, Arden and Priscilla's youngest granddaughter."

The woman, who appeared to be sixty or so, said, "Pleased to meet you," also in English.

"This is Sally Yoder, a cousin of yours," Rosene said. "She's visiting from Ohio."

"Nice to meet you," I said. "How are we related?"

"I'm first cousins with your grandfather," Sally answered. "Beth Zimmerman was my mother—she married John Yoder and they moved to Sugar Creek. I'm visiting my sister, who moved here from Ohio forty years ago."

There were so many relatives I'd never heard of, let alone met.

"I've been telling Treva about the olden days," Rosene said, "and thinking about Zeke. Did your mother hear from him over the years?"

"Who?" Sally asked.

"Zeke Zimmerman. He was the youngest of the siblings.

He worked on our farm with Jeremiah for several years, up until the time he left."

"Okay," Sally said. "I do remember her mentioning a younger brother who left. I don't remember ever meeting him, though. I'm not sure if she corresponded with him or not. She wrote to so many people."

"Any chance she saved her letters?" Rosene asked.

Sally shook her head. "No. I don't think so. When was he last heard from?"

"He was still in California around the time your grand-mother Elizabeth passed away. That was the last I heard." Rosene sounded so sad.

"So many have died or moved away," Sally said. "For how big the family was, only Arden still has a farm in the area, right?"

"Jah," Rosene said. "That's correct."

Sally excused herself, saying she saw someone she wanted to speak to.

"What was Zeke's middle name?" I asked.

"He didn't have one."

"Why not?"

"Not everyone did back then." Rosene shrugged. "Jer-emiah didn't have a middle name either."

"I'm going to keep looking for him," I said.

After the meal, we went home and Rosene took a nap while Dawdi and Mammi read in the living room. I went out to the picnic table and sat, thinking about Zeke. I'd do another search, focusing on California. And Texas. And Tennessee.

My phone dinged in my pocket. Brenna. It was a long text.

Things are going well here. Settling an estate in
Germany is straightforward and seems much

less complicated than it would be in the US. Per
Lena's will and German law, Rosene became
the owner of the house upon Lena's death, and
the money Lena left goes straight to Rosene
too. I've made arrangements to have it wired to
Rosene's account. I'll meet with the lawyer again
tomorrow to finalize the last of the details. I've
selected a company to manage the house as a
rental with a six-month to one-year lease, and
I've decided to have it come furnished, hoping
to appeal to people on short-term assignments
or with contracts in Frankfurt, or those who are
looking to relocate and want to take their time
finding a home. If that doesn't work, I'll look
into renting it out as a vacation home.

Are you free if I call this evening? Right after the
milking is done, so five your time. See if you can
get Rosene and Mammi to go out to the barn
too. I'd like to talk with all of you.

> Thank you for the information. I'll pass it on to
> Rosene. Yes, on your call. I'll let everyone know
> they're wanted in the barn at five.

At five, Mammi, Rosene, and I went out to the barn just
as Kamil was leaving.

"Tell Zaida and Cala hello," I said to him. "And that I'm
looking forward to seeing them tomorrow."

He smiled and nodded.

Mammi, Rosene, and I joined Dawdi in the office, and then
Gabe appeared at the door. "What's going on?" he asked.

"We're expecting a call from Brenna."

"Really? She doesn't like to talk on the phone. Is something up?"

"Probably." I grinned. "We'll—" My phone buzzed. I accepted the video call. "Hello!"

She came into view, with Johann beside her and Natasha behind the two of them.

I held the phone to show Dawdi, Mammi, and Rosene. And then Gabe.

"Is that Gabe?" Brenna asked.

"Yes," I answered.

Brenna waved and said, "Gabe! It's great to see you!"

"Are you in the study?" Rosene asked.

"Yes," Brenna answered. "In your house."

I squinted, trying to imagine Garit in the room, typing away on his thesis, the full bookcase behind him.

Brenna held up her hand. Was that a ring?

"I asked Brenna to marry me," Johann said.

Brenna gushed, "And I said yes."

Behind them, Natasha beamed.

"Congratulations!" I glanced from Brenna to Johann. "I'm so happy for both of you."

"Goodness," Rosene said. "Johann, did you propose in Frankfurt?"

"Yes," he answered. "I wanted to officially ask Brenna to marry me in the city where we first met. I proposed in the garden of your house."

Rosene grinned.

"We're so happy for both of you," Mammi said. Did I sense a hint of sadness in her voice?

"Denki." Brenna brushed a strand of her hair from her face. "It means I'll be staying in Ukraine for good. I know that's not what you planned for me."

Mammi clasped her hands in her lap. "You're a grown woman. You're entitled to your own plans. I'm happy for you."

"Jah," Dawdi added. "We're very happy for you." He sounded joyful.

"When's the big day?" Gabe asked.

"I have something I want to ask all of you," Brenna said. "We'd like to get married on June twenty-second—"

I gasped. "That's so soon."

Brenna smiled. "We want to get married on the farm."

There was a moment of silence, and then Dawdi said, "We're delighted you want to be married here."

This time, Johann smiled while Brenna clapped her hands together. She continued, "We can get a marriage license at the courthouse. Johann's passport is enough identification." Brenna looked at me. "Treva, will you be around? Could you help us plan it?"

I was supposed to be in Alaska by then. And yet I found myself saying, "Of course." I couldn't miss out on Brenna and Johann's wedding.

"Thank you," Brenna said. "We want a small and simple ceremony." She glanced at Johann. "Although we've just made the engagement formal, we've been talking about marriage for a while. I've thought it would be good to have someone in the area to help plan the wedding."

"I'll see to whatever you need. Just let me know." I shifted my gaze. "Can you come too, Natasha?"

"Yes," she answered. "I can."

"I'll call Ivy next," Brenna said. "And then Gran." After a few more minutes of chatting, Brenna ended the call, and the others went into the house.

I stayed in the barn to think for a minute. Misty and Shawn's daughter was getting married the first part of May. Could I go to Alaska to help with that, come back to Lancaster County to finish the details for Brenna's wedding, and then return to Alaska by the fourth week of June to stay? Would it be worth it to Misty and Shawn to only employ me for four months? Would it be worth it for me to fly out twice? The tickets would be expensive. I'd give it more thought and then text Misty tomorrow.

I wasn't shocked Brenna and Johann were getting married, but I was surprised they were coming to Lancaster County for the ceremony. Surprised—and pleased. I guessed Brenna would want photographs. I hoped Dawdi would be okay with having a photographer on the farm as long as none of the photos were of Mammi, Rosene, or him. I'd ask Brenna what kind of food she wanted. Maybe Olena, a Ukrainian woman we knew through Brenna's friend Marko, could make a Kyiv cake. Perhaps she'd be interested in catering the wedding dinner too. That might be a nice touch for Johann and Natasha.

Or if they wanted a traditional Amish menu, maybe Sharon could help. Perhaps that would work for the rehearsal dinner. I sent a text to Brenna with my questions and also asked what ideas she had as far as an officiant. She texted back.

> I like the idea of an Amish menu for the rehearsal dinner—it will just be our family and Natasha and Johann. And we think Ukrainian food would be great for the wedding dinner. I'll send you Olena's number. Would you ask Pastor Mike about marrying us? I'd like that.

Staying on the topic of love, my thoughts shifted to how sad Rosene seemed when talking to Sally about Zeke. I needed to find out what happened to him. Rosene deserved some closure.

I'd go by the library on the way home from the refugee

center the next day and try again. There had to be information somewhere about what happened to Ezekiel Zimmerman from Lancaster County, Pennsylvania.

Monday morning, Kamil came into the kitchen for breakfast for the first time, even though Dawdi invited him to every day. He was quiet but smiled several times and spoke about his work on his family farm.

"I milked the goats," he said. "By hand. Your way of milking is much easier. Plus, cows aren't as wild as goats."

Dawdi agreed.

"Although you should consider raising goats," Kamil said. "Most of the refugees I know prefer the meat. You'd have a ready market."

When I arrived at the refugee center, Zaida and Cala were preparing the meal in the kitchen. Both gave me hugs. Then Zaida said, "A couple of the other volunteers would like to come to our next refugee dinner. They saw the article in the paper."

"The article?"

Zaida motioned to the counter. "You haven't seen it?"

I shook my head as I walked across the kitchen. It was about the dinner at our house. Drew didn't name Dawdi and Mammi, but he did write about Rosene and use her full name. There was a photograph of Zaida and Cala but no photo of Rosene, of course.

I read the article. Drew included parts of Zaida and Cala's story and mentioned that Rosene had been volunteering to help refugees in Lancaster County since 1948. He then added how much Carol Smith enjoyed hearing the refugees' stories. *"My Amish ancestors were some of the very first refugees* to this area," Smith said. "I was happy to meet the Hamad family and to be able to hear their story and help welcome them to Lancaster County."

I looked up from the article. "Nice."

Zaida and Cala both grinned. "Would Saturday work for a dinner?"

"I'll ask Mammi and Dawdi and text you this afternoon." Dawdi had wanted to host another one and invite people from church. It would be better to do it now rather than closer to when I would be going to Alaska.

After finishing at the center, I sat in the parking lot, trying to figure out exactly what to text Misty. I felt as if I were making excuses. I had to remind myself they weren't excuses—they were reasons I had no control over. I wasn't justifying. I was explaining.

I started my text by saying that my middle sister just announced she was getting married June 22 on our grandparents' farm in Lancaster County, then added,

> Could I come the week before Lindsay's wedding, help through the wedding, come back home, and then return June 24? Let me know your thoughts.

Then I headed to the library. First, I hopped on an address app and put in Ezekiel Zimmerman. Several listings appeared, but none for a ninety-one-year-old.

Next, I searched *Ezekiel Zimmerman, California, obituary*. Charles "Zeke" Zimmerman popped up, but he was born in 1952. The next entry was for Ezekiel "Billy" Zimmerman. He was born in 1902 and died in 1947. Next was Robert Lewis "Zeke" Zimmerman, but he was born in 1975. I couldn't find any Ezekiel Zimmerman that met Zeke's information. I kept at it but changed the search to Texas. When nothing credible appeared, I widened my search. I found an Ezekiel Zimmerman in Bellevue, Washington, who was the executive of a meatless patty company. Another in Boise, Idaho, who worked for a computer chip manufacturing company and had won an employee of the year award. I kept searching.

After an hour and a half of looking, I came across an article from 2003 in the *Fairbanks Daily News* about a Zeke Zimmerman in Anchorage, Alaska, who had retired at the age of seventy-five from the Alaska Department of Fish and Game. I did the math. He was born in 1928, the same year as Rosene's Zeke.

Could this be the Zeke I was looking for?

My phone dinged with a text from Misty.

> I talked things over with Shawn, and we can make that work. The planning for the wedding is done, but we'll need you to confirm with the vendors the week before and work with our chef and kitchen staff on the rehearsal dinner and wedding dinner. We'll also need you to do the day-of coordination. Then you can finish the planning and coordinate the other events and the five other weddings we have over the summer. The first one is June 28.

> Thank you! That sounds like a great plan.

And it did, except that I'd be using a large portion of my summer wages to finance my flights. But it would be worth it.

I searched for airline tickets and purchased one departing on May third and returning May twelfth, a day after the wedding.

Then I continued my search for Zeke. No Ezekiel Zimmerman showed up in Fairbanks. I expanded the search to all of Alaska. Only a football player popped up.

I hopped onto an address app and narrowed the search to Fairbanks, Alaska. Nothing. Next, I put in Juneau. Same thing. Next, Anchorage. Nothing again. I went back to the article to see if it had a byline. It did—and an email address. I sent the reporter a quick email with a link to the article and asked if he knew if Zeke Zimmerman was still alive, and if so, where he lived. I also asked if the Zeke he interviewed happened to mention where he grew up or if he grew up Amish.

It was a leap—but it was all I had.

· 27 ·

I spent the next week planning Brenna's wedding and preparing for another refugee dinner. Zaida invited two women from the refugee center. I invited Ivy and Conrad, and they invited Pastor Mike and his wife, Ruth, from the Mennonite church. After hearing back from Brenna, I'd planned to contact him about officiating Brenna and Johann's wedding. I'd wait and ask on Saturday in person.

Every evening I went out to the barn to check my email to see if the reporter from Fairbanks had replied, but there was nothing.

On Wednesday, I drove Dawdi to the homes of four of the Amish families in our district he thought would benefit from the refugee dinner. We repeated our process from two weeks before. Three out of the four couples committed to attending. I knew Dawdi was respected in our community, and seeing him in the homes of others always confirmed that. He had a dorky side but also a side that really connected with others. He was the closest I'd ever see to my own father as a seventy-five-year-old.

On Thursday, I took Rosene to her cardiac rehab appointment. On Friday, as I weeded the garden, Gabe headed toward me. "Want some help?" He wore a baseball cap, a sweatshirt, and jeans.

"Sure. If your back is okay."

"I'll give it a try."

I gave him the hoe I was using and then went to the shed and retrieved another one. When I returned, I took my sweatshirt off and tied it around my waist, over my jeans. The day had grown warm.

Gabe asked, "Have you decided not to go to Alaska?"

"No, I'm going."

"What about Brenna's wedding?"

"I'll come home for that."

He gave me a puzzled look.

"What?"

"I don't understand why you're going there when you have the farm and your family here."

I dug my hoe into the soil between two rows of beans. "I just keep wondering if there are better options for me."

He shook his head. "What could be better than this farm?"

"How would I know if I don't try something different?"

Gabe, who worked a row over, scraped the weeds with his hoe and shook his head again.

"Ivy says I have FOBO—fear of better options."

"That's funny. I haven't heard of that." But he didn't laugh. "I think I have a FONO."

I stood up straight. "What's that?"

"Fear of no options."

I shot him a sympathetic look, but he had his head down.

"Do you think the best decisions in life are the easiest or the hardest?" he asked.

"I have no idea."

"Let's take your decision." He stood and leaned against his hoe. "Would it be easier to go to Alaska or stay here?"

"Easier to go to Alaska," I said. "I'm ready for something different. Staying here would make me sad."

Gabe held the hoe in one hand and took his baseball cap off. "That makes me sad." He flipped the cap around, with the bill in the back.

"Why does that make you sad?"

"I'll miss you."

Surprised, I said, "Aww, don't get sentimental."

"I can't help it," he said. "You're the next-generation Rosene. You bring people together. You're the hub."

That surprised me so much I didn't know how to respond. Finally, I said, "I've never seen myself that way, but thank you."

Gabe started weeding again, and I got back to work too.

A few minutes later, Gabe broke the silence. "I've been thinking about the store. Brenna, when she thought she'd take it over, wanted to take it online. Adding local Amish products—jams and jellies, honey, handcrafted toys, potholders and dish towels, handmade soup mixes, that sort of thing—would be a good idea too if you decide to take it over. They could be sold in the store and online. I think those additions would draw more tourists in, but also cater to shoppers from afar who can't visit Lancaster County but would still like to purchase a little bit of the experience."

"Those are great ideas, but I'm not interested in managing the store."

"Why not?"

"It's not that I don't like it, but I like the farm better. I feel caged in when I work in the store day after day. But you should talk with Mammi about your ideas."

Gabe kept weeding. "No. I don't think it's my place."

"You should," I said. "Maybe she'd hire you on full-time to manage the place so she could retire."

"I'm afraid if she did it would only be because she felt sorry for me."

"Mammi and Dawdi don't feel sorry for you. They appreciate you." When he didn't respond, I asked, "What would be easier for you? To stay here on the farm and manage the store or to go somewhere else?"

Without missing a beat, Gabe said, "Definitely to stay here. That would be a dream come true." Then, without as much as a segue, he asked, "What happened with you and Pierre?"

"Wait. What?"

"What happened with you and Pierre?"

"That seemed a little abrupt—and personal."

Gabe grimaced. "Sorry."

Actually, the question didn't make me that upset. It seemed like something the old Gabe would ask. I decided to give him an honest answer. "I didn't want to stay in Haiti, and he didn't want to leave."

"I'm sorry," Gabe said.

"Thank you." I hesitated a moment. "It wasn't meant to be. . . ." My voice trailed off. Being home made me realize I wasn't ready to make a monumental decision like that yet anyway. I still had a lot I needed to figure out.

Gabe asked, "Any hope one of you might change your mind?"

I smiled a little. "No." I used to imagine being married to Pierre and the two of us living on the farm. Safe. But his parents wouldn't be safe. He'd worry about them every day, unable to see to their needs. It would have been a miserable life for him. How would I feel if I'd never be able to see my family again? Not able to help care for Rosene. Not able to see Mammi and Dawdi grow older.

Love was complicated. It wasn't nearly as easy as I'd thought it would be.

"Besides," I said to Gabe, "Pierre is already seeing someone else. A nurse midwife who plans to stay in Haiti."

"I'm sorry," he said again.

I managed a genuine smile. "No, don't be. I want what's best for Pierre. I really do."

As Gabe and I worked in silence, Dawdi came out of the stable, leading two workhorses.

I called out, "What are you doing?"

"I need to spread manure on the south pasture."

I stepped to the edge of the garden and yelled, "Have Conrad do that on Saturday."

Dawdi held the reins and took a handkerchief out of his pocket. "I don't want to take up his weekend time."

I lowered my voice and said to Gabe, "I'm going to go help Dawdi."

"I'll keep weeding."

We needed six horses altogether, so I headed straight to the stable. Dawdi had already filled the massive barrel-like tank with the slurry mixture of manure, so once we had the horses hitched to the spreader, we headed toward the pasture.

That was the easy part. The job required quick-footedness to stand on the platform, drive the team, and make sure the spreader was working properly. We both stood on the platform, which had a railing around the front. That made me feel a little better. If Dawdi lost his balance, he had something to grab. He drove the team while I stood behind him. When he stopped the team at the gate, I jumped down and opened it. Once he was through, I closed it.

Now came the tricky part. With the flip of a switch, the sprayer opened up on the backside of the barrel. Dawdi had started making and using the slurry mixture a couple of years ago instead of just spreading manure from a low wagon, as he'd done for years. The slurry mixture had its advantages, but it seemed a little precarious to me. The massive barrel wasn't nearly as stable as the low wagon, and there was more stopping to fix the line or nozzle.

When Dawdi stopped the team so the tank was positioned at the end of the pasture, I opened the nozzle. Then I jumped on the platform, and Dawdi said, "Walk" to the horses and they started forward, picking up speed a step at a time. I kept an eye on the tank to make sure everything was working correctly.

I didn't mind the scent of the manure. It was mingled with the smell of the pasture and the grass and the soil and the wide-open space. Above, the sky was a brilliant blue and the sun was shining.

When we reached the other end of the pasture, Dawdi called out, "Ha!" for the horses to turn left. Then he pulled on the reins for a sharp left, and we headed down the field.

I had liked helping spread manure from the time we moved to the farm. I liked any work out in a pasture or a field. Dragging. Mowing. Planting. Harvesting.

I liked it all.

Halfway down the pasture, the spray stopped.

"Hold up," I said to Dawdi. "I need to check the nozzle."

"I'll do it." He handed me the reins. But as he took a step to the edge of the platform, he stumbled and lost his balance.

I lurched for him, dropping the reins as I did. I managed to grab his arm and pull him backward as I held on to the rail. We both fell against the rail, startling the horses, who pitched forward. I scrambled for the reins, but they fell off the railing.

"Hold on," I said to Dawdi, who had managed to reach a standing position. I jumped down from the platform and ran to grab the lead horse's bridle, bringing him to a stop. The others followed. Dawdi then stepped down from the platform and retrieved the reins.

He began to laugh as we resumed our places on the platform. I scowled.

"Come on, Treva," he said. "You have to admit that was comical."

"No. It was scary. You would have fallen off the platform. What if the horses took off?"

"You had the reins. You would have stopped them. You chose to grab me instead."

"You could have twisted your ankle or hit your head," I barked. "What if you'd been alone?"

"Well, I wasn't. You were here with me."

I headed back to fix the nozzle.

When I returned, he'd grown more serious. "I'm not asking you to keep a secret or anything. But don't tell Mammi. I'll mention it to her in a few days. She's been worrying excessively lately, mostly about my balance."

Alarmed, I asked, "What's wrong with your balance?"

"Nothing, except that I'm getting older. It's perfectly normal."

Farming wasn't exactly safe work. There was machinery. The fact it wasn't modern didn't make it any safer. And there were big, unpredictable animals, both workhorses and cows. And fertilizers and chemicals and weather. It seemed so idyllic, but it wasn't. Farming was a dangerous occupation, even for the young.

I didn't tell Mammi what happened, but I kept thinking about it through the rest of Friday and into Saturday, up until the time Zaida and Cala and their three helpers stepped into the kitchen with their baskets of food and table decorations.

Before we served the meal, I asked Pastor Mike if he would marry Brenna and Johann. After asking a few clarifying questions, he said he'd be honored to. I gave him details about the wedding—small, simple, and on the farm.

The second refugee dinner was another big success. As Ivy helped me with the dishes afterward, she said, "You've brought life back to the farm."

"What do you mean?"

She glanced around. Mammi and Dawdi were getting ready for bed, and Conrad and Gabe were taking down the tables and chairs in the living room.

She leaned toward me. "It was kind of boring around here when you were gone. I think Mammi, Dawdi, and Rosene were a little depressed without any young people here, especially after Gabe left too. Now there are refugee dinners and tourist dinners and Gabe and Drew living on the property." Ivy smiled. "It makes me sad to be leaving."

I put a plate in the drying rack. "You'll do the same in Oregon. You and Conrad will get involved in our old church, maybe with the youth." My eyes began to blur. "You'll be like Mom and Dad."

"No," Ivy said. "We'll never be like Mom and Dad. But hopefully we'll all have homes like they did, no matter where we are."

After we finished cleaning up and Ivy and Conrad left, I followed Gabe out the door to go check my texts and email in the barn. As we reached the picnic table, it began to rain, and I hadn't grabbed my jacket. "You can check your phone in the Dawdi Haus," Gabe said.

"Thanks." That would save me from getting soaked.

Gabe opened the door and ushered me inside. It was as tidy as could be. No dishes in the sink. Nothing on the counters. The place was immaculate. I'd never thought of Gabe as tidy, but perhaps he'd learned that from being in the army.

I sat down on the couch and took out my phone. First, I checked my texts. Nothing. I sent Brenna a message, saying Pastor Mike would officiate at the wedding. Then I checked my email. I squinted at the inbox. I had an email from earlier in the evening from the reporter in Alaska.

Thank you for reaching out to me. I'm sorry to take so long to respond—this isn't an email address I use very often anymore. I haven't heard from Zeke Zimmerman since I did the feature story on him. He never mentioned to me that he grew up Amish, but he did say he'd moved to Alaska from California in the early 1970s. He's a remarkable man. Funny and charitable. I did some sleuthing and can't find an obituary for him, nor can I find an address for him in Fairbanks. I sent an email to the last address I have for him but haven't heard back. If I do, I'll send him your email address and he can contact you directly.

"Is everything all right?" Gabe asked.

"Jah." I slipped my phone into the pocket of my apron.

As I walked to the house, I pondered whether I should say anything to Rosene. The email certainly wasn't definitive.

Perhaps I could look for this Zeke Zimmerman while I was in Alaska.

When I reached the house, I heard noises in the downstairs bathroom, and Rosene's bedroom door was open. A minute later, she came out, wearing her nightgown and bathrobe.

I motioned toward the living room, and she followed me. I told her about the email. "It *might* be him," I said. "How many Zeke Zimmermans could there be who were born in 1928?"

She sat down in the rocking chair. "If it is, he's most likely still alive."

Now I just had to figure out how to find him.

· 28 ·

I spent the next week performing my usual obligations, getting ready to go, and planning ahead for Mammi, Dawdi, and Rosene while I was gone. I didn't tell Mammi about Dawdi's near-fall in the pasture—I trusted he did. But I did tell Gabe as we sat at the picnic table Monday afternoon.

"If he decides to spread, spray, or drag any of the pastures while you're gone, I'll go with him," Gabe said.

"I don't want you to hurt your back."

"I won't lift anything unless it's an emergency. I have another two weeks until I'll be cleared for that."

I took Rosene to her cardiac rehab on Tuesday and picked up her prescriptions. I hoped she'd tell me more of her story from 1949, but she dozed on the way to her appointment and on the way home too. On Wednesday, I weeded the garden again, with Gabe's help, and dusted and cleaned the floors in the store. On Thursday, I shoveled out the horse stalls in the stable. Gabe helped by manning the wheelbarrow. It didn't hurt his back to dump it after I filled it.

On Friday, Gabe gave me a ride to the Philadelphia airport for a 6:00 a.m. departure. I had a layover in Chicago and then arrived in Anchorage eight hours after that.

Misty picked me up. With the time change, it was only two in the afternoon, so we stopped for lunch and then at a warehouse-type store to pick up supplies for the resort and the wedding and loaded them into her SUV.

As she drove to the Resort of the Midnight Sun, which was a half hour from Anchorage, she briefed me about the wedding. I'd need to call the vendors to confirm the plans and ask about any last-minute details, work with the manager of the resort to double-check on the staffing for the wedding, and work with the chef to double-check menus. Lindsay wasn't flying in until Wednesday.

"She works in Seattle as a techie. Because it's her first year at the company, she doesn't have much vacation time and wanted to save it for the honeymoon." The groom and his family were flying in on Thursday, the rehearsal dinner would be Friday, and the wedding Saturday. Then there would be a brunch on Sunday morning. I'd need to check with the groom's mom about the rehearsal dinner when she arrived to see if she had any special requests.

I took notes on my phone as Misty talked.

"Oh, and order two table arrangements for the rehearsal dinner from the florist when you call her." Misty spoke quickly and efficiently. This was a different side of the woman who had spent most of her time in Haiti rocking babies.

As we left the city behind, I marveled at the beauty. Thick woods of evergreen trees. An entire horizon of snow-topped mountains. Lush meadows with patches of snow. "Is that a bear?" I pointed toward the meadow.

"It's just a brown bear," Misty said, "and a small one, at that." She pointed ahead. "A moose is over on the left."

Sure enough, a moose sauntered alongside the road.

When we reached the resort, Misty backed up to a garage

door. It opened, and Shawn stepped out from a large shed with shelves full of supplies.

I jumped down from the truck and gave him a hug. "Did you change your mind? Are you here to stay?" he asked.

"No," I answered. "I'll be here until Sunday after the wedding. Then I'll return in late June."

He smiled. "Let's get this stuff out of the truck. Then Misty can give you a tour."

The resort was beautiful. On the other side of the warehouse was the building Misty referred to as the Big Lodge. She led me around to the front. The lodge was made of huge logs. The front porch had rocking chairs and couches and groups of chairs. Today, it was nearly forty degrees, but it seemed too cold to hang out on the porch. I imagined in a month or two it would be warm enough.

Off to the side was a deck with an archway. Misty pointed to the area. "We sometimes have weddings out here in July and August. We also have outdoor dining on the nicest days. We'll put tables and chairs up in June and put out patio heaters. Sometimes guests just like to bring their morning coffee here and enjoy the outdoors."

Misty opened one side of the double front doors. I stepped inside. Timbers of Sitka spruce—I remembered Misty's description of the lodge from what she shared in Haiti—framed the ceiling, with a long log down the middle. More groups of chairs and sofas decorated the lobby, with a long counter to the left. A wide, open staircase led to the second floor.

"We'll have Lindsay's wedding in here. She and Shawn will come down the staircase and then into the dining hall, where we'll have the ceremony." Misty motioned to her right.

I followed her. Groups of people sat at several of the

wooden tables, and two waiters worked the floor. "We'll have around seventy-five guests, so not a large wedding. The dance floor will be in the back." The dining hall was large and would easily accommodate that. "We're renting white chairs for the ceremony and tablecloths—the rental company is in the wedding binder. You'll need to call to confirm that they're delivering on Friday morning."

I followed Misty into the kitchen. The chef was a woman named Marci, who appeared to be in her fifties. She greeted me with a hug and then said, "You just tell me what you need, honey. We do everything from biscuits and gravy to gingered wild salmon."

Misty led the way out of the kitchen. "We'll go upstairs to see one of the guest rooms. From there, we'll go to the fourth floor, where the employee rooms are."

The guest room had two queen beds with wooden frames and a weaving of spruce trees above each. The view from the window was of the lake. I could make out a few boats on it and cabins around three-quarters of the lake. On the fourth floor, she opened a door at the end of the hall. "This is your room."

We stepped inside. It had a single bed, a dresser with a TV above it, a desk, a closet, and a bathroom with a shower. It was simple but more than adequate. On the bed was my bag.

"Shawn brought it up," Misty said.

We took the elevator down to the first floor, and then I followed Misty out of the building to a golf cart.

"Let's go see the lake," Misty said. "It's stocked with trout, but fishing doesn't start until June. It gets as warm as the low sixties in July, sometimes higher. Then it starts cooling down again. By October, we're back down to highs in the lower forties, like now."

The lake came into view again. Misty stopped the cart at what she called the Lake Lodge, and we went inside. It was much smaller than the Big Lodge.

The young man behind the counter smiled and said, "Hello."

"This is Craig," Misty said to me. "He's worked for us the last few years." To Craig, she said, "This is Treva. Shawn and I volunteered with her in Haiti. She's here to coordinate Lindsay's wedding, and then she'll return in June for the rest of the season."

"Great," Craig said. "You'll really like it here. I know I do."

"Thanks." The lodge had equipment for rent on one side—canoes, kayaks, paddleboards, bikes, life jackets, and helmets. On the other side was a coffee and snack bar, and there was a café in a back room, with knotty pine paneling and rustic tables and benches.

Misty said, "We'll have the rehearsal dinner in here. It doesn't open for guests until June, so Marci and her crew will be in charge of that meal too." She motioned to a door in the rear of the café and then led the way onto a boardwalk that expanded into a deck at the edge of the water and then into a dock that went out over the lake.

"We use the deck for weddings too," Misty said. "We're really trying to market the resort as a destination wedding spot, June through August, with a Midnight Sun theme. And also for family reunions, work events, and other kinds of gatherings. We have three family reunions this summer and already have four booked for next year."

It was exciting. Working at the resort would give me experience coordinating events and maintaining a property. I could work at the resort for seven months each year. And then what? Find a job in Anchorage? Rent an apartment? Go back to the farm, as long as Dawdi and Mammi still owned it? Or go stay with Ivy or Brenna for five months?

I didn't need to figure that part out now.

I spent Saturday going through the wedding binder, exploring the event venues, and making a detailed list of everything to do. In the afternoon, I started calling vendors. Of course, no one answered. They were likely at someone else's wedding. I left messages, introducing myself and saying what I needed.

Sunday dawned wet and windy. I joined Misty, Shawn, and several of their employees in the café for a worship service in the late morning. Misty led singing, and Shawn gave a devotion. Afterward, we ate together in the dining hall, and then, after lunch, I took a nap. When I awoke, a wave of homesickness swept through me as I sat alone in my room. How was Rosene doing? How about Mammi and Dawdi? What about Gabe?

I stood and walked to the window. The rain had stopped. I grabbed my coat, stuffed my phone in the pocket, and went outside, heading for the lake. As I walked, I texted Ivy, asking how everyone was doing. She didn't respond. Then I texted Gabe. He didn't respond either.

Once I reached the lake, I walked down to the dock. An eagle soared over the water and then up into the trees. I checked my phone. No texts, but I had an alert for an email. I opened the app and then let out a squeal. I had an email from zzimmerman.

A reporter in Fairbanks who interviewed me years ago emailed me. I believe I'm the Zeke Zimmerman you're looking for. I did grow up

Amish, in Lancaster County, PA. I worked on the Simonses' family
farm, which my brother Jeremiah and his wife, Clare, inherited,
making it the Zimmerman farm. I'm guessing you must be a granddaughter of Arden. Is he still on the farm? How are Janice and
Lydia? Please tell anyone who remembers me hello.

I quickly responded, saying that I was Arden's grand-
daughter and that Arden was still living on the farm, that
Janice lived in the Big Valley, and that Lydia lived in Canada.
Then I wrote, *Where are you living now?*

I hit Send and then stared at my screen, hoping he would
answer right away.

He did.

Anchorage, Alaska, which is a long ways from Lancaster County.
I'd be tempted to make the trip to see all of you, but I had back
surgery a month ago and am still recovering. Could we talk on the
phone?

I replied.

Yes, I'd love to chat on the phone, but I'm actually thirty minutes
outside of Anchorage right now.

I paused as I thought through my week. I should try to
see him as soon as possible—I'd be busier as the week pro-
gressed. I included my phone number.

Could you call me ASAP? If it works for you, I could get a ride into
Anchorage and see you this afternoon.

I included my phone number. As soon as I sent the email,
I regretted it. Zeke was old. Suggesting I come today might

be more than he could deal with. What a shock to have a great-grandniece contact him and then invite herself over in the same day. But I headed toward the lodge just in case.

A minute later, my phone began to ring. I answered it and was greeted with a booming "Treva! This is your Onkel Zeke! I'd love to have you visit me today!"

After chatting with Zeke for a few minutes, explaining why I was in Alaska, I got his address and told him I'd be there within an hour. I'd reached the lodge. Thankfully, Misty was at the check-in when I stepped into the lobby. I told her I was going to take a rideshare into Anchorage to visit a long-lost uncle.

"You can take my SUV." She reached into the pocket of her sweatshirt. "It's parked in the back lot."

"Thank you," I gushed. That would save me money.

As I reached Misty's SUV, my phone dinged. Gabe.

Everyone's fine. How are you?

Is it okay if I call you?

Right now?

Yes!

Sure.

I climbed into the front seat as I called Gabe.

He answered with a panicky "Are you all right?"

"Yes. I found Zeke!"

"Who?"

"Dawdi's uncle—Rosene's sweetheart from when she was twenty-two. You know. Zeke. From her story."

There was a long pause and then Gabe said, "Wow. That's crazy."

I gave him a quick rundown on the whole story. "I'm going to go see him right now. If he wants to talk to Rosene, could I text you? And could Rosene use your phone in the Dawdi Haus or barn? It's only three here—so seven your time. I'll let you know what Zeke says ASAP."

"Sure," Gabe said. "I'd be happy to help. If Zeke doesn't want to talk to Rosene, make sure and let me know how your visit with him goes."

"I will." Just having Gabe know where I was going and to have him interested made me feel supported.

Twenty-five minutes later, I pulled into the parking lot of an assisted living facility, jumped down from the SUV, locked it, and headed toward the front door of Sitka Creek Assisted Living. I entered through sliding doors into a lobby. Several elderly people sat on the couches and chairs. The floor was tile.

A man in a wingback chair pushed himself up with the help of a cane. He was tall and slim, with thick gray hair. He wore dark brown slacks and a forest green quilted jacket with a tan shirt underneath it. "Treva?" He smiled.

I nodded. "You must be Zeke."

He took a step toward me. I put out my hand, but he said, "May I give you a hug?" I agreed, and he gave me a half hug. He was clean-shaven and smelled of soap.

When he let me go, he wiped at his eyes with his free hand. "It's been so long since I've seen anyone from home," he said. "I forgot what it means to see family."

I replied, "It means everything."

"Let's go into the dining hall to talk." Zeke's eyes sparkled. "They have soft serve ice cream available twenty-four hours a day."

Once we had our ice cream and sat down, Zeke said, "I was afraid to ask this earlier. Is Rosene still alive?"

"She is." I explained about her recent heart attack.

His eyes grew watery again. "Well, that's both good news and frightening news." He took out a handkerchief from the inside pocket of his jacket and wiped away his tears. "Where is she living?"

"On the farm. She never left." I took a bite of my chocolate soft serve.

"Not even when she married?"

I shook my head. "She never married."

He stared down at his ice cream and then took a bite. After he swallowed, he said, "That surprises me. There were plenty of young men in my group who were interested in her. Ones who deserved her far more than I did."

That surprised *me*. "She's been telling me her story, starting in 1948. She's in the summer of 1949 now—not once has she mentioned any young man but you." My face grew warm as I realized perhaps I'd shared too much.

Zeke closed his eyes.

I reached out and put my hand on his arm. "Everything okay?"

He opened his eyes. "Yes. I just needed a moment."

"Would you like to talk with Rosene?"

"Now?"

"Maybe," I said. "I told Gabe, someone who lives on the farm but is not Amish and has a phone, that I was coming to see you. He's on standby to see if Rosene would like to speak to you."

"Goodness," Zeke said. "Why, yes, if Rosene would like to speak to me, of course I want to speak with her."

I pulled out my phone. "I'll text Gabe."

He responded immediately.

I'll go to the house and ask Rosene.

When I relayed Gabe's message, Zeke said, "Would you mind if we go to my apartment? If she's willing to speak with me, I'd rather not have the conversation here."

"That's a good idea," I said.

We bussed our half-eaten bowls of ice cream and then, as we walked down the hall, Gabe texted back.

Rosene said yes but wondered if we could do a video chat. We're on our way to the Dawdi Haus.

Let me know when she's ready. We're on our way to Zeke's apartment. I'll ask him about video chatting.

"Would you like to do a video chat?" I asked Zeke as he stopped at a door at the end of the hall.

"Of course." He hooked his cane in his left elbow, unlocked the door, opened it, and motioned for me to go in first. I stepped into a cozy living place with a recliner, small couch, coffee table, desk with a laptop on it, and bookcase. Off to the right was a small kitchen, and to the left was a short hallway with two doors.

Gabe texted.

We're in the Dawdi Haus. Call when you're ready.

I liked Gabe's text and then said to Zeke, "Rosene is ready. I can place the call and then step out into the hall and give you privacy."

"I'd prefer you stay," Zeke said. "I'd like you to listen."

He sat down on the couch. "I'm feeling a little nervous. If you listen, you can answer any questions I have afterward about the conversation."

"Sure." I sat down too and placed the video call to Gabe's phone.

When Gabe answered and his face filled the screen, I said, "Hi, Gabe. Zeke and I are here. I'm handing the phone to him."

"Hi, Treva," Gabe replied as Zeke took the phone. "And hello, Zeke. It's nice to meet you. Rosene is sitting next to me."

Rosene's face appeared. "Hello, Zeke." She took the phone from Gabe. "Is it really you?"

"It's really me. And I know it's you—I'd recognize you anywhere." Then he quickly asked her about her health and, of course, she downplayed the heart attack.

"I'm doing fine," she said. "How are you?"

He explained about his back surgery. "But I'm definitely on the road to recovery."

For the next twenty minutes, as Zeke and Rosene talked, they both transformed in front of my eyes. How Rosene, the kindest and most loving person I knew, could become even more so was beyond me, but that's what happened. Plus, I'd always seen glimpses of the girl Rosene used to be through the ways she reveled in the beauty of nature and storytelling and relationships, but as she talked with Zeke, it was as if she were twenty-three instead of ninety-three. Her eyes shone. She held her head high.

Zeke seemed to bloom too. He became even warmer than he'd been with me and more animated. At times, I thought his face might break from the grin that spread across it as he listened to Rosene.

They talked about both the past and the present. They hadn't spoken in over seventy years, and yet they sounded as if it had only been a short time. Toward the end, Zeke said, "I know you can't travel here with your recent health problems, and I can't travel alone yet. But I hope we can see each other in person sometime soon."

"I'd like that too," Rosene said.

"In the meantime, I want to give you my phone number. You can call me anytime from the barn phone—I'm assuming that's where it is."

Rosene nodded.

"I'll call you right back," Zeke said, "so you don't have the expense."

"Thank you," Rosene said. "Gabe has a pen and a piece of paper so I can write your number down."

Zeke rattled off his phone number and then they said their good-byes and ended the call. I let out a sigh of relief. The phone call couldn't have gone better.

Zeke handed me my phone but didn't say anything, so I stayed quiet too until my phone dinged. It was Gabe.

Rosene wants to know if you told Zeke about Drew.

No.

She wants you to—if you feel like you can. Otherwise, she'll talk with him on the phone about it. But she thinks the sooner he knows that Drew is looking for his grandfather, the better. Zeke is the only one who can help Drew find the answer, one way or the other.

I stared at my phone.

"Treva?" Zeke stared at me. "Is something the matter?"

I turned toward him. "I have something I need to talk with you about. A man is staying on the farm who thinks you might be his grandfather."

Zeke's brows came together. "Seriously?"

"Yes. Drew Richards is his name. His father was born in Tennessee but was adopted by a couple in Wisconsin. All Drew's father knew about his biological father was that he grew up Amish and his last name was Zimmerman."

"I've never been to Tennessee. . . ." Zeke rubbed his chin. "However, I did know a young woman in Texas who was from Tennessee." He hesitated. "I left when her boyfriend, who she had failed to mention previously, was returning to San Antonio. When was Drew's father born?"

"December 1949."

Zeke leaned forward in his chair. "Where does he live now?"

"He passed away," I said. "Three years ago."

"What a shame," Zeke said. "We could have done a DNA test."

"You still can. Drew submitted his DNA to an ancestry app. You can do the same. It takes four to six weeks to find out, but you'll know for sure if your DNA is a match."

"Can I order a test online?"

"Yes." I shared the app Drew had used.

Zeke stood, sat down at his desk, and opened his laptop. Then he logged onto the website. After a few clicks, he opened up the desk drawer to his right and took out a wallet.

As he clicked through the order, I thought about what Zeke said to Rosene about him not being able to travel *alone*. He didn't say he couldn't travel.

What if he flew to Pennsylvania with me? I cautioned

myself to slow down. I'd need to check with Rosene before asking Zeke to come visit.

A couple of minutes later, he'd ordered and paid for his DNA test. He turned toward me. "It should arrive by Thursday."

"Nice." I stood. "I should get going, but I would love to see you again before I go."

He pushed himself up with his cane. "I'd like to see you too. I hate to have you coming into Anchorage. I imagine the resort you're working at for the week has a restaurant?"

I nodded.

"Why don't I take you out to dinner one night this week?"

"That's a great idea. Tomorrow night or Tuesday night would work best."

"Let's make it Tuesday night," Zeke said. "That will give me more time to digest everything that's happened today and see what questions I might have for you."

"Perfect." I found the resort's website online and sent it to him. "Would six o'clock work?"

"Yes," he said. "I'll meet you in the restaurant."

"Denki," I said.

He grinned. "No. Thank *you*. I've been longing for something more, but I was feeling frozen here." He laughed. "No pun intended." Then he grew serious. "I think you may have just changed my life."

· 29 ·

The next morning, as I sat at my desk making more phone calls to vendors, I felt intense loneliness again. Granted, later in the summer, I wouldn't be spending as much time in my room alone. In fact, later in the week, I wouldn't be either.

I couldn't judge the job by the first day, but I couldn't help comparing it with the Zimmerman farm. The biggest difference so far was that on the farm I was usually working with someone—not working alone—whether inside or outside. I missed Rosene the most. If I was home, surely she would have told me more of her story from 1949 by now. She'd left me hanging. Did she make it into East Berlin? Did she find Esther? I shivered. My loneliness in Alaska and my dilemma of what to do next with my life paled in comparison with what Rosene, Esther, and Martha had faced.

No doubt, Rosene was thinking about me—and Zeke—as much as I was thinking about her. I needed to send her an update. I texted Gabe. First, I let him know that the conversation about Drew had gone well and that Zeke had ordered a DNA test from the ancestry app.

> Would you tell Drew about Zeke? Make sure
> to tell him we won't know if he's the right Zeke
> Zimmerman until the DNA results are available.
> And would you ask Rosene if she wants me to
> invite Zeke to come home for a visit? I don't
> know if he'd want to, but I wanted to check with
> her before I asked him. If she's okay with it and
> he wants to, he could fly home with me next
> week.

Gabe replied,

> I'll do that. I'm working in the store this morning
> but will see Rosene at lunchtime.

I smiled at the thought of Gabe having lunch with Dawdi, Mammi, and Rosene.

Just after noon, Misty texted me.

> Come on down for lunch. Bring the binder and
> give me an update.

As soon as I sat down, Misty asked, "How was it seeing your uncle?"

"Great," I said. "He left Lancaster County in 1948 and hasn't seen anyone in his family since."

"What?"

"Isn't that crazy? I tracked him down through an article a reporter in Fairbanks wrote about him years ago."

Misty shook her head. "Wow."

"He's going to come out and have dinner with me tomorrow, if that works for you."

Misty frowned a little and then said, "Sure. Things won't get busy until Lindsay arrives on Wednesday. Oh, I forgot to tell you. I need you to pick up her dress this afternoon." She looked down at her phone. "I'll text you the address of the seamstress. We had some last-minute alterations that needed to be done."

The rest of lunch was spent updating Misty on the vendors and then me taking more notes as she gave me additional instructions. Then I drove her SUV into Anchorage to get the dress. When I returned, I made more phone calls. Around four, Gabe returned my text.

> Sorry it took me so long to respond. Rosene went into town to volunteer at the refugee center today, so I didn't see her until supper. I asked her about Zeke coming for a visit, and she said she'd like that. In fact, she asked if she could use my phone and gave him a video call to ask him. It sounds as if it's all set. You just need to text Zeke information about your flight. He'll look for a ticket as soon as he has the details. And then the two of you can work out the details when you have dinner tomorrow.

I held up my phone, kissed it, and said out loud, "Thank you, Gabe!" There was nothing more exciting than bringing two sweethearts together after seventy years.

I texted Gabe back with a big thank-you but no kiss.
He replied with,

> This is exciting! Good work!

> Thank you for your part! We make a good team!

Gabe texted a smiley face.
I kind of wished he'd sent a heart.

The next night at dinner, Zeke said he'd been able to get a ticket on my flight, which left Anchorage at 11:25 p.m. Sunday night. "I also managed to get in to see my doctor today, just to make sure I'm fit to travel. He said I am."

"That's great," I said. "How long will you stay?"

"I'm not sure." He had a distant look in his eyes. "It's funny because I've been thinking a lot about home lately. A few months ago, I even did an internet search for Rosene. Nothing came up—I surmised she'd married years ago and had a different last name, and whether she'd passed away or was still alive, I wouldn't be able to find her. I did find Arden at the farm—the actual address has changed over the years. Anyway, I've wondered a few times if I should go home while I still can." He focused in on me and smiled. "And here I am, going home for a visit, knowing Rosene and Arden both want to see me. Thanks to you."

I smiled back.

He glanced around the dining hall and out the window toward the lake. "This is a beautiful place."

I agreed. It seemed he wanted to lighten the conversation, so I asked, "What brought you to Alaska in the first place?"

"After a few years, I moved from the Los Angeles area to northern California and began fishing and hunting a lot," Zeke said. "I got my GED and then went to the college in Arcata and got a bachelor's degree in wildlife science. I was looking for a job in California or southern Oregon when a buddy who had moved to Alaska let me know the fish and game department was hiring in Fairbanks. I applied and got the job."

"Nice. How did you adjust to the winters?"

"It took a while," he said. "The summers were so glorious that it made the winters worth it. And soon I took up skiing, both downhill and cross-country, and snowshoeing. In a short time, I loved the winters too."

Our waiter came and took our orders. Then Misty stopped by our table, and I introduced her to Zeke.

He stood and shook her hand, giving her one of his sweet smiles. "I'm so pleased to meet you," he said. "You have a lovely place here. Do you have time to join us?"

Misty thanked him and then sat down. She and Zeke chatted for a few minutes about the resort. When she stood, she said, "I'm so glad you two got connected."

Zeke beamed. "So am I."

After Misty left, I said, "I've only been here three days, and I'm already homesick. One of the things I'm looking forward to the most in June when I return is that I'll have more time with you. I'll actually have a relative here."

His face froze for a moment. He took a drink of water and then said, "Rosene and I had a long chat today. I talked with Arden too."

"Oh?"

He nodded. "They both asked me to return to Lancaster County, to the farm."

Shocked, I managed to ask, "And you're going to?"

"Well, for a little while. If I decide to stay for good, I'll find an assisted living place nearby." He grinned as our food arrived. "I don't want to overstay my welcome."

As we began to eat, I was at a loss for words. But after a couple of minutes, I shifted into planning mode. "What will you take with you?"

"My clothes. A few books. Important papers," he said. "Whatever I can fit into a few checked bags. I'm not going to keep my place here."

"What about your other things?"

"I'll donate them," he said. "Hopefully the front desk will have the name of someone I can hire to help. I'll need boxes and someone to fill them and haul them away."

I wished I'd have the time to do that for him, but I'd be busy. I wouldn't be able to help until Sunday afternoon, just a few hours before we'd need to get to the airport. "Will you need a wheelchair in the airports?" I asked.

"Yes," he said. "I already arranged for that. We'll need an extra-large rideshare vehicle to get to the airport, to accommodate my luggage, and we'll need to check everything at the curb. You won't be able to wrestle everything into the airport by yourself."

It seemed Zeke was a planner. I liked that.

After we finished dinner, we sat in the lobby for another half hour. I told him about Brenna's upcoming wedding. "You'll get to meet her and Johann when they arrive. And you'll meet Ivy and Conrad, who is Gabe's brother, right away. But then they're moving to Oregon in June."

"That's a shame," he said.

"I think so too."

"And you'll be coming back here to Alaska?"

I nodded, fighting the lump in my throat. "But I'll return to Lancaster County once the resort closes down for the season." I surprised myself by saying that out loud. Would I? Was that really my plan?

On Wednesday morning, a pipe broke in the café kitchen. Misty needed to find a plumber, so she sent me to the airport to pick up Lindsay. I liked her—she was a lot like Misty. Warm, kind, and enthusiastic. I gave her updates on the vendors, and she thanked me profusely. I spent the afternoon in the dining room with Lindsay, going over the layout for the wedding and the order of events. I'd coordinate the ceremony, welcome the vendors, get the wedding party what they needed, and oversee the reception.

The more I delved into the actual coordination of the wedding, the more I marveled at Misty trusting me to take on the responsibility. I wasn't sure what I did in Haiti to inspire such confidence in her, but I knew I could accomplish the tasks. I just wished I had some time to go into Anchorage and help Zeke too.

On Thursday, I felt homesick again. After I spent the summer and fall in Alaska, would I want to return the next year? I'd lived in Oregon and didn't want to go back there, at least not permanently. I'd worked in Haiti for six months and didn't want to stay. What about Alaska?

I was in my room when my phone dinged with a text from Zeke.

The DNA test arrived. I spit in the vial and sent it back.

I leaned forward in my chair. Zeke would get his results, but I wouldn't be with him to find out if he was Drew's grandfather. I'd be back here in Alaska, alone.

· 30 ·

O n Friday morning, I had a text from Gabe.

> Zeke called me this morning. He hurt his
> back last night filling boxes to give away.
> He took a muscle relaxer and is resting today.
> He didn't want to bother you—but I don't mind
> doing it, lol. He asked for prayer.

> I'll pray. I wish I could go help him!

Gabe liked my text but didn't respond. I had assumed that Zeke found someone to help him pack but maybe he hadn't.

I spent part of the morning talking with the mother of the groom about the rehearsal dinner and then setting everything up in the café. When the floral table arrangements hadn't arrived on time, I'd called the florist. There had been a mix-up. I borrowed Misty's car and headed into town, resisting an intense urge to check on Zeke.

Upon returning to the resort, I put the flowers on the tables in the café, and I still arrived in the dining hall in time for the rehearsal. Afterward, I hurried down to the café before the wedding party and family members to make sure everything was ready.

As everyone arrived and I directed them to their seats, Misty whispered, "You're doing a great job. Thank you."

I appreciated her affirmation, but I didn't feel as if I were doing a great job. Partly because I didn't feel that connected to what I was doing. When I watched Misty attend to tasks at the resort, she appeared to be absolutely invested. Of course she was. It was her property. Her business. Her responsibility.

I silently recited a verse from Colossians. *Whatever you do, work at it with all your heart, as working for the Lord. . . .* I needed to do the work as if I was absolutely invested. Lindsay and Misty both deserved that.

On Saturday morning, I awoke at five thirty and showered. Then I texted Gabe and asked if he'd heard from Zeke. He didn't answer.

All through the day, as I supervised the dining hall setup, checked in with vendors, checked on Lindsay and her bridesmaids, made sure the wedding party had their charcuterie boards for an afternoon snack, and then hurried to my room to change into my dress and heels, I checked my phone for a text from Gabe. Nothing.

I tried not to think about Zeke. Was he in pain? What would I need to do Sunday to get him ready to go?

Finally, I forced myself to set aside my worries about Zeke and concentrate on Lindsay's wedding. Like any wedding, there were a few glitches—the florist went to the Lake Lodge instead of the Big Lodge. The photographer was a half hour late. And the maid of honor couldn't find her makeup bag. But everything came together. The day was in the low fifties, which was downright warm, so the pre-wedding photos were taken outside. It was a little awkward having the guests in the lobby watch Shawn and Lindsay come down the open staircase and then hurry to their chairs in the dining hall, but it worked out.

As I watched the ceremony, tears filled my eyes. The wedding was aesthetically beautiful, with huge bouquets of pink peonies up front and a white arch with twinkle lights intertwined through the lattice. Misty's shoulders shook a little as Lindsay recited her vows. Shawn put his arm around her. I thought of my parents but then quickly put the memory aside. I couldn't afford to grieve them now.

I shifted my thoughts to Brenna. I was learning so much from this experience that I'd be able to use for her wedding.

When I fell into bed that night, I checked my phone one last time. Finally, I had a text from Gabe. A photo. I squinted. Gabe had sent a picture of Zeke and him . . . in Zeke's apartment. I sat up straight.

> Rosene sent me to help Zeke get packed and fly home with the two of you. We'll see you tomorrow—no rush. I've got this under control.

I fell against my pillow with a smile on my face.

When I arrived at Zeke's place the next day, Gabe had left to buy a couple of big suitcases, and Zeke, whose back was better, was going through his books. He had a few he wanted to take, including Jack London's *Call of the Wild* and a well-worn Bible. He held up the Bible. "My mother—"

"Elizabeth."

"Yes. Your great-great-grandmother." He smiled. "She gave me this Bible before I left home the second time. We had German Bibles in our home, but this one is King James." He turned his desk chair toward the bookcase and sat down, the Bible still in his hand. "However, I didn't start reading it until I moved here, thirty years after she gave it to me."

"What made you start reading it?"

"One of my co-workers invited me to his church in Fairbanks." Zeke flipped it open. "It was a nondenominational church with an eclectic group of congregants. A few people born in Alaska. Some Native people. But mostly people like me who found our way here."

He held the Bible toward me, showing the inside page where his mother had written his name and then hers. He put it in his lap. "The first time I made my way to California, I felt as if I was personally discovering a new world. Rosene had lived in Germany and then come to Lancaster County. She'd been to Philadelphia. She went to New York first when she returned to Germany. I'd never been anywhere. I had no idea what I was missing." He shook his head a little. "I felt as if my church and family had been lying to me about how fascinating the world was—the mountains and forests and ocean. Basically, I was content in Lancaster County before I knew what else was out there. I would have been happy to live there forever, but once I saw more of the country, I couldn't stay."

"FOMO."

He laughed. "What?"

"Fear of missing out. You had a fear of missing out."

"I suppose you're right."

"I have a fear of better options," I said. "I can't seem to decide what to do with my life because I'm afraid whatever I decide, I won't choose the best option."

"Ach," Zeke said. "*Ach*." He laughed. "I haven't said that in years." His eyes twinkled. "You know, usually the options we choose aren't set in stone. We can change our minds, if needed."

Was I on the verge of changing my mind? When I told Misty good-bye and that I'd see her in June, it felt a little hollow. But I wasn't sure what good staying on the farm would do. If Dawdi ended up selling it, I couldn't stay there either.

But what if Dawdi would turn it over to me? I knew as much about the farm as Conrad. If I farmed it, Dawdi could supervise me for the next few years. And maybe Gabe would stay on and help. He could manage the store and help with the milking.

But that was something to think about at a different time. Right now, we needed to get Zeke's apartment cleaned out. Gabe had already done the kitchen.

"He took the boxes to drop off at a donation center on the way to the store," Zeke said. "He also took clothes I no longer need. I'll leave the books I don't want for the library here, and one neighbor wants my desk and another wants my recliner and couch. The director said they'd use my bed frame and bureau."

On top of his desk was a photograph box. I pointed to it. "Are you taking that?"

"Yes." He opened it and held up a photo of him surfing. Then he held up photos of birds, fish, flowers, deer, moose, bears, and Alaskan landscapes. "Although I'm not sure what will happen to them after I'm gone."

"I'll keep them. In the meantime, I can make a collage of some of them for you."

His eyes filled with tears. "Thank you," he said. "I've never had anyone to leave anything to before."

"Why didn't you ever marry?"

"There were a couple of times I thought I might, but then I just couldn't do it." He put his hand to his chest.

Alarmed, I asked, "What's going on?"

"Sorry." His hand slid to his side. "I'm just trying to manage a lifetime of emotions."

As we continued going through his things—tax records, insurance papers, and old check registers—we talked more.

"After I came to the Lord, I considered writing to Rosene," he said. "I thought about going home and seeing if we could pick up where we left off, but I couldn't imagine joining the Amish then. And I couldn't imagine Rosene leaving if she had joined. Mostly, I figured she would have married, and it would be very unfair of me to show up like that."

"Why did you leave the faith?" I asked.

"I couldn't join the Amish church," he said. "I couldn't even join the Mennonite church. I saw enough of the world to believe both churches in Lancaster County were insular, although I was probably wrong. I was a skilled observer as a Youngie, but not much of an evaluator. I failed to see nuances. I also failed to ask questions." He rubbed the back of his neck. "I didn't know what it meant to be a follower of Christ—I just thought it meant being Amish or maybe Mennonite. I'm not saying that people who belonged to the Amish church didn't follow Christ. They did. Our mother did. Jeremiah did. I think our father did, although he didn't talk about it much. It wasn't until I was fifty that I finally understood."

"Would you join the Amish now?"

He cocked his head. "Why do you ask?"

I shrugged. "Just curious."

"I'd have to put some thought into that." He smiled. "I

don't drive anymore, but boy, it sure would be hard to give up my phone."

I laughed. I understood that feeling.

A knock fell on the door. I turned toward it as it opened. Gabe came through, carrying two large suitcases. "Treva!" He put the suitcases down and gave me a hug. Then he high-fived me. I laughed. The old Gabe was definitely back.

Once we'd packed Zeke's luggage, including another duffel bag and a medium-size suitcase, I ordered an extra-large rideshare vehicle to get everything to the airport. Once we arrived, Gabe sat with Zeke while I checked in the luggage. Then we secured the wheelchair he'd reserved. However, they were short on staff, and no one came to push Zeke, so I did, not wanting Gabe to strain his back. We ate before it was time to board and then we were on our way.

When we reboarded our next leg after the layover in Seattle, Zeke fell asleep. He'd managed to get a seat beside me. Gabe was a few rows in front of us. My thoughts fell to the farm and to Rosene and her story. I fell asleep thinking about Germany in 1949. When I awoke, Zeke was standing in the aisle.

"How are you doing?" I asked.

"A little sore. I didn't mean to sleep so long."

I checked my phone. We had another hour until we landed.

At the Philadelphia airport, we had an agent to push Zeke's chair, which meant Gabe and I could both manage the bags, although I did the heavy lifting.

Gabe had called Sharon when we landed. As we made our way outside the airport to the curb, I spotted her van. Rosene stood beside it. She grinned and waved. "Zeke!" Rosene called out. "Welcome home!"

Gabe drove while Sharon sat up front. Zeke and Rosene sat in the middle seat, and I sat in the back, watching the two chatter away. It was as if they'd never been apart. I'd never seen Rosene so animated.

Finally, I forced myself to stop listening, feeling as if I were eavesdropping on an intimate reunion. Gabe caught my eye in the rearview mirror and smiled. I needed to make sure to tell him how grateful I was for his help.

Rosene had brought crackers, cheese, and apple slices to eat in the car until we reached the farm, which I was grateful for. Stopping somewhere to eat would probably only tire Zeke more.

When Gabe stopped the van near the door, Dawdi and Mammi came down the back steps. Gabe turned off the engine, jumped out, and opened the side door. Then he gave Zeke his arm and helped him down.

Dawdi stepped forward.

Zeke switched his cane to his left hand, and as the two shook hands, he said, "Arden," in a warm and loving voice.

"Welcome home," Dawdi responded.

Mammi ushered everyone into the kitchen.

Zeke stopped in the middle of the room and put a hand on the table. "This kitchen is one of my favorite places in the world. I felt as if I belonged each time I sat at this table." He looked at Dawdi as he came through with one of the big suitcases while I followed with the other. Gabe was behind me with the smaller suitcase.

"Go wash up," Mammi said. "You can reminisce later. We thought you might need an early dinner."

Zeke laughed. "I like you, Priscilla. You remind me of Monika."

Rosene had moved to an upstairs bedroom, and we put Zeke in the spare bedroom on the first floor. After we washed up, we sat down at the table for beef stew and biscuits, thanks to Mammi. I guessed she'd closed the store for the day. As I looked around the table, I wondered if Dawdi had felt abandoned by Zeke as a boy. I guessed Rosene did, but she'd been so gracious to him, so eager to get him home.

I was coming to love Zeke, but he hadn't hurt me. I wasn't sure I'd be as forgiving if he had. The next morning, Zeke slept through breakfast, and I sent Gabe in to make sure he was still breathing. After everyone else left, I asked Rosene if she resented Zeke for leaving as he did.

She gave me a puzzled look. "Why would I?"

"You loved him. You never married anyone else. His leaving changed the trajectory of your life."

She smiled a little. "Zeke wasn't following Christ then. I had no business marrying him. He needed to go out into the world and find himself and his place. It took him a while, but he accomplished that."

"Wow. I guess that's what true love is, right?"

She patted my shoulder. "It's exactly what you did with Pierre."

"I didn't grow up with Pierre. You grew up with Zeke. You had loved him for years."

"I don't think that made it harder to let him go," Rosene said. "If anything, it might have made it easier."

"Why is that?"

She didn't answer me for a long moment. "Let me think about that more. Maybe as I tell you the rest of my story it will make more sense."

By the time Rosene and I finished the breakfast dishes, Zeke was up and ready for the day. All he wanted was a cup of coffee.

"Are you ready to meet Drew?" I asked.

"My maybe-grandson?"

I nodded.

"Absolutely."

"I'll walk over to the store and see if his car is there." I didn't want to text him if he was doing an interview.

It was a beautiful day, in the low seventies. It almost seemed tropical after Alaska. Drew's Prius was parked in the far corner of the lot.

I took out my phone and texted him and then stepped through the back door of the store as the clocks struck nine. Mammi and Gabe were doing the inventory before the shop opened at ten.

Gabe turned and asked, "Is Zeke up?"

"Yes. I just texted Drew but haven't had a reply from him."

"He was down about fifteen minutes ago and asked about Zeke," Mammi said. "You know, I think they have the same build. And maybe the same eyes."

"Do you think so?" Drew walked toward us from the back door. He smiled. "Sorry to sneak in."

"Are you ready to go meet Zeke?" I asked.

"I am."

Ten minutes later, we sat at the kitchen table with Rosene, Dawdi, and Zeke.

Drew asked Zeke, "Is this awkward for you?"

"No." Zeke paused a moment and then said, "I'm too old to feel awkward. I want the truth, as you probably do." He leaned backward in his chair a little. "It would have seemed quite scandalous in 1949. And don't get me wrong, I feel badly, even now, for what grief I may have caused a young woman. If I am your biological grandfather, your biological grandmother would be a young woman I met and spent time with in Texas. Her name was Susanna Green. She lived in San Antonio, where I worked a construction job. She was a few years older than I was and a telephone operator. I do remember that she grew up in Tennessee."

"Were you in a serious relationship?"

"Not really."

"Why did you leave San Antonio?" Drew asked.

"Well, I hadn't planned to stay. And when she told me her boyfriend was moving back to San Antonio from Houston, I left the next day, feeling like a fool." He raised his brows. "Which I was."

I thought of Rosene, on the farm, ill and trying to recover during that same time. And Zeke, leaving Texas for California.

"Thank you for sharing that," Drew said.

"I ordered a DNA test through the ancestry website you submitted yours to," Zeke said. "I'll let you know when I get the results."

Drew, who sat around the corner of the table from Zeke, leaned toward him and asked me, "Do you think we look alike?"

"You're both tall and slim," I said. "Thick hair. And, yes, your eyes are similar, although Drew's are much darker. I think it's plausible." I glanced at Dawdi. "You don't look much like Zeke, though."

Dawdi smiled. "I was never blessed with the tall genes. I

take more after my Grandfather Simons than the Zimmer-man men."

"Well," Drew said, "I'm grateful to all of you for being so generous with me." He glanced around the table. "I have to be honest—I hope I've found the right family. I couldn't find a better one. To have found a grandfather and cousins . . . that would mean so much. Or might mean so much, depending—"

"We'll just wait and see," Zeke said. "We'll know for sure soon."

Dawdi cleared his throat and then said, "Drew, I want you to know, whether we're related or not, you're important to us. God brought you to our farm for a reason, and we're thankful he did."

That evening, Ivy and Conrad came over to meet Zeke and to have pie. He was happy to meet them and chatted away. He wanted to know more about where we grew up in Oregon and then more about Brenna and why she'd moved to Ukraine and where she was getting married.

I was surprised he remembered everything I'd told him. "She's getting married here on the farm," I answered.

"Aww." Zeke glanced at Rosene. "I remember when Jeremiah and Clare got married here. The bishop allowed it, even though Monika and Ervin were Mennonite. Do you remember, Rosene?"

"Jah," she said. "I do. It was a month before World War Two started."

Zeke sighed. "We certainly are old, aren't we?"

"Yes, we are."

After Ivy and Conrad left, Rosene and I sat in the living room while Dawdi and Mammi went for a walk and Zeke headed to bed.

"Aren't you tired?" I asked Rosene. "I don't want you to overdo it."

"I'm fine," she said. "What I'd like to do right now is tell you more of the story."

I blew out a sigh of relief. "You don't know how much I've longed to hear more. I'd like that more than anything right now."

· 31 ·

Rosene

I waited five minutes from the time Martha left the plane before I followed. When I descended the steps, she was nowhere in sight. But a woman wearing a blue velvet hat was.

"Hallo, Betty," I said.

Betty, who appeared to be around forty, smiled at me. "Did you have a good flight?"

"Jah." I walked beside her across the tarmac to a hangar, where we climbed into the back seat of a car. The driver didn't say anything and neither did we. He drove us to a part of Berlin I didn't remember, through neighborhoods that had been partly rebuilt. I imagined the supplies had been flown in during the blockade. Some buildings were only framed. Others were being painted.

We stopped in front of a large house. Betty thanked the driver and then said to me in English, "Please follow me."

She led the way into the house and closed the door after me. As I followed her into the kitchen, she said, "We have until tomorrow morning. Relax. I'll fix dinner and then you can go to bed. Martha said you need extra rest."

Betty cooked pasta and served it with a salad made of cucumbers and tomatoes. It was simple but delicious. With a full stomach, I put on the pajamas Martha packed and crawled under the down comforter on my bed. The days in Frankfurt had exhausted me. I slept soundly and awoke when the summer sun began creeping beneath the shade in the room. I smelled coffee brewing and got out of bed, washed in the bathroom down the hall, and then dressed.

When I reached the kitchen, Betty, wearing a dress and apron, was cooking powdered eggs, according to the box next to the stove. "I managed to find a loaf of bread this morning." She opened the oven, where two slices of bread were under the broiler. "But not any butter." Obviously the blockade had ended, but food was still scarce. "I'm hoping more supplies will be available soon."

She set the table for two. It didn't seem anyone else was in the house. The eggs had a flat, bland flavor and a grainy texture, but I ate them, along with the dry toast. I started washing the dishes, and then Betty walked down the hall.

She returned wearing a skirt, blouse, and jacket, along with stockings and pumps. "I'll go with you to the border by car," she said. "But I'll need to wait there while you continue on foot. Hide your passport in the false bottom of your purse, along with this file for if you need to break into the apartment." She handed me a small file, and I put it and my passport in the bottom of the purse.

Betty continued, "Use Esther's passport to get into East Berlin. When you return to the border with Esther, have her use her passport and you use yours. If anyone asks, tell them you know Esther from her time in the US. I'll be waiting in the car where I dropped you off."

I put Esther's passport in the main compartment, and then Betty added several tubes of red lipstick and a flask of something to my purse.

"What are those for?" I asked.

"In case guards need some extra encouragement." She closed the purse. "It's a two-mile walk from the border to the apartment building."

I'd been walking at home again. I thought I could walk that far and back.

She handed me a piece of paper. "I need you to memorize these directions to get to the apartment building where we hope Esther is. Martha said she took you to the same place a year ago."

I nodded. "I remember it well."

"And the neighborhood?"

"Jah, although it was mostly rubble a year ago. Has that changed?"

She shook her head. "I can assure you it hasn't changed for the better—perhaps for the worse."

An hour later, I stood in line at the checkpoint to cross into East Berlin. The line was shorter than the line coming in the opposite direction, but it still took an hour. The guard checked the passport and asked the purpose of my trip. "To check on my uncle," I said. "I haven't heard from him for a few weeks."

The guard rifled through my purse and took the flask. He opened it and sniffed it. "I'm confiscating this," he said.

"But it's for my uncle. A gift."

He shook his head. "It's mine."

I began walking, silently repeating the instructions on the map and taking the turns I needed to. Again, the urban landscape was dismal. People still lived among the ruins. An old man sat on a sidewalk with a broken cup in his hand, begging. Two children played tag in the middle of the street.

I kept walking. I missed a turn but then corrected myself. Forty minutes later, I reached the apartment. Again, the hallways were dark. I made my way to the third floor and then to apartment 314. I knocked and knocked. No one answered.

A door opened down the hall, and a woman stepped out. "Esther?"

I turned toward her.

She spoke in German. "Where have you been?"

"At a friend's." I hoped the hall was dark enough that I would pass as Esther.

"Thank God," the woman said. "I thought he locked you in there. How are you?"

"I'm fine." I smiled. "I need to retrieve my things. Is he in there?"

"I saw him leave this morning. But I've heard noises coming from the apartment during the day when he's gone. That's why I thought he'd locked you in there."

I shook my head. "Can you help me?" I didn't want to pull the file out of my purse in front of her.

She said, "Stay put."

She returned a minute later, carrying something in her hand. When she reached the door, she ran a butter knife between the plate and the frame. The lock clicked. She turned the knob, and the door opened. "There you go," she said, pleased with herself.

"*Danke schön,*" I said, wishing I knew the woman's name.

"Be quick," she replied. "You never know when that beast will return."

I shivered and closed the door behind me. I hurried through the apartment, whispering, "Esther, it's me, Rosene." I searched the one bedroom with a mattress on the floor. I searched the one closet in the hall and the cupboards in the kitchen. If the woman next door heard sounds—as long as they weren't from rats—it was likely Esther was somewhere on that end of the apartment. There was a window seat under the last living room window. I opened it. There was one box in it, but that was all. I lifted it out, and then knocked on the plywood bottom.

A grunting sound greeted me. And then another one. I ran my hands along the wood on the bottom and then gasped. Something was pushing the plywood upward.

"Esther?"

More grunting sounds.

I grabbed the plywood and lifted it away. Esther's head popped up. Her mouth was gagged, and her hands tied.

I quickly ungagged her as tears started falling down her face. "How did you get here?" she asked.

I started to untie her hands. "Martha sent me." The rope was knotted several times. "I need a knife."

"By the sink."

As I returned with the knife, she said, "We need to get going. He could return at any time."

I began sawing the rope. Finally, the knife broke through.

She groaned. "He took my passport."

"I have one for you." I gave her my hand to help her out. Esther had lost a considerable amount of weight, and her face appeared gaunt. Her clothes were wrinkled, and she was barefoot.

"Where are your shoes?" I asked.

"He took them."

"We have to walk to the border. I'll go search the bedroom and see if I can find something," I said. I finally found a worn pair of men's slippers in the bottom drawer of the bureau. I also found a woman's sweater that would help cover Esther's wrinkled dress. Anywhere else, she'd be conspicuous, but in East Berlin she wouldn't stand out.

Esther stood by the door. I gave her the slippers.

"I'll go first and wait by the door of the apartment. When you arrive, start for the border, going straight," I instructed. "I'll circle around the block and catch up with you."

~

As I waited outside, someone yelled, "Esther!"

I turned. It was a middle-aged man with a beard. Her uncle? He couldn't be on the sidewalk when she came down. I turned and hurried around the corner of the building. He followed me, yelling, "Esther!"

I hurried across the street, wanting him to keep yelling to warn Esther to hurry the other direction. I slowed my pace, and he grew closer, yelling "Esther!" again.

Then I darted into a store and hid behind a shelf.

"Esther!" he yelled one more time. Then he started walking up and down the aisles of the store. I stayed put, looking at an empty shelf.

"There you are!"

I turned toward him.

"Esther?"

I shook my head and said, "My name is *Roese*." I couldn't think of anything else to say.

He stepped closer and placed his finger under my chin, tilting my head.

I glared at him.

He dropped his hand and took a step backward. With a scowl on his face, he turned away.

I waited until he left the store, and then I continued on down the block, crossed the street, and then circled around. Then I hurried up the street, hoping to find Esther.

After a block, Esther came out from the side of a building. "Is he gone?"

"Jah," I said. "You go first. I'll walk behind you."

I guessed once Esther's uncle discovered she was gone, he'd head to the border looking for her, which might be about now. I wasn't sure if we should go to a different checkpoint or not. If we did, we'd have farther to go before reconnecting with Betty.

"Keep walking," I said to Esther. "But listen. I have some questions for you." However weak I felt from my recent illness, it didn't compare to Esther being locked in a window seat and half starved. "Can you walk to the border?"

"Jah," she answered. "I could fly if I had too."

"Will your uncle head to the nearest crossing?"

She froze.

"Keep walking. . . ."

She did. "Most likely," she said. "That's where he would expect me to go."

"Then we should go to the next one. We'll have to backtrack once we cross the border—our ride is at the closest one."

"I hope he doesn't send one of his comrades to the other crossings looking for us," Esther said. "He has a group of hoodlums working for him."

I hadn't thought of that. I asked, "Do you know how to get to the next checkpoint?"

"I do." Esther turned to the left and picked up her pace, the slippers slapping against the sidewalk.

We finally reached the next checkpoint. I did my best to stand to the side and slightly behind Esther, blocking anyone's view of her unless they were ahead of us in line. Her hand shook as she held her passport. I pulled up the false bottom of my purse and removed mine as discreetly as I could. When we reached the front of the line, Esther showed her passport as someone yelled, "Esther!"

The guard glanced up.

"He's yelling at me," I said. "But my name is Rosene. Not Esther." I quickly handed him my passport and nudged Esther ahead, hoping the guard wouldn't remember that her name was, in fact, Esther.

He didn't seem to. The guard handed Esther her passport, and she hurried forward.

I pulled the lipsticks from my purse. "For your girlfriend," I said. "I know how hard it is to get cosmetics."

He smiled and took them from me. Then he glanced at my passport and waved me through.

As we neared the American guard, Esther's uncle shouted, "Stop those girls!"

"I'm an American citizen!" I said to the guard as I reached him. "That man has been harassing me all day—he followed me here."

The guard asked, "Are you two together?"

"No," Esther replied. "We met in line, waiting."

He glanced at Esther's passport and then mine. "Go on," he said.

Esther's uncle continued to shout.

As we entered West Berlin, I let out a sigh of relief, but Esther grabbed my arm. "That's one of Onkel's comrades."

A stocky man wearing a hat low on his head turned toward us. We turned right, in the direction of the next checkpoint, where Betty waited for us. The man started after us. I grabbed Esther's hand and began to run. Neither of us had much stamina, but I knew I had more than Esther. If only we *could* fly.

Esther tripped over the slippers, but I steadied her. At the next intersection, I heard footsteps behind us and then tires on the pavement and a screech. I didn't want to turn around and face the man pursuing us.

"Get in!" A car door flung open and hit my leg. "Now!" It was Martha, driving a sedan. I yanked Esther and pushed her into the car as the man came around the back. I dove in after her. Martha hit the gas. The car door swung wide, but I managed to grab the handle and pull it shut.

· 32 ·

The man ran after us as Martha accelerated down the street. Esther was already on the floor of the car, and Martha barked, "Rosene! Get down!"

A few minutes later, the car came to a stop. "Stay down," Martha said. "When I say *now* very slowly sit up and then count to a hundred. Then, Rosene, you calmly get out of the car and climb into Betty's car. She's sitting up front with her driver. Esther, you count to a hundred again, and then you do the same."

"And then what?" I asked.

"She'll take both of you to the airport. Once you're in Hamburg, take the train to Frankfurt, to Josef and Lena's. I'll meet you there in a few days."

After a few minutes, Martha said, "Now."

I sat up slowly, and Esther climbed from the floor of the car to the seat. I counted slowly to one hundred and then opened the door, climbed out, and then got into the back of the car I'd been in earlier. As I closed the door and scooted across the seat, the driver started the car. When Esther climbed into the car and closed the door, the driver began moving away from the curb.

Someone shouted, "Esther!"

The man from the other checkpoint appeared behind the car, and the driver accelerated. I couldn't help but look behind us. Martha turned her car around into the street, blocking the man and Esther's uncle, who had appeared beside him. The uncle hit the hood of her car with the palm of his hand, and the other man tried to dart around it. But Martha put the car in reverse, bumping into him. Martha had her window down. "Sorry!"

Esther's uncle reached the back door of her car and yanked open the door. A look of disgust passed over his face. The driver of our car turned left. I craned my neck to try to see Martha, but she and her car were now out of view. Our driver turned right and then sped away from the area. After taking what seemed to be a convoluted route, we arrived at the airport.

Betty stayed in the car, but the driver climbed out and opened the trunk. He took out my suitcase and then opened my door. I slid out, followed by Esther. "Safe journeys," he said in German. "We're grateful for your work."

"Rosene, wait." Betty climbed into the back seat and slipped off her shoes and then her stockings. She scooted across the seat and handed them to me. "I hope they'll fit Esther."

Tears filled my eyes. "Danke."

A few minutes later, Esther and I were strapped into seats on another transport plane, ready to take off. I stuffed the stockings in my purse for the time being, and Esther took off the slippers and put on the shoes. They were perhaps a half-size too big, but they would do.

When we reached Hamburg, I opened the suitcase. On top were two coats, another pair of pajamas, another set of underwear, a skirt, a blouse, and a sweater. Underneath the clothes was a packet of Deutschmarks and a note from Martha. *This is enough for taxi fare, train tickets, and food along the way. I'll see you soon.*

I was miffed with Martha, feeling as if she'd set us adrift, until anxiety filled me again. What might happen to her? I knew I couldn't dwell on that now—I needed to take care of Esther. First, she needed food. And then rest. Even if it took us a day longer to get to Frankfurt.

We followed several soldiers off the plane. One said to the other, "Let's go by the cafeteria first." We followed them into a hangar converted into a cafeteria.

There was a line of people in uniforms but a few civilians too, including women. I stashed the suitcase in the restroom, and then Esther and I went through the line. It was American food. Meatloaf and mashed potatoes. Green beans. Jell-O salad. And soft rolls. Esther and I sat and ate.

"We'll take a taxi to the train station from here," I said. "There's a train to Frankfurt at five. Hopefully we can make it." It was a quarter to four.

"Let's go," Esther said. "The farther we are from Berlin, the better I'll feel."

We had to find a phone in an office two hangars over to call for a taxi. Then we had to walk out to the main road, which was over a mile away. Betty's shoes looked better on Esther's feet, but the slippers had been easier for her to walk in.

Finally, we made it to the train station. I rushed to the booth and bought our tickets. Ten minutes later, we were on the train heading south to Frankfurt.

Esther immediately fell asleep. I took the coats from the suitcase and spread one over the top of her while I put the other one on.

Worry gripped me. Was Martha safe? Had Esther's uncle gotten into her car? What if something happened to her?

It would be nearly ten by the time we arrived in Frankfurt and nearly eleven by the time we reached the house. Would Vater Josef and Lena let us in?

I dozed for a while and then awoke with a start. I longed to be home in Lancaster County. Tears stung my eyes, and I stifled a sob.

"What's wrong?" Esther asked.

Feeling like a fool—what were my losses compared to hers?—I said, "Nothing."

"It's something."

"I'm missing home."

"And Zeke?" She reached for my left hand. "Have the two of you married?"

"He left," I said. "For California again."

"And you didn't go with him?"

"No."

"Rosene." She clasped my hand. "You two were perfect for each other. I thought you'd marry soon after I left."

"A year ago I hoped we'd marry. But things were never the same when he returned from his first trip. He'd changed." Maybe I'd changed too. "I regretted not going with him after he left again, but I don't know if that would have been the right thing to do. He said he'd write, but I haven't heard from him."

"I'm sorry," she said. "Maybe he still will. Maybe he'll tell you to meet him in California, and you'll live happily ever after, like in a Hollywood movie."

I tried to smile as I dried my eyes. "Will you come back to Lancaster with me?"

"I don't know," she answered. "I need to speak with Martha."

Esther was without a home. She had no parents to return to, only an uncle she couldn't trust. Lancaster wasn't home to her. All she seemed to have was Martha.

At least I had one family that loved and cared for me, and a second one that was at least interested in me. I could make a plan for myself, whether to stay in Lancaster County or to leave. It was my choice.

When we reached Frankfurt, I called the Weber home. After twelve rings, Garit answered with a gruff "Hallo."

"It's Rosene. I hope I didn't wake you."

"No. I was writing."

"I'm at the train station and will arrive at the house soon. I have a friend with me. Esther is her name."

"I'll let Lena know," Garit said. He didn't sound happy about it.

When we reached the house, I knocked softly on the front door and then loudly. A light flicked on in the house across the street. Finally, Garit came to the door and let us in. "Lena said to go on up to your room."

I led Esther upstairs. She didn't bother to change into her pajamas and fell into what had been Dorina's bed, exhausted. It took me longer to fall asleep, as I grappled with who I was. A Mennonite young woman from the United States or a German woman from Frankfurt?

I'd just rescued Esther from East Berlin. For some reason, Martha thought only I could do it. And I had.

I stared at the ceiling. What would life be like in Lancaster County for the rest of my life without Zeke? All I'd wanted was to create a home with him, to live together and make a life together, to hope the Lord would bring children into our life, regardless of the fact I would never have our own.

The next morning, when I stepped into the kitchen, Lena

and Garit sat at the table with cups of coffee and a newspaper. Lena turned her head toward me. "Tell me about your friend."

I poured myself a cup of coffee. "Her name is Esther. She's from Berlin and knows Martha."

"Through the Red Cross?"

I nodded. "Esther is a refugee. Her parents were killed during the war."

"What is her last name?"

"Lang."

Garit glanced up from the newspaper. "She looks Jewish."

"Her father was Catholic." I sat down at the table with them.

"Meaning her mother was Jewish?"

I stared at him. "What does it matter?"

He glared at me and returned his gaze to his newspaper. "How long will the two of you be staying?"

I answered, "Until Martha returns."

Garit folded the newspaper. "How long will that be?"

"Not long."

Garit stood. "We're not running a hotel here."

"Rosene can stay as long as she needs to." Vater Josef stood in the doorway. "She's always welcome here. So is her friend and Martha too."

Garit shook his head. "Do you really think Martha works for the Red Cross? There's something more going on."

"It doesn't matter," Vater Josef said. "This is still my house. They're welcome here."

Garit, without saying anything more, left the kitchen. Lena stood and followed, saying, "I need to get to work—to pay the bills around here."

Vater Josef sat down beside me. "I meant what I said.

You're always welcome, although I understand it's hard for you to be here."

"Danke." Was he sincere? Or just an ill old man, regretting what he'd done, but too afraid to say so? I stood and said, "I'll pour you a cup of coffee."

I wished him no ill will. I'd forgiven him as best I could. Did I have an obligation to do more?

Esther mostly slept for the next few days. Twice she came down to eat, but often I took a tray up to my room for her.

Lena complained about not having enough money in her food budget to feed two extra mouths, so I gave her most of the rest of the money in the envelope.

One evening, after I washed the dishes, Garit came into the kitchen. "Where's Martha?" he asked.

"She'll be here soon," I said.

"That's what you said before."

I concentrated on drying the last plate.

"You have no idea how much trouble you've caused this family," Garit said. "Lena and Josef never deserved to be treated this way."

I spun around, clutching the plate with the towel. "Them treated this way? Let's talk about the Kaiserslautern train station. What would you have done with Clare and me if you'd caught us?"

"I don't know what you're talking about." His face reddened.

I deepened my voice. "'Has anyone seen a young American woman with a thirteen-year-old German girl? They're wanted by the Gestapo.'"

"Don't be ludicrous." He crossed his arms. "I wasn't working with the Gestapo. And I didn't go after you."

I put the plate in the cupboard and then marched out of the kitchen.

"If Martha isn't back in two days, you need to leave," Garit called out after me.

I ignored him.

I knew Martha would come to Frankfurt, as she promised, if she could. But my worries were growing. Had something happened to her? Who should I contact to inquire about her? I had no idea who could be trusted and who couldn't.

Finally, I took a taxi to the Red Cross office in Frankfurt and waited in line for two hours to speak to the receptionist.

I greeted her and then said, "I'm the sister of Martha Hall and the sister-in-law of George Hall, who both work for the Red Cross. I need to speak with one of them."

The woman stood. "I'll return in a minute." She turned and knocked on the closed door, then entered the office and closed the door behind her. I stared at the door, willing it to open.

Finally, it did. The receptionist stepped out and said, "Herr Hoffman would like to speak with you."

As I walked into the office, my knees began to shake.

A man wearing a suit stood in the middle of the room. He extended his hand and said, "I'm Herr Hoffman, the new director of the Frankfurt Red Cross. Please sit down." He motioned to a chair against the wall.

I sat.

"I'm afraid I have bad news," he said.

I braced myself, fearing the worst had happened to Martha.

"George Hall passed away three days ago in Berlin."

I gasped. "Was he killed?"

"No. It seems he had a heart condition."

I remembered that Martha had mentioned a heart problem kept him out of serving in the war. "Where is Martha?" I asked.

"That's the problem," Herr Hoffman said. "We don't know. I was hoping you did."

· 33 ·

Treva

W ait," I said as I put the last of the dishes away.
I turned toward Rosene. "George is dead, and
Martha is missing. How can that be?"

Rosene had a sad expression on her face. "Jah, those were
hard times. I mourned George's death and wondered if Martha even knew. Perhaps she'd been captured and was in East
Berlin. Perhaps in Esther's uncle's apartment, in the window
seat, which would have been difficult for her to fit in."

"This is horrible." I placed my hand against the ache in
my heart. Rosene had already lost Zeke. "What happened?"

"I'll tell you more soon." Rosene yawned. "I need to get
to bed."

I watched in disbelief as she shuffled out of the kitchen.
How could she leave me hanging?

The next morning, after breakfast, Zeke said he'd like to
go out to the barn. I said I'd take him and then asked Rosene,
who was doing dishes, if she wanted to go too.

"No." She laughed. "That barn has changed a whole lot

since 1949 but not so much since last week. I'm going to tidy up in here."

"Don't overdo it," I said.

"I won't, ma'am." She shot me a sassy smile.

As Zeke and I crossed the driveway, I held on to his arm while he made his way with his cane. When we reached the barn, Dawdi came out of the milk room. "Zeke, welcome."

"I always knew you'd make a good farmer," Zeke said. "You were enthralled with all of it from the beginning. You'd cry when your Dat wouldn't let you ride on the spreader with him."

"It took years for him to allow me on that piece of equipment."

"That's probably because I was almost trampled when I fell off once," Zeke explained. "That was a tricky machine."

"It was," Dawdi said. "It still is, and I'm getting too old to operate it anymore." He winked at me.

"Yep," Zeke said. "It's time to retire."

Dawdi didn't agree or disagree. Instead, he asked, "Have you been inside a dairy recently?"

Zeke shook his head and smiled. "Not since the last time I was inside this one. I, unlike you, wasn't made to be a farmer."

That surprised me. From everything Rosene had told me, it seemed as if Zeke was a hard worker as a young man and did well at farming.

As we walked into the milk room, Zeke said, "I didn't realize how unfit I was for farming until I tried other things. Farming was all I'd known until then."

"No one here ever saw you as unfit for farming," Dawdi replied. "You were sorely missed. I don't think Dat ever got over you leaving."

Zeke rubbed the back of his neck with his free hand. "That makes me miss Jeremiah. He was a good brother. And a good friend."

"And the best father," Arden said.

"He was a good man." Zeke collected himself for a moment, then pointed to the tubing along the ceiling. "So, the milk goes from the milkers straight to—" he pointed to the vat—"here?"

"That's right," Dawdi said. "It's much more streamlined than it used to be. Of course, we have a bigger herd too. . . ."

A half hour later, as I walked Zeke to the house, he said, "I love this place. It feels more like home than even my own house did, which I understand isn't in the family anymore."

"That's right," I said. "It sounds as if Dawdi is the only cousin who still farms in Lancaster County."

"That's a shame," Zeke said. After a long pause, he said, "When I came home the first time, Mamm blamed the Simonses for me not wanting to join the church. She called them worldly. She saw Monika as being different, running her store and being from Germany. She dressed differently than the Amish women for sure, but even differently than the Mennonite women around here. And it was hard for her to have Jeremiah living with a Mennonite family instead of an Amish one. She wanted him to marry a girl who grew up Amish, not Clare, who became Amish as an adult. But it wasn't the Simonses' fault I left. They were good people."

He stumbled a little, and I held him steady. "The Simonses did give me a glimpse of something more, of possibilities. All of them had traveled. They had a car. And fancier food than we ate. And they had so much going on at the store—people coming and going. And Martha! Oh, dear Martha. She was something. What happened to her?"

"I don't know yet," I answered.

"What do you mean?"

"Rosene is in the middle—well, close to the end, maybe, of telling me what happened in 1948 and 1949. Right now, in the story, Martha is missing in Berlin—perhaps East Berlin."

Zeke shook his head. "See what I mean? Those Simonses had adventures. They inspired me to have adventures of my own. But they didn't inspire me *not* to join the church. It just wasn't meant to be at the time."

"At the time? What do you mean?"

"Oh, I'm just rambling," he said. "Do you think you could help me find a nearby assisted living place to move into in about a month or so? I don't want to wear out my welcome here."

Everyone on the farm seemed to be thriving. Dawdi was thrilled to have Zeke home. Zeke seemed to have charmed Mammi, because she had been on her best behavior. Gabe was back to his old self and was officially working for Mammi in the store again. Kamil seemed more relaxed around us. Drew stopped by the house more and more.

And Rosene seemed to grow younger each day.

Then there was me. I was in a conundrum. When I'd arrived home from Haiti, I couldn't wait to leave the farm. Now I dreaded leaving in June. Misty and Shawn's resort was beautiful, and I'd enjoyed coordinating the wedding and my work for the week. But I missed being around older people. I missed *my* older people in particular.

But what future did I have on the farm?

I took Zeke to visit two different assisted living places.

One was as nice as his place in Alaska and within a half hour of the farm. But he wanted to see a couple more.

On Tuesday at lunch, Dawdi told Zeke to take his time finding a place to live. After Dawdi went out to the barn and Mammi returned to the store, Zeke said, "I really don't want to outstay my welcome."

"Oh, don't worry about that," Rosene said. "Arden wouldn't tell you to take your time if he didn't mean it."

Brenna texted to say Lena's estate was settled, and she wanted to talk to Rosene about it. It was raining that day, so Rosene and I barged in on Gabe instead of going all the way to the barn in the rain. Zeke tagged along. I'd only texted Brenna about Zeke. It would be her first time to meet him by video. I sat in the middle of the couch, between Rosene and Zeke.

At first, the connection was poor, but then it came through. I introduced Zeke to Brenna.

"Hello, niece," he said.

"Hello, Onkel," she answered. "I'm happy to meet you."

"Likewise."

"Gabe is here too." He stepped into the camera field and waved.

I thought about how Gabe was like our Zeke—the farmhand we had a good relationship with and missed when he was gone.

"You should start by telling Rosene about her house," I said. "Then you and I can talk about the wedding. We only have a month. . . ."

Brenna clapped her hands together and grinned, which was so unlike her. She didn't used to show much emotion.

"Rosene," she said, "I think everything is settled. The leasing company has the information they need and will rent the house out on six-month to one-year contracts. They'll be responsible for repairs and will notify me of any issues. The rent money, after their cut, will be deposited directly into your account. And they'll send you tax information that's needed to pay both your German taxes and your US taxes. You'll also need to pay German property taxes. Herr Mayer gave me the name of a tax preparer that he recommends."

"Thank you," Rosene said.

"Lena made several updates to the house about a decade ago. The property company will paint the inside and redo the hardwood floors, which will be done in a few days. Then they'll advertise the property."

"Perfect," Rosene said.

They chatted for a few more minutes and then Brenna said, "Okay. One more thing. Lena left a letter addressed to you in the desk."

"Did you open it?"

Brenna shook her head. "It looks like a personal letter, as if she intended to mail it but didn't have a chance."

"Just bring it with you when you come home."

"I'll do that." Brenna's gaze shifted to me. "On to the wedding plans."

"I should call you back," I said, "after I walk Rosene and Zeke to the house."

"I can do it," Gabe said.

Brenna told Rosene and Zeke good-bye, and then they headed to the door.

As they left and the door closed, Brenna said, "Rosene and Zeke are so cute together."

I laughed. "They're both over ninety."

"So?"

"You're in love. You're projecting."

"I don't think so. . . ." Brenna grinned.

I started watching Rosene and Zeke when they were to-gether. It was obvious they cared for each other, but did they still share romantic feelings after all these years?

Zeke always stood when Rosene came into the room. His eyes sparkled when she spoke. He sat beside her at meals. Even though he hobbled around on a cane, he refilled her coffee and brought her glasses of water and walked with her a half mile each day to build up her strength. He tow-ered over her by at least a foot but hovered when he was close to her, as if his very presence could protect her. One time I observed Rosene turn up her face toward him just as he ducked his head toward her. My heart lurched at the sight.

From the moment Rosene and Zeke heard each other's voices and saw each other again, they'd been connecting. Rosene had paid an exorbitant amount for Gabe to fly out to get Zeke home. Zeke had upended his life to move back to Lancaster County. I thought he wanted to come home—but maybe what he really wanted was to return to Rosene.

Zeke sat on the front porch with her in the afternoon. I wasn't sure what they talked about, but it seemed to be meaningful to both of them.

Life on the farm had a comforting routine, plus the variety of people kept things interesting. Zaida and Cala and the children came out a couple of times while Kamil did the afternoon milking with Dawdi. The children played on the lawn, and Zaida and Cala visited with Rosene and Zeke. Gabe, when he wasn't working in the store, often visited with Zeke and Rosene on the porch or helped Dawdi with light chores.

One afternoon, as I helped Dawdi repair the fence in the south pasture, I brought up the future of the farm. "Would you have offered the farm to just Ivy if she wasn't married to Conrad?"

Dawdi, who held a hammer in his hand, froze. "What do you mean?"

"Did you want to give the farm to Ivy or to Conrad?"

"To both." He hammered the nail in the split rail fence several times and then stood straight with his hand on the small of his back.

I squared my shoulders. "Would you be willing to give the farm to me?"

He cocked his head as he asked, "Once you're married?"

"No. Before I'm married. Even if I never marry." I put my hand on my hip. "Remember, I'm not even twenty-one yet."

He laughed. "Operating a farm is a lot of work."

"I know that," I said. "And you *know* I know that. But I'm strong, and I understand how to operate a dairy farm and manage the land. I could do it if you supervised me for the next few years."

"Are you serious?"

I nodded.

"But you're planning on going to Alaska to work—and then who knows what."

"I *was* planning to go back to Alaska, but while I was there, I realized this land matters to me. It's part of me." I gestured across the pasture. "If allowed, I think I could make a life and a living here and keep it in the family."

Dawdi tugged on his beard with his free hand. "You are serious, aren't you?"

I nodded.

"Well." He spoke slowly. "Think about it some more and pray about it. I'll do the same. We'll talk about this again soon."

When I did the milking with Dawdi that Saturday and Sunday, I quizzed him about things I didn't know. Had he found a new farrier for the horses? Did he get bids on grain and the feed that he didn't grow, or did he always order it from the feed store? If he *could* have a tractor on the farm, would he?

At that question, he said, "Treva, if you end up taking over the farm and you stay Mennonite, I'm fine if you have a tractor. Just don't bring electricity back into the house until I'm dead."

I assured him I wouldn't.

On Sunday, I went to the Amish service to see how people reacted to Zeke. I shouldn't have been surprised that there wasn't any drama. He sat with Dawdi on the men's side. Literally no one remembered Zeke. After the service, he said sitting that long was hard, but he enjoyed the service, even though he didn't remember much Pennsylvania Dutch. However, he said, the meal afterward of bean soup, fresh bread, and peanut butter spread was even better than he remembered as a child.

On Tuesday, Rosene baked a cake for my twenty-first birthday, Mammi made lasagna, and Ivy brought baguettes and a big salad. Everyone, including Gabe and Drew, celebrated with me. And Brenna joined via video to sing me happy birthday.

The next Sunday, I went to the Mennonite church, and Gabe went with me. A couple of times during the service, he leaned forward with his hands clasped together.

I had been so eager to do God's work when I went to Haiti, but I'd left depleted. Gabe had felt far away from God the last few years, but now seemed to have grown closer. It took Zeke years before he truly came to know the Lord. It took some of us longer to return than others.

On the way home, Gabe asked, "What do you think it means to start over?"

"Are you referring to Pastor Mike's sermon from a few weeks ago?"

"Yes."

"Starting over means . . ." I stole a glance at him and grimaced. "Starting over? I don't know. See what Google says."

He pulled out his phone and a minute later said, "To make a new beginning."

I thought about it a second and said, "*To make*. It's deliberate."

"Do you think one can start a new beginning in an old environment?"

"Yes." I reached out and touched his arm. "Especially in a store one has already worked at for the last eight years. Has Mammi asked you to manage the place yet?"

He laughed. "I think that's wishful thinking on your part."

I grew serious. "What steps would you take to make a new beginning, no matter where you land?"

"I'd be more committed to the future."

"What would that look like?"

After a long pause, he said, "I have some ideas, but I'm not ready to talk about them yet."

"Fair enough." I wasn't ready to talk with him about asking Dawdi for the farm yet either. What if Dawdi's answer was no? What would I do instead?

On Monday, I finished planning and confirmed the details

for Brenna's wedding. Dawdi approved of having a photographer as long as they only took pictures of the wedding party and Englischers, which made me sad. I'd really hoped for a photo of Rosene with Zeke.

That afternoon Drew and Stephanie stopped by and both Rosene and Zeke talked about life on the farm during and after World War II, and Zeke talked about Jeremiah. Zeke talked about what it was like to be harassed for not being a soldier.

"I remember the POWs harassing you. Did other people too?" Rosene asked.

"Jah," he said. "Sometimes when I was driving a buggy or wagon on the road, men would yell out their truck windows at me."

"You weren't even eighteen when the war ended," Rosene said.

"Jah," Zeke said. "But I was big. I looked older. It was hard for other people when they thought we Amish weren't doing our part. I understood that. Their loved ones were dying."

"It was a hard time," Drew said, "for everybody."

Zeke said, "It wasn't hard for me, except for having Jeremiah gone. I didn't mind people harassing me. I understood."

"I never knew you felt that way," Rosene said. "I was just so glad you were safe on the farm."

"And then I wasn't safe on the farm," he said. "I was out in the big, bad world, but I soon realized it really wasn't that big nor that bad. Sure, there were bad people who did bad things. But there were more good people. The Englischers, generally, weren't nearly as bad as I expected. Many were closer to God than I was and much more sincere. They understood salvation when I didn't at the time. They cared about their neighbors. And they cared about me."

I headed into the kitchen to start dinner, and Gabe followed me in.

I asked, "Want a cup of coffee? I'll heat up the pot."

"Thanks." He sat down at the table. "I really like Zeke," he said. "He's straightforward. It's like he really knows himself. Do you think he was always that way?"

I shook my head. "I think he was a typical guy when he was younger." I gave Gabe a sassy look. "Sorry."

He rolled his eyes at me. "No offense taken."

I sat down at the table. "He left without settling things with Rosene. He said he'd write—but it seems he didn't. I don't think he was very self-aware back then."

"What do you think made him change?"

I leaned toward Gabe. "A whole lot of years."

He frowned. "That's not very encouraging."

"And God. And maybe learning to be honest about things." I stood, retrieved two mugs, and stepped to the stove. "Why do you ask?"

Gabe put both of his hands flat on the tabletop. "I'm just trying to figure out what to work on first." He shot me a grin. "I'll save aging for later." His face grew serious. "I've learned a lot from the story Rosene is telling and also from spending time with Zeke. I can relate to him."

I gave Gabe a thumbs-up. I was learning a lot from Rosene and Zeke too.

The next day, as I drove Rosene home from her last cardiac rehab appointment, I told her I'd had an email from Brenna. "She said your house in Germany has been rented out to a couple from the Netherlands with four children. The wife is teaching at the University of Frankfurt for a year."

Rosene exhaled, as if in relief. "That's perfect. How wonderful for there to be children in the house again. Dorina and I were the last—and that was eighty years ago."

"Did you ever think of selling the house?" Before she could answer, I winked and said, "You could take Zeke on a year-long cruise."

Rosene waved her hand at me, as if telling me to stop. Then she said, "I think the bishop would object to that."

I laughed. "I think so too." Then I changed the subject. "I've been thinking about Mammi and Gran growing up as friends here in Lancaster County. Mammi mentioned that the first time she ever visited the store, your clock was chiming the hour, and that it was the only clock in the store at the time."

"Jah," Rosene said. "I was there that day with Arden and Janice. Clare was tending the store, and the children and I were on a walk and stopped in to say hello. Priscilla came in with her mother. A year later, Priscilla and your gran started school with Janice. They became close, but Priscilla and Laurel were particularly close. Arden was in the third grade. They all ran around together as they grew up."

"When did Dawdi and Mammi start courting?"

"Well, not until they were eighteen or so, but I think Arden only had eyes for Priscilla since he was a boy."

That made me feel warm inside.

"Priscilla's parents loved her, but her father was ill most of her growing up and her mother wasn't a warm person—no doubt she was worn down from caring for her husband," Rosene said. "Clare and Jeremiah looked out for Priscilla. And Laurel's love and Arden's attention helped her too. Priscilla was quiet, but she would light up in the store when the clock chimed. She always really loved that."

"Interesting," I said. "Why did you put the clock in the store instead of the house?"

"That's a bit complicated. Would you like me to tell you the end of the story?"

"Jah," I answered. "Of course."

· 34 ·

Rosene

I stopped and sent a telegram to Mutter on my way home from the Red Cross office, saying it was from Martha and that we'd decided to spend more time in Frankfurt. I didn't want to worry my parents. Then, as I took a taxi back to Vater Josef's house, I did my best not to burst into tears. Weakness was scoffed at in this home. If I arrived in tears or even with a red face, Lena and Garit would be disgusted with me.

I couldn't trust them with the information that George had died and no one knew where Martha was. Without Martha to hold them accountable, would they kick Esther and me out of the house? I believed Garit might, but I couldn't know for sure. And so far, he didn't seem to control the household. Vater Josef did—but just barely.

I wasn't even sure if I should tell Esther, at least not without first having a plan for the two of us. And to execute a plan, I needed money, and the only way I could get money was to send another telegram to Vater and Mutter and ask them to wire me the cost of two airline tickets. But that would be an astronomical amount for them.

When the taxi pulled up in front of the house, I paid the fare and climbed out. Then I stood and stared at what used to be my home, listening to the fountain in the middle of the street. I decided to simply say the director of the Frankfurt Red Cross didn't have the information I needed. If Martha had been kidnapped and taken to East Berlin, wouldn't someone have reported that they had her? Wouldn't it be an international scandal? Unless they'd done worse than kidnap her.

I couldn't rush to the worst conclusion.

I cooked dinner that night—a roasted chicken, which was a treat in postwar Germany, and scalloped potatoes like Clare made. Thankfully, Lena had purchased the groceries. After we ate, Esther excused herself and went upstairs, while Lena and Garit went for a walk to discuss his thesis.

Vater Josef said, "I'll help with the dishes."

"I can manage," I said.

"No. I want to." He stood and began slowly clearing the table. As we worked, he said, "There's something I need to talk to you about."

"Oh?" I hoped it wasn't anything serious. I had enough troubling issues to deal with as it was. I began running the dishwater.

"It's about the Simonses—about Ervin, in particular." He took a clean towel from the drawer. "I used to believe Ervin was an unsophisticated man—a bumpkin of sorts. I found him quaint when I first met him when he came to study here in Germany. He was the son of a farmer. I was the son of a professor. He was from a rural area in the state of Pennsylvania. I was from the city of Frankfurt." Vater Josef dried the first glass and then continued. "I had recently converted to the Mennonite faith, believing that the theology better reflected the teachings of Christ. When Ervin enrolled at the university with the others from the US, I found all of them antiquated in their thinking and stuck in their ways. The Mennonites in Germany seemed much more adaptive and progressive than their American cousins. I attributed that to the persecution the Mennonites in Europe had already endured, whereas the Mennonites in the United States hadn't been challenged in the same ways. It's no surprise I was shocked when Monika Kaufman—my own Rose's sister—fell in love with Ervin and then married him and moved to Pennsylvania." He continued drying the glasses and then started to put them away.

"Put them on the table," I said. "I'll take care of them." He seemed too weak to be helping with the dishes, let alone putting them in the cupboards.

"Ervin seemed to be simple," Vater Josef said, "and yet he understood things about human nature that made him leery of the Nazis from the very beginning. I, desperate for Germany to rise again, to become unified and economically self-sufficient, was willing to ignore Hitler's idiosyncrasies—what I thought they were at the time. Now I see it was so much more than that."

He put a plate on the table. When he reached the drying rack again, he said, "You're probably wondering why I'm telling you this."

I wasn't. I just wanted him to stop. But I didn't say that.

Without waiting for a response, he said, "I was deceived by Hitler and the Nazis. I put my trust in their ideology instead of in the Lord. That was my fault. And it tainted everything, including my relationship with you. I'm sorry."

He took another plate from the rack without looking at me. "I wasn't a good father to you, nor to Dorina."

I drew in a breath. No one in my German family ever mentioned Dorina.

"I didn't protect the two of you. I made horrible decisions. I'm thankful to Ervin for taking my place. I'm grateful you have him and Monika as your parents. And grateful for Clare and Jeremiah and their children, and for Martha too."

Did I have Martha? I couldn't think of that now.

I inhaled, taking a moment, debating what to do. I thought of Joseph's words in scripture: *Ye thought evil against me; but God meant it unto good.* Except this Josef, my father, hadn't meant it for evil—although clearly it had been evil. He couldn't see the truth because he'd put his hope in an evil man and an evil regime. He'd been deceived. But it did help that he'd apologized.

"Thank you," I managed to say. "For your words. They help."

———

The next morning after breakfast, Lena left for work, Garit—who had been avoiding me—retreated to the office, and Esther went upstairs to rest, leaving Vater Josef and me at the table.

"I need to tell you something," I said. "I understand you were deceived by Hitler and the Nazis, and you weren't alone in that. I don't hold it against you. Ervin has been a good father to me, and I'm very appreciative, but at some point, as I processed my grief in your allowing the doctors at the Institute to sterilize me, I came to trust God as the Father I could always rely on. I trusted He would provide what I needed. When I needed it."

I paused, silently repeating my words to myself. When it came to marrying or never marrying, could I trust that God would provide what I needed, when I needed it? "God always meets those needs through other people."

Vater Josef nodded again.

"And right now, it seems Martha may have been detained for some reason. I'm not ready to go on without her—I don't want to return to the US and take Esther with me and have Martha show up with a different plan." I folded my hands together on top of the table. "Are Esther and I welcome to stay here longer, without knowing when we'll be leaving?"

"Of course," Vater Josef said. "I was sincere when I said you're always welcome here, and so is Esther. My home is your home." He coughed and then pushed himself up from the table. "I'm going to go rest for a while."

I did the dishes and started sweet-and-sour red cabbage for lunch to go with the cheese Lena had purchased the day before. I also had dough rising for bread.

At lunchtime, Esther stayed in our room, and Garit took a plate of food into the study, leaving Vater Josef and me alone again. As we ate, he said, "I also need to apologize for not intervening last year when Lena verbally attacked you."

"I imagine it's hard for you to be stuck between your daughters."

He nodded. "And I think it's hard for you to realize everything Lena has gone through, everything she's done to keep me alive and get Garit into university and maintain her work. She's done good things, translating for the Nuremberg Trials and now working with refugees."

"No doubt," I said.

"She misses you. It broke her heart to have you leave. She always felt you preferred Clare."

I did prefer Clare. Lena had never been warm to me. I didn't say that, though.

"I hope you and Lena can talk before you leave," Vater Josef said. "She's more like me. You are more like your Mutter. Lena's intentions are good, but she's ruled by her head—not her heart."

I stared at my red cabbage.

"You have a good heart, Rosene," he said. "I can tell by the way you care for Esther and by your concern for Martha and the rest of your family."

It took me a long time to fall asleep that night. Should I try to talk things through with Lena? Would it do any good or only make things worse? And what would I do if Martha didn't return? I couldn't make myself think about what might have happened to her.

In the middle of the night, someone whispered my name. "Rosene, wake up."

I turned toward the voice and then sat up.

"It's me. Martha."

I reached out in the darkness. She grabbed my hand.

"Are you all right?"

She sobbed. "I couldn't make myself send a telegram about what happened. I decided to come straight here as soon as I could."

"I know about George," I said. "I'm so sorry."

"How do you know?"

"Herr Hoffman at the Frankfurt Red Cross office told me. I went there to try to find you or George."

"Esther's uncle and his colleague managed to pull me from the car I was driving at the border and drag me into East Berlin. They kept me there, and then Russians questioned me for several days," Martha said. "The Red Cross became involved right away, and the US State Department. Finally, I convinced the Russians I was a Red Cross agent, solely concerned about a missing refugee. I didn't find out about George until after I was released. I'm having his body shipped to Chicago."

"Was he that ill?"

"We thought he had several years left—we didn't think it would happen this soon."

I scooted over in my bed. "Get in," I said. "Try to sleep. We'll talk more in the morning."

Esther was overjoyed to see Martha the next morning. "Are we going back to Berlin?" she asked.

"No," Martha said. "I can't. I can't say much—except that the information you gave me about your uncle's travels and what I observed while I was in East Berlin has been helpful."

"We can't return even to work for the Red Cross in West Berlin?"

"No," Martha said. "I'm no longer working for the Red Cross."

Alarmed, I stuttered, "Wha-at?"

"It's all right." Martha smiled gently. "I'm going to London to work with another group that works with refugees." She turned toward me. "You did a good job getting Esther out of East Berlin. Exceptional, really. This new agency I'm joining needs help in their London office. Would you be interested?"

I hated to think of Martha as a widow, by herself. But I didn't see living in London as a life I wanted.

"What about me?" Esther asked.

"You could come to London with me too," Martha answered. "Are you interested?"

Esther asked, "Would I be able to help refugees there?"

"Yes," Martha said. "And there's a synagogue not far from the office. The Jewish community isn't large, but you will be welcomed."

Esther answered, "I like the idea of being in a big city. When would I go?"

"Soon. I'll connect you with a colleague there who could help you get settled."

I asked, "If I decide I want to go home, when would I leave?"

Martha gave me a caring smile. "Whenever you want."

"When will you be home again?"

"I'll go to Chicago for George's funeral." Her voice wavered as she spoke. "I'll have to work out the details with his parents."

"I'll meet you in Chicago," I said. "For the funeral." I'd ask Clare to go with me.

"You don't have to do that," Martha said.

"I want to."

"I don't think you're going to take up my offer of a job in London, are you?"

I shook my head. "I'm going home. At least for now."

Martha made arrangements for Esther in London and bought her an airline ticket and then tickets for the two of us to New York. A couple of days before we were to leave, Vater Josef said he had something more he needed to tell me. He motioned for me to sit at the dining room table, across from him.

He whispered, "I wish you would choose to stay here."

"I can't." It would crush my soul. "I'm going home. I probably won't be back."

"I won't see you again."

"Not on this side of heaven," I said. "But we'll meet again."

He smiled a little. "We'll see if the grace I've prayed for will be granted."

That made me sad.

He leaned forward a little and spoke in a normal voice. "I had an uncle I didn't know well on my mother's side who passed away at the end of the war. It turns out I was his only living relative. He had the foresight to deposit his savings in a Swiss bank before the war. I only recently inherited the money. When I pass away, Lena will inherit this house and the little bit of money that I've managed to hold on to through the war and our economic woes. But I've divided my inheritance between you and Lena, although she doesn't know about it yet. I'll tell her after you leave. I've already wired your half to Monika to put in the bank for you," he explained. "I want you to have money of your own so you're not dependent on others, especially if you never marry."

Dumbfounded, I didn't respond.

He winced as he stood. Then he walked to the dining room linen closet and took out a box. "I have one more thing for you."

He staggered a little under the weight, so I hurried to take the box. It was heavy but not horribly so. I placed it on the table.

Vater Josef opened it and took out a mantel clock. It was made of cherrywood, and it had both a moon phase and a calendar on the face. I'd never seen such a clock.

"This sat in the parlor of my childhood home," he said. "It was a gift from my father's parents when he married my mother. I believe it was made in 1885." He paused. "I want you to have it. My parents had been gone for twenty years by the time you and Dorina were born."

I marveled that he'd said her name again. Something had changed inside of him.

"I want you to think of me and your mother and of Lena," he said. "I want you to know you once had a lovely home in Germany, and that you were deeply loved. I want you to remember how the death of your mother and the war changed all of that." He put the clock in the box. "But mostly know that wealth can quickly vanish. So can relationships. And communities. Even countries. What you have is time. Use it wisely."

"Danke," I said. "I will. And I'll remember you and the early truths I learned about the Lord in this home—and the later truths I learned from the Simonses."

Esther left Frankfurt for London, and then a couple of days later, Martha and I started our trip home. From New York, Martha flew to Chicago, while I took the train to Lancaster. It wasn't until five weeks later that Clare and I took the train to Chicago for George's funeral. We stayed in a hotel room with Martha. I dressed Mennonite. Clare dressed Amish. And Martha wore Englisch clothes—a black dress, a coat, pumps, and a hat with a veil.

The funeral was September 22, 1949. The next day, as we headed to the train station in a taxi, we heard President Truman on the radio, saying, "We have evidence that within recent weeks an atomic explosion occurred in the USSR."

I stared at Martha as I listened. She didn't look surprised. What kind of spying had she been doing in Berlin? I'd read that the Soviets had captured German scientists—and Esther said her uncle guarded scientists. Were some of them being held in eastern Germany and helping create a nuclear bomb for the Russians?

I felt sweaty and chilled at the same time.

Clare reached for my hand and squeezed it. I knew she was thinking of her children. First, the US had an atomic bomb—and used it on Japan. Now the Soviet Union had an atomic weapon too. Would they use it on us?

The Cold War had escalated. I'd never wanted to get home to Lancaster County as badly as I did at that moment. Zeke was gone—and for the first time, I knew for sure I didn't ever want to go after him, even if he wrote. I needed to let him go—and get on with my life as a single woman in Lancaster County, living on the Zimmerman farm.

Martha continued working in London until 1952. After that, she became a photojournalist and covered conflicts around the world, from Korea to Central America. She never married again and seemed content with her life. She only returned to Lancaster County a few times, but we corresponded regularly. Esther stayed in London, married, and had a family. She was active in her synagogue until she died in 1997.

As it turned out, the Displaced Persons Act of 1948 only allowed 200,000 refugees into the US, and nothing guarded against the entry of Nazi collaborators who had lied their way into displaced persons camps. The majority of Jewish survivors, after three to five years in camps, immigrated to Israel.

Through the years, I didn't think much about my visit to Frankfurt in 1948—it was too painful. I managed, mostly, to block it out. Instead, I focused on the visit in 1949. Although my relationship with Lena was still strained, I tried not to think about her much.

But it was that time with my German family that convinced me to join the Amish church. I felt the safest with the Amish and appreciated the way they embraced nonresistance. They truly believed in turning the other cheek and loving their neighbors. That was where I belonged, where my most important work was. I was more than an Aenti to Arden, Janice, and Lydia. I was a second mother. And then I was a second grandmother to Isaac too. I was where I belonged.

· 35 ·

Treva

T hose are all of my memories of that time," Rosene said. "I continued to volunteer at the refugee center for a couple more years and then again in the 1970s after Vietnamese boat people arrived in Lancaster County. Then, it wasn't until Iraqi refugees started arriving around 2005 that I started volunteering again." She sighed. "Jesus might as well have said, 'The refugees, along with the poor, will always be with you.' That's what happens when countries keep attacking each other."

I nodded in agreement. "What about the clock? Why did you put it in the store instead of the house?"

"I wanted to be reminded to use my time wisely, but I didn't want to hear it ticking every second of the day or striking every hour. I didn't want to forget Germany—but I also didn't want to think about it constantly either." Rosene paused a moment and then said, "For a long time, it was the only clock in the store, but when Priscilla took over, she added more and more. They sell quite well." She smiled wryly. "I think your Mammi has been thinking a lot about time the last few years. We all have."

I had too. Wasn't that what my FOBO was about? I had limited time. If I didn't make the best decision now, I would be wasting time. But that wasn't the way God worked. Our decisions weren't wasted as long as we grew from them.

"What agency was Martha working for?"

"I'm not sure," Rosene said. "She never said. And I have no idea how long she worked for it, whatever it was."

"When did she die?"

"In 1985, in Nicaragua, where she'd been covering the revolution. She'd come down with pneumonia. Unfortunately, there wasn't much medical care available, and she became septic. She was only sixty-two. I wished she'd lived to see the end of the Cold War. I've been the only one left of our generation in the US all this time."

I clarified, "Except for Zeke."

She smiled. "You're right. Except for Zeke."

"What about baby Lydia? What happened to her?"

Rosene exhaled slowly. "While Arden and Janice both joined the church at eighteen, it was the mid-sixties when Lydia became an adult. She went on a Mennonite mission trip with a friend to Ontario, Canada, to work with Indigenous people there, wanting to do something 'real' to help others. She ended up marrying a Canadian Mennonite man, and they moved to the Northwest Territories. He became a bush pilot, and they left the ministry. They had five children."

"Is she still alive?"

Rosene nodded. "We exchange Christmas cards."

My heart lurched. "She was like your own baby. You must miss her."

Rosene smiled, a little woefully. "Babies grow up. They

choose their own lives. She used to come home and visit every few years, but after Clare and Jeremiah died, she came less and less. It's understandable. It's a long trip, and they've never had much money. When I offered to pay for her travel, she declined. I didn't offer to go there—it's much easier to go to Germany than where they live. I'd have to take a bush plane for the final leg to their home. The weather is unpredictable, and there are a lot of delays. Of course, there are only a few months of the year that I would have attempted to go at all." Rosene shrugged. "She's seventy-one now, which is hard to fathom. I relish her Christmas cards and news. She's a grandmother and a great-grandmother. Three of their five children and all of their grandchildren are in the area, so she and her husband will be well taken care of in the years to come."

I thought about my idea of going to Alaska and how hard I thought it would be on everyone. But they'd gone through it before. With Zeke to California. With Lydia to Ontario and then the Northwest Territories. With Dad to Oregon. Even with Janice marrying and moving to the Big Valley. She stayed Amish, but she also left. Some Youngie stayed—some didn't. That's the way it had always been. What I decided to do was entirely up to me. They would miss me, but no one would stop me.

But I was beginning to understand why Dawdi, Mammi, and Rosene had invested so heavily in Ivy, Brenna, and me. We were the future of both the Simons and the Zimmerman families. We were all that was left to carry on their farm, their faith, and their memories.

The next day, I went to the library hoping to find information about both Martha and Esther. Who were they really working for? I knew for this research, I needed to start with a librarian. After I explained that I was looking for possible federal agencies my great-great-aunt had been working for during the Cold War, the first librarian referred me to another one with a quick "She's our history expert."

"You're in luck," the second librarian said. "Intelligence and policy documents have recently been declassified in the US, Germany, and Great Britain. We have a database available. You can search by agency, country, or first and last names. Or all three."

"There are three women I would like to research," I said. "Martha Simons Hall, who was American. She worked in Berlin, Hamburg, and London. It seems she may have had knowledge in 1949 about the Russian development of their atomic bomb before it became news in the US. Esther Lang, who was German, is the second woman. She worked in Berlin and London. And Lena Weber Becker, who was also German. She worked in Nuremberg and Frankfurt."

The librarian jotted down the information as I spoke. When I finished she said, "I'll look up their names in the database. While I do, I have two books that might interest you. The first one is *Western Spies in the Two Germanies*, which is about American, British, and West German spies who collected information on Russian maneuvers in East Germany, along with their acquisition of science that contributed to their nuclear weapons." She tucked her pencil behind her ear. "And the second one is *The History of the CIA*. I'll be right back with both."

I thought it interesting that she thought I needed to read about the CIA when I hadn't mentioned the agency. But Rosene had learned in 1948 about the CIA, although at that time she didn't believe Martha was working with them.

Five minutes later, I sat at a table and skimmed through the first book, reading about the science, weapons development, and military capabilities of the Soviet Union and how the West gathered the intelligence they needed. According to the sources, a host of spies were used in East Germany, from refugees to employees of charitable organizations to CIA agents to double agents.

I switched to the second book. The CIA had been founded in 1947 as part of the National Security Act and grew out of the World War II Office of Strategic Services. The CIA was under the National Security Council and advised the organization on intelligence matters. It became the US's pre-eminent intelligence service.

If the CIA advised the NSC on intelligence matters, then obviously agents gathered intelligence information. Esther had some sort of information Martha and Stephen Wilson needed, and it most likely had to do with Russia. I shivered. Information that she somehow knew because of her uncle, who was working for the Soviets. He probably discovered she was a spy and that was why he detained her in his apartment. It seemed plausible that Martha was working for the Red Cross *and* for the CIA while she was in West Berlin, which meant she was violating the Red Cross edict to remain neutral. Perhaps they'd realized what she was doing when she was detained in East Berlin and let her go because of it.

So many had hoped the end of World War II would bring peace, but instead a new war had waged. A cold war. And it appeared Martha—and Esther too—had been a new kind of soldier. Or, perhaps, the oldest soldiers of all. Spies.

What had convinced Martha to go against the tenets of nonresistance to work as a spy? Perhaps she saw herself as a peacemaker, as someone helping to prevent a nuclear war.

I kept reading.

"Treva," the librarian said an hour later. "I've found some information. I'll start with Lena Weber Becker." She sat down beside me. "She worked for a European agency, Relief for Refugees, as a translator. But she also worked for an agency that predated the *Bundesnachrichtendienst*, or the West German Federal Intelligence Service, as a translator. Mrs. Becker continued until her retirement in 1984."

I blinked rapidly, trying to process what she'd said. "Lena worked for a Nazi officer during the war. Do you think it's likely someone could go from working for the Nazis to working for a federal intelligence agency?"

"Yes," the librarian said. "I think that's plausible. Especially if she was in a secretarial role for the Nazis. That was a fairly common role for a young woman during that time."

I was shocked that Lena was assisting spies, translating information gathered by spies, or perhaps doing some sort of spying herself. But all along, the worry, for the Weber family and other Mennonites, had been the threat of Russia. A fear of Stalin was why they'd chosen to support Hitler in the first place. It made sense that the fear of Stalin had only grown worse as the Cold War grew more intense.

"It's interesting," the librarian said. "Lena worked at the IG Farben Building in Frankfurt from 1949 to 1955. It served as the European center for the American armed forces—and as the headquarters for the CIA."

"Did she work for the CIA?"

"I can't find any record of that, but it's likely the work she did was shared with the CIA." She slid a couple of pages with the information about Lena over to me. Then she held one more paper up and said, "The CIA recently digitized their records too, although I couldn't find Lena nor Esther in those records. In fact, all I could find on Esther was that she worked for the same agency Lena did, Relief for Refugees, but in London. Martha Hall worked for that same agency in London from 1949 until 1952."

"Really?" I hadn't expected to find out Lena worked for Relief for Refugees too. Perhaps the three of them had collaborated without Rosene ever knowing about it.

The librarian nodded and continued, "However, a Martha Hall is also listed as a CIA agent in Germany, in Berlin and Hamburg, from 1947 until 1949. And then in London until 1952. After that, she served in Korea and then in Vietnam. She died in Nicaragua in 1985."

I was first shocked but then not surprised. "Yes," I said. "That's the Martha Hall I'm looking for. Although I thought she became a photojournalist after 1952."

"It appears that was her cover—and a good one. Enough so that when she resigned from the CIA in 1966, she continued working as a photojournalist for nearly two more decades. I read in the material I found that over fifty American journalists have been identified through the years as working covertly as CIA agents during the Cold War. In later decades, the numbers were curtailed due to pressure by the Senate Select Committee on Intelligence, but the practice continued." The librarian glanced down at the document in front of her. "It appears Martha Hall was compromised in East Berlin in 1949."

No doubt that was when the Red Cross discovered what she was doing and likely let her go. She knew the risk she was taking, but she had lost both George and the work she loved at the same time. However, she immediately found other work with a refugee agency. Either she hid her intelligence work or the agency allowed her to do it.

I reported what I found to Rosene as we sat at the kitchen table that afternoon and I showed her the documents.

She leaned forward in her chair. "Back then, I was surprised Lena was working to help refugees after the war. But now I'm shocked to think she was helping West Germany collect and distribute intelligence during the Cold War. I wish I would have known that sooner."

"What about Martha? Are you surprised she was working for the CIA?"

"I knew she was working for someone—and even wondered at times if it was for the CIA. It makes sense working as a photojournalist was a cover, although a working one. Now I wonder if Relief for Refugees might have been a cover too—for all of them."

I agreed.

"I imagine Martha was conflicted. The CIA had plenty of controversies through the years. I'm guessing there were times when her ideals were compromised, but she must have believed for a time that the good she did outweighed the harm. Perhaps an imbalance led her to resign when she did." Rosene sighed. "Martha was always one of the bravest people I knew. I guess I'll never fully understand just how brave she was."

"I'd say you were pretty brave too," I said to Rosene.

She smiled. "I did have a moment way back when, didn't I?"

I laughed and said, "You certainly did."

The next day, as I weeded the garden, Rosene sat down at the picnic table. It appeared she was soaking up the sunshine, but after a while, she called out, "Come join me. You need a break."

As I sat down across from her, she said, "It appeared you were deep in thought. What about?"

"Just about how Christmas in Oregon a year and a half ago was when I first met Pierre. It had seemed like such a magical time. Conrad was there with Ivy. And Johann had come from Ukraine, although he and Brenna weren't dating yet. I barely knew Pierre, but already we liked each other. It was so fun. But Pierre won't ever be a part of *us* again."

"He'll always be a part of that memory."

I shrugged.

"Some of my fondest memories are with people who passed through my life but didn't stay," Rosene said. "Dinners around the table, interactions, adventures—all of those events have value. We may never see any of the tourists from the dinner we had, and yet we'll remember them. Zaida, Kamil, Cala, and the children might move to New York and start a restaurant with Kamil's brother, and yet we'll treasure the time we had with them. I always held on to my memories of Zeke and carried them with me. I never wanted to forget him. And now he's back."

"Pierre and I won't ever be reunited. He's moved on. I haven't."

"Carry what you learned from your relationship with Pierre with you. And be open to God's plans for you."

"I am," I said. "And I'll be open to being single, like you. And open to doing a benefit dinner for the orphanage in Haiti. There's a large Haitian diaspora in Lancaster County, especially the city of Lancaster."

"Jah," Rosene said. "There is. It really is about loving others. Sometimes that love is for only a short time. Sometimes it's for a lifetime. The important thing is to love and value the people who come into our lives, whether it's for a short time or a long time." She tipped her head a little. "I've finally been able to tell Zeke my stories. I think telling you girls helped me be able to tell Zeke all of it, something I should have done when we were young." She met my gaze. "Speaking of my story, I have several scrapbooks about Martha. Photos she took. Articles that have her pictures in them. Postcards she sent." She smiled up at me. "I'd like you to have them. In fact, I want you to have the scrapbooks—to keep those memories for the next generation."

Tears stung my eyes. "Denki," I said. "I'll share them with Ivy's baby someday—and with the other children our family will be blessed with."

On the third Sunday of June, six days before the wedding, Gabe rode with me to the Mennonite church. We sat with Ivy, Conrad, and Sharon. Pastor Mike preached about love—how we were created to be loved by God and love God, and that the world will know we are His disciples by our love for one another. "The attitude of love is the essence of true belonging."

I repeated what he said silently—*The attitude of love is the essence of true belonging*—and then thought of Rosene. She belonged because she loved. I whispered to myself, "True belonging comes from loving others."

I belonged on the farm. It was where I was most rooted in the love of family and others. It was where I was the most rooted in serving others. It was where I was most rooted in God's love. Whether Dawdi would give the farm to me or not, I would stay—as long as I could.

After the service, I gave Ivy a big hug and whispered, "I love you. And I love your baby. And I'm really sad you're moving—but also really happy for you."

She hugged me back and held on. "I'm going to miss you."

"I'm going to miss you too."

As I let go of her, I caught Gabe watching us. And smiling. He seemed taller. And more confident. Perhaps the sermon had spoken to him too.

I asked Gabe to drive home so I could send a text to Misty.

> I'm not going to be able to take the job after all. I've decided to stay on the family farm and do what I can to help my grandparents. I'm grateful for the experience coordinating Lindsay's wedding and hope you'll be able to replace me soon.

It wasn't until Gabe turned onto our lane that my phone dinged. Misty.

> Thank you for letting us know. We enjoyed having you here for Lindsay's wedding and appreciated the good work you did. We wish you all the best and hope our paths will cross again.

I loved her text and then let out a sigh of relief, grateful that she'd been understanding.

That afternoon, Rosene took a nap while Zeke, Gabe, and I sat on the porch. Zeke cleared his throat and said, "Treva, I can't thank you enough for tracking me down. I was fine with my life in Alaska, but being home is . . ." He exhaled slowly. "It's more than I ever thought I'd have again."

"Have you decided on an assisted living facility yet?" I asked.

He grinned. "You know what I've been thinking?"

"I have no idea."

"That I would join the Amish church now to marry Rosene if she'd have me." He chuckled. "I can't drive anymore anyway, and I can barely hear music. And I'm sure I'll figure out how to live without my phone and laptop." Then he grew serious. "No, the truth is I've enjoyed going to services, I appreciate the community, and I believe—at this point in my life—I can best worship and serve God by going back to my roots and joining the church," he said. "Do you think Rosene would have me?"

I was sure she would, but I said, "All you can do is ask."

· 36 ·

Gabe helped Dawdi and me with the milking that afternoon. After we finished, Dawdi told me that he'd had a phone call from Kamil when he first came out to the barn in the afternoon. "The family is going to move to Buffalo. His cousin found a place for their restaurant."

"Oh, I'm sad," I said. "But happy for them." I thought about what Rosene had said about loving people who come into your life, whether it's for a short time or a long time. The Hamad family had been part of our lives for a short—but important—time.

Gabe had supper with us, and then he and I went for a walk up the lane. "Can we speak hypothetically?" I asked.

"Sure."

"I'm trying to figure out if I was in charge of the farm what I would do to increase revenue and get the work done without making the seventy-something-year-olds and the ninety-three-year-old work so hard."

"I'm all ears," Gabe said. "What are your plans?"

"Basic things such as trying to increase crop yields to produce more feed—maybe even enough so that we can sell some of it." We turned right, toward the covered bridge.

"And building a calf barn where they'd be together inside with feeding-on-demand stations instead of outside in the elements."

"Why?" Gabe asked.

"It increases weight gain," I explained. "And the calves are healthier when they're together."

"That makes sense."

I continued, "I'd also do little things, such as continuing to rent out the apartment above the store and doing more tourist dinners, if your mom would like to keep helping."

"I think she would," Gabe said.

"I also thought I could partner with the refugee center to do more benefit dinners—perhaps four a year." Two children in a passing buggy waved at us. We both waved back as I said, "We can continue to provide a venue for local people to meet refugee families and contribute to the center."

"That sounds like a good idea too," Gabe said.

"After Brenna's wedding, I'd like to evaluate offering the farm as a wedding venue too."

Gabe groaned. "I don't think Priscilla would go for that. I'm not even sure Arden would. And even if they did, I doubt their bishop would."

"I hear you." I stepped to the left as we reached the road and Gabe followed. "But what if they were okay with it?"

"Wait," Gabe said, "are we not speaking hypothetically anymore? Is Arden going to give you the farm?"

My face grew warm. "I wasn't going to tell you, but I asked him for it. He hasn't given me an answer yet."

"Wow." Gabe paused for a moment. "Would you become Amish?"

"No," I answered. "No matter what Dawdi decides, I'll join your Mennonite church soon."

He sounded confused. "*My* church?"

"Yes," I said. "The one you grew up in. The one you've been attending again now for a while."

"Hmm . . ."

"If it's not your church, what is it?"

"I was so determined to leave it behind," he responded. "But I guess you're right. It is my church." He grinned. "So, you plan on joining *my* church?"

"Jah, that's what I said." I bumped into him with my arm. "And neither Pastor Mike nor any elder there is going to protest if I coordinate weddings."

"Don't you think Arden and Priscilla's bishop would object?"

"There are a few people in their district who host Englisch tourists, even overnight, and other events on their farms," I replied. "I think their bishop might be fine with us hosting weddings."

"I would be available to do the milking since Kamil won't be around much longer," Gabe said.

I grabbed Gabe's arm and pulled him off the edge of the road as a car buzzed by, going too fast. "Great," I said. "I don't know if I should be thinking about what I'd do with the farm or not. Do you think Dawdi would turn it over to me?" When he didn't answer, I asked, "Would you want him to turn it over to me?"

Gabe laughed. "Sorry. I was just wondering, if you took it over, whether you'd let me stay in the Dawdi Haus."

"Of course," I said.

"Then, yes." He bumped against me. "I want Arden to turn the farm over to you. You'd do a great job running it."

Monday was drizzly and cold, but my weather app claimed it would be warm and seventy degrees by Saturday. I was counting on it. After mucking out the horse stable, I heard Zeke call out my name as I headed to the barn. Rosene stood beside him by the door.

As I veered their way, Zeke and Rosene walked down the steps. When I reached them, Zeke said, "I have my DNA results. But I haven't opened them yet."

He glanced at Rosene. "Should I look at them now?"

"The sooner the better," she said.

He pulled his phone from his pocket. I stepped back, not wanting to see anything he didn't want to share. He read, "One hundred percent Northwestern European. Ninety-five percent French and German, from the Canton of Bern." He looked up. "That's where the Amish originated."

I nodded.

He glanced down and clicked on something and then said, "DNA relatives. First one. Andrew Richards, grandson." He raised his head. "I'm Drew's grandfather." His hand dropped to his side. "I wish I would have known I was a father sixty-nine years ago instead of finding out now. But I hope it will bring some closure—and connection—to Drew."

I asked, "Do you want me to text Drew?"

"Could you share his number with me?" Zeke asked. "I'd like to text him. I'll ask him to stop by when he has a chance."

"Why don't we ask Drew and Stephanie to come to dinner?" Rosene suggested. "Ask Ivy, Conrad, and Gabe too."

"I'd like that," Zeke said. "I'll text all of them."

When Drew and Stephanie arrived at the front door for dinner, Zeke met them at the door and gave Drew a hug.

When Zeke let go of him, Drew said, "Does this mean I am your grandson? Or that I'm not?"

"You are," Zeke answered. "Welcome—officially—to the family."

Stephanie beamed and hugged Drew too.

After we gathered around the table, Dawdi led us in a silent prayer. Once he finished, I looked at those surrounding me. In May, I'd acquired an uncle. And now, in June, I had a cousin. Ivy and Conrad were moving, but I wasn't losing them. I'd welcome a niece or nephew soon. And I'd gained a good friend in Gabe. He was someone I could truly rely on.

Ivy and Conrad left soon after dinner. Everyone else went out to the front porch, except for Stephanie. She helped me with the dishes. As we worked, she said, "Drew has been restless ever since I met him, as if something was missing from his life. Staying on your farm has been healing for him. Thinking Zeke might be his grandfather helped even more. I can tell, just from observing him at dinner, that knowing Zeke is his grandfather has already brought him to a better place."

"I'm so glad." I put a plate in the rack. "You know what would make us even happier?"

"What?" Stephanie asked.

"If he stays here in Lancaster County."

Her eyes sparkled as I met her gaze. "Has he said anything about our plans?"

I shook my head.

"Then I won't say anything." She picked up the plate. "But I will say he has a lead on a job in this area." She grinned.

"I can't wait for a formal announcement." Maybe I'd be coordinating another wedding on the farm soon. Of course we'd invite Drew and Stephanie to our holidays and family dinners. Not to be too practical, but maybe they would live close enough that Drew could help with the milking when needed. He seemed to enjoy it. I loved how our family kept growing.

Brenna, Johann, Natasha, and Gran arrived on Wednesday. After she led the others upstairs to their rooms, Brenna delivered the envelope from Lena to Rosene as she, Zeke, Gabe, and I sat at the kitchen table.

"Denki." Rosene tucked it into the pocket of her apron.

I could hardly contain myself. "Aren't you going to read it?"

"Jah . . ." Rosene glanced around the table. "Do you want me to read it now?"

I nodded. So did Zeke. Brenna sat down beside me.

Rosene took the envelope out, opened it, and then pulled out the letter. She read it silently first and then cleared her throat. I thought she was going to read it out loud. Instead, she opened her mouth but then closed it. Then she said, "On my three trips to Germany and encounters with Lena, I longed for her to apologize to me, to acknowledge what I'd lost. When she died, I knew I'd never have that. I was wrong."

She stared at the letter for a long minute and then handed it to me. "Treva, would you read it?"

"Jah." I took it from her and read aloud.

"My Dearest Sister,

I was never maternal toward you, not like Clare, but I did love you. After Mother had her last seizure and died, I pulled away from you and Dorina, afraid I was going to lose both of you too. Ironic, isn't it? My pulling away contributed to me losing you. I supported Father in the decisions he made about your medical care. I didn't even attempt to talk him out of having you and Dorina participate in the study. Long after I had an idea what the Nazis were doing with the disabled, I still didn't protest against you going to the Institute.

I don't expect you to forgive me, but I am sorry. I have been since the translating I did at the Nuremberg Trials and realized the atrocities the Nazis committed. But for some reason I couldn't bring myself to say I was sorry to you the three times I saw you, not even in 2014, when I knew I needed to. Nor did I write it in a letter.

For years, it seemed better to move on. We were all trying to do that. Garit and I were, at least. We both specialized in denial. At the end of his time, Father tried to sort out his trust of the Nazis with what he'd allowed to happen to Dorina and to you. I understand that now as I face my own last days.

Garit was at the Kaiserslautern train station looking for you and Clare after you left the farm—I assumed you'd been at the farm. I overheard you talk with him that day in 1949. I knew he'd gone after you back in 1939. I think 'moving on' was his motivation to not admit it to you. Or his shame. Or denial. Or all three.

I can't defend what I didn't do when you were only a child or what I didn't say when you were a young adult and also five years ago, when we were both old. But before I go to meet my Maker, I needed to write to you and ask your forgiveness.

With love,
Your sister Lena"

I looked up from the letter. Brenna was crying. Both of Rosene's hands covered her mouth. Zeke's eyes brimmed with tears. And Gabe leaned against his chair with a sigh.

"That was unexpected," Rosene said.

Zeke put a hand on her shoulder. "God's grace knows no bounds or time."

She reached over with her hand and clasped his. As her other hand fell from her mouth, she reached for the letter. "All these years, I grieved Dorina while I felt angry at Lena. Now it feels as if I can finally grieve Lena too. She cared enough to make amends. I forgave her as much as I could through the years. I do believe, now, forgiveness will completely replace the last of my hurt and anger."

Zeke patted her shoulder.

She turned toward him. "It feels like a happy ending to my story."

I said, "Your story isn't over."

Rosene smiled as Zeke patted her shoulder again. And then she began to laugh. We couldn't help but join her.

The next two days were filled with wedding tasks. Brenna and Johann got their marriage license and met with Pastor Mike. I confirmed with the vendors. On Friday afternoon, Gabe helped me put up the archway and attach the twinkle lights on the inside of the tent I'd had delivered. After a brief rehearsal and a typical Amish dinner that Sharon and Gran cooked, Ivy spent the night with Brenna and me on the farm while Johann, Conrad, and Gabe stayed at Conrad and Ivy's apartment.

As the three of us settled in the big bed in my room, Ivy said, "Remember our first night on the farm? When I came down the hall to sleep in here with the two of you?"

"Yes," Brenna said. "We couldn't have imagined where we

are now. Coming here turned out to be what was best for us. Gran was right. It was what we needed."

"I never would have guessed that we'd grow so close to Mammi and Dawdi," Ivy said. "Although it was obvious Rosene was someone we could count on from the start."

"And now we have Zeke," I added.

Brenna said, "And Drew."

"And Conrad and Johann." Ivy propped her head on her hand.

"And Gabe." Brenna smiled at me. "He's changed. A lot. For the good, don't you think, Treva?"

"I do."

Brenna chuckled. "Anything I need to know?"

"No." I gave her a sassy look. "Except that I'm only twenty-one."

She laughed.

I rolled over and stared at the ceiling. "But I think I'm beginning to realize how old—or young—I am doesn't matter. I can do more than I ever imagined." I rolled to my side and glanced from Ivy to Brenna.

"Yes!" Brenna's eyes sparkled. "You're right. That's true for all of us. God provides what we need. He leads us to do more than we thought we could."

Ivy patted her stomach. "God has been good to us. We have a baby on the way and another marriage to celebrate. All three of us are doing well. Let's count our blessings."

"Which will always include Mom and Dad," I said.

"Absolutely," Ivy and Brenna responded in unison.

After a moment of silence, I asked, "Do you know the hymn 'By Evening's Light'?"

"I remember Dad singing that when I was little," Ivy said.

"I don't remember it," Brenna said.

"Apparently Martha and Rosene used to sing it, including when they were fleeing Berlin in 1948."

"Wow," Ivy said. "You'll have to tell us more of the story sometime."

"I will." I sat up as I began to sing. "'Brighter days are sweetly dawning, Oh, the glory looms in sight! For the cloudy day is waning, And the evening shall be light.'"

As I sang the chorus, Ivy joined in. "'Oh, what golden glory streaming! Purer light is coming fast; Now in Christ we've found a freedom, Which eternally shall last.'"

Eternally. I felt as if I had a glimpse of that on the farm—Rosene's stories, memories of Mom and Dad, holding on to the time our elders had left with us, thinking of Ivy's baby. Time marched on, bathed in Christ's light.

I'd never seen the farm look as beautiful as it did the next day. I'd planted fuchsia geraniums and white lobelia in the pots on the porch and around the tent that we'd rented. The archway was at the front of the tent, with branches of pink and white blossoms intertwined through the lattice.

As I walked down the aisle in my modest light pink dress, I passed a handful of guests from the Mennonite church. Sharon and Olena. Then Drew and Stephanie, who sat beside Rosene and Zeke. Natasha. Dawdi and Mammi. Gran. We were small for an Amish/Mennonite family, but growing.

Ivy and I stood with Brenna, and Gabe and Conrad stood with Johann. Pastor Mike read from 1 Corinthians 13, concluding with "And now these three remain: faith, hope and love. But the greatest of these is love." Then he spoke about the sacrifices of love and submitting to each other and putting your beloved first. "Marriage is never about competition. Remember, what's best for your partner is what's best for you too." He went on to talk about the importance of community and finding a place to belong as a couple. Then Pastor Mike said, "Repeat after me."

As Brenna and Johann said their vows, I closed my eyes and said a silent prayer of thanks. If I ever had a happily-ever-after, it wouldn't mean any more to me than Brenna's did.

Olena, with help from a couple of women she knew, prepared a delicious Ukrainian meal, along with several Kyiv cakes. After the guests left, Sharon, Natasha, Drew, and Stephanie headed to the kitchen to help clean up.

Dawdi said, "Girls, could we talk for a few minutes?"

Gran, Mammi, Rosene, and Zeke already sat at the first table under the tent. Johann, Conrad, and Gabe were talking at the edge of the tent. Conrad said, "We'll give you some privacy."

"Actually," Dawdi said as he pulled a second table next to the first, "we'd like you to join us." The six of us pulled up chairs to the second table.

To the west, the sun had started to set, and the lights in the tent grew brighter. Once we were seated, Dawdi said, "We want to talk about the future. Laurel, why don't you start?"

Gran folded her hands together. "As you all know, Ivy and Conrad are moving to Oregon to operate the farm. We would like to deed the property to them, if that's acceptable to Brenna and Treva."

"Yes," I said, "of course." Brenna nodded in agreement.

Gran gestured toward Rosene.

"I would like to deed the Frankfurt house to Brenna. She'll be the closest to be able to rent it out or live in it in the future or whatever she wants to do with it." She glanced from Ivy to me. "If the two of you agree."

We both nodded.

"My turn." Dawdi focused on me. "Treva, I've put a lot of thought into this. I do want to turn the farm over to you, and in a few years, deed the property, including the house and store, to you. I trust you to manage it and continue its operation. I'll be here to guide you as long as I'm able."

My heart swelled with gratitude. I would do my best to care for the farm and for my elders. Both would be privilege. "Denki."

Dawdi grinned. "Someday the farm will be yours." He turned toward Gabe. "As far as the store, Priscilla has asked Gabe to manage it so she can retire right away. And he accepted."

Gabe gave me a nod, which I responded to with a smile.

Dawdi continued, "We want each of you girls to have a property. Along with the money from your parents that was put in trusts for the three of you, you'll have a good start on life."

"Thank you," Ivy said. "I can't imagine our lives without you."

"Same." Rosene grinned.

We all laughed. I was grateful for some levity, as I expected my sisters were too. "What about you?" I asked Rosene. "What are your plans?"

She leaned toward Zeke. "After seventy years, we've come full circle."

Zeke shifted so his arm touched Rosene's. "I've decided to join the Amish church. I've already spoken with the bishop. He's never had anyone want to join at my age, but he said after I go through the classes, we'll talk again." Zeke took Rosene's hand in his. "And then I'll be asking Rosene to marry me for the second time."

She turned toward Zeke and smiled. "And I'll be saying yes."

Gabe grinned at me, and I smiled in return, pleased that he and I had played a role in bringing Rosene and Zeke back together.

I tilted my head as Gabe held my gaze. Did I have romantic feelings for him? It would be easy to on a night like tonight. I wasn't sure, but I did see him as a business partner when it came to the farm and store. We'd start there.

No matter what, I finally saw a future for myself. It was okay to choose the option right in front of me. Rosene had shown me that.

I picked up my half-full glass of punch. "I propose a toast to Mom and Dad. I know they'd be happy for us—for all of us. And maybe even a little amazed at how everything turned out. I'm guessing they never would have predicted that Ivy would want the tree farm in Oregon. Or that Brenna, the homebody, would make her life in Ukraine. Or that I would be farming the land where they first met as babies and played together as children."

I raised my glass. "But here we are. My toast is a prayer of thanks. For Mom and Dad—may their memory always be with us. And a prayer for the rest of us—that we would follow where God leads in the time we have left."

Author's Note

World War II was the deadliest conflict in history. Seventy to eighty-five million people worldwide perished during the war, and as many as sixty-five million people were displaced in Europe alone. Nearly everyone in the world was impacted in some way by the war. It ended with the horrific nuclear bombings of Hiroshima and Nagasaki that, instead of bringing peace, introduced a new and possibly more deadly conflict—nuclear war.

By Evening's Light explores how the beginnings of the Cold War, a term used by 1947 to describe the chilly relations between the US and USSR made even more so by the USSR's development of an atomic bomb in 1949, impacted survivors of World War II, including my fictional character Martha Simons Hall, who grew up Mennonite but left her church and took a job with the International Red Cross after World War II ended.

Martha ends up, in her IRC work, acquiring and passing on information to US intelligence agents. Although certainly not common, there is a history of people working for the International Red Cross who were involved in espionage. In the 1920s, a small spy ring of International Red Cross workers in Switzerland spied for Comintern, an organization that advocated for worldwide communism and was affiliated with the Soviet Union's Communist Party. In 1941, David Bruce, who had been the chief delegate of the American Red Cross in Britain, became a member of an American intelligence agency. And several International Red Cross workers in North Africa were accused of spying for the Germans during World War II, and one was eventually executed. These accounts, along with those of people working for missions and other nonprofit organizations spying for the US during World War II, in the years after, and during subsequent US wars, also inspired me as I imagined the stories of Martha, Esther, Rosene, and Lena during their time in Germany at the beginning of the Cold War.

Besides exploring the first years of the Cold War, *By Evening's Light* also follows the Zimmerman and Simons families and friends and acquaintances in both the contemporary and historical threads as Youngie in both generations are faced with decisions centered around leaving or joining their Anabaptist churches, their convictions around the principles of nonresistance, and their responsibilities to those displaced by violent and prolonged world events. Members of both generations work with refugees in Lancaster, Pennsylvania, a place often referred to as America's refugee capital. The city has been welcoming refugees for over three hundred years and has resettled twenty times more refugees per capita than the rest of the nation. The "refugee dinners" in *By Evening's Light* were inspired by real events in Lancaster County that brought refugees and locals together to share meals and life stories.

Some of the resources I used in researching *By Evening's Light* include *The Origins of Totalitarianism* by Hannah Arendt, *Destination Elsewhere: Displaced Persons and Their Quest to Leave Postwar Europe* by Ruth Balint, *The German*

Christian Movement in the Third Reich by Doris L. Bergen, *The City Becomes a Symbol: The U.S. Army in the Occupation of Berlin, 1945-1948* by Donald Carter, *Britain and the International Committee of the Red Cross, 1939-1945* by James Crossland, *The Sisterhood: The Secret History of Women in the CIA* by Lisa Mundy, *Humanitarians at War: The Red Cross in the Shadow of the Holocaust* by Gerald Steinacher, *Double Crossed: The Missionaries Who Spied for the United States During the Second World War* by Matthew Avery Sutton, *The Secret History of the CIA* by Joseph J. Trento, *The Cold War: A World History* by Odd Arne Westad, and a variety of newspaper and magazine articles, along with information from the National Archives. I particularly appreciate Odie Miller sharing some of her childhood memories of living in Germany during the Cold War.

As always, I'm thankful to my husband, Peter, for supporting my writing, assisting with research, and functioning as a sounding board when I get stuck. I'm also grateful to my dear friend Marietta Couch for being a resource when it comes to Anabaptist beliefs and practices and for reading my manuscripts and offering her insights. Any mistakes are my own.

I'm thankful for my agent, Natasha Kern, for representing my Amish Memories series and for her encouragement throughout the last five years. I wish her the best!

I'm immensely thankful for my editors, Jennifer Veilleux and Rochelle Gloege, for their help shaping and developing the story, and all the good people at Bethany House for their work on making this novel a reality.

Above all, I'm grateful to God for giving me the opportunity to write my stories and to my dear readers for reading and sharing my stories. Thank you!

Discussion Questions

1. At the beginning of *By Evening's Light*, even though she loves Pierre, Treva doesn't feel she can stay in Haiti. Do you think she does the right thing in leaving? Why or why not? She's not content to stay in Lancaster County either. What is her motivation to leave again? What stops her? How does she handle the change in plans? Has there been a time you ended up staying somewhere you had intended to leave? What were the circumstances? What was the outcome?

2. *By Evening's Light* is a dual-time story with a historical and a contemporary thread. Which story resonated with you the most? Why? Which character did you find the most likable? Which character did you identify with the most?

3. In the historical thread, Rosene doesn't want to return to Germany to see her biological father and sister in 1948, but Martha thinks it will be good for her. Do you think it was beneficial for Rosene to see her family? How did her trip in 1948 compare to her trip in 1949?

4. Rosene feels shame from being sterilized by the Nazis as a young teen and believes she is "damaged." How does this change her relationship with Zeke? Why does she ultimately decide not to go after Zeke, even though she still loves him? Do you think she should have gone west with him?

5. How does Zeke change throughout the story? Do you think Rosene did the right thing in reconciling with him after decades of being apart? Why or why not?

6. In what ways is Treva's time in Alaska fulfilling? In what ways is it disappointing? How does she compare the resort in Alaska to the Zimmerman family farm in Lancaster County? What does she learn from her time in Alaska?

7. What role does Gabe play in Treva's decision about her future? What does she learn from Gabe? What impact does Gabe showing up in Alaska to help Treva take Zeke back to Lancaster County have on her?

8. Why is it important for Drew to find his biological grandfather? What impact does finding Zeke have on Drew? What impact does finding out he is a father and grandfather have on Zeke?

9. Martha is involved in intelligence work for the US while working for the International Red Cross in Germany. What are some outcomes of her intelligence work? What is her motivation in feeding information to the CIA?

10. What are some of the similarities between Rosene's historical story and Treva's contemporary story? What are some of the differences? What does Treva

learn from Rosene's story? What lessons have you learned from the stories of elders in your family?

11. *By Evening's Light* explores Amish and Mennonite young people grappling with remaining in and committing to their Anabaptist churches or leaving and making a new life in the Englisch world. If you had grown up in an Anabaptist community, do you think you would have stayed or left? Why?

12. Rosene serves refugees in Lancaster County, periodically, throughout her adult life. In what ways did volunteering help her as a young woman? Why did she choose to continue serving refugees as an older woman? What volunteer work have you done? Did you find it rewarding? Why or why not?

13. Treva and her sisters will need to care for their three aging grandparents and perhaps their Aenti Rosene too in the near future. Do you believe the three young women are obligated to care for the elders in their family? How have the current elders in the family taken care of past elders—and also taken care of Ivy, Brenna, and Treva? How, from what you know, does the care of elders in Amish communities differ from the majority of the US population, generally speaking? What are some of the differences in resources between the two groups?

14. Near the end of the novel, Treva recalls that Rosene and Martha sang an old hymn, "The Evening Light," by the side of the road as they were fleeing Berlin. Treva then sings the song to her sister the night before Brenna's wedding. What did the song symbolize for Rosene and Martha in 1948? What did

it symbolize for Treva in 2019? What is your favorite
hymn? What meaning does it have for you?

> Brighter days are sweetly dawning,
> Oh, the glory looms in sight!
> For the cloudy day is waning,
> And the evening shall be light.
>> From the hymn "The Evening Light"
>> by Daniel S. Warner (1885)

Leslie Gould is the #1 bestselling and award-winning author of over forty novels, including the Sisters of Lancaster County series and the Plain Patterns series. She holds a bachelor's degree in history and an MFA in creative writing. Leslie enjoys research trips, church history, and hiking, especially in the beautiful state of Oregon, where she lives. She and her husband, Peter, have four adult children and two grandchildren.

Sign Up for Leslie's Newsletter

Keep up to date with Leslie's latest news on book releases and events by signing up for her email list at the link below.

LeslieGould.com

FOLLOW LESLIE ON SOCIAL MEDIA

Leslie Gould Author   @LeslieGouldWrites

More from Leslie Gould

When Ivy Zimmerman's Mennonite parents are killed in a tragic accident, her way of life is upended. As she grows suspicious that her parents' deaths weren't an accident, she gains courage in the story of Clare Simons, a woman who lived in pre-World War II Germany. With the inspiration of Clare, Ivy seeks justice for her parents, her sisters, and herself.

A Brighter Dawn
AMISH MEMORIES #1

Mennonite Brenna Zimmerman's life grows complicated by her feelings for a Ukrainian soldier and her friendship with an Afghanistan War vet. But she's inspired by the story of her Amish relative's experience during World War II. How will Brenna find the courage to give up the comforts she craves for the life she truly wants?

This Passing Hour
AMISH MEMORIES #2

Dumped by her fiancé a week before the wedding, Savannah Mast flees California for her Amish grandmother's farm, where she becomes unexpectedly entangled in the search for a missing Amish girl. When she discovers her childhood friend Tommy Miller is implicated as a suspect, she must do all she can to find the Amish girl and clear his name.

Piecing It All Together
PLAIN PATTERNS #1

BETHANYHOUSE